As a child, Kate Tremayne was fascinated with Greek mythology and from that grew her love of history and tales of valour and adventure. That passion for historical adventure, weaving fictional characters into real-life history dramas, is the driving force behind her writing. Her childhood holidays were spent in Cornwall and she still makes regular pilgrimages to the land whose beauty and atmospheric moods have always haunted her.

Married with two children, Kate now lives in Sussex. She has written seventeen novels under a different name.

Also by Kate Tremayne and available from Headline

Adam Loveday
The Loveday Fortunes

The Loveday Trials

Kate Tremayne

headline

First published in 2001
by HEADLINE BOOK PUBLISHING

First published in paperback in 2002
by HEADLINE BOOK PUBLISHING

6

ISBN 978 0 7472 6412 5

Typeset in Times New Roman by
Letterpart Limited, Reigate, Surrey

Printed in Great Britain by
Clays Ltd, St Ives plc

HEADLINE BOOK PUBLISHING
A division of Hodder Headline
338 Euston Road
London NW1 3BH

www.headline.co.uk
www.hodderheadline.com

For Chris – my long-suffering husband   for his patience and support.

ACKNOWLEDGEMENTS

To the unsung heroines at Headline for their professionalism and support. Shona Walley, Andi Sisodia, Jane Morpeth, Rhian Bromage and also Yvonne Holland. And to my wonderful agent, Teresa Chris, who is my guiding light.

Also a special thank you to my not so ancient mariner, Tony Pratt, for help on all things naval.

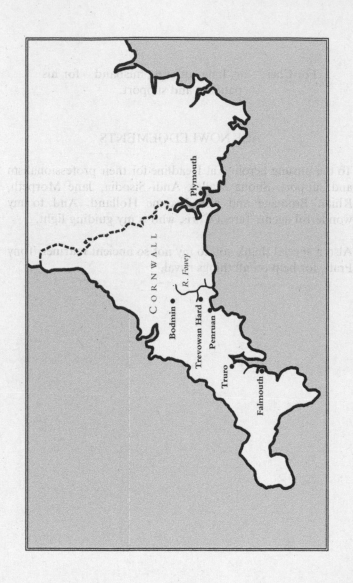

THE LOVEDAY FAMILY

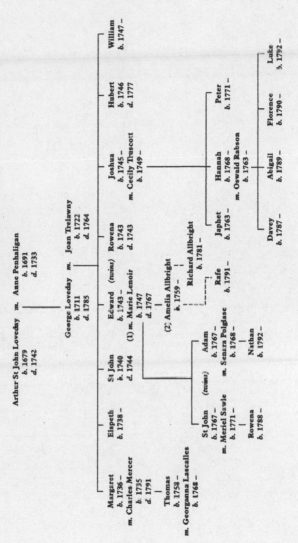

Chapter One

January 1793

The two riders halted at the top of a craggy tor. The salty tang of the sea was strong on the breeze, and the undulating coastline of steep cliffs and jagged outcrops of granite rocks was less than an hour's ride. The morning mist had lifted and as the sun rose higher it warmed the chilled bodies of the riders, and patches of vibrant blue widened in the sky above them. Plumes of steam rose from the rocks and gorse, and pheasants fed on the dried wildflower seeds scattered amongst the heather. The travellers were tired and their muscles ached from a week of riding over tracks made treacherous by mud and rain.

The man unwound the muffler around his lower face and smiled across at his wife, who was carrying his month-old son wrapped in warm blankets. Adam Loveday's dark-fringed eyes sparkled. 'We are almost home, Senara, my love.'

He laughed as he surveyed the landscape he had not seen for several months, and felt his heart stir with the thrill and expectancy of his homecoming. Along the coast the tall chimneys of Trevowan rose above the trees. The sight of the house and estate of his birth swelled his heart with pride. There was no other place like Trevowan. It was his haven, his sanctuary and his obsession.

1

The sea, with its white-tipped waves crashing on to the rocks, was another vision which lifted his spirits. The sea was also in his blood, whether he was sailing it as a merchant adventurer, or working on the ships being built in the family shipyard. As he exchanged smiles with the woman he loved, and had finally won as his bride, emotion almost unmanned him. In that moment his world was complete and fulfilled.

In two hours he would present his wife and son to his family at Trevowan. First they would stop at Marincr's House, his home at the yard, and refresh themselves for the journey and change their travel-stained clothes. He had sent a messenger on ahead for his family to expect him tomorrow, but he had not wanted to tell them of his marriage and son in a letter, only that he had found Senara. They had made better time on the roads than he had expected.

Senara was looking pale and her smile was strained, prompting him to say, 'Are you nervous? My family will come to love you as I do. There is nothing to fear.'

'Is there not? I cannot believe that your family will accept a gypsy as your wife. I fear we acted too rashly by taking our vows at Avebury . . . Your father will not see our union as legal.'

'Do you see our union as legal?'

'Of course, because it followed our old customs. But—'

'Which is precisely why we shall retake our vows at Trewenna church,' Adam cut across her protest and misgivings. He would not listen to caution. He was too exultant. 'I love you, Senara. Our son will one day inherit the Loveday yard. Nathan is my future and my father's first grandson. Our line is assured.'

He reached across to squeeze her hand on the reins and could not resist stroking the cheek of the sleeping Nathan. 'Nothing is going to come between us. I've spent six months searching for you after you ran off believing that I would

2

marry a woman of my class. Does that not prove that you are the only woman I want to be my wife?'

'I ran away because I loved you too much to be the cause of a rift between you and your family. I fear the consequences of our marriage, not for myself but for you.'

Her words were sobering. Senara's intuition was rarely wrong, but Adam remained optimistic. He was confident about his marriage. He was too realistic to believe it would not present some problems, but they would not be insurmountable.

'Together we can conquer anything,' he smiled. 'The Lovedays are always united. It is our strength.'

The shrill blast of a huntsman's horn destroyed the peace of the countryside. A stag with ten points to its antlers broke through the cover of a copse, bounded over the heather, leaped across a stream and pounded up the side of the tor towards them. The animal was in his prime, strong, fast and magnificent. As he sped past, terror showed in the whites of his eyes and his breathing was heavy. Within moments the baying hounds appeared, and behind them over fifty riders spread like a comet's tail across the moor. Some skirted the copse, whilst the bolder riders were emerging from the trees.

'That's Lord Fetherington's pack.' Adam rose in his stirrups to study the huntsmen. 'Aunt Elspeth is bound to be with them.' He felt his gut tighten with apprehension. Elspeth could be more formidable than his father at times. This was not how he wanted to introduce Senara as his wife. He was looking for other members of his family when he heard Senara's mare whinny in fear.

Senara had edged her mare, Hera, closer to the protection of a tall standing stone. The hounds were massing around them as they pursued their quarry. Hera – unused to the excited, noisy hounds – reared and pawed the air with her hoofs. Senara clutched Nathan tight to her breast.

Adam jumped to the ground to grab Hera's bridle and bring her under control. He was terrified that Senara would be thrown or Nathan injured. Whilst he ducked to avoid Hera's thrashing hoofs, he clung on grimly to the reins, and spoke soothingly to the mare as the last of the hounds pushed past. His arms strained in their sockets as he forced the mare on to all fours and gradually she quietened.

'Are you all right, Senara?' Nathan was crying after the rough jolting and Senara was rocking him in her arms. She nodded, too shaken to speak.

'Good Lord, if it isn't Adam.' The man's voice was breathless from exertion.

Adam froze. There was no warmth in his father's voice. Edward Loveday's face was flushed from the ride and splashed with mud.

Elspeth was with her brother. 'And as you feared, Edward, he is not alone.' Her voice was loaded with accusation. 'What is the meaning of that woman's presence, Adam?'

Edward and Elspeth were glaring at Adam. He was shocked by their manner but other riders were now thundering past, making Hera skittish. Adam was forced to give all his attention to the mare and lead her closer to the protection of the Druid stone to avoid Senara being jostled. Adam's elder twin, St John, also joined them, followed by Edward's wife, Amelia, who stared at Adam's family with growing horror.

Adam stood tall and tense, his anger rising at the manner of their greeting. 'I said I would return once I had found Senara.'

'She's holding a child.' Amelia looked close to swooning. 'A bastard. Oh, Adam, the shame of it.'

'My son is no bastard. Senara and I are married. Nathan was born a month ago.'

There was a moment's stunned silence. Then Elspeth

4

snapped. 'How dare you marry without your father's blessing? And to this . . . this . . .'

'Careful how you speak of my wife, Aunt,' Adam challenged.

Elspeth glared at Senara. 'You are no better than that other fortune-huntress who snared St John for a husband. Used the same ruse too by the look of it.' She rounded on Adam. 'I thought you had more family pride. I will not tolerate this shame brought upon our family again. I will not receive her.'

'But you've always liked Senara. You spoke highly of her when she treated your mares,' Adam was stung to protest.

Elspeth's glare was scathing. 'I have no quarrel with Senara Polglase as a servant.' Her piercing stare pinioned Senara. 'Once I had thought you an exceptional woman. You have betrayed the trust of our family. That is unforgivable.'

She wheeled her horse and galloped off. Edward's anger was as lethal as his sister's, though it carried a chilling disdain. 'Where were you married? Some backwater church by a drunken priest, the same way as St John, was it? Clearly you were not proud of your actions for you to marry in secret.'

Adam's mind reeled under his father's scorn, his anger defensive. 'We intend to restate our vows at Trewenna church before our family and friends. I thought I had your blessing, sir. You knew my intention was always to wed Senara.'

Edward inhaled sharply and his stare was glacial and unnerving. 'You are of age, but I thought you would remember your duty and come to your senses. I will not countenance it. You bitterly disappoint me, Adam. You know the financial problems we are facing. It was your duty to marry a woman with a dowry.'

'The prodigal son returns to find he has lost favour.' St John looked delighted.

Adam ignored his twin, his forthright stare on his father. He had never seen Edward so furious nor so ready to judge him. They shared the same dark, lean good looks but now both their faces were chiselled and bleak with tension. 'Then there is nothing more to be said, sir. You will be informed of the date we are to retake our vows. Your grandson will be christened at the same time by Uncle Joshua.'

'A gypsy's brat is no grandson of mine.' Edward was white-lipped and condemning.

Adam flinched, but continued to hold his father's glare. Amelia pushed her mare between the two men. She was casting anxious glances at the last of the huntsmen riding past. 'Edward, people are watching. This is not the place.'

Edward swept a disparaging gaze over Senara, who kept her head lowered. Her face was shadowed by the hood of her cloak as she soothed Nathan's cries. 'I expected better judgement and loyalty from you, Adam. Attend me at the yard office tomorrow. If you come to Trevowan, you will come alone.'

Adam strove to keep his voice calm but found it was trembling. 'I will enter no place where my wife is not welcome. In the circumstances it would be inappropriate for us to lodge at Mariner's House. Until the service Senara and I will take rooms in Fowey. Naturally I expect the support of my family at Trewenna church in one week's time.'

'You will get no blessing from me on this marriage,' Edward proclaimed. 'I thought you had more pride in our name . . . in your family.'

Adam had heard enough. His temper was dangerously close to erupting and a glance at Senara saw how close she was to tears. His concern was for his wife. 'I am very proud of my family – Senara and my son, Nathan. If you cannot accept them then that is your sad loss, sir.'

Keeping hold of Hera's bridle, Adam mounted his horse

and led his wife and child away.

'Edward, you cannot let them go like that.' Amelia was shaken by the events. She had always tried to reconcile the differences which arose in the family but any form of scandal appalled her. She was shocked by Adam's marriage and agreed with Elspeth's sentiments, but from the curious glances they were attracting there would be gossip. She did not believe a family's problems should be displayed in public. She held back her own misgivings and humiliation to diffuse the scandal she feared would erupt.

'I will not discuss it, Amelia. Adam knew my views. He has betrayed his heritage.' Edward touched his spurs to Rex's sides and sped after the hunting field.

Distraught, Amelia turned to St John. 'Go after your father. Edward forgave you. You must make him see reason.'

St John regarded her without compassion. 'Adam stole my birthright when his scheming made Father change his will and I lost half my inheritance as the elder son. Why should I interfere?'

'Because Adam is your brother. And we must avoid a scandal.' Amelia struggled to control her emotions, which were threatening to destroy her composure. She was shocked by the marriage. She was also embarrassed by the curious glances they had received from the other members of the hunt. She hated scenes or to be the butt of gossip. 'Has your father not enough worries over finances and problems at the yard?'

'The yard is Adam's responsibility, not mine. Let him come grovelling back to Father if he wants to keep his inheritance. I have slaved on the land this last year to help Father recoup some of the losses after Uncle Charles's bank failed. What has Adam done in the last months to help the family? Adam did not consult me when he schemed to steal the yard from me. He can go to the devil for all I care, and take his ill-gotten bride and brat with him.'

His virulence alarmed Amelia. She had not realised that St John hated his brother so much. This rift in the family could destroy them.

'Adam, you must go after your father.' Senara pulled on Hera's reins in her alarm. 'You must reason with him. You cannot mean to throw away your heritage and all the work you have done for the shipyard. More importantly, you cannot disregard the love you have for your family.'

'If they make me choose, it will be you, not them.'

His face was ashen against the darkness of his hair, tied back in a queue. Even the crescent star on his cheekbone was more prominent in his anger. What alarmed Senara most was that his mouth was drawn into a stubborn line. She was appalled to have her worst fears realised. 'There must be no talk of choices.'

'Once you and Nathan are settled in Fowey I will speak with Uncle Joshua about our wedding and the christening. The rest is up to Father.'

Her heart ached at the torment she could see behind his eyes. 'And is not your uncle dependent upon the goodwill of your father for an allowance? He cannot live on his meagre stipend. It is not right to place him in that position.'

'I was hoping Uncle Joshua would make Father see reason.' Adam's voice was weighted and he lapsed into a troubled silence. How could his father be so stubborn?

He stared unseeing at the landscape as they left the moor to take the ferry across the river to Fowey. He was furious with his family. He had assumed that his father would accept his marriage as he had accepted St John's.

That Edward had not, roused Adam's sense of injustice. Senara's gypsy blood had never been an issue to him – it was her integrity and honesty, the very essence of her gentle

8

nature, which had made him fall in love with her.

Adam glanced at Senara. The sun-blessed olive of her skin and hair the colour of rich, warm earth was an exotic and earthy beauty, but now the usual serenity in her green eyes was haunted by worry.

'I will never fail you or Nathan,' Adam promised.

'That is not my fear. Your father loves you too much. His pain is as great as yours – but it must be you who heals this breach. Do not give him an ultimatum.'

Adam did not answer. His anger was as yet too hot to be cooled by reason. They passed the track leading to Trevowan Hard, and he could hear the distant ring of hammers as the men worked on the ships in the yard. Were they working on his designs for the new cutter? And what had happened to *Pegasus* in his absence? *Pegasus* had been the first brigantine built in the yard to his own design. She had proved herself to be fast for her size, and before he left the yard merchants had begun to show interest in placing orders for others to be built. Had the business received those commissions?

Sailing *Pegasus* as a merchant captain had once been Adam's dream for his future. Those plans had changed when his ship designs had won his father's approval. Edward had changed his will to ensure that Adam would inherit the yard. Before that the estate and yard had been linked, the elder son inheriting both, ensuring that one supported the other in times of hardship.

Adam would give up the yard for Senara but no one could take *Pegasus* from him. It had been built and paid for from a legacy left him by his Great-uncle Amos. With *Pegasus* he could support a wife and child. Yet what of now? His travels had left him with less than two pounds in his pocket. He frowned, realising that his family could not have afforded for *Pegasus* to lie idle. Had his father engaged a captain to sail her? And, if so, when would his ship return? He would also need to raise the capital to invest in a cargo for her next voyage. All his past profits had been given to his father to keep the yard solvent when they had faced ruin.

And now his father chided him for lack of family loyalty . . . Again his anger surfaced. He had all but beggared himself to ensure the yard was saved from bankruptcy. He would have done so again if his family had needed such a sacrifice.

Senara interrupted his thoughts. 'Before we cross the river to Fowey I would like to visit my mother and Bridie.'

'Of course. I am sure Leah's welcome will be warmer than my family's.'

Senara was disheartened by his heavy tone and tried to lighten his mood by reason. 'Your father was taken by surprise – the circumstances were unfortunate – and too reminiscent of St John's marriage. St John had to wed Meriel because she was with child. Perhaps he feels that you were also trapped into marriage by the arrival of Nathan.'

'He knows I intended to wed you.'

Senara dropped the subject. The hard edge which had entered Adam's voice disturbed her. He was a man of fierce family pride and loyalty. A rift with his father would crucify him.

They had entered the wood and now rode along the path by the stream which led to her mother's cottage. A spiral of smoke rose from the chimney and a dog from within the cottage barked a warning of their approach. It was a simple two-roomed dwelling with a thatched roof, wild honeysuckle growing over the door and a fenced herb garden. Across the clearing from the house was a small barn which housed a goat and donkey, with a hayloft above. The cottage door was opened and a huge mastiff bounded out to prance around Hera's hoofs. He was salivating with excitement, his scarred

face contorted as his tongue lolled from his vast jaw. The
stooped figure of Leah appeared at the door. Her thin face,
wrinkled from the years she had spent with the gypsies on the
road, broke into a smile.

'Angel! Behave yourself!' Leah shouted at the dog. 'Down,
boy!' The mastiff sprawled on the ground, his body wriggling
as he eased himself forward to greet his mistress.

Adam dismounted, took Nathan from Senara and helped
her to the ground. Senara paused to stroke Angel, who,
despite his fiendish appearance, was as gentle as a lamb with
her family. The dog regarded Adam through his single eye
and licked his outstretched hand. His injuries were from his
days of bull-baiting before Senara had saved his life after his
owner had left him for dead.

While Adam tethered the horses to the fence, Senara
embraced her mother. Leah pulled back from her and wiped
a tear from her eye.

'So your handsome captain found you. That is good.
Come in out of the cold; you must be frozen.' She looked at
Adam and the bundle in his arms. 'That will be my grand-
child then. Not that Senara told me she was expecting when
she left – but I had guessed.'

Adam held the child out to her. 'His name is Nathan.
Senara and I were wed by the ancient rites at Avebury stone
circle. We will retake our vows in Trewenna church as soon as
I can arrange it.'

Leah lifted a grey eyebrow, then took Nathan in her arms
and kissed his brow, her face glowing with emotion. 'To have
wed Senara at Avebury was a bold step and will be frowned
upon by your family. They'll not be so accepting of Senara's
beliefs.'

'They need know nothing of them,' Senara declared. She
had given serious consideration to this matter. 'I respect
Joshua Loveday as a parson of great compassion for

11

mankind. Did not the master he serves preach tolerance and acceptance?'

'Aye, but the teachings of a master and the actions of his followers sadly don't always follow the same road,' Leah responded as she led them into the cottage. 'You would not have come here if you had not already visited your family, Cap'n Loveday. Have they accepted Senara as your bride?'

'They will.' Adam's terse statement was delivered in a voice which indicated the subject was not open for further discussion.

'Where's Bridie?' Senara was puzzled that there was no sign of her sister.

'She be down on the shore looking for mussels for the cooking pot.'

Senara glanced around the room. She had been away for eight months and little had changed. Her old potter's wheel stood in a corner. There was the table, two chairs, a stool and a small cupboard. Two rag rugs were on the floor, and through the open door of the bedchamber she could see the double bed had a patchwork quilt made by Leah. An iron kettle stood on a trivet by the hearth and a large cauldron hung on a hook over the fire. It contained a thick pottage of simmering vegetables and the appetising smell filled the room.

There was a squawk from the rafters, and Senara looked up and held out her hand to the magpie, who regarded her warily.

'Have you forgotten me, old friend?' she chided the bird. He fluffed out his feathers and, after regarding her with his head on one side, swooped down to land awkwardly on her hand. The bird had only one leg, having lost the other in a snare. Senara stroked his white breast before he flew back to the rafter. There was no sign of the owl who used to live in the house.

Seeing her gaze, Leah said, 'The owl took a mate. They are nesting in the barn. There be several wild animals in there that Bridie be tending. She has your skill with healing.'

'Why did she not take Angel to the shore?' Senara was concerned. 'I left him as protection for her.'

'The foolish dog will not stay out of the water no matter how cold it be and he can barely walk for days after. Charity is with her.'

Senara frowned and noticed the grey mingled with the brindle of the dog's muzzle. There was the sound of frantic barking and the scampering of paws as Bridie's dog, Charity, tore into the room. The crossbred spaniel almost knocked Senara over and received a warning growl from Angel and a cuff from his paw which quietened her.

'Senara, Cap'n Loveday, how wonderful you be back.' Bridie Polglase stood in the doorway and put her wooden pail of mussels on the table before she threw herself into her sister's arms.

Senara hugged Bridie, then held her at arm's length. 'My, how you have grown!' The change in her half-sister was dramatic. Bridie had always been small for her age but now at fifteen she had reached five foot. Always slender, she had a trim figure which was showing the softer curves of womanhood. There was a new confidence about her and she held herself upright with a wooden staff. Her gait was slow but with the aid of the built-up shoe which she always wore, she no longer dragged her weak leg. Also the deformity of her right shoulder was no longer so apparent as she held herself straighter. But it was her face which had changed the most, though it was still elfin in its appearance. Her green eyes were large and round and her mouth red and sensuous. She was fast growing into a beautiful young woman.

Bridie curtsied to Adam where a year ago she would have

flung herself at him in her excitement at seeing him again. 'Good day, Cap'n Loveday.'

Adam suppressed a grin and put his hand to his heart and bowed formally to her. 'Your servant, Mistress Polglase.'

Bridie looked flustered. Senara laughed. 'Do not tease her so, Adam.'

'I but show her the respect due to a beautiful young maid. She will soon be breaking men's hearts. You will have to watch over her, Leah.'

'Bridie don't care to mix with others. She has her work to do here, making baskets, tending the vegetables we grow and she's been making pots like Senara taught her. Our needs be simple – they always have been.'

Bridie belatedly noticed the baby Leah was rocking in her arms. Her eyes widened in astonishment. 'Do that be Senara's child?'

'Would you like to hold him? His name is Nathan,' Senara answered.

'But a baby, Senara . . .' Bridie looked uncertain. 'Is that why you went away?'

'The child was part of it. Captain Loveday is my husband.'

Bridie's eyes widened further. 'But they be saying at Trevowan Hard the Cap'n would never wed you. That he'd come back and wed his cousin, who he was to wed afore.'

'That proves it does not do to heed gossip,' Adam said.

'I knew the Cap'n wouldn't have betrayed you.' Bridie gazed in wonder at the child in her arms. 'He be so tiny and so perfect. Can I see him often? I could come to Mariner's House after my work here be done.'

'Do you no longer attend the school at Trevowan Hard?' Senara asked.

Bridie shrugged. 'I can read and write, which is more than most of the pupils can do. What more learning do I need?'

Senara glanced at Leah, whose expression was resigned.

Senara guessed that since she and Adam had left the yard, Bridie would have been taunted for her deformity and the way they lived. Bridie would have felt more comfortable away from the jeers and ridicule, and preferred to live in seclusion as they had in the past.

Senara stroked her sister's brown hair, which hung loose to her elbows. 'I shall visit you often but we may not be living at Mariner's House. We will be staying for a while in Fowey.'

'Why you be living in Fowey?'

'That's enough of your questions, Bridie,' Leah rebuked, and there was an anxious light in her eyes as she regarded Senara. 'Your sister has been journeying for days and must be tired.'

'We should leave soon or we will not get to Fowey before dark,' Adam reminded his wife.

Nathan began to cry and Senara took him from her sister. 'I will feed Nathan before we go, then he will be settled for the journey.'

'You will both eat before you leave,' Leah insisted. 'The soup be ready and will keep the cold at bay.'

Adam nodded. 'Thank you. I'll go and water the horses.'

Leah followed him as he led the horses to the stream. 'I know it bain't my business but you wouldn't be taking lodgings in Fowey if things were right with your family.'

'We had a chance encounter with my father and he was angry. I pray that in time he will see reason.'

'And if he does not . . . ?'

'I will not forsake my wife and child. I shall call on my uncle tomorrow to arrange Nathan's baptism and for Senara and I to restate our vows. I hope you will attend the service.'

'That be most kind of you, Cap'n Loveday, but I wouldn't presume to impose myself upon your family.'

'It will be a simple ceremony, and you have every right to attend. Nathan is your grandson. It will mean a great deal to

15

us both. And there is one more thing I must make clear now. You and Bridie will never want for anything. Even had we taken up residence in Mariner's House, it would no longer be right for you to work as my housekeeper. Or to work at all.'

'I do not want your money, Cap'n Loveday. You've done right by my Senara.'

Adam shook his head. 'A Loveday does not take his responsibilities lightly. I would be insulted if I could not provide for my wife's family. There will be no more discussion on the matter.'

On his arrival at Trevowan, St John flung the reins of his horse to Jasper Fraddon, the head groom. He hurried to the Dower House, which had been given to him on his wedding, expecting to find Meriel already there. She was a poor horsewoman and did not like hunting.

'Where is your mistress?' he demanded of their maid, Rachel.

'Mr Basil Bracewaite did call on her, sir. Got himself one of those fancy coaches and he took her out for a drive. Mistress said she'd be gone but an hour.' The thin, plain maid had no liking for her mistress and her expression was sly as she informed him, 'That were two hours gone, sir.'

'The roads are barely passable for coaches. Bracewaite must be mad.' St John was displeased. He changed his riding clothes and, when Meriel still had not returned, became impatient. He was eager to tell her about the meeting with Adam, and his father's anger.

It was almost dusk when Meriel finally came home. There was mud on her cloak and gown and several blonde curls had fallen around her face where the pins had dropped from her coiffure.

'What happened to you?' St John was suspicious of her dishevelled state.

'Basil lost a wheel on his phaeton and he all but turned us over. He had to send the groom back to fetch another carriage from the stables. The fool could have killed me. I am bruised and ache all over.' Meriel did not meet his gaze and called to the maid to prepare her bath.

'What were you doing driving with Bracewaite? He was supposed to be with the hunt.' St John disliked her superior manner.

She rounded on him with narrowed eyes. 'At least Basil does not leave me to my own entertainments whilst everyone else joins a stupid hunt. That's the last time I allow him to drive me.'

'Bracewaite is a philanderer,' St John accused. 'You should not have gone out with him in the first place. Have you no care for your reputation?'

'You act as though I have encouraged the man in some way. He was kind enough to consider that I might be in need of diversion.' Her contempt lashed him and she flounced from the room.

St John glared at the closed door. Meriel's moods were becoming impossible and had slowly strangled the love he had once felt for her. The financial crisis the family had faced had shown him how shallow was his marriage. Now he acknowledged that Meriel had never loved him, only the wealth and status he could give her. The knowledge flayed his pride, and the love which had held him in thrall of her since their marriage choked on its final breaths. Meriel must learn her place.

And she would not be the only one to get her come-uppance. His ill-humour lifted. Adam had displeased their father and was no longer the favoured son. If Adam was in disgrace, then their father would change his will and the shipyard would again be part of St John's inheritance.

He rubbed his hands together. He heard Rachel Glasson

drag the hip bath across the floorboards in the bedchamber above to position it before the fire. He waited until the maid had completed several journeys carrying hot water up the stairs before he entered Meriel's bedchamber and dismissed Rachel who had just finished unlacing Meriel's corset.

At St John's approach Meriel grabbed a robe to press against her body. Her voluptuous figure was revealed through the fine silk of her chemise, and her blonde hair had been freed from its pins to curl seductively around her heavy breasts. Her beauty was alluring and still had the power to enslave him, but to his cost he had learned how cold and calculating was her heart. Greed was the only passion which governed her. His anger sparked and he snatched the robe from her grasp. 'Why do you hide yourself from me?'

'I dislike being spied upon when I am bathing. Am I allowed no privacy in my own home?'

'A loving wife would be pleased at her husband's attentiveness.'

Meriel glared at him. 'I am bruised and weary from the accident. Have you no consideration?'

'Madam, you forget the lowly status from which I raised you.' His smouldering resentment gathered force. Too often, she forgot her place and the honour due to him. Too often, she did not hide the distaste she felt at his touch. She had shamelessly encouraged Bracewaite today. She did nothing without a motive – nothing without plans for her own self-aggrandisement.

'Is Bracewaite your lover?' He grabbed her wrist.

'You're hurting me.' Her voice was scornful and unafraid. 'I am no man's mistress.'

'You mean you will accept no man as your master.' St John pulled her against him. 'Answer me, is Bracewaite your lover?'

'You know me not at all if you think that.'

He stared into her lovely face. Her eyes were defiant. 'I know you for a cold-hearted fortune-huntress with a hunger for jewels. Your morals can be bought for the right price.'

His cheek stung from her slap and he jerked her hard against him. 'At last! Some true passion from my frigid wife!' He could feel the heat and soft curves of her figure against his body, and cursed the ease with which she could still arouse him.

Aware of his body's response, she tensed in his hold. He knew that look. If he forced himself on her she would be submissive and unresponsive, and he would take no pleasure from her. Yet when she chose, for a matter of her own gain, she could be an ardent lover.

He stepped back from her. Now he wanted her on his terms.

'A pity your absence from the hunt robbed you of meeting Adam and his family. You would have enjoyed Father's response. He was furious.'

'Are you raving? Has Adam returned? But he has no family. How could he?'

St John grinned and walked to the door. 'He has returned with a wife and son.'

Meriel ran after him and caught his arm. Her face was pale. 'You're lying.'

'Why should I lie?' He shrugged off her hand. 'Your bath is growing cold. We can talk later.'

'Tell me now.'

He sat on a padded armchair by the hip bath. 'I will tell you while you bathe.'

Meriel scowled, then turned her back on him, unfastened the ribbon of her chemise and let it fall to the floor. He caught a brief glimpse of her porcelain flesh before she stepped into the bath, and drew her knees up to her chin, hiding her body from him. 'I want to hear about Adam. Who has he married? It's not that slut Senara, is it?'

St John did not answer but kneeled at her side and began to soap her shoulders. She groaned in frustration. 'It is Senara, isn't it? That's why Edward was so angry.'

St John ran his fingers along her arms and across the top of her breasts.

Irritated, Meriel slapped his hand away. 'Was it Senara?'

'Yes.' He studied her flushed face. 'Why does that bother you so? Had Adam married a woman of our class who brought a rich dowry to our family, he would be firmly ensconced as Father's favourite. Today, Father sounded as though he was about to disinherit Adam. I shall have the shipyard, as is my right.'

'Edward would never disinherit Adam.' Meriel stopped pushing St John's hand away from her breasts. 'And you said Adam was with his family. Did you mean Senara has borne him a child?'

'A son, apparently.'

A flicker of pain crossed Meriel's face. 'Adam has a son.' Her eyes glittered in a way which sent a shiver through St John and then her head flopped forward on to her knees. 'Edward will never disinherit Adam, who has given him the grandson who will inherit both the estate and the yard. Adam's child will take our daughter's birthright, as Adam took yours.'

St John gripped his wife's arms, the flesh turning white beneath his fingers. 'Then damn you, woman, give me a son. I won't work all my life to hand over Trevowan to any son of Adam's. I must have a son.'

St John's outburst roused Meriel from the pain of his revelations. She had loved Adam since she was a child, and had seduced him, hoping that he would marry her. Instead he had become betrothed to his French cousin Lisette and then rejoined his ship as a naval lieutenant. Meriel had then discovered that she was pregnant. Knowing Adam would be at sea for at least a year, she had played on the twins' rivalry and seduced St John, then claimed that her child was his.

Her love for Adam had soon turned to hatred at his rejection of her. The thought of his son robbing Rowena of her birthright was more than she could endure. Rowena was almost five now, so why had she, Meriel, not conceived another child? Dr Chegwidden had declared that, after Rowena's protracted birth, Meriel may never conceive again. But what did that old fool know? She was only one-and-twenty, and was strong and healthy. Meriel was adept at playing the seductress. She manipulated men and revelled in the power she had over them. She had been foolish to deny St John his rights so often and hinder her chances of giving him a son.

The last two years had seen a curtailment of many of her dreams of riches. The near ruin of the family had meant drastic sacrifices by everyone to ensure that they did not lose everything. There had been no jewels and fashionable gowns: even her servants had been cut to a single maid. Meriel had been expected to do her own housework and even raise chickens to be sold at market.

It was far from the life of luxury she had planned, and she had taken her ill humour out on her husband. It made no difference that others had sacrificed as much, if not more, in the last two years. Aunt Elspeth had been forced to sell three of her beloved mares, which meant she had to cut back on the days that she could hunt. That had made the old harridan even more difficult to live with, for hunting had taken the place of a husband and children in Elspeth's life. That Amelia, who had brought a fortune with her on her marriage to Edward, must now live on a pittance left Meriel unmoved. Amelia seemed to blossom under adversity and had taken up beekeeping, her honey much sought after at the markets.

Meriel studied St John through lowered lashes. His gaze, hungry with desire, was travelling over her naked flesh. The man who should have provided her with a life of luxury slaved on his father's land as hard as any labourer. Every six weeks, weather permitting, a smuggling run would be made and he would be absent for two nights. The profits from that should have kept them in comfort. St John was sparing with her allowance, yet he spent several evenings a month gambling and consorting with his friends. It infuriated Meriel that she was excluded from that circle. To ease her boredom she flirted with men. She loved to lead them on, promising much but offering nothing but a stolen kiss or the mildest of liberties. She needed their admiration, but she would not give them her body, even though more than one had tempted her with expensive presents.

It was time for change. Drastic change. She had begun to suspect that St John took an occasional mistress. That had not troubled her, for it meant he did not bother her with his attentions. Belatedly, she saw the error of her tolerance. Another woman took away Meriel's power over her husband.

She shivered in the now cool water and rose to stand naked before her husband. She heard his breathing deepen. Why couldn't she love him as she had loved Adam? St John was an inch taller than his twin and from his work on the land he had a lean and athletic body. He was dark and handsome, as were all the Loveday men, though his eyes were slightly more hooded and there was a weaker line to his jaw than either Adam's or his father's. St John had changed since their marriage. Before then he had been weak and a wastrel. Smuggling had hardened him and made him less easy to manipulate. She must regain her control.

She held out her hands for him to help her from the bath and a smiled played over her lips. 'Neither Adam nor his son will ever take that which is ours. I will give you a son.' She stepped into her husband's embrace and began to kiss him.

St John lifted her and carried her to the bed. She surrendered to his loving, her eyes closed as she silently chanted a litany. 'Let me bear a healthy son. Let me bear a healthy son . . .'

When St John slumped over her, she opened her eyes and found him staring into her face. His expression was ruthless when it should have been filled with adoration. Something about his manner alarmed her.

'I need a son, Meriel,' he demanded, and his eyes were glazed with desperation. 'You would be foolish to deny me your bed in future. Too much depends upon it.'

He got up and left her. The evening was still early and Meriel heard the front door close as her husband left the house. His manner and desertion chilled her with dread. She had believed that St John was so in love with her that he would accept any treatment she meted out. But his hatred for Adam was driving him harder to prove himself the better man. He had changed and she was frightened.

23

Chapter Two

S ince the evening was still early, St John rode to Fowey where he knew a card game would be in progress. He was in a restless mood after Adam's return. The favoured twin had fallen from grace and St John felt the need to celebrate. He felt lucky tonight.

The tavern in Fowey was a regular haunt for St John and his friends. The private room attracted merchants and land-owners intent upon an evening of gaming. To St John it had become a place to escape the complaints of a discontented wife and the constraints of a life which was becoming daily more onerous.

After three hours of play St John was in a buoyant mood. There was a pile of two hundred guineas in front of him from his winnings. The low-beamed ceiling of the panelled room reflected the heat of the roaring fire and the men had removed their jackets, relaxing in shirtsleeves and long embroidered waistcoats. Their faces were flushed from the excitement of the gambling and good brandy.

'Luck seems to be smiling on you, Loveday.'

The cold belligerent voice behind him made the hair on St John's neck crackle. For a moment the room seemed to rock and the ground give way beneath him with the violence of a landslide. The pleasure of the night was gone.

Affecting an outward show of calm, St John glanced over

his shoulder at the man he knew to be his enemy. Thadeous Lanyon was short, with a beer-barrel stomach and bulbous, hooded eyes which now glinted with malice.

'Lanyon, it is not often we see you away from counting the profits in your coffers,' St John jeered.

Two of St John's companions sniggered, the others made a show of studying their cards. Lanyon was a man who instilled fear in many. He lived in Penruan – a village a short distance from the Loveday estate of Trevowan – where the Lovedays owned several properties. Lanyon appeared outwardly to be a respectable merchant, but St John knew him for a smugglers' banker who financed several gangs.

'Many are jealous of my success.' Lanyon made the comment sound like a threat. He was overdressed in a gold-braided jacket and elaborate cravat. A large ruby pin gleamed like the eye of Cyclops from its centre. Lanyon's short, powdered wig emphasised his heavy jowls as he went on, 'Yet I succeed when others fail. Though you prosper from the looks of it, Mr Loveday. Strange, when one hears rumours that your family be in financial difficulties.'

St John felt sweat trickle down his neck as he held Lanyon's hostile stare. 'What difficulties would they be? Have you not recently taken possession of a cutter built in the Loveday shipyard? Though I hear the revenue cutter, which we also built, is pursuing the vessels of free-traders.'

'Be amused while you may, Loveday.' Lanyon leaned closer to whisper in his ear. 'There be money come your way by an ill wind. I've an unforgiving memory. You keep poor company in that of your brother-in-law Harry Sawle. The man should take care who he makes his enemy.'

St John shrugged. 'Harry is his own man and, unlike many of the fishermen in Penruan, he is not in your debt. You have no power over him.'

Lanyon showed two missing front teeth as he grinned

sarcastically. 'Do I not? Sawle lost his intended bride to me. He'll lose much more if he doesn't learn respect.'

Lanyon left the room but St John could still feel the malevolence of his presence. He played recklessly to boost his confidence and, in consequence, the cards changed. Within an hour his winnings and own stake money of thirty guineas had been lost.

Damn Lanyon, he fumed. The smuggler was too full of his own importance. Yet despite his bravado, St John was alarmed that Lanyon may suspect that he was now involved in smuggling with Harry Sawle. After finishing another brandy St John's confidence returned. Why should he fear Lanyon? Had not Harry Sawle and himself ambushed and stolen one of Lanyon's cargoes last year? That had been in retaliation for Lanyon informing on an earlier run of theirs to the excise men. St John had been careful to cover his tracks where his smuggling was concerned. The good name of his family must be protected.

His partnership with Harry Sawle sat ill with him. Harry had a violent streak and, since they had ambushed Lanyon's cargo, Harry had begun his own vendetta against Lanyon – to the point of taking Lanyon's wife as his mistress. That Harry had courted Hester Moyle for years before she had married Lanyon made the rivalry between the two men more dangerous. If Lanyon ever suspected that Harry and Hester were again lovers, he would think nothing of having them both murdered.

St John scowled as he regarded his empty purse and rose from the gaming table. 'That's me finished this night.'

'But it is early, my friend.' Percy Fetherington looked appalled. 'Time enough for you to win back what you have lost.'

St John waved his hand in dismissal. 'I have a business appointment early tomorrow.'

As he passed through the taproom, the tobacco smoke, acid smell of poorly trimmed candles, slopped ale and press of sweating bodies clawed at his throat and eyes. Outside, the town was in darkness. A church clock struck one o'clock, its chimes sinister in the thin mist swirling around the roof gables. An occasional lamp burned outside a tavern, inn or the grander houses, creating a pool of light amongst the obsidian shadows.

There was a bite of frost in the air and, shivering, he fastened the buttons on his caped greatcoat and patted down his high-domed beaver hat. He had stabled his horse at an inn in the next street and he began to walk briskly.

Then he heard a footfall behind him. He froze and spun round. There was no figure visible in the poorly lit streets and no sound, yet his senses were now alerted. The smell of an unwashed body wafted to him. Ice coated St John's spine and his heart thumped in mounting fear as he proceeded. Within seconds he knew that he was being followed.

He took to his heels. Two sets of running steps now hammered on the cobblestones behind him.

'Don't let him get away or we won't be paid,' a rough voice ordered.

St John's lungs were bursting and his feet slithered on the icy cobblestones. Twice he wrenched his ankle and almost fell. The second time he was limping badly. Fear pulsed through his veins. The men were gaining on him.

Without slackening his pace he fumbled to tear open his greatcoat where he carried a dagger in an inside pocket. His speed and cold fingers hampered him.

Before he could free the dagger, a cudgel slammed down upon his shoulder. The pain made him stumble. He recovered his balance and the dagger was in his hand as he spun round to face his attackers. Two thickset men loomed from the shadows both armed with cudgels, St John lashed out and

27

felt his blade slice through the flesh of a shoulder. The man cursed and staggered back, while the other assailant swung his weapon down on to St John's wrist, knocking the blade from his grasp.

Instinctively, St John kicked out, his boot catching the second man in the groin. His attacker fell to the ground, groaning. He collided with his injured companion, bringing him down too. It had been a lucky strike. St John knew he was no match for the men in a prolonged fight and, with the brief reprieve, he turned and fled.

Angry shouts followed him. The sound of pursuit spurred him faster. The pain in his chest was excruciating but he dared not rest, though his legs were beginning to weaken and threatened to betray him. Ahead he saw an alley and, in desperation, sped down it. It backed on to walled gardens. With the last of his strength, he shinned over a wall and lay panting on the ground.

The moment he dropped out of sight, his attackers entered the alley and blundered past his hiding place. Within a few yards he heard them stop.

'He ain't down here,' one wheezed. 'Must be 'iding. You try over that wall there . . .'

There was a crash as the man knocked over something within the garden two houses away. A dog barked from inside the building and a light appeared at a window.

'Who's out there?' a man shouted, raising a window sash and thrusting his head through. His nightcap fell off his bald head and he cursed. 'There's footpads about. Let the dog out, Bob, lad. That will see the thieves off. I'll summon the watch.' His voice resounded through the night. 'Thieves! Watchman, to me.'

More windows were opened and further shouting added to the outcry.

The dog was barking frantically and as St John heard the

scraping of bolts, there was a clambering from two gardens away as his assailant leaped back over the wall and ran off. As he drew level with St John, who had flattened himself against the wall, St John heard him order his accomplice, 'Run for it! We ain't getting paid enough to get arrested and send to Botany Bay.'

Although the men slunk away, St John remained in his hiding place. If he was discovered he could spend a night in the gaol on suspicion that he was the thief. Fighting to control his laboured breathing, he did not move until he heard the watchmen arrive and set off in pursuit of his attackers.

St John realised that he had had a lucky escape. Only one man would pay to have him attacked and that was Thadeous Lanyon. Lanyon must suspect that he and Harry Sawle had stolen his cargo during the ambush last year. Therefore Lanyon would want St John dead. And Lanyon would not now let the matter rest once he learned St John had escaped. If St John did not want to spend the rest of his life awaiting an assassin's blow, the smuggler must be dealt with.

After a sleepless night Adam prepared to leave the inn on the slope above the quay at Fowey to ride to Trewenna Rectory. Senara was suckling Nathan at her breast. She was still in her nightgown and robe, her brown hair cloaking her shoulders and trailing to her hips. The vision of his wife and son made Adam pause with love and wonder.

'I am in awe that I have a son.'

She smiled. 'Then for Nathan you must swallow your stubborn pride and speak with your father. You will never be happy until you make your peace with him.'

He did not answer and began to pull on his boots. When he next glanced at the bed, silent tears were running down Senara's face. 'This is everything I feared would happen. I

29

should never have agreed to the service at Avebury without your father's blessing.'

'You must not blame yourself, my love.'

'But I do, and as long as you and your family are at odds, I will not be at peace with myself.' Her tears splashed on to Nathan's face and he stopped suckling, his deep fathomless eyes gazing up at her without judgement. His brow wrinkled as though he sensed her pain. She kissed his temple and he resumed his feeding. Unlike her child she could not be reassured. When she gazed at Adam the rigid set of his shoulders showed her the intensity of his pain.

'Adam, this rift with your family will eventually destroy us. You will realise all you have lost because of me and you will come to hate me.'

He took her in his arms but she would not let him silence her with kisses. 'Go to your father. Ask for his forgiveness.'

'No.' His pain and anger at his father's response to his marriage blotted out reason. 'He had no right to treat us as he did.'

'He had every right,' Senara reasoned. 'All his hopes for the future of the yard were with you.'

He shrugged on his jacket in silence, eventually saying, 'First I must visit Uncle Joshua.'

The morning was overcast and a cutting wind now blew straight off a turbulent sea. The grey stone rectory at Trewenna was not much larger than a cottage and was set within an acre of garden. As Adam approached he noticed that the garden was ploughed and given over to growing vegetables. There were rows of winter cabbages and turnips. A dozen hens pecked at scattered seed and a nanny goat was tethered beneath an apple tree. With all the economies made by the family last year, Edward had been unable to maintain the allowance given to his younger brother. Clearly they were supplementing their meagre stipend by these changes.

The back door to the rectory was open and the short, plump figure of his Aunt Cecily came out and picked up an armful of logs from the pile stacked against the wall. At Adam's approach, she dropped the logs as she held out her arms in delight.

'Praise be that you are home. We have all been worried about you. Even Japhet had no word of you in all his travels. He has been to all the horse fairs in four counties.'

Adam dismounted and embraced his aunt. He doubted that his older cousin would have frequented the places where he had been searching for Senara, apart from the horse fairs. Japhet was the wildest of Adam's generation of Lovedays and made his living as a horse trader and also by gambling.

'Come inside, your uncle will be pleased to see you. He is writing his sermon for Sunday.'

Uncle Joshua had heard their voices and had risen from his desk to greet Adam. He was wearing a red silk dressing robe over black knee breeches and waistcoat. His bagwig was on a wooden wig stand on his desk and his cropped hair was thinning at the temples and splattered with grey.

'My dear boy, this is a joy.' He clasped Adam's shoulders. 'So long without a word. Your father has been worried.'

'That was not the impression I received. Father was far from pleased that I have returned with a wife and son.'

'A wife and son, you say. And would this wife be Senara Polglase?'

'Yes, my son was born a month ago.' Adam stood stiff-backed with defiance. 'I had no knowledge that Senara was expecting a child when she left, and she had no intention of seeking me out if I had not found her. She too believed that marriage between us was impossible. Nathan must be baptised and Senara and I will retake our vows at the same time and the marriage noted in the parish register.'

'Then you are not yet wed.'

Adam became defensive. 'Not by the laws of the Church, but we married according to the custom of Senara's people. I consider those vows binding and there were witnesses. I would have our union blessed by the Church and to ensure that there is no doubt upon the legality of our marriage. And who else would I ask to officiate at two such important events in my life other than my uncle?'

Joshua continued to frown and looked troubled. 'When did you plan for these ceremonies to take place?'

'Next week.' Adam stood with his shoulders squared and chin jutting, his manner imperious.

'But what of the banns? You cannot be legally wed so soon.'

'Since our vows have already been exchanged that constitutes a marriage. The service would be a formality.'

Joshua frowned and Adam persisted: 'I will delay no longer. I had no wish to dishonour my father's wishes, but it would be a greater dishonour to abandon the woman I love who has now borne me a child.'

'I suppose in the circumstances this procedure is legal. For a couple to take their vows before witnesses is to enter into a contract of marriage which would be upheld in a court of law. But you place families who have long been your friends in an awkward position that they must receive Senara. Out of respect for your father many appear to accept Meriel, but to be forced to do so again with Senara may be expecting too much.'

'Senara has no wish to inflict her presence upon anyone who does not wish it. She prefers to live quietly.'

Uncle Joshua studied his hands for a long moment as though they would give him guidance. 'There is also the question of Lisette. There have been many difficulties with her whilst you have been away.'

'Is Lisette still at Trevowan? I had hoped she had gone to

London where Aunt Margaret would have launched her into society and a new life.'

Joshua shook his head. 'Since you rescued Lisette from France, she has made life difficult at Trevowan. But she is Edward's niece and he feels responsible for her. Though Edward has not encouraged her, Lisette remains unshaken in her belief that you would still marry her. She refuses to acknowledge that she ended your betrothal by her marriage to the Marquis de Gramont.'

'She should have come to terms with the truth by now. I know what she suffered in France was hideous, but she is safe and loved here.'

'Edward fears for Lisette's sanity.' Joshua regarded Adam gravely. 'Her moods are volatile and at times she has had to be sedated and locked in her room. In her fragile state of mind . . . well, who knows how she will react to news of your marriage?'

'Then the sooner she accepts the situation the better.' Adam hardened his heart against Lisette's suffering. He could not allow an unstable woman to undermine what he believed was right. Lisette had been the cause of Senara leaving Cornwall. When *Pegasus* had docked at Trevowan Hard after Lisette's rescue, Senara had overheard Lisette's delirious announcement that she and Adam were to wed. It seemed she was still causing trouble now.

Joshua fiddled with the quills in their stand on his desk. 'It is not as simple as that. Lisette idolises you for the way you saved her. Many of her outbursts and erratic behaviour are because you are not at Trevowan. She rides the countryside calling for you. Twice Edward has had to send out search parties as she has not returned by night. Both times she was found the next day lost on the moor and in a terrible state. And there have been other incidents.' He spread his hands and sighed, his expression troubled. 'Suffice to say that her behaviour has been a trial to your family.'

Adam was shocked by Lisette's conduct and, with a grimace, recalled her outrageous behaviour in France when they had been stopped by rebels. Her language had been profane and obscene. 'Perhaps the nuns who cared for her in France were right and she should be committed to an asylum. I thought once she was living in the love and protection of our family, she would recover.'

'We must pray that in time she will. But Lisette is not the only worry your father has to deal with. He has been under a great strain with problems at the yard – lost orders, mounting debts, worries over St John. Your twin is much embroiled with Harry Sawle and smuggling. Meriel encourages him, of course.'

Adam folded his arms and leaned against the wall beside his uncle's desk. 'It was not my intent to add to my father's worries. But why should I bear the brunt of his censure when St John does not?'

'Because he always expected more from you. You were the one upon whom he built his dreams for the future.'

Adam gave a heartfelt groan and ran his hand over his dark hair. 'Have I not done all I could to save the yard? My designs have brought it to greater eminence.' Adam stared out of the window to the tower of Trewenna church, rising above the yew trees in the churchyard. His anger subsided but not his frustration. He refused to feel guilty for marrying Senara.

When his emotions were under control, he asked, 'How bleak are things at the yard? I thought our finances were recovering.'

'The yard has only received one new order since you left. One customer could not meet his instalments after a ship of his was lost at sea. The ship is left unfinished and Edward is barely managing to meet his debts. It will be years before

Amelia's investments are restored. She is receiving no income from her own estate.'

Adam paced the room. He had hoped that by now their finances would have become more stable. Yet this was a difficult time. The economy was volatile. The price of copper and tin were low, and taxes were high, affecting the import of foreign goods. The King's bouts of madness did not help the stability of the country, and the politicians were jousting for power between themselves – either flattering the Prince of Wales or plotting to depose those close to the King. There was rumour that war with France was imminent now that their King was imprisoned.

Adam was aware that the current political situation could cause problems but trusted his father's judgement to surmount them. 'There is my ship, *Pegasus*. Surely Father has not let her lie idle.'

Uncle Joshua brightened. 'Indeed not. Your Uncle William has captained her. With England at peace, the navy has put many of her officers out to grass. William was moping at Trevowan for two months before your ship returned from a short voyage to Rotterdam. The reputation of *Pegasus*'s speed goes before her. William drummed up some cargo and sailed with her to Venice. She should be back by the middle of February.'

Adam's heart sank. That was four weeks. If his father remained against him, he needed to provide his family with an income. Yet any voyage would mean he was away from Senara for months at a time.

Uncle Joshua regarded him thoughtfully. 'I will talk to Edward if you wish, but it would be better coming from you. He will have slept on your homecoming and all that entails. You may now find him more accepting.'

'And if not, will you still perform the ceremony for us? And Nathan's baptism?'

35

'I would be remiss as your religious guardian if I did not.'

'Then let it be one week from today.' Adam strode to the door. 'I have some things I need from Mariner's House. If Father is at the yard I will talk to him there.'

As Adam left, Cecily came in to put her arms around her husband. 'I heard everything from the kitchen. I never thought Adam would be the one to cause so much worry. This has come at a bad time for Edward. Perhaps once your brother gets used to having a grandson all will be forgiven.'

'Not a grandson with gypsy blood. To have first St John and now Adam marry beneath them will be a bitter blow to Edward.' Joshua could understand his brother's anger. 'It was Adam's duty to marry a woman with a dowry and position which would have ended this financial crisis the family faces.'

'But I had no dowry, and you took me as your bride,' Cecily reminded him.

'You, my dear, were the respectable daughter of a parson. As a younger son I had no expectation of riches. Senara is a lovely woman and has many good qualities, but you cannot deny her heritage. Even if Edward accepts her, many of our neighbours will not. Edward has much need of these people's goodwill if he is to recover from the ruin which could still so easily engulf him. If the yard was to lose orders because of a customer's prejudice against Adam's wife, it could bring disaster to us all.'

St John was becoming adept at subterfuge. Once a week he rode around the perimeter of the estate checking dry-stone walls and satisfying himself that any work to be completed that week by the labourers had been carried out. If a meeting with Harry Sawle was necessary, it would be pre-arranged during this time. Today they were to meet at the bridge over a stream in Four Acre Wood.

As St John cantered over the land he noted that a beech tree had blown down in a recent storm and had damaged a cow byre in the top meadow. The storm had also caused a ditch to overflow and flood a quarter of another field and the sheep must be moved to higher ground.

He entered a wood and frowned at seeing that several young trees had been chopped down and dragged away to fuel a thief's winter fire. The wood was near a track, and fresh wagon ruts were visible. He would alert Dick Nance, the son of Isaac, their bailiff, to patrol the wood at night. Dick had taken on the role of gamekeeper after several farm hands had been laid off last year.

Even though he knew that none of his labourers was near Four Acre Wood, St John scanned the landscape to ensure he would not be observed before approaching the bridge. To his annoyance Harry was not there. St John was angry after the attack on him last night and was in no mood to be crossed. The clock tower of Penruan church chimed the hour and St John checked it against his own fob watch. Harry was late. It began to drizzle and the clock had chimed the half-hour before Harry rode over the bridge. St John was cold, wet and in a surly mood.

'You're late.'

Harry shrugged. His hair, several shades darker blond than Meriel's, was plastered to his scalp and the rain had moulded his jerkin to his muscular form. His face, which had been battered in many fights, was ruggedly handsome. 'I bain't a man of ease and luxury like yourself. I still have a fishing smack and a catch to land. It would look suspicious if I gave up the life which brings me an honest income.' He pulled a leather pouch from inside his jacket. 'That should make your wait worthwhile. Two hundred and thirty guineas' profit from the last run, and another cargo due next dark of the moon, seas permitting.'

'The winter storms have already delayed one cargo and part of another was swept away so that we barely broke even.'

'Hazards of the trade,' Harry grumbled. 'The revenue cutter has been vigilant along this coast. We've been lucky not to lose more. They confiscated a cargo off Mullion Cove and another near Mevagissey. None of those cargoes was paid for by Lanyon. I reckon the new officer be in Lanyon's pay.'

'Would it not be worth our while to bribe him, if he can be bought?'

'This man is a stickler for the rules. Lieutenant Beaumont bain't the type to take no ordinary bribe.'

'Lanyon is getting too big for his boots.' St John's anger flared. He still ached and had a sore shoulder after his ordeal. 'Lanyon had two men set on me last night in Fowey. I got away unscathed after a fight. Lanyon thinks he is beyond justice. But he will not get away with trying to have me killed.'

'It be time Lanyon were dealt with once and for all.' Harry's voice was low but laced with threat.

Despite his anger, St John looked aghast at his companion. He knew how Harry dealt with enemies and he did not want any part of murder. Lanyon must be punished by the law. 'Forget it, Harry. Lanyon's wife is your mistress – is that not revenge enough?'

Harry shook his head. 'No man gets the better of me.'

'Let the law deal with Lanyon,' St John advised. 'He's bound to overreach himself soon. We'll find a way to inform the authorities about him.'

'Don't you want that bastard dead for what he did to you? And what of your father? Lanyon tried to ruin him by calling in a loan early.'

'There are ways and means to get back at Lanyon. Murder is not one of them.'

Harry gave an unpleasant laugh. 'I'm not a patient man, Loveday.' He kicked his horse into a canter and sped off.

St John stared after him with a shiver of alarm. Harry was ruthless and without remorse. He was also a hot-headed fool. The pouch of guineas weighed heavily in his jacket: money which brought him freedom from the financial constraints his family had placed upon him. It was money for pleasure to enjoy his life to the full, as was his right as a gentleman. But would the cost be too high?

Adam approached the Loveday shipyard with a heavy heart. It had begun to rain and he pulled the brim of his hat further over his eyes. The thickness of his greatcoat protected him from the cold and wet. His thoughts were as bleak as the weather. His pride demanded that his wife was accepted as an equal by others – yet he was realistic. It would happen slowly, perhaps over some years. Senara had the grace and dignity to overcome prejudice eventually.

The shipyard was awash with mud churned up by the winter rains. Despite the downpour, the yard was busy with men clambering over the scaffolding around the ships' cradles; others were at work in the sheds or smithy. To prevent the scaffolding around the vessels becoming slippery with mud, planks had been put on the ground around the two cradles. One cradle held a partly built brigantine – on which it looked as though work had been abandoned. The other held the sleeker lines of the latest cutter Adam had designed. There were also plank walkways from the worksheds to the cradles.

Piles of tree trunks with their bark removed lay in a field for seasoning. The curved trunks used for the ribs and knees of the ship were set apart from the straight ones. Two plough horses were dragging a tree trunk by chains to the saw pit. Adam passed by a file of men trudging through the mud carrying sawn timber from the saw pit to the shaping sheds.

The rain kept the shipwrights' and labourers' wives and children inside the dozen cottages which formed a hamlet within Trevowan Hard. There was also the Ship kiddleywink, a tavern which also doubled as a general store. From the schoolhouse Adam heard the children shouting out an answer to a question. The sound of Solomon's hoofs squelching in the mud was lost amid the general clamour of rasping saws and banging hammers. As he passed the work-sheds there was the smell of heated iron, sweat and wood smoke. The air of the yard smelled of a mixture of fresh-cut wood, wet rope, tar, and the mud and salt from the tidal inlet of the River Fowey.

When he drew level with the single-storey cottage which served as the yard office, he saw the door was shut and no smoke came from the chimney. His father was not working at the yard.

Adam sighed. However difficult the interview may prove, he wanted it over with. He put Solomon in an empty stall in the yard stable, loosened his girths and placed a blanket over him for warmth, before walking to Mariner's House. The door was never locked, even during his long absences. Although it was the largest dwelling at the Hard, it was unpretentious. Mariner's House had been extended from a cottage when Adam had taken up residence after leaving the navy and joining his father to work in the yard. Although he loved his home, Trevowan, the conflict between him and St John had made it easier to live here.

The house would be adequate in which to raise a family, with four bedrooms, a parlour, a dining room, a study and kitchen. In the roof were two rooms for the use of servants. The house was gloomy, for the shutters remained closed against the winter storms, and without a fire it smelled musty from lack of use. It was sparsely furnished and the furniture was covered in dustsheets. He opened a shutter in the parlour to let in some light.

In his months searching for Senara he had travelled with little baggage. His clothing had become worn and travel-stained and he needed fresh shirts which had been left here. The wardrobe was empty, but he found everything packed away in a cedar chest which protected the material from the damp and moths. He packed some essentials into his saddle-bag and, returning to the parlour, was about to close the shutter when he heard a familiar bark. Scamp, his liver and white part-bred spaniel, from the same litter as Charity, was running towards the house and Edward was walking to the office from the stables. Edward glanced across at the house but did not halt in his stride and disappeared into the office. He would have seen Solomon in the stable and so knew Adam was at the yard.

Scamp ran in to greet Adam, wriggling on his back in his delight at being reunited with his master. When Adam was away the dog stayed at Trevowan. He patted the spaniel, then picked up his saddlebag to stride purposefully to meet his father. Scamp ran to the woodpile on the scent of rats or rabbits.

Several shipwrights had noted Adam's presence and called out greetings. He gave them a cursory nod, too preoccupied to be more genial. Adam knew each worker by name and usually concerned himself with the men and their families' welfare.

Adam rapped on the office door and entered without waiting for his father's response. He dropped his saddlebag on the floor and closed the door but did not move further into the room. His father had lit the fire and was seated at his desk. There was accusation in Edward's stare as he regarded Adam in silence. The tension in the room was ominous as the blue eyes of father and son locked in condemning stares.

'There is no ship in the dry dock.' Adam finally attempted

41

a neutral conversation. The building of the dry dock had been undertaken at great expense. The money needed to repay the loans raised had caused many of the financial problems before Adam left. It was a bad sign that the dry dock was lying idle.

Edward sat back in his chair, his expression harsh. There was a hollowness to his cheeks and deeper lines around his mouth and eyes. The strain of the last months was evident.

'You knew my intentions when I left,' Adam went on. 'I had hoped, if not for your blessing, then at least your acceptance.'

'And what must I accept? That my son has followed some ridiculous romantic ideal and has forgotten all family loyalty and obligation?' Edward rose, his hands clasped behind him in an imperious pose. 'I did not cast aside family tradition to name you as heir to the yard, only to have it pass to a gypsy's brat.'

'Who is your grandson, sir,' Adam replied with equal heat.

'And, if I remember correctly, he is also the grandson of a hanged horse thief – a rogue – a vagabond.'

'Who was innocent of that crime. Yes, Senara's father was a gypsy – a horse trader, an opportunist with a keen eye and a cunning mind to survive. Many a Loveday has deemed such attributes qualities to prize.' Adam was breathing heavily, his hands clenched as he struggled to remain civil. 'My great-grandfather for one. And Japhet and St John can hardly be called law-abiding. Many would claim them as rogues, but not vagabonds because they were born to a respectable family. Great-grandfather was a buccaneer, a womaniser, and a gambler before he married Anne Penhaligan solely for her money and the land of Trevowan.'

'Your great-grandfather married into one of the oldest families in Cornwall – an example you would have done well to follow. If St John does not have a son, the estate would have passed to you or your son, as well as the yard. But I will have no gypsy as an heir to Trevowan – is that clear? It will go to Rafe.'

Adam held his father's enraged stare. He had found it hard to accept that St John would inherit Trevowan, the estate and house he loved, but whilst St John remained without a son there was still a chance that the land he coveted would one day be Adam's own. Trevowan and the yard were his heritage. Injustice blazed through him that his father would even consider taking it from him. 'My half-brother is not a year old. Are you prepared to gamble he has the aptitude to run a shipyard?'

'I pray he grows up to know his station and duty,' Edward raged. 'I will not give my blessing on this marriage.'

Adam lost his temper. 'Would you prefer that I lived openly with Senara as my mistress and raised a brood of bastards, for that would have been the alternative?'

'Then you are a fool.'

'If it is foolish to honour and respect the only woman I will love, then I am proud to be such a fool. I have a son any man would be proud of and he will be brought up to revere the Loveday name and his heritage with pride.' Adam was breathing heavily as he outstared his father.

Edward Loveday did not look away and his eyes sparked with outrage.

Adam said with passion, 'Nathan's baptism will take place at Trewenna church in a week. Senara and I will also retake our vows. If my family does not stand by me in this, I have no course but to turn my back on them. Good day, sir.' He picked up his saddlebag and marched from the office.

Halfway across the yard the master shipwright, Ben Mumford, caught up with him. 'Glad you be back, Cap'n. You've been sorely missed. There be a problem with the rudder on the cutter we be working on. I need your advice.'

'Speak with my father,' Adam snapped without breaking his stride. 'It is no longer my concern.'

'But, with respect, Cap'n, Mr Loveday can see nothing wrong with the workings. We've redone the work twice and still it bain't right.'

Adam had reached the stable and turned to study the cutter in its cradle. His father marched from the office to the smithy next door to the stable without looking in Adam's direction. Edward's face was rigid with anger.

It was matched by Adam's fury and he answered Ben Mumford curtly. 'We had this problem before and I updated the plans.'

'Then those plans be lost. And we be falling behind with the work.'

Adam turned to leave and Ben put a hand on his arm to stop him. 'Cap'n, the rudder! What's to be done about it?'

Adam swallowed his anger to focus on the problem. The rudder had been a new design and it was pride which spurred him to correct any fault in it. 'I'll take a look.' He threw his saddlebag on to the floor of the stable and headed back to the cutter. A half-hour later he had solved the problem and drawn a rough sketch of the work to be carried out. 'Keep that with the original plans. I haven't time to draw up a complete set.'

His anger towards his father had not abated and every moment he spent in the yard was like salt to an open wound. Shipbuilding was in his blood. The yard was his pride. The rivalry with his older twin had always stemmed from the knowledge that St John was heir to both the estate Adam loved, and the shipyard. When Edward had made Adam heir to the yard, St John had never forgiven his twin and their rivalry had intensified.

For Adam the prospect of inheriting the shipyard was the culmination of a dream. During his years in the navy he had used his knowledge of ship construction to sketch vessels from around the world. His ambition was for the Loveday yard to build larger ships, their reputation one of the finest in England. He also had not given up hope that he would one day be master of Trevowan. It was not easy to walk away from all that.

His father came out of the office and paused at seeing Adam still in the yard.

'The Cap'n 'as sorted the problem with the rudder, sir,' Ben Mumford shouted.

Edward nodded and went back into the smithy. Adam glared after him and marched to the stable. Anger burned through him at his father's stubbornness. He had been prepared to gamble everything to win Senara as his bride. And it looked like that was exactly what it had cost him. Everything. He was unprepared for the pain which skewered him. To lose the yard was bad enough, but Trevowan was not a dream he could easily relinquish.

But if he had to, he would. His father had until Nathan's christening to make his decision. If Edward Loveday was not at the service, Adam would leave the district and make a home for Senara elsewhere. He still had *Pegasus* and she would provide him with a living as a merchant captain.

Adam had taken a room at the Ship Inn, a popular tavern converted from the townhouse which had once belonged to the Rashleigh family, not far from the Town Quay. Fowey had a natural harbour and was far enough from the mouth of the river to provide a safe haven for ships. Apart from its fishing industry and shipyards scattered along its river, Fowey was a thriving port with ships exporting tin and china clay mined in the area. The port was surrounded by low-lying hills and was cradled between the arms of two headland points, each with armed forts. The harbour was further protected by a chain which linked the two forts and which was raised each evening to prevent unwanted shipping entering the port.

By land Fowey was cut off from the rest of Cornwall, its only approach road a narrow winding track. To avoid any slight to Senara, Adam had sent out invitations only to those neighbours he believed regarded him highly enough to accept his bride, also to workers, tenants and villagers who were always included in family celebrations. He had asked his old friend Sir Henry Traherne to stand as godfather to his son. He had sent word to his Aunt Margaret living in London and his cousin Thomas and his new wife, but did not expect them to attend at such short notice as many of the roads would be quagmires at this time of year.

Sir Henry's wife and her mother, the Lady Anne, were indisposed with a fever of the lungs, but Sir Henry's sister-in-law, Gwendolyn Druce, who also lived at Traherne Hall, had spent Christmas with friends in Truro and her invitation had been forwarded to them. Squire Penwithick had sent word that he would attend but that his wife was also indisposed. Adam controlled his anger; at least Sir Henry and the squire's presence would give a show of acceptance from amongst Adam's neighbours. Lord Fetherington had sent his apologies, declaring he had business in Truro.

The next day Adam's cousin Hannah arrived unexpectedly at the inn. Adam was out trying to get a cargo for *Pegasus*'s next voyage. Senara received Hannah with some trepidation, nervous that Adam was not present. Hannah Rabson swept into the bedchamber of the inn where Senara was nursing Nathan.

'I could not wait until the christening to see my new cousin. I called at the Rectory and Mama was full of the news of your wedding. You look glowing, Senara. How could Uncle

Edward treat Adam so scurvily? I have come from the yard after telling him he will regret his actions.' Hannah eased back the shawl which was wrapped around Nathan and which partially obscured his face. 'The little darling has a shock of dark hair and I swear he has Adam's mouth.'

Senara laid Nathan on the bed. She liked Hannah but her forthright manner was daunting. 'May I ring for some refreshments for you, and take your coat? Come sit by the fire. You must be frozen. The sea mist can chill to the bone at this time of year.'

Hannah shrugged off her thick coat, pulled off her gloves and went to stand with her back to the fire. 'Once I have warmed my hands I must hold my cousin. Some mulled wine would be most acceptable.'

Senara pulled the bell rope and smiled awkwardly at Hannah as she waited for the maidservant to appear. Hannah was two years younger than Adam and had been married for six years to Oswald Rabson. In that time she had presented her husband with two sons and two daughters. Her hair was dark but the firelight caught its coppery tinge, and she had inherited the striking Loveday looks of high cheekbones, sensuous mouth and a noble Grecian nose. She had a darker complexion than most women of her class, for Hannah was a farmer's wife and worked as hard in the fields as her husband. There was a redness to her hands which she did not trouble to hide and which showed her hard work on a farm that struggled to support them.

Hannah chuckled. 'Oh dear, you look quite stricken, Senara. I never meant to make you feel ill at ease.'

'No you do not. You are kind – very kind. More than I deserve.'

'Stuff and nonsense. I could give my family a tongue-roasting for the way they are behaving. Elspeth has always been a dragon. But I thought Uncle Edward—'

47

Senara interrupted. 'Please do not speak against them. They are good people.'

The maid arrived and Senara ordered some wine and some saffron cakes for her guest. 'I am very honoured that you have called upon me, Mrs Rabson.'

'None of that Mrs Rabson nonsense. We are cousins now. You must call me Hannah.' She picked up Nathan and laughed as he opened his eyes to frown up at her unfamiliar face. 'He is perfect. Adam must be so proud. And St John will be envious that Adam has a son and he does not. Their rivalry in all things is as fierce as ever. Not that Rowena is not a delightful child. She is a lovely girl. Another true Loveday.'

Hannah's effervescence was as disconcerting as it was heart-warming.

'I am sorry that Adam is not here,' Senara said. 'He will regret having missed you.'

Hannah sat by the fire and smiled at Senara. 'It gives us more time to get to know each other. You must have a poor opinion of us Lovedays.'

'Indeed not,' Senara protested. 'It is what I feared could happen if I married Adam. I have no wish to drive a wedge between him and his father.'

'Edward expected too much from Adam – I suppose because St John is often a disappointment to him. His pride is injured and the Lovedays have more than their fair share of pride. Adam loves you, and if you can make him happy that is all that is important.'

Senara sat on the edge of the bed, unsure what to say. The maid brought the mulled wine in a pewter flagon and a dish of saffron cakes. Senara poured the wine, then handed a glass to Hannah, but some of it spilled on her hand.

'My gracious, you are trembling. Am I such an ogress?' Hannah laughed and glanced around the room. 'This is too bad. You have a lovely house at the yard which you should be living in. An inn is no place to rear a baby.'

Senara blushed. 'It is all we can afford at present. All Adam's money was used to pay off the debts of the yard . . . That was as it should be. He lost so much income during the time he was looking for me. And I did not make it easy for him. I should have had more faith . . . But I am content here. I have all I need.'

'But not all you deserve as Adam's wife.'

There was the sound of footsteps on the stairs and the door opened to admit Adam. His expression had been drawn with worry but on seeing Hannah it brightened. 'Dear cousin, this is a pleasure.'

'I wanted to welcome Senara to our family and see my baby cousin. He is adorable. And so good-natured.'

'He takes after Senara in temperament,' Adam grinned.

Hannah stood up and Senara took Nathan from her to put him into the drawer which acted as his cradle. Stacked against a wall were the shaped pieces of wood which Adam was carving to make a proper cradle for his son. Hannah saw them and frowned. 'My baby Luke is still in our cradle or I would loan it to you.'

Adam kissed Hannah's cheek. 'I have not congratulated you on the birth of another son. You seem to thrive on producing children, and look as radiant as ever.'

'Enough of your flattery. I am as weary as a crone.' She battled constantly against tiredness. This winter Oswald had suffered much with the ague, leaving many of the farm jobs for her to contend with. 'I came to suggest that the wedding and christening feast be held at our farm. We are close enough to Trewenna church to make it convenient.'

'I had thought to hire the parlour of the inn at Trewenna,' Adam replied.

'I will not hear of it and, having seen how cramped your

quarters are here, I insist that you live at the farm. We have two spare bedrooms and one can be made into a parlour to give you peace from my noisy brood.'

Adam shook his head. 'Thank you, Hannah, but we could not impose.'

Hannah struck Adam playfully on the arm in feigned exasperation. 'You are my cousin and will not be imposing. It is the perfect solution. Return with me now and Senara and I can start on the baking for the celebrations. With less than a week we have no time to spare.'

Adam looked at Senara, who nodded acceptance. Hannah had made a generous offer, and it would be rude to slight her by refusing. And it would not be for long. Senara had already decided that if Adam had to go back to sea to make a living, she would live with her mother and Bridie.

Adam grinned at his cousin. 'You always were exceptional, Hannah. I am in your debt.'

'The Lovedays always stick together and if your father chooses to forget that, I do not. Besides, I think it may make it easier for him this way to accept what is inevitable. You could hardly expect him or Amelia to attend a celebration held in an inn.'

'I expect nothing from my father.' Adam went to saddle the horses.

Chapter Three

Senara was kept too busy baking and helping Hannah at the farm to feel awkward in the company of her family. Oswald Rabson accepted their arrival and raised no objections at his wife's plans.

'Hannah will enjoy your company,' he greeted her warmly. 'We are isolated here in winter if the roads are bad.'

Senara liked Oswald. He said little, content to listen to conversation rather than talk. He was a wiry man, with amiable though rugged features. His brown eyes were gentle and adoring whenever he gazed at his wife. Beneath the weathered complexion there was a splash of high colour on his cheeks. Senara was concerned when she heard him coughing through the night, and she feared that he was suffering from consumption. She had herbs which would ease Oswald's discomfort but there was no remedy to cure such an ailment, which was made worse by the damp and mist.

The farmhouse was an old timber-framed, wattle-and-daub construction dating back two centuries. The flagstones were worn from the passage of feet, and draughts crept through the diamond-paned windows and under the doors. Even the fires in the bedchambers and living rooms did not keep away the persistent damp.

Senara helped Hannah milk the cows. They had no

51

milkmaids and only Aggie, a general maid, and Dick and
Mab Caine to help them. The married couple lived in a tied
cottage and worked in the house and farm. They were
middle-aged and surly and did their work with an air of
being constantly put upon. Mab Caine's narrow ferret
features had looked horrified on encountering Senara in the
kitchen for the first time.

'Senara and my cousin Adam will be staying with us, Mab,'
Hannah explained. 'We are to hold the feast following their
wedding here in three days. You can start cleaning the front
parlour. Aggie will help you. Adam and Oswald cleared it
out last night.'

The parlour had been used as a storeroom for some years.
Mab grumbled beneath her breath as she shuffled through
the house. When she passed Senara she made a furtive sign of
the cross as though warding off evil. 'I bain't taking no
orders from 'er. I got enough to do.'

Hannah blocked her exit from the kitchen. 'You will treat
Mrs Loveday with respect, or you will answer to me, Mab.'

'Some say she be a witch. What if she do put the evil eye
on me?'

'There's some as would say it would be an improvement,
Mab Caine.' Hannah pushed her through the door. 'Enough
of your nonsense.'

Aggie giggled as she followed the older woman. She was a
frail-looking young woman not much older than Bridie.

Hannah shook her head and laughed. 'Pay no mind to
Mab or Aggie, Senara. The poor lass is woolgathering most
of the time. Mab is never happy unless she is moaning.'

Adam had taken the farm wagon into Fowey to collect the
rest of their belongings from the inn. He also purchased a list
of provisions suggested by Senara, who did not want the
expense of the celebrations to fall on the Rabsons. It had
taken the last of his meagre funds.

Hannah protested when Adam unloaded the wagon and piled into the kitchen flour, spices, currants, meat, fish, fowls, vegetables, kegs of wine, brandy and cider.

'How many do we cater for?' Hannah asked.

'We may be shunned by the gentry but I have received well-wishes from the shipwrights and people of Penruan. Our wedding seems to be the gossip of the district. Even if it is curiosity which brings people to the church, all are welcome, and will be given refreshment to bless our union and the health of our son.'

Senara sighed as Adam left the room. His intentions had been admirable but he had no idea of the amount of work involved for the women. 'Hannah, shall I ask Adam to take the wagon to fetch my mother and sister to help with the baking?'

Hannah was storing the provisions in the pantry and called back, 'We could do with the extra help.'

Leah arrived an hour later and rolled up her sleeves. She set herself and Bridie to pluck the two dozen ducks, pheasants and hens which had been purchased from a butcher and which had already been hung. A pig had been slaughtered and was slowly cooking on a spit over a fire in the yard. Every quarter-hour when the grandfather clock chimed in the parlour, Senara ran outside to turn the spit handle so that the meat did not burn.

Throughout the morning there would be a hesitant rap on the door and the wife of a shipwright or tenant of Trevowan shyly offered her services. Keziah Sawle, the wife of Meriel's oldest brother, Clem, arrived with Meriel's mother, Sal, from Penruan. Keziah was not a local woman and foreigners were always treated with suspicion. But Keziah did not care whether she was accepted or not, and was regarded with awe by the villagers. She had also stood up for Senara when the fishwives of Penruan had turned against her, naming her a witch and wanting her driven from the district.

'We wanted to show our support, my lovelies.' Keziah unwrapped several goat cheeses, which she made from the milk from her own herd, and laid them on the table. She was a buxom woman with a mass of curling red hair tied back with a scarf.

Sal Sawle placed four large pies on the table. 'They be rabbit caught by our Harry. And I'll send along six fresh loaves on the day. It bain't right that Edward Loveday has accepted our Meriel as St John's bride and he be said to have turned against Adam. Adam has always done right by us. I wish you both well. There'll be many turned out from Penruan to wish you happy on the day.'

'Thank you both,' Senara said, overcome with emotion.

'And who is running the Dolphin Inn with you here, Sal?' Hannah asked.

Sal chuckled. 'My Reuban may 'ave lost his legs, but since he be so fond of drinking the profits, I told 'im it be time he got behind the counter again. Harry has rigged him up a seat on wheels, so he can push himself along. It will do the ol' misery good. He's been moping too long since Thadeous Lanyon's coach ran over 'is legs.'

At the laughter ringing in the kitchen, Davey and Abigail, Hannah's two eldest children, ran excitedly around the skirts of the women until Hannah chased them out to search for hen eggs in the barn.

Later that morning Pru Jansen from the Ship kiddley at Trevowan Hard appeared with her daughter, Carrie, and two other wives from the yard.

'We wondered if you could do with some help,' Pru volunteered.

'The more the merrier,' Hannah said with a laugh.

Senara dabbed a tear from her eye. The support of the local women was unexpected and meant a great deal to her.

★ ★ ★

To be married in a suitable dress troubled Senara as she did not want to shame Adam. She knew that Adam's funds were low and it would be impractical for him to buy her a new gown. Living with the gypsies had taken a toll on her best green woollen dress, and the only decent gowns she possessed were the two summer gowns Adam had bought her last spring. Apart from being unsuitable on a frosty morning, Senara's figure had not yet returned to normal after the birth of Nathan, and they did not fit her. Hannah had offered Senara her best velvet gown of burgundy, which was showing wear. That did not trouble Senara, but the difference in their heights meant that the gown did not reach Senara's ankles. Even so, Senara was grateful.

While Senara had been feeding Nathan on the morning of the celebrations, there was a commotion downstairs in the farmhouse and Hannah burst into the room, looking jubilant. She was carrying a parcel wrapped in calico. 'This has been sent by Amelia. There is a note. It must mean that Edward has forgiven Adam – that he will be at the wedding.'

'I hope so, for Adam's sake.' Senara took the note. Her smile faded as she glanced back at Hannah. 'Amelia says that since Adam has seen fit to invite so many guests, his bride must appear worthy of her husband.'

Senara laid the now replete Nathan on the bed and unfastened the ribbon on the parcel. A dress of royal-blue velvet edged with silver was revealed and a hooded cloak of navy velvet lined with cony was beneath it. 'How can I accept this? It is too expensive.'

Hannah was frowning. 'Amelia is aware of the viciousness of gossip. These are from her wardrobe, though have scarcely been worn. Do not build your hopes that it means she has accepted the marriage.'

'Then I shall not wear her clothes.'

'It would be a pity not to.' Hannah held up the beautiful gown. 'View this offering as a conciliatory gesture. Perhaps it means that Uncle Edward is mellowing. If they turn up at the wedding and you are not wearing it, they might take offence.'

'And I am not supposed to?' Senara was angry.

'Sometimes our heart has to be larger than others'.'

Senara laughed. 'That sounds like something my grandmother would say.'

Separately wrapped beneath the cloak was a smaller parcel. It contained the Loveday christening robe and cap, the ancient lace yellowed with age.

At noon, as the wedding party approached Trewenna church, Senara felt faint. She was tired from the days of baking and a sleepless night with Nathan. To honour the custom of the groom not seeing his bride on the day of the wedding until the service, Adam had spent the night at Trewenna Rectory. Senara rode to the church in the Rabsons' farm wagon. Bridie had spent the previous day decorating it with boughs of holly and ivy, and had scoured the woods for snowdrops to make her sister a bridal posy. Other snowdrops were woven into a garland of ivy for Senara's hair.

When Senara appeared in Trewenna village a cheer went up from the people gathered to watch the wedding. Senara recognised shipwrights and their families from the yard, and fishing, mining and farm families from nearby villages and hamlets, especially Penruan.

'So many people,' she gasped to Oswald. She had asked him to escort her to her husband's side.

'Adam has always been popular and many will want to wish him well.'

At the church Senara handed Nathan to Cecily Loveday, who had come to the lych-gate to meet her. The church gate had been decorated with love-knots of white ribbon and posies and nosegays made from the roses Sir Henry Traherne had sent over from his hothouse.

On trembling legs Senara walked up the path on Oswald Rabson's arm to where Adam was waiting in the porch of the church. Beside him was Cecily's eldest son, Japhet, who must have returned to Trewenna last night.

Japhet softly whistled his appreciation as he watched Senara approach. 'It is time you made an honest man of Adam, Senara.'

Adam stared at her with such naked love in his eyes that Senara felt her throat close with emotion and she feared she would never be able to speak her vows.

Harry Sawle, Meriel's brother, was another to run an appraising eye over Senara. 'Here be your maid come at last, Adam. We be wondering if she'd thought better of it and found a more handsome rogue to wed.'

Clem Sawle added to the jesting. 'A christening and a wedding on the same day. Didn't think the Lovedays needed such economies to cheat your friends out of two celebrations.'

Barney Rundle from Penruan shouted, 'Cap'n Loveday be a wise man. Makes sure he 'as a son to follow him afore he do shackle himself to a bride. Got the right idea 'as the Cap'n.'

'You be making the Cap'n blush,' Ben Mumford chortled.

The ribaldry was as much part of the wedding as the service itself. Adam smiled at his bride and whispered in her ear, 'You look beautiful, my love.' But as he scanned the people packed into the churchyard a shadow returned to his eyes. His father and immediate family were absent.

Joshua Loveday stepped forward and began the service. After the couple had spoken their vows in the porch of the church, a cheer went up, and Adam and Senara then processed to the altar to receive the blessing. Once the register was signed they proceeded to the font and realised that a hush had fallen over the gathering.

Edward, Amelia, St John and a sullen-looking Meriel were standing at the back of the church. Edward's expression was unreadable and he stared at the font, not at the christening party. There was a strained falseness to Amelia's smile and St John glared at Adam with open displeasure. Once the baptism service was over, Hannah, as Nathan's godmother, lifted him from Senara's arms.

Edward held himself stiffly and made no sign of greeting the couple. To Senara's relief, Adam addressed his father. 'It means a lot to me that you are here, sir.'

A muscle pulsated in Edward's jaw and his voice was far from welcoming, 'Since my niece so forthrightly reminded me, we Lovedays are united as a family. I hope you will resume your place at the yard, Adam, and that you and your wife will live at Mariner's House.'

Edward clearly had not given the marriage his blessing, but he would also wish to avoid unnecessary gossip which an obvious rift in the family would cause.

'Thank you, sir. Will you and the family be joining the celebrations at the farm?' Adam asked.

'I see no cause for celebration. But St John will stay for the sake of appearances.'

Adam felt his anger surfacing and struggled to keep a hold on it. Too many eyes were on them: many were openly curious, but others were waiting to speculate on any dissent. The Loveday yard finances remained unstable. Adam's reputation as a skilled designer had enhanced the yard's reputation and brought in orders. If word got out that father and son were estranged, the future of the yard could be in jeopardy. Adam changed the subject to another matter which troubled him.

'Richard is not present. I had thought my half-brother

bore no ill will towards my wife.'

'Richard is in the navy.' Edward remained curt. 'He joined as a midshipman last August when you were away. He sailed with the fleet which took prisoners to Botany Bay so his first voyage is an extended one. He is not expected back for many months. Amelia is upset over his absence, but it will be the making of the lad.'

'It was the life he wanted,' Adam said with a smile. 'He will do well.'

'Edward, we should get back to Trevowan.' Amelia stepped forward, and her stare upon Adam was cool. 'Lisette has been difficult since your return. Last night we were forced to lock her in her room and she set fire to it. Fortunately, the dogs smelled the smoke and little damage was done. She needed an opiate to calm her. Elspeth is sitting with her.'

'I am sorry to hear that,' Adam replied. 'She must be a great worry to you.'

'It is rather late in the day for you to show concern,' Edward snapped, and strode away to talk with Joshua.

When Amelia made to follow him, Senara said, 'Thank you for the loan of the gown and cloak. I will return them to you tomorrow.'

Amelia cast a critical eye over Senara. 'You look well enough in them. Keep them.' She struggled to be civil. The shame she felt at this unsuitable marriage had not abated. Her parents had been devoutly religious and she had been brought up in an atmosphere which harshly condemned any laxity of morals. Amelia had tried to be more compassionate of others' failings but her upbringing was too deeply ingrained to overlook Adam's actions. She did not believe it right to marry beneath one's class – and Senara carried the stigma of gypsy blood, who were reviled as tinkers and vagabonds.

Squire Penwithick was shaking Adam's hand in a bluff and hearty manner. He had a girth measurement to match his middle years and his jowls wobbled as he moved. His pale eyes were enclosed in flesh, the lids weighted down by grey tufted brows, and he peered short-sightedly through the spectacles perched low on his nose.

'You have won a beauty for your bride. Glad to see you back in Cornwall, my boy.' He tipped his hat to Senara. 'I wish you happiness, my dear. I ask your pardon that I cannot stay for the celebrations; my wife took a fall at the last hunt and is confined to her bed. I see young Dr Chegwidden over there. I must ask him to call on her.' The squire used his staff to push his way through the people clamouring for a sight of the bride and child.

Sir Henry Traherne stepped in front of Senara and kissed her cheek. 'The Lovedays get all the prettiest women.'

A bold laugh followed and Japhet Loveday spun Senara round to face him. 'Hands off her, Henry. I'm the one who urged this lovely woman to marry Adam last year before all this foolishness caused by Lisette. I should claim the first kiss.' He kissed her full on the mouth with lingering intensity. When he drew away, he ran the tip of his tongue across his lower lip. 'Mm, you taste sweet as honey. You watch your step, Adam. I can't believe I allowed my cousin to win this woman's heart from under my nose and I did not put up a fight.'

Adam laughed. 'You cannot love every woman who crosses your path. Some have more discerning taste.'

'We did not think you had heard of our wedding,' Senara said. 'Your father was not sure where we should send an invitation.'

'I was in Truro and saw Gwendolyn Druce at a ball in the assembly rooms. I travelled back from Truro in her coach. She is here somewhere. My worthy sister has probably way-laid her.'

Adam caught a glimpse of the copper-haired Gwendolyn whispering and laughing with Hannah. There was an air about Gwen which was different. She had always been shy and self-effacing, and although not conventionally pretty, she had striking features and a kind and generous nature. She was also an heiress and it surprised Adam that she remained unwed. She kept glancing in Japhet's direction. At seeing Adam watching her, she blushed and waved.

'And should we be expecting an announcement between you and the lovely Gwen, Japhet?' Adam teased. 'You were spending a fair amount of time with her before we went to France.'

Japhet looked shocked and scratched at his narrow black side whiskers. 'You've bees in your head if you think there is anything between Gwen and myself. We have been friends for years.'

'Since when did you have a woman as a friend?' Adam chided. 'You cannot set eyes upon any attractive woman without attempting to seduce them.'

'There's been nothing like that between Gwen and myself.' There was an amused twinkle in his eyes. 'Gwen is a good sort. We indulge in some harmless flirtation but I respect her too much to want to endanger her reputation.'

'You could do a lot worse than marry Gwen, Japhet.'

'Four hours wed and you would see every bachelor in Cornwall settled. Few will be fortunate to achieve the happiness you have found, cousin.' Japhet favoured Gwendolyn with a long assessing look and smiled when he caught her glance upon him. 'Besides, Gwen deserves better than me.'

Adam shook his head in mock reproof. 'I never thought to hear you utter such sentiments. Are you sure you do not care for her?'

Japhet laughed. 'I adore all pretty, witty and intelligent women.'

Adam slapped him on the shoulder. 'I had not realised that you were so selective.'

Japhet grinned, but before he could reply there were cries from outside for the bride and groom to appear.

Gwendolyn rushed forward to kiss Adam's cheek. 'I wish you every happiness, Adam. I'm sorry that my sister, Roslyn, will not receive Senara at Traherne Hall. Henry is furious with her but she will not be swayed, nor will my mother. I hope I may be permitted to call upon you and Senara at Mariner's House?'

'Of course, Gwen. Your friendship means a lot.'

Senara had been standing quietly, ill at ease in the presence of Adam's family and friends. Gwendolyn smiled warmly and kissed her cheek. 'Do not be upset by those within our society who would snub you. I am sure in time you will win them round.'

Gwendolyn squeezed her hand and moved on to converse with Japhet. When he raised her hand to his lips, her complexion glowed with an iridescent pink flush.

The bride and groom continued to receive the well-wishes of people in the church and as they passed St John, he swept Senara a mocking bow. When he turned to Adam, his features were burnished with malice. 'Don't think Papa has forgiven you. You are no longer his favourite.'

Meriel had followed Amelia from the church to avoid congratulating the couple, but was standing in the doorway glaring at them from a distance.

Adam ignored his brother. He was in too good a humour to have St John ruin it. He signalled to Leah to pass him the salver of crib cake, which had been cut into small pieces, and he handed a portion to everyone they passed. As Adam gave some to Meriel he asked in the time-honoured tradition, 'Pray that the baby receives the Good Lord's grace and will grow hale and hearty.'

Meriel took the offering but, when no one was watching, crushed it and dropped the crumbs on the ground.

It took half an hour for Adam and Senara to walk through the press of well-wishers to reach the decorated wagon which would drive the bride and groom back to the Rabsons' farm.

'Do you think we have enough food for everyone?' Senara voiced her concern to Hannah. 'Adam has invited them all back.'

'There is more than enough,' Hannah reassured. 'And the barn has been swept and cleared for the dancing. I knew everything would come right.'

Senara's cheeks were flushed with excitement. 'I still can't believe how kind everyone has been.'

'Are you happy, my love?' Adam raised her fingers to his lips.

'That bain't no way to kiss yer bride, Cap'n,' Clem shouted. 'She deserves a proper kiss, not that simpering courtly posturing. Give her a proper kiss or there be many a man who'll do it for you.'

Adam grinned and Senara felt herself drowning in the love shimmering in his eyes. Then he kissed her until they were both breathless, to the cheers and whistles of the people on foot around them.

'I am happy. This is so much more than I expected,' she answered with a contented sigh.

Adam refused to allow his father's coolness to spoil his wedding. Throughout the feasting and dancing, the guests were boisterous, their mood jovial from the amount of cider consumed.

The dancing in the barn began early and, despite the cold, everyone was soon sweating from their exertion as they joined in the country reels played by a fiddler.

St John was furious that his father had insisted that he

remain until Uncle Joshua and Aunt Cecily left. Two hours had passed and they showed no sign of leaving.

Japhet was in his element, flirting and dancing with all the single women. As he spun his partner in a country reel, Japhet called out, 'Not dancing at your twin's wedding? Shame on you, St John.'

'Don't you dare leave my side.' Meriel linked her arm through her husband's. 'I refuse to dance with such common people.'

'You grew up with many of them,' St John reminded her.

'They are dirty and uncouth. I was never like them.'

'No, they know their place and accept it with good grace. You, madam, are never anything but discontented.' St John was now bored in Meriel's company. To witness Adam's happiness was nauseating.

When St John saw Thadeous Lanyon arrive, he almost marched out. He would not stay in the room with the man who had tried to have him murdered.

Clem Sawle paused as he danced past with Keziah. 'Why the long face, St John? This be your brother's wedding. Has Lanyon's presence got you fired up?'

When St John glowered at him, Clem lowered his voice. 'Harry told me what happened in Fowey. You can't let him think he has the upper hand or he'll crush you.' Clem grinned. 'Ask his wife to dance, that'll rile him. He's stopped all other men from dancing with Hester, but he can't refuse you. You be the brother of the groom.'

'You will not dance with Hester Lanyon,' Meriel decreed once Clem had gone. 'Lanyon will then expect me to dance with him and I will not tolerate his dirty paws on me.'

'I intend to snub the upstart. It would give me pleasure if you refused him. That will show him his place.' St John raised his wife's fingers to his lips in mock courtesy. He was angered by Lanyon's presence, but open confrontation with the man would solve nothing. It would only give Lanyon the satisfaction of knowing the attack had unsettled him. There were other ways to ensure Lanyon regretted his actions.

Adam surveyed the guests, noting with sadness that none of the more eminent families had attended. A few of the middle-class families such as the chandlers and timber merchants with whom the Lovedays did business were here. He saw that his cousin, Pious Peter, had arrived and was talking to his father, Joshua. He hoped that Peter was not going to cast a cloud on the merrymaking and start lecturing his guests on the sins of drink. Japhet, who was dancing with Gwen, bent to whisper in her ear and Gwen left him to lead Peter into the next dance. He protested, but Gwen was persistent and he appeared to relax and almost to be enjoying himself. Was the twins' younger cousin finally becoming human?

Senara broke away from the dancing to join Adam and was holding her side and breathing heavily from exhaustion. Adam was concerned. 'Are you certain that you are not overtaxing yourself. It is little over a month since Nathan was born.'

There was devilment in Senara's eyes. 'Gypsy blood has some compensation. We are a hardy breed. It is wonderful to see so many people enjoying themselves. Even your cousin Peter is dancing.' She laughed. 'I thought he believed dancing and music were servants of the devil to tempt mortals to sin.'

Adam laughed. 'For years Peter's preaching and pontificating has stretched the family's patience and tolerance.' He watched the awkward steps of his cousin. Peter was now twenty-one and Adam wondered if he was still celibate. Peter was constantly at loggerheads with his older brother, Japhet, whom he condemned as a reprobate.

'Peter has no need of a lonely bed this night.' Senara seemed to have read Adam's thoughts. 'There's many a maid casting inviting glances at him. He has the same handsome looks as his brother, but unfortunately none of Japhet's grace or easy charm.'

'It's time Peter learned to enjoy himself. He takes religion and life too seriously.'

Senara studied the younger cousin. 'But he'll never entirely rid himself of the fanaticism which drives him.' She saw Thadeous Lanyon standing to the far side of the barn with his wife. Hester looked miserable. 'There's a man who is truly touched by evil. Why did you invite him?'

'Lanyon is a prominent figure in Penruan. I saw no need to make an enemy by slighting him.'

Japhet bowed to Senara and led her back on to the dance floor. Adam remembered his own duty and danced with Gwendolyn.

'Your presence here means a great deal to me. Many of our class have made their excuses.'

Gwendolyn held his gaze with an open honesty. 'Senara has snatched up one of Cornwall's most eligible bachelors. That will have displeased many a matron. And, of course, their daughters are heartbroken.' She smiled to brighten his mood. 'Also it is unfashionable for a man to be in love with his wife, as you so undoubtedly are with Senara.'

Japhet spun past them and Gwendolyn's stare followed him for some moments, prompting Adam to remark, 'Japhet is a fool not to see your qualities. He's very fond of you.'

'And more fond still of his freedom. I have resigned myself that marriage is not for me.'

'I thought it was the craving of every woman.'

Gwendolyn glanced over at Hester. 'What use to marry one man when one's heart belongs to another?'

Adam followed her gaze and frowned. Once Hester had been vivacious and full of laughter. Since her marriage to Lanyon she cowered at the slightest sound and no longer looked anyone directly in the eye. She was dressed in a pink satin gown festooned with gold bows and her underskirt was of gold cloth. Her attire was more suitable for a ball than a wedding, and her neck and wrists were glittering with diamonds. While Hester kept her eyes frozen to the floor, Lanyon kept a tight grip on her arm, and twice Adam saw the woman wince. When she did raise her eyes, it was to glance towards Harry Sawle, who was flirting with Molly Nance, the daughter of Trevowan's bailiff. At the sight of them, Hester looked even more miserable.

Molly was clearly enamoured of Harry and enjoyed the attention he was paying her, though Isaac Nance was keeping a stern eye on her, disgruntled that a man of Harry's hard-drinking and womanising reputation had singled out his daughter. Twice Sarah Nance had put a restraining hand on her husband's arm. If Isaac confronted Harry it would end in a fight.

But it was Hester's unhappiness which most concerned Adam; she was concealing it badly. Her love for Harry was stark in her eyes. If Lanyon suspected that Hester loved another, her life would become even more wretched.

The dance ended and Adam chose Hannah as his next partner. She was watching the dancers as the music changed tempo to a more stately pace. 'St John is asking Hester to dance.'

Adam saw St John draw Hester away from her husband even as Lanyon protested. Lanyon started forward to stop him, then thought better of it. When the two men locked glances the antagonism between them was palpable. St John had deliberately provoked Lanyon.

'There's no love lost between Lanyon and St John,' Hannah observed. Her voice dropped to a whisper. 'Is it because St John has joined the free-traders?'

Adam had unwittingly become involved in a raid St John

and Harry had made on Lanyon's cargo last year. When both Harry and St John had been shot, Adam had taken them to Senara, who had saved Harry's life. Harry was a dangerous influence on St John. There was no mistaking the change in his twin, for there was a time when St John would have avoided any confrontation with a man as treacherous as Lanyon. St John, formerly an indolent dissolute, had become more his own man, even a force to be reckoned with.

'Father forbade St John to continue in the trade,' Adam replied. 'Does he continue?'

Hannah shrugged. 'St John would not confide in me. But according to Japhet, he is rarely short of funds at the gaming tables. With so many economies at Trevowan, such money does not come from the estate. Recently, St John returned from Truro claiming that Lanyon had tried to set his bullies on him.'

'Then St John is a fool to provoke him.' Adam saw Lanyon heading towards Meriel, but she turned her back on him as he approached. To avoid looking ridiculous, Lanyon had engaged in conversation with Mr Snell, the parson of Penruan church. St John had also seen the incident and was grinning.

'Something unpleasant is going on between them,' Adam said.

Halfway through St John's dance with Hester, Harry Sawle cut in. Immediately Hester became agitated. Harry had been drinking heavily. He pressed her close and bent his head to whisper in her ear.

There was an outraged shout from Lanyon, who marched towards the couple. Adam excused himself to Hannah and, to avert an unpleasant scene, cut through the dancers to reach Hester before her husband. 'My turn now for a dance, Harry. I don't want any trouble at my wedding.'

'Wait your turn, Loveday. I'll dance with whom I wish.'

Harry was belligerent. Adam took Hester's hand and moved between her and Harry, his voice low with warning as Lanyon was nearly upon them. 'You are deliberately taunting Lanyon. It will be Hester who pays for your conduct.'

Adam twirled Hester away from both her husband and her lover. A backward glance showed Harry shoot Lanyon a challenging glare. Harry turned his back on Lanyon and cut in on Senara, who was dancing with Sir Henry.

Hester was close to tears. 'Thank you for stopping Harry doing anything foolish.'

'Harry can look after himself. If he truly cared for you, he would not put you in danger. You should forget him.'

'I hate Thadeous,' she confided, and Adam could feel her trembling.

'Then you should leave him, but not for Harry. That can only end in bloodshed.'

Her answering look was despairing. 'Thadeous would never let me go. He'd kill me first. Harry is all that makes my life bearable.'

Adam was appalled at the risks Hester was taking. The dance ended and Adam returned Hester to her husband. 'Your wife is a credit to you, Mr Lanyon. She dances beautifully.' He hoped the compliments would dispel the banker's anger. 'And are you satisfied with the performance of the cutter we built?'

'She sails well enough.' Lanyon was sullen. 'I wish you and your wife happiness, Captain Loveday, but you must excuse Hester and myself. It is time we left.' He virtually dragged Hester from the barn in his haste to leave.

Adam was distracted by the younger children running around amongst the dancers. He smiled at the way his niece Rowena pursued them, though one arm remained held tight against her side. The useless hand, damaged at birth, was hidden by a trailing sleeve. When the dancers became more boisterous and Rowena was knocked to the ground, St John strode across the floor to rescue her and kept her, protesting, at his side. Rowena did not appear to have been harmed and her tears were from anger at not being allowed to join her cousins.

Senara was kept from Adam's side as each dance was claimed by a different man. Japhet had danced with her several times but St John had so far ignored her. Adam's anger rose at his twin's behaviour. Meriel was looking mutinous and kept signalling to St John that they should leave. She had refused all offers to dance with the men of the estate, shipyard, or from Penruan.

Adam was gallantly dancing with Bridie for the second time. The young girl's face was radiant with happiness even though the dance steps were difficult for her to master. He led Bridie back to Leah and next chose Meriel.

'I have been remiss in not asking you to dance. Are you not enjoying yourself? You have not been dancing despite a stream of men clamouring for your hand.'

'I have danced with those men of importance. I do not dance with yokels. It is not seemly.'

Her haughty demeanour made Adam laugh. 'Have you not yet learned that self-importance is a sign of bad breeding? Humility is the prerequisite of good manners.'

'How dare you lecture me? Keep your lessons in manners for your gypsy. She has need of them.' She made to pull away from him, but Adam kept a tight grip on her hand, his expression serious.

'I had hoped that you would be an ally to Senara. You have ignored her all day.'

'What have I in common with a gypsy?' Meriel spat.

His grip tightened on her fingers and she winced. 'Little, it would seem, for Senara is a woman of compassion. She would never, by either word or deed, do harm to another.'

'I am not a hypocrite. Edward and Amelia attended the service to put a semblance of respectability upon your marriage. They were appalled at your actions.'

He was goaded to sarcasm. 'And my father was not when St John was forced at gunpoint to wed you? I married Senara of my own free will.'

'At least St John was honourable enough to marry me. Unlike you, who abused the love I gave you.'

Her tart response startled him. 'You did not love me, Meriel. Marrying St John with such speed proved that. How long after I left did he replace me as your lover?'

The statement bleached the colour from her cheeks. 'Everyone knows I was carrying St John's child. My brothers would not allow me to bring shame to our family.'

'But is Rowena his child? I have always had my doubts. She was born nine months after you and I—'

'How dare you suggest . . . ?' Her cheeks regained their colour to flare to an alarming red. 'Rowena is St John's child. He ravished me a month after you rejoined the navy. She was an eight-month baby. I fell down the stairs.'

Her vehemence increased Adam's suspicions that Rowena could be his child and not his brother's. Yet that was a secret best kept locked away. He regarded the dark-haired girl, who was giggling excitedly as she played chase with Davey and Florence Rabson. Rowena was an engaging child and Adam had always been fond of her.

He abruptly changed the subject. 'I will not have you slighting Senara. You could make it easier for her to be accepted by our friends. I know how vicious your tongue can be – take care that you do not use it against my wife.'

'I speak as I find,' she defied him.

'My brother does not know that we were lovers, does he?' Adam's voice was low.

'You would not tell him!' Her eyes rounded in alarm. 'Not after all this time.'

'It is not something I'm proud of. Accept Senara and, when necessary, ensure that others accept her. Then I shall have no need to speak of that other matter to my brother.'

Meriel glared at him. 'You will regret threatening me.'

'All I ask is that you are civil to my wife. Is that so much?'

'I will be civil – do not expect more from me.' Her voice sounded as though she was being slowly strangled. Her eyes narrowed with malice. 'You think you're so clever, but my word will carry little weight. There is one in our family who poses a greater threat. Lisette was screaming all last night that she would kill any woman who became your bride.'

'The ranting of a deranged woman. She will not harm anyone.'

'Will she not?' Meriel's lips curled back. 'She hates Senara. They had to lock her in her room for she was threatening to stop the wedding by declaring it illegal as you are betrothed to her. Then she set fire to the room, screaming that she could not live without you and they would all die with her.'

Adam was shocked, realising that Amelia had not told him the whole story. Meriel was gloating.

'Everyone knows that it was Lisette who ended our betrothal by marrying another,' he reminded her.

Adam was sickened by Meriel's spite. He had lost his infatuation for her the moment he learned she had tricked St John into marriage and chosen the heir of Trevowan rather than a naval lieutenant.

'I heard from Japhet what Lisette was like when you found her in France,' Meriel took pleasure in informing him. 'She should be locked away in an asylum. She is capable of anything.'

The dance ended and Meriel flounced away. Adam had not expected today to be easy but there were now undercurrents to it which would need all his and Senara's resilience to overcome.

Chapter Four

'I can't go on like this any more, Harry,' Hester sobbed
against his shoulder.

They were in the hayloft of the Dolphin Inn where Harry
still lived with his mother and crippled father. It was not an
ideal meeting place, for Hester was fearful of discovery.
Throughout the summer and early autumn they had made
love in the woods of the coombe or on the beach, but such
trysting places were unsuitable in winter.

Hester's sobs increased. 'I rarely see you. Why can't we just
run away and start a new life far from here?'

'Because this be my home.' Harry kissed her. 'And there be
nowhere we could go that Lanyon won't find us. We need
money and my contacts in the free trade be in Cornwall. You
must bide your time a while longer.'

It was a week since the wedding and this was the first time
that Hester had been seen outside her house. Lanyon had
gone to Liskeard on business. Hester had added some
laudanum drops to her maid's secret cache of gin and had
left her snoring and slumped across the kitchen table. Phyllis
Tamblin had been engaged by Thadeous, supposedly to help
in the shop and the house. Within weeks of her arrival the
young woman had been installed as his mistress in their
home and also as her husband's spy upon his wife's activities. It was that which Hester found hardest to bear. She was

74

relieved not to have Thadeous's nightly affections forced upon her, for his lust was as voracious as it was brutal.

Even in the dim light from the lantern hanging on a beam, the yellowing marks on her jaw and eye bore testimony to Lanyon's displeasure that Hester had danced with St John and Harry at the wedding. Her husband had accused her of leading St John on, screaming that if she even so much as looked in Harry Sawle's direction again, both she and he would find themselves food for the fishes. Lanyon never made an idle threat.

Hester regretted her hasty marriage to Lanyon. She had wed him out of fury when Harry had betrayed her with another woman. Harry had never been faithful during all the years of their courtship, though he had declared that she was the only woman he loved. Each year he put off plans for their wedding, taking Hester for granted. When Lanyon had set out to woo her, he had been kind and generous with gifts and compliments. She had encouraged him as a means to make Harry jealous, but Lanyon hated the Sawles and he had no intention of allowing Hester to use him. Hester had been no match for Lanyon's devious scheming. Before she had realised what was happening, the wedding was planned and, without her actually consenting to a service, she found herself before a parson in Truro. When she had tried to protest, the look in Lanyon's eyes had alarmed her.

'Make a fool of me, would you? I think not, if you wish to see another sunrise. And I can ruin your father's chandler's business, leaving him and your sister destitute.'

Too terrified to protest, she had married him, and from that moment a churning nausea had never left her stomach whenever her husband was near her. Harry was her salvation; without him she would have taken her life to escape the misery of her existence.

Through eyes blurred by tears, Hester searched Harry's

face, which was in partial shadow, telling her nothing of his true mood. But when had she ever really known Harry's moods? He was secretive by nature and, in his own way, was just as dangerous as Lanyon. She had loved him since she was a girl and he had been her only lover before she wed Lanyon. He was rugged and handsome and, although cavalier in his affections, his anger at her marriage had proved how much he loved her.

Harry could see that Hester was close to breaking point. They had kept their trysts a secret for a year, but sooner or later they would be discovered. That did not suit his plans. Hester had not served her purpose. Harry wanted revenge on Lanyon – cuckolding him was not enough. Lanyon had stolen Hester from him. Lanyon had crippled his father. Lanyon had become the most influential leader of smugglers in the district – where once the Sawles had ruled. It was time that Lanyon learned that the Sawles gave up nothing.

'Lanyon will get what's coming to him,' Harry promised. 'I need time to ensure that no suspicion falls on us and that Penruan remains a safe place for us to live.'

Hester clung to him. 'Thadeous will never allow me to leave him. He'll kill us, Harry.'

'Not if he dies first.'

Hester stepped back from him, her eyes wide with horror. She was fearful for Harry if he carried out his threat. 'But everyone knows of your rivalry. You would be the first they'd suspect if anything happened to Lanyon. What use is Lanyon's death, if you be hanged?'

'That's why the timing must be right. I bain't gonna swing for that bastard.'

There was a giggle below them and both froze as Mary Lee, the new barmaid, leaned against the stable door. Harry peered over the edge of the hayloft and saw Don Roche, the younger brother of the village cobbler, framed in the

doorway. Don had been at sea for the last seven years as a
sailor on one of the great clippers. He had returned to
Penruan, declaring he was finished with such a life, and had
taken work on Basil Bracewaite's estate as a farm hand.

'You following me, my pretty?' Don Roche said with a
chuckle. 'I not be a man who'd disappoint a wench if she 'as
a mind for some sportin'.'

'And what would I be wantin' with a man who has a
woman in every port?' Mary leaned back against the door
frame and thrust out her chest in provocation, her manner
belying her coyness. 'I know the reputation of you sailors.
You be wicked men who'd lead an innocent woman astray.'

'But I've done with the sea,' Don drawled. 'How about a
kiss?'

There were further giggles. Harry, who had enjoyed several
romps with Mary in the hayloft, did not want the couple
discovering Hester here. He was about to drop down into the
stable and order Mary back to work, when Sal's angry voice
came from the inn kitchen.

'Mary, where the devil are you, girl? There be a taproom
full of thirsty fishermen come in on the tide. Get yourself in
here, or get yourself another job.'

Mary sighed. 'I'd better go or Sal will have my hide. But I
finish in an hour, my handsome.'

'Happen I might still be interested,' Don stated, pushing
her up against the door and pressing his body into hers.

'Mary!' Sal yelled. 'If you've seen my Harry I could do
with his help, as well. Reuban has passed out drunk and is
useless.'

Grumbling, Mary left the stable and Don Roche followed
her.

Harry sank back on to the straw. 'It be too risky to meet
here. Perhaps we had better not see each other for a while.'

Hester started to cry.

77

'Do you want to ruin everything?' Harry lost his patience. 'It be foolish to see each other until Lanyon be dealt with.'

'I love you, Harry. I need to be with you.'

'Sweetheart, there be too much at stake.' He kissed her with passion to silence her protests.

Instead of being calmed, Hester sobbed louder. 'I think I be again with child. Your child. Lanyon beat me so badly I miscarried last time. We should go away . . . hide somewhere.'

'Once Lanyon knows of your condition, he'll leave you alone.' Harry had been worried that Hester was becoming less rational. Living with Lanyon could not be easy, but it had been her choice. Anger smote him. He had not forgiven Hester for betraying him. Forgiveness was not in his nature. But he needed her to exact his full revenge upon Lanyon. With Lanyon dead Hester would be a wealthy widow, and he had his eye on all Lanyon's property, not just his wife. 'Lanyon's had three wives and you be the only one to get with child. It's what he wants most – an heir to pass on his ill-gained riches. Obviously, he bain't capable of siring one, but a man like that would never admit it to himself. You'll be safe until the child be born.'

As he climbed down to the stable and checked that no one would see Hester leave, he was exultant. To fool Lanyon into believing the child Hester carried was the smuggler's was a subtle revenge upon his enemy. Soon his revenge would be total. He would have not only Hester, but also everything Lanyon had worked for would be his.

Whenever Adam saw his father at the yard, the strain on Edward was obvious. His temper was short with the workers, and he had drawn up punishing schedules so that the cutter they were building would be finished by Easter. February was not a month known for its benevolence. The men were used to working in the winter downpours of rain, but the last week had been blustery, with constant sleet lashing the workers. One man had been knocked unconscious when a pulley rope broke and the heavy iron hook swung free, injuring him and a colleague. They'd been fortunate not to be killed, but only one had recovered sufficiently to work. Several shipwrights were labouring with the malignant ague, their constant coughing fits slowing their pace.

Both Adam and Edward worked alongside the shipwrights as the upper and poop decking was hammered into place. Once when Adam had worked with his father, they had shared an easy camaraderie. Now Edward worked in silence, breaking it only to shout his impatience at the men, with Adam receiving the sharpest lashing from his tongue.

One afternoon, when the weather was particularly bad, there was a cry, and an apprentice carrying some planking fell from the slippery scaffolding.

'Young Wakeley's bin hurt bad,' a man shouted above the wind and rain.

Edward threw down his hammer. 'At this rate the cutter will never be finished.'

His father's lack of sympathy shocked Adam. It was so unlike him. Adam shinned down the scaffolding and pushed through the men standing round Tim Wakeley. They boy was conscious but his face was twisted in pain and from the look of his arm it was broken. There was also a deep gash on his brow, which was bleeding profusely.

'I can't see nothing,' the youth sobbed.

'Can you get up, Timmy?' Adam asked.

He made to move, gave a scream and vomited violently. 'Aw, it hurts. Me arm hurts. Why can't I see?'

Adam kneeled beside him. 'You've banged your head. You'll be all right, Timmy.'

The boy clutched his arm, his eyes wide with fear. 'I ain't gonna be blind, Cap'n, am I?'

'You'll be fine, Timmy.' Adam raised his head to order two men, 'Get him on a stretcher and back to his house. Take it easy; his arm is broken. And send for my wife to tend him.'

Senara arrived at the Wakeley cottage at the same time as the men carrying Timmy on a broad plank. His father, Seth, was hobbling over from the carpentry shed where he had been working on the ship's carved rail. The mud made a squelching, sucking sound each time he raised his peg leg.

'How be the lad?' he demanded.

Senara was trying to examine him on the table of the single downstairs room. The cottage was gloomy, with light from only a small window. Her work was made more difficult by the family and friends crowding into the room. 'He needs rest and quiet, Mr Wakeley.'

'I can't see, Pa.' Timmy twisted from side to side, holding his injured arm. There was a large purpling bruise on his temple. 'I be blind.'

'I think Dr Chegwidden should be called out,' Senara said. 'A head wound should be seen by a physician.'

'I can't pay no physician's fees.' Seth bent over his son, smoothing back the hair on his brow. 'You do what you can for the lad, Mrs Loveday.'

'My skill is not enough this time. I can tend a broken arm but his skull could be cracked.' She looked over Seth Wakeley's head to Adam, who was herding the others from the cottage.

He came back to stand beside Senara. 'You treated my concussion when I'd been set upon. Do what you can for the lad.'

She drew him aside. 'I do not want such responsibility, Adam. What if he is blinded or dies from some internal injury I do not detect?'

'Chegwidden will not come unless he is paid. Given the choice, I would rather be in your hands than that butcher of a doctor.'

Adam left the cottage and discovered that the men had stopped work for the day as the weather had worsened. He saw his father heading for the stable and went after him. Edward was saddling up his hunter, Rex, and did not pause when he saw Adam enter the stable.

'The men are being pushed too hard, sir. There will be more accidents if we continue as we are.'

'I have no choice. If the cutter is not delivered on time there is a penalty clause in the contract and we will lose a great deal of money – money which is needed to meet the loans I still must repay.'

'We have never had a penalty clause in a ship's contract before.'

'We were a small yard, building fishing smacks and an occasional schooner. The merchants who want the larger ships have always dealt with the bigger yards. It is all very well for you to design a ship which will outsail others of its class, but owners demand deadlines from a company they have not dealt with before. When the customer learned that you were not in charge of the project, he wanted to pull out and get another yard to build a similar vessel.'

Adam had not considered this during his months away. Edward continued to rage at him. 'I convinced the customer that we would finish on schedule and the penalty clause was my guarantee.' The pent-up anger and frustration of months erupted. 'You pushed for the contract in the first place, Adam. You knew how important it was. You should have been here to see it through. A new design brings unforeseen problems. Most of our shipwrights have only worked on small craft. There have been many mistakes which have cost us dear.'

'But when I left, I thought the yard's finances were stable. When Cousin Thomas married the daughter of another banker, I thought the family no longer faced ruin and that gradually our position would improve.'

'We were teetering on the brink of bankruptcy then and little has changed. Thomas is slowly recovering the money we lost, but the dividends do not meet the interest on the loans. Had my son followed his duty and married an heiress, the crisis we now face would have been averted.'

He swung on to Rex's saddle and glared down at Adam. Adam had never seen him so angry. 'Now you are back, get the problems with the cutter put right. I've received word from home that Lisette has gone missing again. St John has gone off God knows where, so I have to arrange a search party. When Lisette returns I want you up at the house to explain to her the reasons for your marriage and why you allowed her to believe you and she were still betrothed when you brought her from France. If she's not capable of acting with reason, then I will have no choice but to commit her to an asylum. May her father, my dear friend, and her mother, your own mother's dear sister, forgive me. For I have failed them.'

The tirade stung Adam as laceratingly as the leaded tips of a cat-o'-nine-tails. As he watched his father canter out of the yard, his head bowed against the rain, Adam let out a harsh breath. His anger at his father's attitude to his wedding had blinded him to possibilities that they could still be in danger of losing the yard.

He closed his eyes against a rush of guilt. He had vowed that his wedding heralded a new beginning. He had won the woman he loved and that same determination would drive him to make amends to his family and ensure that the yard was again solvent.

He entered the yard office and began to examine the books and contracts. When he finished he was shaken by the list of accidents, faulty fitments, late deliveries and two cancelled orders which had beset the yard in recent months. The delays to the cutter were listed, often the result of careless errors in the reading of the original design. The innovations he had made should not have been that complicated, but wood had been cut the wrong size, wasting valuable timber, and other errors had crept in once the pressure to complete on time had increased.

He would consult Ben Mumford at Mariner's House this evening, and they would go through every detail of the plans together. In the morning he would examine every timber and fitment of the ship. At least Timmy Wakeley had recovered his sight and Senara had earlier sent him word.

His head ached from working over the close writing on the plans and ledgers, and when he returned to Mariner's House he found it empty. Even their maid, Carrie, the fifteen-year-old daughter of the Jansens who ran the Ship kiddley, had left for her home. She would have kept Nathan with her. Adam guessed that Senara must still be tending young Timmy. He threw another log on the fire and flopped into an armchair with only the flames of the fire to light the room.

He started at the sound of the door opening and realised that he had fallen asleep. Scamp, who was asleep at his feet, sat up and growled.

'Is that you, Senara?'

There was no answer and when he went to investigate he found the front door was open but there was no sign of his wife. 'Must have been the wind,' he murmured as he closed the door after Scamp had run out into the night.

The strengthening wind caused an unfastened shutter to clatter against the window in a bedroom and a mournful lament echoed from the chimney.

Adam went to fasten the shutter and halfway up the stairs a voice, soft as a spectre, called, 'My love, my love. Come to me.'

He grinned and took the stairs two at a time, intrigued by

the game Senara was intent on playing. The embers in the bedchamber grate glowed red, providing a feeble light. The green brocade curtains from the four-poster bed billowed in the breeze from the window and Adam could just perceive that Senara lay across the covers, her naked body masked by partial shadow, her face hidden by her arm.

Adam laughed. 'My sweet love, what ruse is this to tempt an honest man from his labours?'

'Love me! I am forever yours.' The voice was muffled.

'Shameless wench,' he chuckled as he gathered her into his arms and kissed her with passion. 'You are frozen,' he whispered as his hand travelled over a rounded hip to take her breast. With a curse he stood up. This woman was not Senara.

The figure rose up, crawling towards him with her arms outstretched. 'Do not deny me, Adam. I am yours. I was always yours. Only yours.'

He backed away. 'Have you no sense of decency, Lisette? Get yourself dressed and out of here.'

'But you want me. I saw it in your eyes – heard it in your voice.'

'I thought you were my wife. What the devil are you about?'

'But I am your wife. We were betrothed – a contract which was as binding as a marriage service.'

'That contract was broken when you wed another, Lisette. The choice was yours.' He had reached the door and she launched herself from the bed to wrap her arms around him. Her body was icy where it touched him, yet she seemed unaware of the cold.

'You lie. That was not a marriage, it was a penance. You are my true husband.'

She squirmed against him, the strength from such a petite figure surprising as he tried to push her away. She was pulling

84

at his shirt, ripping it in her fervour, her mouth hot against his flesh. Unwilling to hurt her, Adam tried to be gentle as he shoved her away. He grunted in pain as her teeth fastened on to his shoulder, drawing blood.

'Little vixen.' His anger got the better of him, and he picked her up and flung her on to the bed, then stepped back from her. 'Get dressed and get out of here. You must accept that I am married to another. When you are dressed I will take you back to Trevowan.'

He shut the door behind him and heard her scream of rage as he ran down the stairs. The door opened and she stood naked at the top of the stairs, her brown hair, cropped short when she was a prisoner of the rabble in France, was wild and her eyes large and feral.

'I will not leave.' She was breathing heavily, her voice rising in hysteria. 'This house was to be our wedding gift from your father. It is my house.'

'I will not talk to you until you dress.' Adam was at a loss at how to deal with her. In this unstable frame of mind he did not trust her. He had believed himself a man of the world, and was far from inexperienced with women but being confronted by a naked, demented woman, who was also a member of his family, left him totally perplexed. He dared not walk out on her, for he feared how she would react, yet the need to avoid a scandal was also important. As he struggled to find a way out of this problem, her manner changed. Without shame she pursued him down the stairs.

'Are you afraid of me, Adam? Do you fear your whore will leave you if she discovers that we are lovers?'

Decency demanded that he avert his gaze, but he dared not take his eyes from her after the way she had thrown herself at him earlier. 'We have never been lovers, Lisette,' Adam snapped, now incensed. 'And never refer to my wife as a whore. I will not talk to you until you dress yourself.'

She reached out for him and he evaded her and stepped into the parlour. Despite the cold he was sweating profusely. He had to get her calm and back to Trevowan. But how?

'But I have no wish to talk.' She spread her arms wide, her nubile body golden in the light from the fire. 'Why do you not want me? Am I ugly? Do you think that I could not give you pleasure? They have tried to stop me coming to you, *mon chéri*. Nothing can keep us apart now.'

'Lisette, you must accept that I am married to another. This conduct is unworthy of you. You are acting like a harlot.'

Her face contorted with rage and her hands came up like talons to strike out at him. '*They* called me a harlot, a whore . . . those *canailles*. Those pigs. They called me names while they defiled me.' When she could not reach Adam, who kept side-stepping to avoid her, she began to scratch at her face and breasts and to scream obscenities in French.

'But you must not punish yourself.' Adam gripped her wrists to stop the frantic clawing. This depraved woman sickened him, but once she had been so sweet, so innocent, beautiful and fragile as a porcelain figurine.

'But you loved me, Adam,' she sobbed. 'When I was wretched and frightened and feared they would kill me, I clung to that. I knew you would come for me – that you would love me again.' She flung back her head, her screams rising in hysteria.

To silence her he had no choice but to slap her. Lisette reeled back against the arm of a chair and fell sobbing into it. Adam snatched up a cloak from the peg by the door and threw it over her. 'Cover yourself and remember who you are,' he raged. 'You shame the memory of your parents by your conduct.'

She stopped sobbing to look up at him. The wildness left her eyes and her expression was one of a wounded child. 'I only wanted you to love me, Adam. Everyone hates me. I wanted everything to go back to how it was. Then I could forget . . .' She began to tremble with reaction, her face awash with tears. 'How can anyone love me now? Why did Etienne make me marry that monster?'

'Your brother has much to answer for.' Recalling the horrors she had endured in France, Adam's pity was roused. At least now she was calmer, and he again tried to reason with her. 'I love you as a cousin, Lisette. And no one hates you. Go upstairs and dress. I will say nothing of this to Father. The family want to help you, but you must see that your actions make it difficult for them.'

'Do you want to help me, Adam?' Her voice was childlike.

'Of course. Go and dress. I will take you home to Trevowan.'

She remained crumpled on the chair and Adam went to his bedchamber in search of her clothing. All he found was a muddy cloak and nightdress, its hem ripped and sodden. There were not even any shoes. He took Senara's spare woollen dress from its hook and some thick stockings, and threw them at Lisette.

'I'll wait outside while you dress. How did you get here?'

'I rode but the stupid mare took off before I could tether her.' She held up the dress. 'Whose is this? I won't wear anything that belongs to your gypsy.'

'Then wrap yourself in my cloak. Though what Father will say when you arrive home in such a condition will not be pleasant. To be honest, Lisette, he despairs that if you do not change your unladylike behaviour, he will have no choice but to have you committed to an asylum.'

'He would never do that.' She was shocked, and discarded her hysteria and defiance. 'Edward promised my father that he would look after me.' She had at least wrapped the cloak around her now and stood shivering by the fire. 'But then he

87

promised that we would marry.' A sob tore from her. 'I can trust no one. You all hate me.'

She made to dash past him. Adam made a grab for her and the cloak came away from her fleeing figure in his hands.

'Stop, Lisette. Be sensible.'

There was a cry from outside and as Adam ran into the yard he found Senara grappling with the Frenchwoman. Lisette was screaming abuse at Senara and scratching at her face with her hands. Without hesitation Senara slammed her fist into the woman's face and she crumpled unconscious on the ground. She strode past Adam, looking furious.

'Get her back in the house before the whole yard sees her,' she ordered.

Adam flung the cloak around Lisette and carried her back into the house.

'What has been happening here?'

'I found her naked in our bed. She has lost her wits. I know how it must look, my love, but you must believe me . . .' He lowered Lisette's still-limp body into the chair by the fire. Scamp had returned and, at seeing Lisette, he growled then slunk into the kitchen, making Adam suspect that Lisette had mistreated Scamp when he had been at Trevowan.

'I do not believe that you have been unfaithful, Adam, if that is what you fear. Your aunt's horse, Bracken, was careering round the yard without a rider when I left the Wakeleys' cottage. One of the men managed to catch her and put her in the stable. The mare had been viciously beaten with a whip and needs tending. From the racket coming from this house, I suspected that Lisette had shown up, but not the extremes that the woman would go to.'

Senara was staring down at the scratches and cuts on Lisette's feet. She put her hand to the Frenchwoman's brow. Her usually open expression revealed no emotion. 'It is surprising she has no fever. Put her into the bed in the back bedroom. She's in no fit state to travel.'

'Lisette is not staying here. How can you even consider it after the way she has acted?'

'She's your cousin, and she is a very disturbed woman.'

'I'm not having her under my roof.' Adam stepped back from Lisette, suspicious that her unconscious state was a trick. 'I do not trust her. What if she attacked you? She is capable of it and she hates you because you are my wife.'

Lisette moaned and stirred. 'Adam, you have not left me, *mon chéri*?'

'I'll take her back to Trevowan,' he said. 'There's a search party looking for her. I do not want to leave you here with her.'

'Adam.' Lisette pushed herself upright in the chair, and the moment her gaze fell upon Senara her face twisted with venom. 'You whore witch. You stole Adam from me. I curse you. I curse you a hundred times.'

'Lisette, that is enough!' Adam turned on her. 'If you want my help you must accept that Senara is my wife.'

'Never. Never. Never!' She thumped the arms of the chair in her fury.

'Then I shall never see you again, Lisette.'

For a moment her eyes were wild, then the lids lowered but not before Senara had glimpsed their cunning. Lisette stood up and wrapped the cloak around her, her poise now one of regal dignity and her voice pleading and childlike. 'My head hurts. I do not mean to act so badly, Adam. All I want is for you to love me, for your family to love me. You must never say you will not see me, Adam. I know I do bad things, but that is not me. That is that other Lisette – the one who has such terrible nightmares.'

The swift changes of mood were a sign of her illness of which the nuns who had been caring for her in France had warned him. 'I will see you if you act like the sweet cousin and gentlewoman who was such a delight to us all.'

'You are not going away again, Adam. I know you have *her*. But I will still see you, will I not?'

'If you remember how a gentlewoman should behave.'

She nodded. 'You have come home, that is what is important. You will love me again if I do all you say.'

Adam sighed. 'We will all love you, Lisette.'

'And I must go back to Trevowan. Uncle Edward will not be pleased if he sees me like this. He will want to lock me away.' She giggled and picked up Senara's woollen dress. 'I must look respectable when I return to Trevowan. You will not say anything to Uncle Edward, will you? I promise I will be all you want of me, Adam.'

Adam looked across at Senara for guidance but she merely shrugged. His father should be told and he wondered just how unacceptable Lisette's behaviour had been in the past. Yet his own conscience troubled him. If he had not insisted on a delay to their wedding none of the horrors she had faced in France would have happened. And there was also the guilt which came with relief that, loving Senara, he now knew he could never have been happy with Lisette. 'I will say nothing if you make your peace with my wife.'

Senara made to protest but Adam was insistent.

Lisette pouted and turned to regard Senara. 'I have behaved badly. I ask your pardon.' She hung her head, pleading for forgiveness like a child.

'We will forget this unfortunate incident,' Senara replied, but she was not fooled by the Frenchwoman's manner. 'I must attend to Bracken.'

Senara could feel Lisette's hatred as a living, palpable thing, waiting like a viper in the shadows for the moment to strike.

Chapter Five

A dam was shocked at the state of Bracken when he saw the mare in the stable. She was snorting and kicking up her straw. There were a dozen deep, bloody gashes along her flank where she had been whipped. Such unnecessary cruelty was inexcusable. Bracken was a spirited mare, too spirited for Lisette, who had never been an accomplished horsewoman.

'What possessed you to ride Bracken so hard?' he snapped at Lisette when she appeared to show no remorse at the injuries.

In the dim light of the single lantern hanging in the stable, Lisette stood with her arms folded. 'That monster tried to throw me. Elspeth is too soft with her mares. It is a brute.'

'She is Elspeth's favourite, and my aunt does not like others to ride her. Meriel's mare is a quieter animal. No animal deserves to be treated this way.' Adam stroked the mare's nose to calm her. 'Elspeth will never forgive you for this.'

'I hate her,' Lisette scowled. 'She treats me like a child.'

'Because you act like a spoiled child when you do not get your own way.'

Senara entered the stable, carrying her box of herbs and salves. She offered Bracken a carrot and turned her back on Lisette to tend the animal's wounds. 'It will take a week or

91

more for these cuts to heal. Three of them need stitches. I will need someone to hold the horse steady while I work on her.'

'I'll do that, Mrs Loveday,' offered Mike Fletcher, the blacksmith. The thickset, bearded man was currying Damsel, one of the shires used in the yard for pulling logs.

'I'll saddle up Hercules for Lisette to ride.' Adam entered the stall of the second shire horse and heaved a saddle over Hercules' broad back.

Lisette stamped her foot, causing Bracken to shy, and Senara was knocked against the wooden side of the stall. 'Why can I not ride on Solomon with you, Adam?' Lisette demanded. 'I do not wish to ride that ugly beast. And that is a man's saddle.'

'Bracken's side-saddle is too small for Hercules. You will have to ride astride. You should have treated Bracken more kindly.'

Adam pushed on Bracken's rump so that Senara was no longer trapped. She was unharmed but tight-lipped with annoyance. Senara ignored Lisette and spoke soothingly to Bracken.

Adam added, 'And I will not burden Solomon with an unnecessary double load.'

Lisette remained petulant though her voice became wheedling: 'I am sorry, Adam. You are right. Do not be cross with me. I will do whatever you ask of me.'

Senara frowned as she saw the Frenchwoman ride away at Adam's side. She was not fooled by Lisette's compliance. The woman had wrapped herself in an air of tragedy. What she had suffered in France and survived was to her credit. She needed love, compassion, sympathy and understanding to ease the inner torment of her suffering. Yet her difficult behaviour was only turning people against her. Lisette had always been selfish, her needs more important to her than consideration for the feelings of others.

Senara had seen this at the time of Adam's betrothal to the Frenchwoman. Lisette could change roles and moods to please her father, brother, a Loveday, or even a stranger. Senara had once seen an exhibit in a travelling fair. The lizard creature was from Madagascar and on the point of dying from being fed the wrong food. It was a chameleon and capable of changing colour to be as one with its surroundings. The creature was beautiful, fascinating and exotic, but behind its beauty was lethal intent. Its ability to blend in with its surroundings allowed it to devour an unsuspecting prey. Lisette was a chameleon. She had always been sly, using her moods to win approval, but it was what lay behind that intent which alarmed Senara. Tonight more than cunning had driven Lisette – there had been madness in her eyes. An unstable woman like that could never be trusted, and to have treated Bracken so severely meant she was capable of great cruelty.

It had been dark for two hours when Adam and Lisette arrived at Trevowan. Only two of the windows showed light within. The gables and tall chimneys were black against a starlit sky. A single candle burned in the hall, dappling the black and white marble floor and throwing eerie shadows up the curving staircase.

Lisette hung back. 'I will go to my room.'

'No, you will face my family and apologise.' Adam took her elbow so that she could not escape.

When they entered the winter parlour with its Chinese wallpaper of peacocks he found his family gathered. Amelia was sewing a garment for baby Rafe, Elspeth was reading and Edward was pacing by the window. He saw them first.

'Thank God she's been found. Where was Lisette?'

'Lisette paid us a visit at Mariner's House,' Adam replied.

Edward turned on his niece. 'Have you any idea the worry you have again caused us? Go to your room at once.'

Lisette stamped her foot. 'I will not be treated like a child. Am I prisoner in your house? I wanted to see Adam. You would not let me. If I had told you where I was going you would have stopped me.'

'That is enough of your insolence, Lisette.' Edward was struggling to control his anger.

Adam attempted to diffuse the tension. 'Lisette, apologise and assure my family that you will not act so thoughtlessly again.'

Her mouth pouted in mutiny.

'Remember your promise to me,' he reminded her.

She wrung her hands and lowered her gaze to the floor. 'I ask your forgiveness, Uncle Edward. I was thoughtless. I do not want you to hate me.'

'And you took Bracken.' Elspeth heaved her slender body to her feet and banged her walking cane on the floor. 'How dare you? You are a thoughtless, selfish baggage. After all this family has done for you, you repay us with ingratitude, and behave in the most shameless manner.'

'Oh, I say, Elspeth, that is a bit strong. The poor girl looks done in.' William Loveday stepped out of the shadowy recess where he had been pouring himself a drink. William's presence meant that *Pegasus* had docked.

'We have all been worried,' William continued. 'Lisette is safe. Surely that is the main thing. Best to sleep on it.'

'Trust you to defend her, William,' Elspeth snapped. 'The minx can do no wrong in your eyes. All you see is a pretty face.'

William strode to Adam and Lisette and smiled down at the woman. William was Edward's youngest brother and, at forty-four, was tall and lithe, and his short dark hair was still thick and without grey. There was a more boyish roundness to his handsome features than either of his brothers'. His complexion was nut brown from his years at sea, making his blue eyes piercing in their intensity. They were smiling with indulgence as he regarded his French niece.

Lisette was subdued and refused to meet anyone's gaze, and Elspeth continued to complain at her lack of gratitude.

William, who was so austere when in command of a ship, was obviously charmed by Lisette. 'The girl has asked our forgiveness. Perhaps you overreacted, Edward. It is obvious she would want to see Adam. She has endured many traumas in the last year. We must all be patient with her.'

Lisette stood on her toes to kiss his cheek. 'Dear William, you are always so kind. So understanding. When did you arrive?'

'An hour ago. And everyone was worried about you. Edward has been out searching the moor.'

Lisette looked all sweet innocence. 'I had not realised that a visit to Adam would cause so much worry to the family.'

'Indeed you would not.' William patted her hand. 'But it is not done for a woman to ride unchaperoned.'

'I never mean to act badly, truly I do not.' Lisette ran to Edward and kissed him. He remained rigid and unaffected by her charm. 'I ask your pardon, my dear uncle. But for you I would still be in that dreadful convent in France. I was wrong to run off to see Adam and not let someone know where I had gone. I will go to my room. I am tired.'

Edward remained stern. 'First you must apologise to Amelia. She has been distressed at the worry you have caused.'

Lisette bowed her head and clasped her hands together at her waist. 'Dear Aunt Amelia, I know that sometimes I behave badly.' She began to sob. 'I do not want to. I get frightened. I hear the mob shouting for my blood . . . The terror is too much to bear . . .' She fell at Amelia's feet, weeping.

'You must learn that we are not your enemies.' Amelia held back from comforting her. 'And you must act as a gentle-woman.'

Lisette sniffed. 'I will try. I do not want you to hate me. If only my dear papa were alive . . .'

William stooped to help her to her feet. 'We do not hate you.'

Edward tapped the mantel shelf with his fingers, uncomfortable at her emotional display. 'Go to your room. I expect an immediate improvement in your conduct.'

Lisette hurried away.

'Not so fast, young lady,' Elspeth challenged, but Lisette ignored her and left the room. 'Come back here! I have not finished with you.'

'Let her go, Elspeth.' Amelia put a hand to her temple and rubbed it as though it pained her.

Edward watched Lisette's departure with suspicion; Elspeth through narrowed eyes.

Amelia sighed and added, 'At least she has come to no harm. But she was barefoot?'

'Her shoes and stockings were sodden. They were left at Mariner's House by mistake,' Adam improvised.

'The minx is up to something.' Elspeth massaged her hip. 'Edward and William are fools if they believe that false contrition.'

William scratched his chin. 'Before I went to sea, Lisette had been acting almost normal. The poor girl has been through so much.'

Elspeth rounded on him. 'She is too demanding of one's time: always wanting praise or compliments, and sulking if she does not get her way. Her tantrums are deplorable. I am going to the stable to check on Bracken.' Her step was stiff with pain from her hip, injured years ago in a riding accident.

'Bracken is still at the yard,' Adam said.

Elspeth banged her cane on the floor. 'If that baggage has hurt my darling mare, she will live to regret it. How bad is Bracken?'

'Senara is tending her. A few cuts.'

Elspeth stamped across to him and jabbed him in the chest with the silver handle of her cane. 'I lay much of the blame of this on you. How badly is Bracken hurt? And don't lie, Adam. A few light cuts would not stop you returning Bracken to her stall. I shall see for myself in the morning.'

'Lisette took a whip to her.'

'And I shall take a whip to that young lady.' Elspeth's face whitened with rage. 'I have never whipped any of my mares. The girl is unstable. She must be locked up for her own good, Edward.'

'I say, that is too harsh,' William protested. 'She used to be such a sweet, gentle girl. Give her time.'

Edward shook his head. 'I fear Elspeth may be right. Her behaviour has been more erratic since she learned that Adam has married. Her remorse tonight is different from her normal manner.'

'Surely that is a sign that Lisette intends to change her ways. She is calm enough now,' William insisted.

'What happened at the yard?' Edward regarded Adam coldly.

Adam had witnessed enough of Lisette's behaviour to realise that she was causing many difficulties for the family. Neither was he fooled by her demure manner – it was as unnatural as her conduct had been at the yard. He did not want to lie, but the truth would have been unacceptable to Edward. 'Lisette was upset and volatile when she arrived. I had trouble reasoning with her. She is convinced that everyone hates her. She has promised to behave in a more circumspect manner in future.'

'What did she do and how did you effect this startling transformation?' Edward's eyes were dark and condemning. 'When she is upset, she gets hysterical and no one can reason with her.'

'She took some persuading, but as you saw, she now seems to accept that I am married.'

Edward clasped his hands behind his back. 'Why do I feel that you are not telling me the whole story?'

'I promised Lisette that I would not be leaving again.'

'But with *Pegasus* moored at Fowey awaiting unloading, where does that promise stand?'

'Obviously, I had not expected my ship to dock so soon. And I had to say something to calm her.' Disliking the cross-questioning from his father, Adam turned to William Loveday. 'I am delighted your passage was so swift.'

'*Pegasus* is at her best under full sail in strong winds.' William scanned Edward and Adam's faces and frowned at their hostility. 'Your ship seems to have wings when she skims through the waves. I have never had such a swift passage through the Bay of Biscay. A naval frigate is cumbersome by comparison.'

Elspeth startled each man by rapping him painfully on the arm. 'With all this talk of ships have you forgotten the issue of this night? Lisette. I will not tolerate her conduct any longer. What do you intend to do about her, Edward?'

Tension tightened his features. 'She will have one final chance. We knew it would be difficult when Adam returned, especially with a wife. She deserves at least some time to come to terms with that knowledge.'

Amelia nodded. 'I will make this plain to her tomorrow—'

'She is a cunning, deceitful minx,' Elspeth interrupted. 'I

do not trust her. And I think you will rue the day you allowed her to continue to live here.'

'And you are a wizened, sour old maid, Elspeth,' William returned, but with some humour to take the sting from his words. 'Have you forgotten what it is like to be young and in love?'

Elspeth glared at him over the top of her pince-nez. 'No, I remember well the pain of thwarted love – was I not jilted a week before my wedding? But I never forgot that I was of gentle birth, or the conduct society expected of me.'

'Not everyone is as resilient as you, Elspeth.' William regretted his outburst. He had been only nine at the time Elspeth had been jilted, and already a midshipman serving at sea. He had not seen the misery and humiliation Elspeth had suffered. He put his arm round her. 'Your pardon, Elspeth. My words were thoughtless. You have always been strong. Lisette is not.'

Elspeth shrugged off his hold. 'There's no fool like an old fool where a pretty face is concerned. Or, I begin to suspect, no fool like a Loveday. I was beguiled by a handsome adventurer and bigamist, and in recent years St John and Adam have put beauty before duty. Take care, William, that you do not fall foul of the same snare.'

William laughed. 'I am a confirmed bachelor.'

'No, brother, you are a man and a Loveday.'

When Edward retired for the night and joined Amelia in their bedchamber, his wife was lying back on the pillows reading. She looked pale and tired.

'Can you not sleep, my love?'

'It has been another trying day.' Amelia put the book aside. When Edward went into his dressing room to disrobe, she wiped a tear from her eye. She had endured deprivation in the last year without complaint. She had mediated in the

99

growing disruptions in family life with equanimity, but this latest conflict was becoming too much to bear. Throughout her marriage to Edward she had tried to be strong. There had been many shocks waiting for her in Cornwall. When he told her of the circumstances of St John's marriage, she had been appalled as much by the immorality of St John's conduct as by him marrying out of his class. She had accepted it, knowing that even the most respectable family had occasional lapses. Then she had come to Cornwall and Adam had been openly conducting an affair with Senara, and Japhet had morals no better than a tomcat. This had shocked her but again she had accepted the lapses, realising that the Lovedays were passionate by nature and more unconventional than she was used to.

However, Lisette's behaviour had horrified her. The woman was a wanton and had been caught in an unseemly manner with one of the grooms. With all the worries Edward was dealing with she hid the extent of her mortification. For Edward's sake she tried not to judge his family. It had not been easy. She had also hidden the shame she felt at Adam's appearance with a son and Senara as his wife. Her gift of a gown to Senara had been to shield the family from further gossip and avert a scandal. Venomous tongues would revel in a family torn apart by conflict.

Edward came back, got into bed and put his arm around her. 'Are you still awake, my love?' He kissed her hair. 'Without you I do not know how I would have coped. You are my strength.'

Amelia moved into his arms. It was the reassurance of his love which made everything bearable. When Edward made love to her, he awoke her own sensuality, giving her pleasure in a way she had never before experienced. It made her more determined that the family must be united again, their vendettas and discord resolved. The Lovedays were a passionate

breed of men, but passion had many sides: it could raise
them in love and honour, or turn to anger and enmity. This
was her greatest fear.

Meriel was seated in front of her dressing table, admiring
the sunlight catching the emerald and diamond drop earrings she was wearing. The pale morning sun threw a lattice
pattern from the leaded window across the clutter of
perfume bottles, and powder and patch boxes. She savoured
this morning ritual when she was alone. The earrings suited
her colouring and were by far the most handsome she
possessed. It was wearisome that she could never wear
them in public or when St John was present. They had been
a gift from Lord Fetherington, the ageing roué who had
been pursuing her for over a year. Not that she had
succumbed, but it was becoming more difficult to entice
these trinkets from him, when all she would allow him was
a hurried kiss.

She draped a ruby bracelet over her wrist. This was a gift
from Basil Bracewaite, her latest admirer. He could be generous but he was becoming impatient at the way she evaded his
lecherous attention. She would have to be more careful with
Bracewaite. Sex was repulsive to her, but she enjoyed the
admiration of wealthy men and the power it gave her over
them. If they were foolish enough to press gifts upon her, she
was too acquisitive to refuse.

She smiled as she held up to the light an emerald pendant,
the stone the size of a duck egg. This was no gift but an illicit
acquisition which she had found on the floor of a hallway
during a visit last summer to Lord Fetherington's house in
Truro. It had belonged to some old harridan of a viscountess,
one of a dozen other house guests. The woman had twice
insulted Meriel and refused to sit at cards with her. The
viscountess had not discovered the pendant missing for two

days, then raised a hue and cry over its loss. A maid had been dismissed without references over its disappearance. Meriel experienced no twinge of conscience at the maid's misfortune. The pendant was her security. She may not be able to wear it, but it would fetch a good price. Harry had contacts for such a sale. Her brother's dealings had expanded beyond smuggling to selling goods lifted by a band of pickpockets working in Fowey and St Austell.

Lost in her contemplation, she started as she heard footsteps approaching outside her door. She snatched the earrings from her ears and threw the other jewels into an ivory trinket box. The bedchamber door burst open and St John bellowed at her, 'What is the meaning of these bills? Do you mean to have me thrown in debtors' prison?'

Before facing her enraged husband, she drew a discarded fichu across the box to hide it from his attention. She dabbed a powder puff against her cheek to regain her composure. That had been a narrow escape for she was terrified St John would discover her trinkets. Her expression was puzzled innocence as she turned and stared up at St John's flushed face. 'My dear, whatever is amiss?'

'These damned bills which have arrived from milliners, shoemakers and dressmakers in Bodmin.'

'Oh, those. Lady Traherne was so persuasive. How could I act the pauper and not purchase them, when her ladyship insisted that they were basic necessities?'

'Roslyn Traherne has a fortune. We do not. How am I to be expected to meet these accounts? I said you could purchase a hat since Roslyn insisted on you accompanying her.' He waved the papers under her nose. 'You purchased two hats, two silk petticoats, a pelisse, a muff and walking shoes.'

Meriel pushed some blue hair bows on pins into her blonde hair and studied her reflection in the mirror. 'It is not fitting for your wife to be seen in shabby clothes.'

'You have a wardrobe full of clothes, none of which is shabby. You know our present circumstances.'

'I did not marry you to live in rags.' She picked up a fan and hurled it at him.

St John caught the fan and flung it on the pink satin coverlet of the bed. 'And I only married you because your brother was pointing a shotgun at me. Little pleasure or comfort I have received from the bargain.' He stared at the pink wallpaper and bed hangings which Meriel had purchased since she had moved into her own bedchamber three months ago. His frustration increased his anger. 'And since Adam has wed his gypsy, Father is not slow in reminding me again how I also failed in my duty to marry an heiress. Had I done so there would be no question of Adam inheriting the yard. I lost half my inheritance because of you, madam.'

'You forget that I was carrying your child at the time of our wedding.' They fell into the regular pattern of arguments.

'And you've been barren ever since. You could not even produce a son.' St John opened the door to admit the maid, Rachel Glasson. 'Everything on these bills purchased in Bodmin is to be returned to the shops.'

'But they will never refund the full price. How dare you shame me this way?' Meriel raged. 'And you said I could have a new hat.'

'Your greed has lost you that privilege. In future there will be no more shopping excursions unless I accompany you. Rachel, check that *everything* goes back.'

At being so shamed in front of their maid, Meriel hurled a perfume bottle at St John. He side-stepped and it broke against the wall.

'Smashing things of value in our home will solve nothing.

It but proves how little you appreciate what you have.' He turned on his heel and strode out of the door.

Meriel was alarmed. Until now she had always been able to manipulate St John. But then he had been weak and dissolute. His time with the smugglers had changed him.

She ran after her husband, along the corridor and down the stairs. 'St John, forgive me. I have been foolish.' She caught up with him as he was walking out the front door. 'Of course the purchases must go back. I should never have let Lady Traherne persuade me. It was a matter of pride that we could still afford such things.' Her eyes pleaded with him to forgive her. 'I wanted to make you proud of me, St John; be a good wife to you.'

'Madam, all you have ever wanted is to flaunt your position in public. My wishes – my desires – have always been furthest from your thoughts.'

There was an excited cry and Rowena trotted across the lawn on her Shetland pony. 'Papa, see how well I ride. Fraddon says I no longer need the leading rein. Come watch me.'

St John's expression softened with love as he regarded his daughter. Rowena's dark hair hung around her shoulders and she wore a blue riding habit. She sat straight and proud in the saddle. She had hooked the reins through the fingers of her weak hand.

'Come watch me, Papa?' Rowena's looks were all Loveday but her manner was pure Meriel, always seeking attention. St John laughed, finding this no fault in his daughter. 'Is that riding habit becoming too small for you? You are growing so fast. We must send for the dressmaker to measure you for a new one.'

Rowena smiled. 'I love you, Papa.'

'And I you, my angel.'

Behind them Meriel scowled. Rowena could get anything

she wanted from her doting father. She realised with shock that it had been months since St John had looked at her with anything close to affection. Since the arrival of Adam with a son, St John had come to her bed more often, demanding her compliance. She had submitted with sullen ill grace. Was she allowing her discontent to make her careless?

That evening St John dined on his favourite dishes and wine specially chosen by Meriel. The meal mellowed St John's mood but the game pie was overrich for her taste and sat heavily on her stomach. St John did not speak to her throughout the meal and when she set out to seduce him, he took her with a cold, emotionless passion.

Meriel was shaken. St John acted as though he no longer cared for her. She had to regain his love or her power over him was lost.

All that night she lay sleepless, her stomach churning with nausea. She hoped St John was suffering similar effects of the game pie. The morning light made her head throb and with a groan she listed the tasks which were expected of her — feeding and cleaning out the hen coops, collecting the eggs and storing them in straw baskets to be taken to market. She hated the work imposed on her by Edward when they had faced ruin last year. That Amelia happily tended her bees and collected their honey, or Elspeth spent hours making preserves when the fruits were in season did not placate Meriel. She had married to escape the drudgery of her work in the inn.

The queasiness of the night intensified. An hour ago St John had left to work on the estate. If she did not tend to the poultry it would be noted and she would face the censure of her father-in-law. Aware that after yesterday she needed to regain her husband's favour, reluctantly she swung her feet from the bed. A rush of nausea caught her unawares and she barely had time to reach for the chamber pot under the bed before she was sick. She retched until her stomach ached and finally dragged herself up and pulled on her plain work dress.

She walked precariously towards the poultry coops, fighting against another wave of nausea. Damn St John and his penny-pinching! This was not the life of a pampered lady which she craved. As she stooped to release the catch on the chicken pen, her senses began to swim and she collapsed on the ground. There was a cry from Rachel Glasson, who was attacking a rug with a cane beater as it hung over a line.

'Mistress Meriel be taken ill. She's done collapsed.'

Rachel ran to the main house to fetch Winnie Fraddon. They found Meriel holding on to the chicken pen for support. There was vomit over her skirt. Meriel pushed back a tress of hair which had fallen over her eyes and glared at Winnie's stout figure.

'That game pie was off that you cooked last night. Are you trying to poison us?'

'Weren't nothing wrong with that pie. Family ate the same as you last night and none of them be sick.'

'Fetch Chegwidden, I'm dying.' She clutched her stomach and groaned.

Winnie eyed her with a grin. 'You bain't dying. Looks to me you be breeding. I can always tell. Master won't be pleased at having to pay Chegwidden fees for a touch of morning sickness.'

Meriel stared at her as though the cook had gone mad. Then she gave a smug smile. She was never ill, and to be sick with such violence had only happened when she was pregnant. 'Send for young Dr Chegwidden. His fool of a father said I would never conceive another child. I feel too ill to work. I shall go and rest until the physician arrives.'

St John arrived at the Dower House as Simon Chegwidden was leaving. 'You are to be congratulated, Mr Loveday. Your wife is with child. But every care must be taken of her. I understand your daughter's birth was most protracted. Mistress Loveday must rest – no strenuous work whatsoever.'

In her bedchamber Meriel heard the doctor talking to St John. She pulled the covers up with a sigh. Today and every day for the next few months she would not rise until noon and, to ensure the safe delivery of her child, she must be waited on and pampered. She carried the next heir to Trevowan. Any work could be fatal to the child, could it not?

Chapter Six

The Dolphin Inn was not a place St John cared to visit. That it was owned by Reuban Sawle, who was sour-tempered and vengeful since his accident, made it even less appealing. But he needed to see Harry urgently.

As he turned from the headland path to enter the village of Penruan the wind gusted with renewed vigour and made the breath catch in his throat. The sea was a murky pewter with a heaving swell. The fishing fleet was snuggled within the harbour arm, the smacks swaying tipsily as the wind rattled through their rigging. A warning bell on the buoy beyond the headland rocks clanged incessantly, its sound mournful as a death knell. The cluster of cottages around the horseshoe-shaped harbour clung like barnacles to the side of the coombe, and thin spirals of smoke rose from the chimneys to mingle with the persistent sea mist.

The Dolphin sign creaked overhead. Its paint, flaked and faded, displayed an indistinct blur of grey against a splattering of blue sea. There was a lantern in the window of the inn, the only light visible within the dwellings of the village. Dark would not fall for another hour, and rushlights and candles were a luxury after a poor winter of fishing. It would have been a good night to land a cargo, the activities less likely to be observed on so rough an evening. But Harry had sent word it had been delayed and St John was desperate for money to settle an overdue gambling debt. Creditors could wait for their money, but a gaming debt must be paid immediately or honour was lost.

The low ceiling beams made the inn gloomy, and the two small windows permitted only a dismal light. The lime-washed walls were darkened to amber from the years of tobacco smoke and fires. There was a wooden settle by the fire and benches around the walls, with a few stools and beer barrels serving as tables. Tallow candles spluttered behind two glass lanterns, highlighting the weather-worn features and gnarled hands of the drinkers. The air was musty from the wet clothing drying on the fishermen, and the smell of stale fish which pervaded every crevice of the village.

St John coughed as the fetid air choked him.

'It bain't often our high and mighty son-in-law sees fit to grace our home.' Reuban Sawle glowered at him from his perch behind the bar. His face was cadaverous, the hooded eyes sunken with pain and his toothless mouth twisted with bitterness. His legs ended abruptly before the knee, and he was propped on a high stool which had been fitted on to a trolley so that he could pull himself around the taproom.

'On your own, Reuban?' St John's question was an indirect way of learning Harry's whereabouts. He could not ask openly with a dozen fishermen supping their ale, for he did not want his name linked with Harry's smuggling activities.

'And who else would be working here? Not one of my sons. They think such work beneath them. Got notions above themselves, they 'as.'

'You should be proud of your sons. Clem, he has done all right for himself since he married Keziah, and Squire Penwithick speaks highly of Mark's work in his stables.' St John attempted civility. 'I thought Harry still helped out when he was needed.'

Reuban spat on the floor, his tone sarcastic. 'What you

drinking? As heir to the Lord of the Manor you'll be wanting to buy a round for every man here.'

The heads of a dozen fishermen present turned to St John in anticipation. They had all worked as tubmen to land-smuggled goods, carting inland the kegs of brandy, tea and silks to safe places. Some lived in cottages owned by the Lovedays. St John tossed some silver on the bar with ill grace. This was an expense he could ill afford, but since his rivalry with Lanyon had flared, it was a matter of honour to win the popularity of the locals. Lanyon had been buying up property in the village and had had three cottages built for renting out to establish himself as a prominent landlord. He saw himself as as important as the Lovedays. St John could not tolerate that. Lanyon was also a clutchfist. Largesse was the privilege of the landed gentry, as were good breeding and manners – both of which Lanyon lacked.

'Give each man a brandy. May it cheer and chase the cold from his bones.' He decided to enjoy his moment of generosity and use it against Reuban: 'Have one yourself, Reuban. Though I doubt a whole keg would ever rouse any warmth or cheer in you.'

'And what I got to be cheerful about?' Reuban hawked and again spat on the floor. 'I got a daughter with her nose stuck so high in the air she never visits. Never brings a crumb of comfort to ease my misery. An unnatural wretch, that what she be. And unnatural sons who have no thoughts but for theyselves.'

As Reuban scooped up the silver a woman sauntered to St John's side. 'Bain't you gonna buy me a drink, me 'andsome.' Mary Lee thrust out her large breasts and eyed him boldly.

St John ignored her. Though passably attractive, Mary had a rank smell about her, her dark hair hanging in greasy rat's-tails from her mobcap.

'You bain't 'ere to act the whore.' Sal came into the taproom and pushed Mary back towards the kitchen. 'There be dishes need washing.' Sal turned her attention to St John, her expression curious. 'Meriel bain't sick, be she?'

'No. I was on my way back to Trevowan and Prince lost a shoe. I left him at the smithy and thought a brandy would warm me. Actually, Meriel is expecting again.'

'Our gracious son-in-law is about to become a father again,' Reuban roared. 'Now that will be another round of brandy for all to wish the new babe well.' He held out his hand as St John dropped more coins on the bar.

'I be pleased for you and Meriel,' Sal stated. 'Pay no mind to Reuban's grumbling. 'Appen he got reason to moan about 'is lot.'

From the corner of his eye, St John saw Harry watching him from the kitchen door. With a jerk of his head Harry indicated that St John meet him outside in the stables. St John tossed back the brandy. 'Prince should be ready by now.'

'Good health to your child, Mr Loveday,' a fisherman called as he left.

St John had never been as popular as Adam with the men of Penruan and he warmed to the mark of respect. He tipped his hat to Sal, who looked pale and ill from overwork. Her face was wrinkled and distrustful as a crone's, her body a shapeless mound of sagging flesh where once there had been voluptuous curves.

'What be so important that you risk us being seen together,' Harry jeered when they entered the stable. St John hid his irritation. Harry may be his business partner but they did not like each other. Harry did not trust St John's motives for his involvement with the smugglers. He thought he did not have the backbone when it came to a fight. Even though St John had been wounded trying to save Harry when his partner had been shot, the wariness remained between the two men. St John did not trust Harry, because he was a violent, cold-hearted man who used people for his own ends.

'I need a loan. I've a gambling debt to meet. A hundred pounds.'

Harry gave a harsh laugh. 'You want me to loan you money? What about the money for the next cargo? I bain't gonna put up the money and you expect to cream off the profits.'

'I'll have the money for the next cargo out of the profits from the landing which should have taken place tonight. This loan is a separate matter. You've loaned money to others. You see yourself as another Lanyon, don't you?'

St John resented having to ask Harry. Harry and Meriel were leeches sucking his integrity and honour from him.

Harry disappeared and came back with a leather pouch. 'I want thirty per cent interest for every month the debt be outstanding.' He opened a new ledger and wrote the amount and interest in the columns. Harry, like all the fishermen, had been illiterate until his sister-in-law, Keziah, had taught his brother Clem to read and write. Harry had asked her to teach him. The ledger was proof of his progress.

'That's robbery,' St John fumed.

Harry grinned. 'Legal robbery. Take it or leave it. Lanyon would charge another five per cent. You could always go to him.'

St John snatched the pouch and rode out of the stable yard in a fury. If he was not always so short of money, he would abandon his partnership with Harry. Smuggling was no life for a gentleman. Between Meriel's greed and Harry's wild schemes, St John felt too often that he was being manipulated by the Sawles. It was time for that to change.

Japhet was restless. He found life at Trewenna Rectory dull.

112

His parents were visiting a dying parishioner and, despite the persistent fog that had drifted in when the rough winds died down, Peter had left at first light to preach in St Austell as it was market day. There was to be a hunt and ball at Lord Fetherington's manor over Easter, but no other entertainments until then. He could always visit Hannah, but he had spent the last three days at the farm after learning Oswald had been struck down with a fever of the lungs. Rarely a winter passed without Oswald being ill now and he had a persistent cough. Hannah was reluctant to accept Japhet's help but he hated to see his sister struggle with the work on her own. She had sent a note this morning saying that Oswald was better and for Japhet to enjoy his time at his old home.

Japhet tossed a pair of dice on the table, wagering with himself whether the numbers would be odd or even. It did not keep him occupied for long and he considered riding over to Traherne Hall to visit Sir Henry. Gwen could always be relied on to amuse him – though it meant he would have to endure Lady Traherne and her mother, the Lady Anne's, waspish tongues. On his last two visits to the Hall Lady Anne, suspicious of his reputation and motives, had been determined that he and Gwendolyn were not to be alone together.

So that left Fowey as a place of diversion. Japhet remembered a certain accommodating Kitty Veryan, a captain's wife whose husband was away at sea. His interest quickened. The captain was not due back from a voyage to the East Indies for another month. With the prospect of dalliance his mood lifted and he frowned when he heard a rap on the door.

'Gwen, this is an unexpected pleasure! And in such dire weather too. This fog makes riding dangerous.'

'I never rode faster than a trot. I needed to get away from Roslyn's constant complaining. Have I caught you about to go out?' She glanced at his hat clasped in his hand.

'Nothing that I cannot delay. Riding becomes you: you are prettily flushed and quite seductively breathless.' Slowly he appraised her trim figure, his smile rakish and approving. 'You are more beautiful each time we meet.'

Her colour heightened in a flattering fashion. 'I came to tell your mother that the miller will deliver a sack of flour every week to be distributed to the needy. I was shocked to learn that the high price of grain means so few families can afford it.'

'Such generosity should not go unrewarded.' He stood closer to her and lifted a copper ringlet to feel its silky texture.

'I expect no reward from those less fortunate than myself.' She looked suddenly distressed and clamped her hand to her mouth. 'Oh, you do not think they will see it as patronising or interfering? That was never my intent.'

Gwen was easily discountenanced. Since childhood, her domineering sister and mother had tried to suppress her natural vitality and compassionate nature, and it had robbed her of confidence. Somehow that was part of her charm. Japhet was attracted to beautiful women, but so often they bored him after a short acquaintance. Gwen was different. She never ceased to surprise him.

'They will see you as a saint. Mama cannot praise you highly enough.'

'I do not deserve such praise.' She became flustered and would not meet his gaze. 'A bag of flour takes little enough from my allowance. Being an heiress has some benefits.'

'I can think of no one I would praise more.' He took her hand and raised it to his lips. He could feel the rapid fluttering of her pulse beneath his fingers. The downcast eyes hid her expression and he lifted her chin in his hand. Her gaze met his for the briefest moment. Its radiance was

114

searing. Then as quickly she looked away.

'Is your mother at home?'

'I am alone.'

'Oh . . .' The soft gasp was torn from her and he saw her swallow.

His finger traced the line of her jaw and again her gaze lifted to his, its luminance startling. Then, again, her lashes hid her eyes from him.

'Why will you not look at me, Gwen?' He was both amused and perplexed.

Her laugh was strained and she moved away from his touch.

'Do you fear me?' he was stung to ask.

She did not reply straight away, but fidgeted with the tassels of her cloak.

'Mama has forbidden me to talk with you at Lord Fetherington's hunt ball. She was furious that we spent so much time together at Adam's wedding. And that we met in Truro. She says my reputation will be damaged if I am seen with you.'

She expected him to be angry, or protest, or even ridicule her mother, but instead he shrugged. 'Lady Anne is right. I'm all she believes me to be and more. Yet I would never do anything to harm you, Gwen. Perhaps you should go.'

'Of course, I intrude.' Embarrassment made her awkward and she dropped her riding gloves.

Japhet picked them up but held on to them when she would take them. 'That is not what I meant, Gwen.' The anguish in her eyes prompted him to say, 'I do not know how to be friends with a woman.'

'It should be easy if you do not desire them.'

Her voice was low and as he leaned forward to catch her words, he was assailed by her perfume and the fresh smell of her skin. 'You cannot think that you are undesirable. You are lovely, Gwen. Quite the most witty and captivating woman I know.'

'Flattery rolls off your tongue too easily. It has no substance.'

Her words ruffled his composure. 'What is it you want from me, Gwen?'

She shook her head but refused to look at him, her hands tight upon the gloves which he still held. 'When have I asked anything of you, Japhet? I should leave.' She drew a sharp breath. 'But I will not have Mama dictate who I will or will not talk to during our stay with Lord Fetherington.'

'That's what I love about you, my sweet: you will not be dictated to. You have changed so much in the last two years.' His smile faded and he studied her intently. 'Gwen, I would forgo the pleasure of your company if it means your reputation is being put at risk.'

'But that is so unfair.'

A tear glistened on her lashes and instinctively he took her in his arms. It was inevitable that he would kiss her. A kiss of reassurance and comfort. Brotherly. Yet as her lips parted, moving beneath his to respond with hunger and passion, he was trapped by his sensuality.

Japhet held Gwen tighter, feeling the heat of her body, the curves of her breasts and hips moulded against him. Her fingers curled into the thickness of his hair, binding him closer, and he could feel the clamour of her heart echoing through his body. His world exploded into fire and sweetness as his hands opened her cloak and riding jacket to caress her breast. A raw and primeval passion ensnared his senses.

'Oh, Japhet,' she moaned against his throat.

The sound of her voice reminded him that this was no mere light of love: no experienced courtesan, no neglected wife seeking solace or pleasure, and no woman of questionable morals. This was Gwen. Dear sweet and naïve Gwen. A woman he respected too much to dishonour. It took all his willpower to claw back from the passion consuming him. He broke away from her lips and put her at arm's length.

'Your pardon, my sweet. I should not have—'

'I am not offended.'

Her lovely face was animated, her eyes dark with desire and lips swollen from his kisses. He swallowed against the dryness of his throat and continued to fight against his own desire.

'Gwen, this is wrong. You would never give yourself lightly. I do not want you falling in love with me. You are the last woman I would want to hurt.'

She turned away to adjust her clothing and he saw her shoulders square before she again faced him. Her eyes remained overbright. 'Really, Japhet, I never thought you would take a kiss so seriously. Please give my regards to your mother.'

Japhet frowned. Gwen was no accomplished flirt and her frivolous reaction was unlike her. She hurried out to her horse, her head bowed as she stepped on to the mounting block and swung into the saddle. The morning fog was lifting and Gwen's wild gallop past the church and out of the village drew a half-dozen barking dogs and sent foraging chickens into a frenzy of clucking as they scattered before the flying hoofs.

Japhet swore beneath his breath. He had hurt Gwen. He should have realised that she was beginning to care for him. She was not a natural flirt and he had allowed his pleasure in her company to break his rule of never pursuing unmarried women of his class.

His restless mood increased. Fowey and the now dubious delights of the sea-captain's wife beckoned. He stopped first at several taverns before seeking out Kitty Veryan, having checked that her husband was still at sea.

He was slightly unsteady on his feet when he knocked at her door. The limewashed cottage was in a back street on the hill overlooking the harbour and he approached through a winding alley. It had been two months since their last meeting, before he had gone to Truro. The door was opened six inches and Kitty regarded him warily.

'What would you be wanting after all this time, Japhet Loveday?'

He held up a quart flagon of gin. 'I was wondering if you wanted company. I came as soon as I could. You will have heard my cousin is married. I have been helping my sister on the farm. Have you missed me, sweet Kitty?'

She eyed the gin and ran her tongue across her lips. It was a drink she found hard to resist. The door opened further. 'I doubt you've given much thought to Kitty while you were gallivanting in Truro. You be a wicked man, Japhet.' She took the flagon from him and, without bothering with a cup, drank several mouthfuls. 'But you know how to make a girl happy, I give you that.'

Her thick brown hair was hidden under a lace-edged linen cap, her grey gown was demure and buttoned high to her throat. It fitted snugly over her full breasts, and a clean apron was tied around a waist which Japhet could span with his hands. To the inhabitants of the port she would appear as a respectable matron, keeping herself to herself, and her home tidy as she waited for her captain to return. Japhet knew that her true nature was very different.

Their first dalliance had been six years ago in Bath, when Kitty had been the mistress of one of the City's aldermen. Her protector had caught her with a dragoon officer and finished with her. Three years ago she had married her captain and settled in Fowey, and appeared to live a circumspect and exemplary life. Japhet had renewed their acquaintance six months ago when he had recognised the boredom behind the demure mask. Her conquest had been swift, speeded by the gin which her husband forbade in the house.

'Have you thought of me at all while you were away, Japhet?' There was a mischievous glitter in her eyes. 'I'd been faithful to my husband afore you came back into my life. I promised him I would honour him. He deserved that. Not many men would marry a woman such as me. He has provided for me well.'

'I thought of you often,' he answered without hesitation. A finger stroked her cheek and he pulled the cap and pins from her hair. It tumbled over her shoulders and Japhet kissed her. 'Are we not good together?'

'But my husband be a good man.' The protest was smothered by his lips and her hands pulled impatiently at his clothing. 'No one must know of this.'

'I do not boast of my conquests.' He was affronted, for he had always prided himself on his discretion; a gentleman did not discuss his paramours. 'How long is it before you expect your husband to return?'

'He said end of February or early March.'

'Then we have at least two weeks, perhaps even six. I will be at Trewenna at least a month.'

'But we must take care. David has a violent temper.'

'We will devise a plan. Keep a bunch of dried herbs hanging against the kitchen window while it is safe for me to call upon you. Remove them when your husband returns. I can see it as I approach through the alley.' He laughed. 'It will add spice to our tryst.'

Two days of fog had prevented Elspeth visiting Bracken in the yard stable. The damp air had made her hip too painful to venture out and Adam had assured her that Bracken was recovering. She could not rest from anxiety. Worry for her favourite mare had made her irascible and her ill temper had caused an unpleasant atmosphere at Trevowan. Lisette was constantly in tears and William argued with Elspeth, condemning her harshness towards the young Frenchwoman. Edward no longer found peace in his home and his own temper frequently got the better of him. Amelia worried about her husband's health and her nerves became edgy. The only one who was content was Rafe. His constant smiles as he pulled himself up from the floor, toddled around the furniture and attempted to walk on his own broke through the tension permeating the family.

Elspeth was in the nursery with Amelia when Rafe achieved his first four steps before falling over. Amelia scooped him into her arms.

'You clever, wonderful boy. Richard was thirteen months before he walked and you are still a few days short of your first birthday. Is he not clever, Elspeth?'

Elspeth's smile was tight-lipped. She was standing by the window, searching for signs that the fog was lifting. 'Adam walked at eleven months and St John a fortnight later. He was a lazy child but Adam kept taking the toys from him and it goaded him into walking.' She sighed. 'That was the start of their rivalry. Once a child can walk they are always into mischief. Rafe will be no different. He'll be a constant worry as to what trouble he can get into next.'

'Richard was never any trouble,' Amelia laughed as she stood Rafe up and encouraged him to walk again. 'The only worry he has given me was by joining the navy. That life is so uncertain. I fear that he will be washed overboard, fall from that alarmingly high rigging, or that he will be shipwrecked.'

Overcome with concern for her elder son, Amelia hugged Rafe to her breast. Richard had been her only child for a dozen years from her first marriage, and it was impossible to discard her need to protect him.

'Amelia, such worry will give you the megrims. Richard is a sensible boy,' Elspeth replied absently. 'William joined the navy when just a lad and Adam was not much older. They came to no harm.' She hobbled to the window. 'The mist seems to be lifting. I will go to the yard. If Bracken has been as badly beaten as I fear, that evil madam had better stay out of my sight for I vow I shall take my whip to her.'

Elspeth limped from the room. The dampness of the fog always aggravated her injured hip and her worry had intensified her pain. If the cuts to Bracken had been superficial Adam would have returned her to Trevowan Hard by now. Each step shot needles of fire through her hip. The wild gallop to Trevowan Hard made her light-headed from the pain and Elspeth was forced to cling to the saddle of her mare, Griselda, when she dismounted.

The yard shire horses were working and three stalls were occupied by Edward's horse, Rex, Adam's Solomon and a grey mare which she had seen the Polglase woman riding. There was no sign of Bracken and fear brought an agonised sob to her throat. They would not have destroyed her darling without telling her, would they?

She staggered into the yard and was heading towards her brother's office when she was hailed by Adam. Her nephew jumped down from the ship's deck where he had been crouched and working with a planing tool.

'Good morrow, Aunt.'

'What's happened to Bracken?' Elspeth's voice was high-pitched in her anguish. 'If she's dead I'll have the hide of that evil little vixen.'

'Calm down, Aunt. Bracken is recovering well. Senara is walking her in a field behind the yard. She did not want the mare's muscles to stiffen. She has been well cared for.'

Elspeth was not convinced, and ignored the pain in her hip as she marched towards the field. Several times her foot slipped in the mud and she bit her lip to hold back a cry of agony.

Adam took her arm. He was concerned at the pain etched into Elspeth's face and the frantic glitter in her eyes. He also did not want Senara subjected to one of his aunt's tirades. 'Why not rest at Mariner's House? Senara will bring Bracken to you.'

'Don't talk nonsense. How can I rest until I know my darling is safe?'

'You have always trusted Senara to heal your mares.'

'No one is infallible.' She refused to be reassured.

Senara had looped up the back hem of her woollen dress between her legs and into her front waistband to aid walking through the damp grass. The leather riding boots Adam had brought her protected her legs from the wet. A thick woollen shawl was tied over her head and wrapped across her chest to be tied at her back. She was leading Bracken by her halter and instead of the roughness of a horse blanket over the mare's back, Senara had placed her own cloak to protect the mare from the cold.

As she walked Senara fought against the urge to scratch at her arms and body. Ever since she had donned the woollen dress this morning, which had been returned by Lisette, she had felt uncomfortable. Within an hour her body had become heated, and itched as though she had walked naked through a patch of nettles. It was getting worse and only her resolve to exercise Bracken kept her from running back to the house to change.

Elspeth broke away from Adam to stumble through the long grass. 'Bracken, my poor angel,' she wept as she pressed her face against the mare's nose. The mare whinnied and nuzzled her mistress's cheek.

'She is recovering well.' Senara met Elspeth's blistering gaze. She could feel the woman's antagonism.

Elspeth lifted the cloak and the sheet beneath, which stopped the cloak rubbing on the open wounds. At the sight of the deep gashes and the three rows of stitches in the deepest of the cuts, Elspeth gasped, and tears rolled down her cheeks.

'That wicked, wicked girl,' she sobbed.

'There's no infection and Bracken seems not to have suffered any ill effects,' Senara explained.

'She has been tortured. And she was always highly strung.' Elspeth continued to stroke the mare's muzzle in her distress.

'I'm sure you will give her all the love she needs to recover her trust.' Senara watched Elspeth examine the wounds and gently replace the sheet and cloak.

'You have tended her well. Gypsies have a reputation for healing horses.'

Senara tilted up her chin at the insult but did not flinch from it. 'My grandmother and brother taught me well. I am not ashamed to admit it.'

Elspeth fixed her with a stony glare. 'I thank you for tending Bracken, but this changes nothing. I do not approve of Adam's marriage and I will not be at home if you should call with your husband.'

Senara was glad of the itching on her flesh which distracted her from the cruelty of Elspeth's words. She ironed the emotion from her voice: 'It would benefit Bracken not to travel as far as Trevowan for another week. It will give her cuts time to heal. The stitches could pull apart if she is startled on the road. That is your choice, Miss Loveday.'

'She will stay here.' Elspeth walked away.

Adam could not hold his temper. 'You could at least be civil to Senara. She was up all the first night with Bracken as the mare was so nervous and restless.'

'Have I spoken to her any differently from how I would to any of our servants? I have respect for her healing remedies,

123

but that is her place as far as I am concerned. I will, of course, pay for her services.'

'I do not want your money, Miss Loveday.' Senara stood tall and dignified and concealed her anger. 'I allow no animal to suffer unnecessarily. I would have done as much for one of the wild moorland ponies.'

Elspeth limped away. 'Bracken should not be out of the stable for too long. The weather is too cold for her.'

'That woman is insufferable.' Adam put his arm around Senara's shoulders. 'How dare she treat you in that manner?'

'I doubt she knows how to treat me,' Senara reasoned, and absently scratched at her ribs, which burned in a stinging agony.

The itching became unbearable and she flung Bracken's leading rein to her husband. 'This dress feels as if it is riddled with lice and fleas. I thought your cousin more fastidious in her habits.' As she spoke she scratched her neck and Adam stared at her with alarm.

'Your neck looks raw and there are tiny blisters erupting on your skin.'

Senara ran home and stripped off her gown and her shift. Even the chill of the winter's morning did not ease the heat of her flesh. Her neck, arms and torso felt as if they had been thrust into a furnace.

She studied herself in the small looking-glass on the wall. Her skin had turned a raspberry red and tiny white pustules were breaking and bleeding.

'Carrie, bring me up a bowl of water and a towel,' she shouted to her maid. 'Please, be quick about it.' She rummaged through her box of unguents for a balm of comfrey.

Carrie screamed at seeing the state of her mistress's raw flesh and almost dropped the bowl of water. 'Is it the smallpox? Are we all gonna die?'

'Calm yourself, Carrie. It is not the smallpox and it is not contagious.' Senara examined the woollen gown and found a dusting of greyish powder rubbed into the seams and material. She lifted the dress to smell the powder but could not identify what it had been made from. Yet undoubtedly it was some potent form of irritant which had been applied by Lisette.

Senara heard Adam enter the house and decided that it would be best if he remained ignorant of her suspicions. It would only cause more dissension with the family.

'One of the lampreys we had for supper yesterday must not have been fresh,' she improvised. 'I had a reaction like this once before after eating some.'

'Mistress Loveday, it do look so sore.' Carrie dabbed at Senara's back with a cold flannel.

Adam came into the room. 'Are you sure you are not seriously ill, my love? I'll send for Dr Chegwidden.'

Senara shook her head, which was beginning to throb painfully. 'I have balm to ease the rash. As I don't feel nauseous I'm sure I'll be fine by this evening.'

'Until then I insist you rest. If the rash gets worse, or it is not gone by this evening, Dr Chegwidden will be sent for.'

To Senara's relief the rash and the pain had disappeared an hour before dusk, but locked in her heart was an agony she was too proud to voice: the agony of rejection and of the loathing she had been subjected to by Adam's family.

Lisette had been staring disconsolately out of her bedchamber window as the mist began to thin. She had locked the door and refused to mix with the family who condemned her visit to Adam. The memory made her smile. Adam had been shocked and she enjoyed shocking men out of their complacency. She dismissed her cruelty to the horse, unable to understand their horror at her behaviour.

'I will never understand these English,' she moaned. 'They are so strange about their animals. Yet they do not care how I feel. Is a horse more important than my feelings? *Mon Dieu*, do I not have to accept my life in this wet and dreary country? The English are so cold and reserved – their hearts glacial with no *joie de vivre*. Frenchmen are fiery – their passion volcanic. We French know the importance of pleasure in our lives. I do not wish to understand these silly customs.' She stamped her foot.

Her spirits lifted as she remembered the powder she had rubbed into the dress of Adam's whore – she would never call her his wife. Lisette had purchased the powder last month from a tinker passing through Penruan. At the time she had been angry at Elspeth, who was always punishing her or complaining at her behaviour, and she had planned to use it on her. But she had never had the opportunity. Now Adam's whore knew how much she hated her, that she would always be her enemy. The memory made her laugh – a laugh which was tinged with hysteria, and she clung to the curtain for support.

When Lisette saw Elspeth ride across the lawn, she sobered, her eyes wild as she drew back behind the curtains. She was frightened of Elspeth. The old woman had never liked her. Even as a child when she had visited here, Elspeth had tutted and complained at the slightest thing Lisette did which did not follow English custom.

'I am French. *Vive la France!*' She swung her fist up in an obscene gesture at Elspeth's disappearing figure. Her hands clenched and she beat them against her hips. 'I came here to marry Adam. Instead they treat me as though I am an *enfant*. I am a woman – a woman who needs to be loved as a woman, not as a child.'

She was breathing heavily and striding back and forth in front of the window, her hands flailing as she muttered curses upon the Lovedays. A movement in the garden halted her and she saw William Loveday striding across the lawn towards the cliff path. Lisette's mood brightened. He was the only one of the family who had been pleasant to her in the last days. Elspeth was not in the house to lecture her. She would escape her room and follow William. He would tell her that she was pretty and she would flirt with him. It always made him blush. The French were so good at flirting and the English so poor. She giggled. It would be an amusing afternoon.

She glanced at her reflection in the cheval mirror and frowned. Her gown was plain after the pretty ball gowns she had worn in France. She snatched the fichu from her shoulders to expose the creamy rise of her breasts which were pushed high by her corset. Her giggles were unrestrained as she contemplated following William. It would be such fun to flirt with him. He was her champion, defending her from her enemies.

Lisette laughed as she ran through the house and out into the grounds. She had forgotten her cloak and shivered in the wintry air. The cold did not trouble her. The dungeon in France where the rebels had held her had been icy. Her fury had warmed her, and her need to avenge herself on her tormentors. Two had died by her hand when she had stolen her gaoler's dagger while he was violating her. She had plunged it into his throat and escaped the château. Then she had hidden in the grounds until she had been found by a shepherd, whose desire for her had overridden his prejudice against her nobility. She had stolen what little money and food he had after he had helped her to escape the district. Then she had searched for her brother, Etienne.

But Etienne had not been her saviour. He had shut her away in that prison of a convent and would have left her to rot. He said it was for her own safety. Etienne was selfish.

Had he not denounced his own aristocratic wife to win the approval of the New Regime? He had joined their army. Etienne's betrayal had hurt as much as Adam's. It had been a small revenge on her avaricious brother to steal money and jewels from his hidden cache of property robbed from aristocrats murdered or imprisoned. She had sewn the jewels and money into the hems of her petticoats before Etienne had delivered her to that hateful convent.

She laughed and her dark eyes glinted at the memory of tricking the brother she now despised. The Lovedays thought that her memory had erased the terrors she had endured in France. It had for a time but she had wanted to marry Adam for he would protect her. Therefore, she had continued to pretend that she had no recollection of her marriage to the Marquis de Gramont. She had lost her innocence long before the revolutionists had violated her. Her youth and innocence had been corrupted by her husband, who used her to win favours for himself, and she had discovered a wanton appetite which revelled in the excitement of new lovers she could control.

Now, as she ran along the path that William Loveday had taken, she shut the door on the memories of what had befallen her in France. They had happened to that other Lisette – the feral creature who could not control her moods or desires. That door must remained closed. Locked. The key cast away for ever. If not, that other Lisette would escape to haunt her. The past must be forgotten. But it had taught her how to survive.

Chapter Seven

William Loveday walked along the cliff path to find peace from the tension and disagreements rending his family. Yet solitude also irked him. He was used to a life of action, surrounded by a complement of over a hundred men on his naval frigate, HMS *Neptune*. On board a ship tensions were rife: the men discontent with their rations, the weather a constant challenge to their schedule. There he was in supreme command. His will governed every aspect of the sailors' lives. At Trevowan he felt that he had no right to judge the rules or expectations raised by Edward concerning his family.

Life at sea suited him and he considered himself a tolerant captain, ruling his men by example, rather than by bullying, as was common on other vessels. The sailors were brash and uncouth, but he understood their needs. After a few months at sea any new or press-ganged crew worked as an efficient unit. The officers were often discontent and could be overbearing and arrogant, and it took a different form of diplomacy to keep them in line. Yet William loved the life. It was all he knew.

In the thirty-five years he had been in the navy he doubted he had spent more than fourteen months of leave at Trevowan. He loved his family, but in many ways they were strangers to him, and with the atmosphere of growing

129

tension and arguments, he felt out of place in his old home.

As the youngest of George and Joan Loveday's children, his childhood had been distanced from his two sisters, Margaret and Elspeth. On the rare occasions he saw Margaret, who had settled in London, she had the annoying habit of fussing over him like a mother hen and treating him like a long-lost son. Then there was her infernal interference as a matchmaker to find him a wife. And domineering Elspeth had always been an enigma to him. Her emotions were so closely buttoned she rarely showed affection, and was too hasty with a scathing set-down or reprimand. Yet when he was a child she had been a fun-loving, open-hearted girl who was always laughing and taking joy in the simplest pleasures. She had changed after she had been jilted a week before her wedding. On each leave he had seen her deepening bitterness, her pleasure in life destroyed by a corrosive anger.

This enforced stay on land had been difficult for William and the voyage on *Pegasus* a godsend. Now that Adam was home his nephew would be sailing the brigantine and William would again be left to kick his heels.

He took the path down to Trevowan Cove and sat on a boulder by the cave where as a boy he had played pirates. The sea was murky and heavy, the waves lumbering to shore like cruising whales. The milky sky was free of rain-clouds and there was a stiff breeze. Good weather for full sail, he reflected with a pang of nostalgia. He closed his eyes and could feel again the rise and fall of a ship beneath his feet, and hear the slap of canvas as it billowed in the wind and the creak of ratlines and rigging. The poignancy of the memory made his fist bunch in frustration.

'You're washed up, old man,' he groaned aloud. 'What are you good for now?'

It was a question which had tested him for weeks. The navy could recall him at any time, now France had declared war against England and Holland, but who knew yet if that would be a major conflict? The Revolution had taken its toll on France and her navy. It could all be over in a month or so.

Fortunately, he had always lived frugally. His needs were simple and he had savings enough to support himself in this enforced retirement. He had even offered Edward his savings when he realised that the family was still battling through a financial crisis. But Edward would take nothing until William had insisted. 'At least allow me to pay the interest due on the loan outstanding on the dry dock.'

'It is not your responsibility, William.'

'How so? We are family. Is this not my home?' When his brother tried to protest, William waved it aside. 'Edward, you have never taken money from me in all the times I have stayed here. I would hate to live anywhere but Trevowan. An old tar and confirmed bachelor like myself appreciates the comfort of a family around him when he is on leave. I will be insulted if you refuse my offer of help.'

Edward bowed his head in acceptance. 'Only on condition that this money is considered a loan. I will repay it.'

Yet still this enforced leave and no immediate prospect of a ship had left William feeling like an outsider. Edward was busy at the yard and William knew nothing of shipbuilding, and even less about husbandry, to offer his services on the estate. From a boy he had always known he would join the navy – unlike Adam, who had served an unofficial apprenticeship within the yard because every aspect of shipbuilding had fascinated him. Adam had never wanted to leave his home for the navy, but the rivalry of the twins had driven Edward to separating them. Since St John was the heir, Adam had been sent to sea.

In this moment of honesty, William admitted that he had even less in common with his other brother, Joshua, than with Edward. The caring parson was far removed from the brother who as a child was constantly into scrapes. Joshua had been the cause of many a beating given to both Edward and William himself as he had urged them to join him in his wilder escapades.

William could not shake the despondency which had settled upon him this leave. Every other time he had returned to Trevowan had been a happy occasion. But that was before the family had come close to ruin.

'Edward would have found it hard to deprive his family of their comforts.' William addressed a gull picking at a herring head washed up on the beach. 'And I doubt St John and that wife of his have eased Edward's burden. They are the cause of much of the tension.'

William had been tempted to confront the elder twin about his conduct. He was angry that St John did not do more to ease his father's burden. St John wore their straitened circumstances like a yoke. You could feel his resentment smouldering. And that wife of his was in a constant sulk. Five years into that marriage and William saw little sign of the love which had caused so much upset. And Adam seemed to have followed the same road. No wonder Edward lost patience with his sons.

Yet, in command of a naval warship, William was also judge and jury aboard his vessel. He had learned to take all sides of an incident into account. So what position was he in to judge his nephews? He had loved but once, when he was in his early twenties. Lavinia had been a woman of his class, and an heiress, but her father had deemed a mere naval captain unworthy of his daughter. No one else had touched his heart. The navy and sea were arduous mistresses, demanding all his energy and time. He was resigned to remaining a bachelor with a vague idea of setting up berth with an amiable widow when he finally left the sea for good.

'William!'

He turned to see Lisette silhouetted against the skyline on the top of the cliff. She waved to him and lifted her skirt high to reveal shapely ankles as she walked down the path to join him. Here was another of Edward's problems. The young woman had stirred up high emotions within the family. Yet was she as bad as she was painted? Lisette was such a pretty little thing, with the face of an angel. Even now, after all he had been told she had suffered in France, there was an air of innocence about her. She had been so young to suffer so much. Allowances must be made for her. The incident with Elspeth's mare was reprehensible, and Lisette had assured him that she was overcome with remorse.

William watched Lisette walk daintily down the steep steps to the cove, laughing when her foot slipped and she was forced to run the last twenty yards. William hurried to catch her in case she fell as her feet landed on the soft sand. She clung to him laughing, the scent of lilac blossom wafting from her body and clothes.

'Oh, my gallant knight, you have saved me,' she giggled as she gazed up at him.

He was struck afresh by her beauty, as perfect as a porcelain doll. Her body in his arms seemed as insubstantial as a waif, so fragile it could blow away in a strong wind. He released her to step back and offered her his arm as they walked along the sand. The cove was small and protected by high cliffs on three sides. William frowned when he saw she was not wearing a cloak.

Gallantly he removed his jacket and placed it across her shoulders. She looked even frailer within its broad shoulders and long sleeves. 'We cannot have you catching a cold, my dear.'

'I do not feel the cold,' she replied, but wrapped the jacket closer to her. 'This is so warm, it smells of your cologne and pipe tobacco. It smells like Papa used to.'

Then to William's alarm Lisette burst into tears. 'Oh, Papa. I miss him so much. No one has loved me as he did. Why did he die?'

'You should not upset yourself so.' William was overcome with embarrassment and hesitated before putting an arm round her. 'Do not take on so, my dear.'

'But I miss Papa . . .' Her sobs gathered momentum.

William put both arms around her and her head lay against his chest. 'You will be ill if you do not calm yourself.' He took a handkerchief from his pocket, gently lifted her chin with one hand and wiped the tears with the other. 'There, is that not better?'

She gulped and brushed a hand across her face. 'You are so kind, William. The others do not like me. It was different when Papa was alive and I was going to marry Adam. Then everyone was good to me. They do not want me here.'

'You are mistaken. We are all concerned for your welfare.'

'Only you understand how difficult it is for me, William. The others hate me. I can do nothing right. I should go away.' Her tears welled up and her cheeks were again flooded. 'But where would I go? How could I live without a guardian to protect my reputation?'

'There must be no talk of you leaving, my dear. Our cultures are very similar but there are differences which can lead to misunderstandings.'

'I would do anything to make your family like me again.'

Her tear-filled eyes were pools of translucent pain which made the breath catch in his throat. Her hands moved slowly across his chest, innocent but somehow seductive in their manner. He clasped her hands, intending to ease her away.

Their fingers became entwined and she clung to him, his hand trapped against her breast.

'Will you tell me what I must do, William? You are so wise, so kind. You do not condemn me. I trust you.' Lisette lowered her gaze. 'I do not find it easy to trust men. I have been hurt. Betrayed. Abandoned.' Her lovely face twisted in anguish as she whispered, 'And I have been shamed. Perhaps they think that a decent woman should have taken her life rather than survive. I am a Catholic. To take one's life is a sin. Do you think I was wrong to want to live?'

'Good Lord, no, my dear.' William's face had deepened to a dark red at the implication of her words. It was not a subject a woman should speak of to a man. He was shocked. Yet the French were more volatile and less reserved than the English, and the poor woman had trusted him with her confession. He felt strangely humbled and moved by that trust.

'I have shocked you, yes. Oh my poor, dear William, I did not mean to. I have been indiscreet. You will think I am a fallen women – beyond redemption. I needed to be honest with you. I needed you of all people to understand.' She put her hand to her mouth. 'I could not bear it if you think I am so terrible – that I was to blame for what befell me.'

William coughed, potently aware of the warmth of her body against his, the smoothness of her breasts against the back of his hand. 'I think you have been very brave. How could you have been to blame? You were a victim. You must put all the unpleasantness of the past behind you. Even your months in England.'

'I do not know why I rode off like that the other day. I was upset that Adam was married. It was foolish of me. I knew he did not love me. But I needed to hold on to my dreams of the past. They gave me the strength to survive so many horrors in France. I did not want to believe that was all they were – just dreams. Without Adam I have no place in this family.'

'You will always be Edward's niece. Your mother was his first wife's sister. That gives you a place in our family. No one doubted how fond you were of Adam. I am glad that you have accepted that his life is with another.'

She sniffed delicately and dabbed at the corner of her eye where a tear hovered on her lashes. 'Now I shall beg Uncle Edward's forgiveness. I will prostrate myself at his feet if that is what it takes to convince him I regret how I acted.'

'An apology would be sufficient, my dear. You must remember the reserve of the English.' He smiled to show her he was making a joke of the matter. 'Tell him that you resolve to act as befits a gentlewoman in future and he will forgive you.'

'Is this what you want me to do, William?'

'I want you to do it because you know it is right.'

'You are wise. I will do everything you say.'

'Then perhaps you should consider making some amends to Elspeth.'

She rested her head against his chest. 'What can I do? Elspeth has never liked me. And she can be so difficult.'

'Is it true that you have some money of your own?'

She looked up at him with a wary frown. 'I am not a pauper. Many would consider that I am well provided for.'

'Then you could afford to buy back Elspeth's mare Eglantine from the Rashleighs in Fowey. And so that Edward can raise no objections, you could agree to pay for the mare's upkeep for the next year. That will guarantee you win Elspeth's favour.'

'I do not care for her favour. But she can be very difficult.' Lisette put her head on one side and regarded him through her lashes. 'Would this please you, William?'

'Very much. It would be a generous gesture.'

'Then I will do it. Can you arrange for the purchase of this mare? I shall need to sell a sapphire bracelet which will give me sufficient money.'

William raised her hand to his lips. 'That you are prepared to do so is enough. I will not hear of you making such a sacrifice. I will buy the mare and pay Edward, but it will be our secret that it is my money and not yours. You may need that money in the future. It is your security.'

'William, how wonderful you are.' She flung her arms around his neck and kissed his lips. She did not immediately pull back; her mouth continued with a lingering sweetness until finally she broke away breathless. 'I have never met anyone so wonderful as you, William.'

Before he could reply or admonish her for her astonishing behaviour, she ran to the cliff and up the steps. He watched her until she disappeared. There was a rawness to his emotions which left him shaken. He found he was sweating despite his lack of a jacket, and as he wiped his handkerchief across his brow, Lisette's lilac scent filled his senses. The sooner he found a ship to take him to sea the better. Lisette roused a protective need within him which was too forceful for his peace of mind. At least he had done what he could to heal some of the tensions within his family.

That afternoon William completed his duties on board the *Pegasus*. She had been unloaded and Adam had joined him at Fowey. They had inspected the ship for damage during the voyage, for a sudden squall had split a spar.

'She does not even need to go into the yard for the repairs,' Adam said as they entered the captain's cabin at the stern. 'I'll send a carpenter and two men to do the repairs tomorrow.'

'What do you plan to do next, Adam?' William almost sat

on the chair by the desk and remembered in time that it was no longer his place or right. It made him more aware that his future was uncertain. 'I take it you will be captaining her on her next voyage.'

To his surprise Adam hesitated. 'With a wife and child to support I need a regular income and with things as they are at the yard . . .' He shrugged. 'But it will be hard to leave Senara so soon. And I worry about how she will cope. Our family have not made things easy for her.'

'That is the way of a sea-captain's life. Your wife must have known that.'

'Senara would never complain and expects me to sail as soon as I can find a cargo. But . . .' Adam paced the cabin and indicated that William should sit at the desk.

Once seated William observed, 'Your wife is under the protection of your family by living in Mariner's House. Edward will be there for her if any difficulties arise, I am sure of that.'

'I suppose he would.'

'There have been several problems in the yard, so I gather. That fellow Lanyon reckons his cutter is not handling as it should.'

'There was no problem during the sea trials.' Adam continued his pacing. 'Lanyon would spread rumours like that out of spite. Have there been any complaints from the Excise Office about the cutter we supplied to them?'

'Not that I know of.' William studied the barometer mounted on the wall. 'I did catch a glimpse of this man Lanyon's cutter when she was in the Channel. I was returning to Plymouth in *Neptune*. It looked to me that the cutter was overladen with sail on her bowsprit. I did not think that you would have designed her so. It could make a ship unstable. Has the man changed the rigging?'

'She should be carrying a single narrow triangular sail.'

'This sail was large.'

'Lanyon was angry when he learned a sister ship had been built for the revenue service.' Adam had grown pale at the possible consequences of such changes to the design. 'I'll wager he has gone to another yard to make those changes. Perhaps he thought that by increasing the size of the sail he would get more speed from her.'

William frowned. 'Then the man is a fool. The cutter could capsize in a strong wind with such heavy sail.'

Adam dragged his hands through his hair. 'That would reflect badly on the yard. I shall inspect his cutter and issue a disclaimer – though he rarely has it docked in Fowey or Falmouth. She is based in Guernsey where the free-trade goods are loaded.'

'Have you another cargo for *Pegasus*?' William returned to his immediate concern.

Adam shook his head. 'Unfortunately not. I have neglected my duty by not pursuing merchants for business. I am grateful that you were here to take on the last voyage. That wine merchant could be an important customer as he is extending his business to export to the old colonies of America.'

'Yet such voyages will take you through French waters. With the war, these could be dangerous times.'

'Perhaps now is the time to arm my ship to protect her cargo,' Adam mused. 'I will not skulk in home waters when there are profits to be made.'

William laughed. 'That's the spirit. The wine merchant was satisfied that the voyage was done in the minimum of time. He expected delays because there have been so many storms. But he did not mention another cargo.'

Adam was not daunted. He had had many months while searching for Senara to formulate plans for his ship. 'I have drawn up a list of possible contacts, but it looks as though I shall be tied up at the yard for a week or so.'

'Can I be of service in contacting these merchants for you?' William looked expectantly at his nephew. 'I have too much time on my hands. I know how the *Pegasus* handles and her capabilities as a cargo ship. I could sail her to Plymouth or Bristol. Or do you wish to do that yourself? It is a long time since you sailed her.'

Adam heard the longing in his uncle's voice. 'It could be a voyage we undertake together. It is years since we sailed together.'

William appeared relieved. 'I would enjoy that. Now I have business outside town. Lisette has asked me to buy back Eglantine from the Rashleighs for Elspeth. She hopes that will atone for her treatment of Bracken. She has been very upset over the incident.'

'How is Lisette?' Adam asked.

'She seems to have accepted your marriage. She regrets her actions that night she rode to the yard.'

Adam turned away to hide his discomfort as he remembered how Lisette had tried to seduce him.

'Lisette is determined to win back the family's favour,' William went on. 'I think it is noble of her to buy the mare for Elspeth. She intends to pay Edward the cost of Eglantine's upkeep for a year.'

'That is indeed generous. Let us hope that her changes of heart and manner continue. Until recently her behaviour has been unstable.'

William stood to attention, his voice abrasive. 'I don't think you should be too harsh on her. After all, you could have wed the girl as her father had intended. That marriage was forced on her by her brother.'

Anger flared through Adam. He bit it down. His uncle was stating the opinion of many who did not know the whole situation. 'The betrothal contract was broken by Lisette and her brother, not myself. Many families would not have taken Lisette into their homes after what happened.'

'She is such a frail little thing. I admire her for the courage it must have taken for her to survive.' William stared through the stern window at the busy harbour.

Adam was surprised that William was being so defensive in Lisette's cause. To return to safer ground, he suggested, 'There is another use for *Pegasus* other than carrying cargo. Passengers. Through his bank in London, Cousin Thomas has many contacts among the French. Those who are lucky enough to have escaped prison, at any rate. It is a hazardous voyage, for some English ships have been seized. The most successful place to board the *émigrés* is a remote fishing village or cove, but you need an intelligence network in France to make this work efficiently.'

'You sound as though you have done this work before.'

'Yes. Squire Penwithick needed my help. He runs such an intelligence network for the English Government. Last year he was eager that I pursue my work for him, but my search for Senara took precedence. He may have found others to serve him and have no need of me now.'

William's eyes were gleaming with excitement. 'Another swivel gun or two would not go amiss on *Pegasus* to protect her in such work.'

'The deck was strengthened to take more guns but the cost of installing them was prohibitive.' Adam's enthusiasm made him restless and he paced the cabin.

'Surely the squire could arrange for them to be fitted as a means of safeguarding such a mission.'

Adam grinned. 'You sound as though you would be interested to join me on such a voyage, Uncle.'

'Indeed, Nephew. I was cut out for a more adventurous life than ferrying cargo from port to port.'

Both men laughed and Adam said, 'I shall present my

compliments to Squire Penwithick this afternoon. Let us hope that he has a use for *Pegasus.*'

William rubbed his hands together and became more animated than he had been since his return to Trevowan. 'I shall look forward to such a venture. Much as I love Trevowan, too much domesticity, and all that it entails, does not settle easily with me.'

When William arrived back at Trevowan leading Eglantine, he found Elspeth in a foul mood. He could hear her berating a stable lad for not performing some task to her exacting demands. Elspeth had been riding with Lord Fetherington's pack. With only one mare, Griselda, fit to ride, she would have been forced to return before the end of the day. Griselda would have been too tired to continue when the other riders changed their mounts for fresh ones.

'There you are, Sister. I could hear your dulcet tones from the drive.' William relished a moment of being able to tease Elspeth before delivering his surprise. 'You sound as though the world has come to an end. Yet surely all the lad did was put less bedding in Griselda's stall. Edward was complaining at the cost of straw if he had to buy it in.'

'Don't you dare criticise me.' Her face was pinched with rage. 'You would insist on everything being shipshape on your frigate. My mares deserve the best. Have I not suffered economies enough for my horses? If the lad cannot perform a simple task to my satisfaction—'

William interrupted before she could continue. 'Edward had to let two grooms go last year. But you are right, the grooms do appear to be slacking in their duties. There's a horse been left unattended in the stable yard. Looks to be a fine hunter. I did not think we were expecting guests. Have you any idea whom she belongs to?'

Elspeth stamped past him, yelling at the grooms to tend

the horse. 'I will not endure that a horse is neglected. Oh, heavens—' She stopped in mid tirade and threw down her walking cane to stumble to the mare. 'It is Eglantine. How did she get here? Has she taken flight and returned here instead of her stall at the Rashleigh house? Oh, my lovely girl . . .' The rest of her words were muffled as she threw her arms around the mare's neck and pressed her face into the mane. 'I have missed you so much, my precious.'

After a moment she pulled herself away but kept her head averted from William as she wiped a tear from her eye. 'We will bed her down for the night and send word to the Rashleighs that she is here. I expected more from them. If I had known they would be so careless in their treatment of her I would never have sold Eglantine to them. They will not hear the last of this.'

'The Rashleighs have sold her.'

'What! They promised they would not. That I would have first chance to buy her back.' Elspeth hugged her arms around her waist in her distress. 'That was too cruel of them. I will never speak to them again.'

'I think you will be thanking them.' William could no longer suppress a grin. 'I had the devil's own difficulty in buying her on your behalf. She has proved to be a fine hunter and they did not want to part with her. She is a gift to you from Lisette. She asked me to arrange the sale to atone for the way she treated Bracken. She will also pay for Eglantine's food and bedding for a year, so there will be no reason for Edward to take on the expense.'

'Lisette has done this?' Elspeth shook her head in disbelief. 'I have underestimated the girl. I thought she was spoiled and selfish. Yet to have been so generous as to buy Eglantine . . .' She spread her arms wide and tears flowed down her face. 'It is beyond words to have my darling mare back. I have been too harsh on the poor girl. I too must make amends. I am forever in her debt. I will never say a harsh word about Lisette again.'

'Careful about making promises you will find impossible to keep, Elspeth,' William cautioned his sister.

Chapter Eight

A dam was on his way to talk to Squire Penwithick when he saw Lanyon's coach approaching as it left Penruan. He called out to halt it. Lanyon stuck his head out of the window, his flaccid face mottled with anger.

'I be late for an important meeting, Loveday. Call at the shop tomorrow if you've something to say.'

'You ride in a fine carriage but your manners remain those of a guttersnipe, *Mister* Lanyon.' The title was spat out with contempt. Adam was incensed by the man's rudeness. 'The rigging of the *Sea Sprite* has been changed. If you put more sail on her she could become unstable.'

'Don't know what you be talking about, Loveday.' Lanyon was defensive.

'Captain William Loveday saw the *Sea Sprite* carrying extra sail. He would not be mistaken.'

'What I do with my ships be my business,' Lanyon barked. 'Now get out of my way. I've too important matters to attend upon to be delayed by you.'

Adam lost his temper. 'More important than the lives of your men? I warn you, Lanyon, if the *Sea Sprite* is wrongly rigged she could founder in a storm.'

'Then I shall hold your yard responsible for a poorly designed ship, Cap'n Loveday.' He touched his forelock in mock homage, but his lips were drawn back in a malevolent sneer.

'There is nothing wrong with her design if she is correctly rigged.'

'Drive on!' Lanyon ordered his coachman, and disappeared inside the carriage, and Adam was forced to veer Solomon aside to prevent his gelding being struck by the carriage wheels.

'The yard will not be held responsible for your stupidity and greed, Lanyon,' Adam called after him, fuming at Lanyon's arrogance. But then he pushed his concern aside. *Sea Sprite* was a sturdy ship. He was worrying unnecessarily, being too protective of his own design. It would take an exceptionally fierce storm and high seas to capsize her, and in such conditions an experienced captain would have all canvas furled. It was Lanyon's pig-headed attitude which riled him.

Adam galloped away and did not see the horseman who had taken cover behind a group of hawthorn trees. The rider followed Lanyon's coach until it halted a mile ahead.

Lanyon stuck his head out of the carriage and scowled at the rider, whose thick muffler and wide-brimmed hat partially obscured his sharp features. 'Lieutenant Beaumont, *Sea Sprite* was nearly caught off Gorran Haven the other week by *Challenger*.' Spittle sprayed from Lanyon's lips in his anger. 'I don't pay you to keep away from my landing coves to have my ship given chase to.'

'An overzealous second in command, I fear. Your ship should have landed a cargo the previous week.'

'Any fool would know that those three nights of storms would have prevented a landing.'

The excise officer stiffened with affront. 'And I must be seen to be performing my duty. I cannot avoid patrolling these waters indefinitely. I took care that we did not come close enough to board you. That was not easy; the ships are equally matched for speed.'

'That's why you be paid to stay away. Didn't you know they be sister ships? Both built in the Loveday yard.'

A flush brightened the excise officer's face. 'I did not know *Challenger* was a Loveday ship when I was given her to command.'

Lanyon studied him with interest. 'You have something against the Lovedays?'

'That is my affair, sir.'

'So you've no liking for them,' Lanyon chuckled. 'Be it the Lovedays in general or just Adam you despise?' When Lieutenant Beaumont did not answer, Thadeous Lanyon's eyes narrowed. 'Adam Loveday left the navy in some disgrace. There were talk of a duel with another officer. That officer couldn't have been you, could it?'

Beaumont scowled but did not answer. Lanyon added slyly, 'Do you know that Adam Loveday has a twin – St John?'

'I have no time for gossip, Mr Lanyon. I must rejoin my ship in an hour and you have a payment for me.'

Lanyon took out a canvas money pouch from inside his greatcoat but kept it tight in his hand as he continued to study the revenue officer. 'St John Loveday be married to a Sawle. Word is that the Sawles frequently bring in cargo from Guernsey. Last year the Lovedays were close to ruin, yet St John has money aplenty for his gaming. Now where would that be coming from, I wonder. Seems there be free-traders aplenty in these waters without your vessel troubling the *Sea Sprite*. And who knows what Adam Loveday will be up to now he has his own ship, *Pegasus*. He bain't averse to a run to France.'

'That is interesting news, Mr Lanyon.'

Lanyon tossed the money pouch into Lieutenant

Beaumont's hands. 'I thought you might find it so.'

Lieutenant Francis Beaumont watched the coach lumber away. He had waited a long time to get his revenge on Adam Loveday for the duel which had lost him his commission in the navy.

Adam was admitted to Squire Penwithick's library.

'You have only just caught me, Adam. I am leaving for London.' The squire was sorting through a pile of papers on his desk. He looked tense and worried. 'The news from France is alarming. Now King Louis has been guillotined, I cannot think the bloodshed will end there. The royalists will continue to plot.'

Adam, like most Englishmen, had hoped that the situation in France would become stable and King Louis would eventually regain his throne, if without his previous powers. 'And what news of Marie-Antoinette and the Dauphin?'

'Still in prison. The Dauphin has been taken from his mother. It is said the poor lad is cruelly treated and reviled by his gaolers. Undoubtedly, they will also share the King's fate.' The squire shook his head. 'The new Convention is eager to show its strength. Conscripts are daily swelling the army. I fear the war may be of a long duration.'

Adam nodded agreement. 'I have come to offer my services in getting *émigrés* out of France.'

The squire stopped examining the papers to stare pensively at Adam. 'It would be doubly dangerous now.'

'Yet the nobles of that land continue to be persecuted. More die every day. And those who have escaped arrest must live in terror of what will happen to their families.'

'There are many seeking asylum – and not just the aristocrats. The Terror is spreading. Any who oppose the new regime are imprisoned.'

'I am at your service.' Adam was undeterred.

Squire Penwithick scratched his chin and his tone was accusing. 'I had need of you many times in recent months when you were not here to honour your promise to me. And now you are wed and have a wife and family to consider. I prefer men who are single. A family can make a man cautious, and therein lies a danger to those he serves.'

'I have never been afraid of danger, and my family will be provided for if the worst should happen,' Adam retaliated with heat. 'I realise I did not honour my promise to you, but I could not have foreseen the problems raised by Lisette's arrival.'

The squire shook his head. 'Enjoy your new life, Adam. There is no place for reckless adventure in a new marriage. Especially a marriage for which you have risked so much. Your ship will be blown out of the water by the French if they see an English flag.'

'Have I not proved my worth in the past?'

'Your work for the Government was valuable and Mr Pitt spoke highly of you. But such ventures are more dangerous now. Edward is my friend and he needs you in the yard.'

'With respect, sir, I now have a wife and family to support. I draw no wages from the shipyard because of our debts. Uncle William will sail with me. How long can a return voyage to France take? No more than two or three weeks.'

At the passion in his voice, Squire Penwithick turned away to resume examining his papers. He picked up a handful, tore them in half and threw them on to the fire to burn. Another pile was sifted through and Adam was forced to bite down his impatience. Finally his self-control broke. 'Squire Penwithick, my cousin Thomas has dealings with many *émigrés* through his bank. He would give me the names of their relatives wishing to escape the new regime, but I cannot work alone. You have the network of men in France who can make it possible to bring these people to the coast. I also need papers authorising my duties and the safety of these passengers.' When the squire still did not respond, Adam reminded him, 'You will also need a captain you can trust when your agents must cross the Channel.'

'Are you determined on this dangerous work?' The squire regarded him thoughtfully. 'I understand that your ship needs repairs.'

'Your spies miss nothing.'

'I am kept informed of every ship entering the ports and harbours on the southern shores. How long will the repairs take?'

'They will be finished tomorrow.'

'Is your ship armed?'

'With four cannon below decks. Her decks are strengthened to take more. Uncle William also thought two further guns on the upper deck would be advantageous but I have no funds for these.'

'You would arm her like a privateer,' the squire chuckled. 'She could be mistaken for a smuggler. I hear Lanyon has cannon on board the *Sea Sprite*.'

'With England at war I could apply for letters of marque to board any enemy vessel and claim her as a British prize.' The excitement of such a venture was vibrant in his voice. When Adam saw the squire's lips twitch with amusement he checked his enthusiasm. 'In the meantime I have a living to earn.'

'Then go home now and enjoy your wife while you can. I will send word and instructions from London if your ship is needed.'

'And the installation of the cannon?' Adam persisted.

'You drive a hard bargain. I may need more spies in the naval ports to expand my network. It would not do for a vessel carrying such agents to be unable to defend itself. I shall inform an iron foundry to deliver two sixteen-pounders and two swivel guns before you sail. You can repay the cost when you capture your first French prize.'

Japhet was not given to analysing his emotions or reactions. The incident at the Rectory with Gwen left him vaguely unsettled. Kitty was the diversion he needed. During the next fortnight he visited her on several occasions. She asked nothing more of him than a quart of geneva to cheer her through the long winter evenings. She was often tipsy when he arrived and eager for his embrace. The relationship was uncomplicated and pleasurable, passion unrestrained without emotional ties.

'You be a lusty lover, my fine gentleman,' Kitty chuckled, 'but it be wicked you are to tempt me from my marriage vows.'

'You are too much a woman to be so long neglected,' Japhet whispered against her ear as they rolled across the rumpled bed. The fresh candle they had lit in the bed-chamber had burned low, casting a yellowing light over their naked figures. He was replete and tired, for Kitty had been more than usually demanding.

'Best get yourself off home,' she said, but began to kiss him with growing ardour. 'But then it won't be daylight for another three hours. We've time enough afore the towns-people are out of their beds.'

'What time is the morning tide? It would not do for me to be seen leaving by a fisherman.'

'It were high an hour past,' Kitty giggled. 'No need to worry, the fishing fleet be long gone to sea. Kiss me, my handsome, we 'ave so little time afore David returns, let's not waste it.'

'I shall miss you when your husband returns.' Japhet kissed her with returning desire. 'He's due back any day and this

151

could be our last night together. There's a horse fair coming up next month and I need some stock to sell so I must take to the roads again.'

'Then we best make this a night to remember.' Kitty straddled him, her hair cascading over his face and chest. They were locked in a passionate embrace when Kitty suddenly tensed and stared down at Japhet. 'I heard something. Someone's on the stairs.'

Japhet heard a heavy footfall. He rolled Kitty aside, bounded from the bed and had time only to snatch up his breeches before the door was flung wide. A tall, broad-shouldered, bearded man filled the portal.

'Damn you for a whore,' Captain David Veryan bellowed. 'Yer didn't expect me 'ome so soon.' He pulled a cat-o'-nine-tails from his belt. 'I didn't want to believe the rumours I heard about you on the dock. They were right.'

Kitty's husband rounded on Japhet, who, clutching his breeches in front of him, having had no time to don them, was edging towards the window.

'You'll not escape, you scoundrel,' Veryan growled.

The whip whistled in the air, the lead-tipped thongs slashing across Japhet's buttocks, drawing blood. A fiery agony seared through him as the skin was ripped away. A second blow caught his shoulder and snaked cruelly around his ribs, the flesh torn from the bone. Japhet wrapped his breeches around his arm and raised it to fend off the next vicious lash strokes. The whip raked across his shoulder as Japhet hurled himself at the man.

His flesh was raw and stinging and he could feel the blood mingling with his sweat as he kicked out at the captain. Unfortunately, his sword was on the floor across the room. He managed to heave the bigger man off balance, and darted towards his weapon. Another lashing of the whip peeled three stripes of flesh from his chest. He clenched his teeth to stop himself crying out at the agony inflicted on him.

'Stop it, David!' Kitty screamed, curling herself into a ball on the bed.

'From what I've heard of you, Loveday, you've 'ad this coming a long time.' David Veryan increased the ferocity of his attack.

Twice Japhet evaded his blows, but his hair and sweat were dripping into his eyes and the candle flame was flickering wildly, making it hard to see his opponent clearly. The single candle cast more shadow than light, distorting distance and movement. The captain raised his arm to strike again and Japhet grabbed his wrist, twisting his body in a wrestling hold to throw the heavier man over his shoulder to hit the floor. As the boards shook from the crashing weight, Japhet dived towards his sword belt and drew the blade.

Kitty screamed. 'No, Japhet! Don't kill 'im! He be a good man. We wronged 'im.'

Japhet had no intention of killing the captain in an uneven fight but he knew his own life was in danger if he lost the upper hand now. The captain had rolled to his feet. He was at least five stone heavier than Japhet, and anger would increase his strength. Japhet had to disarm the sailor, yet each movement was torture, and he could feel his muscles weakening. The sword slashed towards Veryan's arm, but became entangled in the whip thongs.

'Heard tell you had a reputation with that sword. You bain't so fancy with it now.' David Veryan yanked on the whip to free it.

The pain flared through Japhet's arm and he feared that the sword hilt would be pulled from his grasp. He clung on, his knuckles locked in a spasm of agony.

Kitty screamed again. 'Stop it! Please! Japhet! David! This is madness!'

'I'll stop when this cur be dead.' Veryan shook the whip free from the blade. 'Then I'll teach my whoring wife never to stray again.'

Japhet had the fencing skills of a gentleman, but during his less savoury escapades he had learned to fight with the survival instincts of the wiliest of rogues. There was little room to manoeuvre a sword in the small bedroom and the blade sliced through the thin bedhangings as Japhet again lunged at the captain to disarm him. But Veryan was faster. The cat-o'-nine-tails swung low, writhing like stinging tentacles across Japhet's buttocks and thighs.

He feinted with the sword and, as the man side-stepped, Japhet twisted and kicked out, his bare feet slamming into his attacker's groin. The captain doubled over and sprawled on the floor, his body jerking as he held his injured member. He grunted like a boar spitted on a pike. Japhet was breathing heavily as he brought the sword round to press against the man's throat. 'Your fight should be with me, not Kitty. I brought her some gin and pursued her.'

'Get out, Japhet!' Kitty screamed. 'David won't punish me more than I deserve. He knows I love him. I'm so sorry, David. I did tell you I couldn't take the long lonely nights when you be at sea. I knew Japhet afore we were wed.'

'I bain't done yet.' Veryan was glaring up at Japhet over the blade.

'Give me your word you will not harm Kitty and I will spare your life,' Japhet demanded.

The captain's face was twisted with fury. 'You stand there mother naked straight from my bed and—'

Kitty was sobbing. 'Don't kill him, Japhet. I beg you, please don't kill him.'

'What's your answer, Veryan?' Japhet demanded, the point of the blade pressing hard enough to break the skin. A trickle of blood ran down the captain's neck.

'Bastard, I'll get you for this.' The man's spittle sprayed Japhet's calves.

'You have the right to name the time, weapon and place if you wish for a more dignified way of settling this,' Japhet challenged.

'Got a reputation for duelling, bain't you?' The hatred in the captain's eyes was intense.

'I'll stand up with you in a fist fight if you wish.'

They continued to glare at each other. Japhet was acutely aware of his nakedness and the absurdity of the position in which he found himself. The raw wounds on his back and chest were throbbing. The pain was so excruciating that he knew he must end this soon, or collapse from the strain. His body and chest were streaked with blood and he could feel the tremors of shock from his injuries begin to overtake his body.

The captain scowled. 'Happen you'll carry a scar or two to remind you that you be a whoring bastard. Won't be easy to explain them away to the next woman you seduce. Get out of 'ere, Loveday. And don't let me hear you've been pestering Kitty again. Next time I shall be carrying a pistol, not a whip.'

'I want your word Kitty will not be harmed,' Japhet insisted.

'She'll feel the back of my hand as she deserves,' Captain Veryan grunted. 'And she'll learn I bain't a man who lets a woman make a fool of me. If I hear you've come near her again, she'll be thrown out on the streets.'

'Just go, Japhet,' Kitty sobbed, and sat up in the bed with the bedclothes pulled to her chin. 'I've been a fool. No rogue, no matter how charming, is worth losing my David over. I never wanted to shame him. Or hurt him. I were just a bit of sport to you, Japhet.'

'No, you were never just sport, Kitty. You're a fine

woman.' Chastened, Japhet withdrew the blade, scooped up the rest of his clothes from the floor, and ran down the stairs. He paused only to don his breeches and shirt before leaving the cottage, and heard Kitty pleading with David to give her another chance. He did not feel very proud of his actions and only hoped that he had not ruined Kitty's life.

The cold air biting into his raw wounds made him stagger, and he clenched his teeth to stop himself groaning as the pain ploughed through him. He was also light-headed from loss of blood. He abandoned trying to struggle into his jacket, the weight too painful for him to bear. He could not return to the Rectory in such a state and took a room at an inn. There he ordered a bottle of brandy sent to his room and splashed it over his wounds to aid their healing. It was like plunging branding irons into his flesh and he stuffed a kerchief into his mouth to stop his cries of agony. The night was cold, but he could not bear a blanket over him and his body was soon burning hot.

Although in pain he kept his wounds hidden for some days, until he found he could not remove his shirt as it had stuck to the cuts. He was also hot and feverish, the room circling crazily each time he tried to stand. A few of the cuts across his ribs were raised and yellow with pus. Those on his back must be worse, for their pain was greater. If his blood became poisoned from the festering wounds it would lead to a slow and painful death. He needed help. It would be humiliating to visit a physician and explain the cause of his injuries. Also he was too ashamed to admit to such injuries to his mother. There was only one person he could trust. Even if that meant swallowing his pride. He rode to Trevowan Hard.

Leaving his horse tied to the fence of Mariner's House, he staggered inside, his legs as insubstantial as reeds so that he clutched hold of the wall for support.

'Japhet . . .' Senara came out of the kitchen, wiping her hands on a towel. There was flour on her cheek from her bread-making. 'What is wrong? You look terrible.'

'A fight. I took a bit of a pasting.' He leaned against the wall, his face flushed with heat and his head throbbing. He had not shaved for a week, and he was conscious that his breath and clothing smelled far from pleasant as the sweat poured down his face and drenched his torso. He swayed as he struggled to pull off his greatcoat and let it fall to the floor, but managing his jacket was too much for him and Senara pushed him towards a chair and slid it from his arms. He did not sit down but held on to the edge of a table.

At seeing several streaks of pus on his shirt, she gasped. 'You are weak as a kitten and have a fever. What happened to you?'

Japhet had closed his eyes as he straightened to tug his shirt from his breeches. When he opened his eyes to watch her, his expression was guarded as Senara lifted the shirt to reveal the long suppurating weals. She put a hand to her mouth. 'You've been whipped.'

'Some would say I deserved it.'

'Oh, Japhet. I suppose you were with another man's wife.'

He did not reply.

'I'll get some warm water and bandages. Can you manage to remove your shirt?'

'No. It has stuck to the wounds on my shoulders and I fear I will need to remove more clothing than just my shirt.' The feverish hue to his cheeks darkened in colour, and he no longer met her gaze as he added, 'I was somewhat compromised when the lady's husband chanced upon us in her bedchamber. The lash marks are low on my back and it is too painful for me to sit. I deuced near passed out on the ride here. But I have no wish to offend your sensibilities. I should have gone to Chegwidden. I was not thinking aright.'

He attempted a wry smile as he made to push his shirt back in his waistband but his face contorted in a grimace and he reeled back against the wall. 'Could you help me on with my jacket?'

'You can't possibly ride to Penruan in your condition. I'm surprised you got this far. Adam sailed for France last week. I do not want any unsavoury gossip so it is as well my mother is here. She is upstairs with Nathan, who will not settle as he has a cold. I will send Carrie to deliver a physic for Farmer Warne's wife, which will make it easier for me to tend you.'

Japhet still looked apprehensive. 'I suppose you must protect your reputation. Your mother is not a gossipmonger, is she?'

'We have shied away from gossip all our life. It's rather late in the day to worry about scandal, Japhet.'

Japhet remained wary and forced a discomfited grin. 'I hadn't reckoned on becoming a public spectacle. This is not a situation I am proud of. I did not know Adam had sailed. I should not have come.'

'I had not thought you bashful, Japhet. And who else will tend your wounds?'

Senara slid Japhet's jacket over his shoulders to hide the blood on his shirt while she called Carrie in from stacking wood cut by an apprentice that morning for their fires. She gave her the physic and told her that when that was delivered she did not need her again that day.

When Leah appeared, Senara explained Japhet's injuries. 'I'll make sure no one comes bursting in unannounced while you tend him. Nathan be asleep now.'

Senara poured Japhet a large brandy to brace him for the ordeal ahead. She helped him into the kitchen and cleared the table of her baking, washed it down and laid a sheet over the top, then ordered him to lie on his stomach. Dipping a cloth in a bowl of warm water taken from the kettle on the

Cornish range, she soaked his shirt and gently eased it from the wounds. It was a slow and painful process and, though Japhet never made a sound, several times he flinched with pain. Finally when the shirt was cut away and the wounds fully revealed, Senara was the one to wince at their extent.

His shoulders were broad and he was unexpectedly muscular for a man who did no manual labour. There were at least thirty stripes, half of them infected, spreading across his shoulders, arms and around his ribs, and several of them snaked down to disappear beneath his waistband. Apart from the flesh wounds, there were several old scars on his torso, clearly from knife or sword cuts and one which was unmistakably a bullet wound.

'You have as many scars as a seasoned campaigner. I'll help you off with your boots and breeches.' Her face burned with heat and she refused to look into Japhet's eyes, embarrassed at having to attend such a virile and handsome man.

He grinned as she tugged at the snug-fitting leather to remove his boots. 'I was never one to choose the easy life.'

The boots put in a corner, Senara took a linen towel from a chest. Japhet sat up and took it from her. 'I can undress myself.' He took the towel she held out to him to wrap around his hips.

Leah returned with Senara to the kitchen and Japhet eyed her warily. 'I trust you not to take advantage of me while I am so vulnerable, Mistress Polglase.'

'Cheeky wretch,' Leah chuckled as she entered the kitchen. 'As if I bain't be old enough to be your mother.'

Japhet was lying on his side on the table with his chest bare and the towel wrapped around his waist. Red lines fanned out from some of the yellowed whip marks. Beneath the black stubble on his jaw his complexion was heated with fever, his brow spangled with sweat, and his heavy-lidded eyes drooped with fatigue.

'Good Lord, those wounds are sorely infected,' Leah sympathised.

Senara began to cleanse the wounds and was concerned at the amount of pus seeping from them. The skin was stretched red and puffy around a dozen of the cuts. The whip must have been filthy. The red tentacles spreading from the wounds warned that the blood had become poisoned. Why had Japhet waited so long before coming to her? If the blood poisoning took hold he could die.

She paused briefly to cut several strands from different dried herbs hanging from a beam in the kitchen. 'Cover them with a finger depth of water, Ma. Then boil them in the small cauldron over the kitchen fire until the water is reduced by half. It makes a strong tisane which will help cleanse the blood.'

She returned to Japhet and finished cleansing the wounds. 'What are your plans for this winter?' She needed to talk to ease the embarrassment of having to lift aside the towel to tend the wounds on his buttocks and thighs.

'I never make plans or promises. They are only likely to be broken. Did I tell you about the incident in Bodmin, when a foppish French *émigré* in his cups mistook a cousin of Lady Chenowith for an actress?' His voice was laboured as he jested to lighten his mortification at the indignity of his treatment. 'The Frenchman propositioned Elsa Chenowith, convinced she had been with a troupe of players in Bodmin last October. Elsa Chenowith is a spirited wench and beat him about the head with her parasol. The hapless Frenchman spent the following day in the stocks being pelted with rotting apples.'

Japhet elaborated in detail until tears of laughter were running down Senara's cheeks and she could hardly see to tend his wounds. Several times he flinched and sucked in his breath when the probing became too painful, but he bore it stoically and did not complain.

When Senara had finished she poured the prepared and now cool tisane into a cup. 'It tastes foul but you must drink it all.'

He sniffed it and pulled a face. 'Smells like demon's breath.'

'Drink it!' Senara stood over him with her hands on her hips. 'It will help fight the infection.'

Japhet tossed it back and his body shuddered with revulsion. 'If I did not know you better I'd swear you were trying to poison me, not cure me.'

'Would you like a spoonful of honey to take the taste away? I always give some to the children,' Senara smiled.

'I'd rather have some brandy.'

She nodded to Leah to fetch it and heard Nathan crying upstairs. 'I'll put some leeches on the swellings and leave them while I feed Nathan. They will draw out some of the poison.' Senara collected several leeches in a glass jar from the water butt outside where she kept and bred them, and held them against Japhet's flesh until they attached their mouths and began to suck his blood.

Leah had brought Nathan downstairs and was watching Senara from the door, her face screwed up with disgust. 'You won't be wanting me to touch them. Makes me go cold just the thought of it.'

Senara shook her head and smiled, remembering that Adam, for all his valour, had a fear of leeches. Leah had also brought down two blankets. 'Mr Loveday will need these if he is not to catch a chill.'

Senara refilled Japhet's goblet with brandy as he lay propped on his side. He showed no sign of being ill at ease in his semi-naked state. 'The table must be uncomfortable but I need you to stay on it until I have removed the leeches.'

'I've had worse places to rest – hedgerows, even the

occasional gutter when drink and fortune went against me.' He rubbed his unshaven jaw. 'I come to you like a common ragamuffin, ill-kempt and carrying the wounds of a punishment rightly deserved. Yet you have not uttered one word of reproof or condemnation.'

'The life you choose to live is no one's affair but your own.' Senara threw the soiled cloths away and washed the bowls. 'We all make mistakes, or do things we are not always proud of. That is life. Your only judge should be your own conscience. If you fail to listen to it, that again is your choice.'

'If I listened to my conscience, I should find life a dull journey, I fear.'

Nathan let out a wail of hunger. 'Rest now. I must feed my son. Then I shall bandage your wounds.'

She fed Nathan and then Leah offered to look after the baby while Senara removed the bloated leeches. A half-hour later the worst cuts across Japhet's shoulders had been bandaged with a poultice and the others on his torso treated with a healing balm before being bound. The ones on his buttocks and thighs were smeared with balm and left unbound. Senara then gave him one of Adam's shirts and left him to dress; then he joined the women in the parlour.

When Senara saw how high his colour had become and the weakness of his walk, she insisted, 'I'll make you up a bed in the back bedroom tonight. You have a touch of fever.'

'I do not want your reputation endangered because of me.'

'You are my husband's cousin – family. And I know that despite your reputation you would never play Adam false. If small-minded people wish to gossip then let them. And Ma will stay. I'll ride over to the cottage and bring Bridie back so that she is not left alone.'

'I have already inconvenienced you too much. I shall stay at the Rectory.'

'And if the fever breaks, are you going to tell Cecily what ails you?' Senara grew impatient. 'Your mother will see the bandages and you can barely hold yourself straight you are in so much pain.'

'Then I will go to an inn.'

'Japhet, I have not spent all this time trying to prevent you dying from blood poisoning for you to neglect yourself now. Your fever will get worse before it gets better. And those dressings will need changing at least once a day. It would also be wise to reapply the leeches daily.'

'I will not put your reputation in danger.' He reached for his jacket which Senara had placed on a peg on the wall and nearly fell. He cursed. 'I am weak as a child. Help me to my horse, Senara.'

'I will do no such thing. If you leave here I shall inform your mother and insist Joshua takes you home for her to look after you.'

Japhet scowled at her. 'You're a hard woman. I will do well enough on my own.' But his legs buckled before he reached the door and it took all Leah and Senara's strength to get him up the stairs to the bed.

Chapter Nine

A week after setting sail, and with favourable winds, Adam and William were sailing off the southern coast of Brittany. They had earlier sighted a French corvette in the waters approaching Brest and had been fortunate to outrun her, taking refuge in an offshore fog.

Adam was tense. This was the third night attempting to bring *émigrés* on board. The last two nights there had been no response to his signals. The squire had warned him it could be a waiting game requiring strong nerves. The French had garrisons all along the coast with dragoons patrolling at night, to prevent those labelled by the Government as traitors to the Revolution from escaping their country.

'We've been lucky so far,' William warned as they studied the sea which was clear of ships. 'The corvette is only the second French ship we've sighted patrolling these waters.'

'Squire Penwithick informed me that the frigates HMS *Conquest* and HMS *Sovereign* are on duty in the Bay of Biscay. Their presence may afford us some protection.'

'If they are close enough,' William replied. 'I suspect it will be our own wits and skill which ensure the success to this mission.'

The fog had lifted with the turn of the afternoon tide and the coast was a purple haze ahead of them. Adam looked at the heavens, where a crimson sun, partially obscured by pennants of clouds, was sliding beneath the horizon. 'There's the headland. Let us hope that the squire's agent ashore is ready for us tonight. Further delay could result in our discovery.'

An hour later, protected by darkness, they weighed anchor in the deeper waters of the cove. The sea rose and fell in a light swell and the moon was half-full – perfect conditions for their work.

'Give the signal, Mr Melthrop,' Adam ordered the first mate.

The cover of a darkened lantern was opened and the light flashed four times in quick succession. Immediately they were answered on shore by two flashes followed by a pause and then two more flashes.

'They are ready for us,' Adam announced, and felt his pulse quicken.

William was scanning the coast with his spyglass. 'Let us pray it is not a trap by the French if they saw our signals on the other evenings.'

Adam gripped the ship's rail as the tension rose. He was straining to hear the sound of a longboat approaching. There was only the slap of waves against the hull, and the creak of his ship's timbers and rigging.

William was pacing the deck with his hands clasped behind his back. 'Where the devil are they? I don't like this delay.'

The silence was oppressive. William halted beside Adam. 'Have the men stand by the guns. We may have been led into a trap. That corvette was too close for comfort. What if the émigrés have been betrayed and word was sent to the French ship?'

'Man the cannon,' Adam ordered. 'No English is to be spoken unless it is an order and the crew will remain silent.'

Then overcome with impatience, he ran to the mizzen mast

and began to climb the ratlines. The coarse ropes were wet from sea spray and slippery under his shoes. He gripped the ropes harder to maintain his pace and his palms stung, softened after months on land. Heights had never bothered him and he had always enjoyed scaling the rigging in the navy. He hooked his leg over the wooden yard, braced himself against the roll of the ship and lifted his spyglass. From this vantage point he had a better view of the expanse of water. Four dark shapes were gliding towards the ship and there was the faint splash of oars. But were they *émigrés*, or French troops in disguise? Adam's throat was dry and his stomach muscles tightened, anticipating danger.

He held his breath as the longboats drew closer. Over a score of passengers were hunched against the cold, some of the men helping with the oars. As Adam studied them, two heads lifted to stare up at the ship's side. The moonlight revealed the face of a woman whose hood had fallen back and she was comforting a child who was sobbing with fright.

Vigilant against every danger, Adam raised the spyglass and moved it eastwards along the coast to a round fortified tower on the next headland. The citadel was too close and *Pegasus* was in range of her cannon. The ship should be shielded from view from the fort by the headland of this cove, but an alert garrison would place men along the coast who would light fires in warning. There was also another fort on the headland to the west, which, if alerted by fire from this citadel, could attack them as they made their escape. And if the corvette was in the vicinity, the guns from the forts would draw the armed vessel to them. That was the greatest danger of all.

Adam returned to the quarterdeck and addressed his uncle. 'Four longboats off starboard bow, sir.'

A voice carried to them in the darkness. 'Ahoy. Ahoy, *mon ami!*'

'What is your business?' Adam replied in French.

'I have a cargo of some thirty souls.'

Adam had not expected so many. Three of the longboats were filled with passengers, the fourth piled high with travel chests. 'Board quickly. I would be out of French waters before dawn.'

Two rope ladders were thrown over the side and the moon revealed pale faces staring up at the tall sides of the ship, many showing fear as the waves pitched them up and down in the water. Several children were present and they were all crying.

'Keep the children quiet,' William ordered. 'Sounds carry at night. Do you want the garrison at the fort alerted?'

Three men climbed on board and leaned over to assist the women. One heavily pregnant woman was sobbing, the roll of the ship making the effort to climb too much for her. Her husband encouraged her, but she was becoming hysterical. 'I cannot . . . I am going to die . . . Henri, help me.' She lost her footing and screamed, clinging on by her arms. Her husband was on the rung beneath her, supporting her around her waist. Together they edged slowly upwards.

'Keep that woman quiet,' ordered William.

The delay was making the other passengers anxious and they were jostling for position on the ladder. An argument had broken out in one of the longboats and too many people were pushing to get to the ropes.

'Children and women first,' William snapped. 'Be patient and get in an orderly line. Too many of you are standing; someone will be knocked overboard.'

The ship rose on a swollen wave and a woman clung to the ladder in terror, too frightened to move. She too was sobbing.

'Get a rope round that woman and haul her aboard,' Adam ordered, 'and, for the love of God, be silent.'

The woman's fear had unsettled the children, who were

bawling with greater intensity. A babble of voices, trying to calm them, only added to the noise.

'Will nothing silence them?' William groaned. 'Do they not realise the danger?'

'Perhaps they have lived through so much already, they can take no more,' Adam observed. Many of the passengers were wild-eyed with fear but to Adam's relief some of the men took control and urged them to speed and silence. Adam was concerned that the party was taking too long to board, when a yellow glow appeared on the shore and flared to an orange brightness.

'That's a warning beacon been lit,' Adam groaned to his uncle. 'Take control of the ship, sir. I'll hurry the passengers.'

'We do not have long, Adam,' William answered, 'a few minutes at most before the fort fires on us. And that beacon could be seen by a French ship.'

Adam ran to the ship's side. Melthrop and another sailor had used their initiative to climb down the second ladder to assist the passengers struggling to get on deck. Mounting a rope ladder was no easy feat, if it had not been attempted before. The ladder moved away from the ship's side as the vessel dipped and swayed in the water. Men, as well as women, found that their feet slipped between the vertical ropes, leaving their legs dangling in the air. The women were hampered by their skirts, and many of the children lacked the strength to haul themselves up the slippery rope rungs.

One woman, a third of the way up the ladder, cried out and fell back into the longboat, rocking it dangerously and knocking one of the oarsmen overboard. The man surfaced and swore roundly as he climbed back on board.

'Faster. Faster! We will be fired on,' the leader of the oarsmen shouted. 'Get the baggage on board. We cannot wait. What is not aboard will be thrown into the sea.'

'No, it is all we have,' a woman sobbed.

Adam ordered grappling irons to be thrown down to the baggage longboat and any luggage bound with rope to be hauled up. 'As soon as the last passenger is on board, we move off. Get ropes tied round the women and children to stop them falling into the sea and pull them aboard if necessary.'

A Frenchman cut through his countrymen's babble to order, 'Be brave, my friends. We have little time. Have we escaped the guillotine to die at the hands of our soldiers?'

His words acted as a panacea and the passengers became more orderly as they struggled to climb aboard.

A flash of orange flared out from the fortress followed by a dull splash as a cannonball hit the water some distance from their bow.

'*Mon Dieu!* We are all going to die! Out of my way,' a terrified young woman demanded. Too frightened to wait for the rope to be fixed around her waist, she pushed aside an older woman, who was slow to take hold of the ladder. In her haste the young woman lost her footing and fell into the icy water.

'Vivienne! The comtesse must be saved,' a man in the boat shouted, and dived in after her.

The woman's head surfaced and then went under again. The man did not reappear.

'The fool! Pierre is a poor swimmer,' a woman yelled. 'Someone save my brother!'

Without hesitation Adam stripped off his waterproof coat, jacket and shoes, and dived into the sea where both people had disappeared. The numbing cold hit him, punching his lungs as he fought to regain his breath. He kicked downwards and felt material wrap around his arm. Blindly, he grabbed it, and pulled until he felt the solidity of a body. His arm circled the figure and he kicked upwards to the surface and took a gulp of air. Arms waved above his head as a man

169

in one of the boats clutched at the body of the woman he had rescued. Gasping and coughing, she was dragged on board.

'Pierre has not surfaced,' his sister wailed, and wrung her hands in despair. 'Dear God, please do not let him drown.'

Another cannonball thudded into the water, this time uncomfortably close. Adam's limbs were growing numb as he took another deep breath and dived. Unable to see in the dark water, he swam blindly, his arms flailing in search of the Frenchman. With his lungs bursting he was forced to claw up to the surface and then made another dive. The cold was fast stripping his body of strength. Each stroke was harder to make, and, with his lungs again bursting, he knew the man had drowned.

The surface seemed far above Adam, and the cold and numbness was all-pervading. It flashed through his mind that drowning could now be his fate. It spurred him to kick harder. But his senses were clouded from the lack of air, and the water pressed heavily upon him, weighted like a lead blanket.

The effort to keep swimming became too much for muscles numbed by cold and devoid of oxygen. As consciousness began to slip from him, a vision of Senara holding Nathan in her arms smote him. She was laughing – reaching out her hand for him to take.

The image brought a glow of energy from some hidden depths within himself. A primeval instinct to survive made his reflexes kick out. Then mercifully he broke the surface and gasped for air. A longboat was some yards away. He had no strength to hail it. The cannon boomed from the fort and there was a loud splash close by. Like a dragon rearing from the deep, the sea thrashed around him, tossing him in its jaws. His head cracked against the side of the longboat and pain shot through his skull. Water rushed into his mouth, nose and lungs and he was again sucked under the waves.

The pain in his head saved him. He was determined not to die and fought his way back to the surface, which seemed an impossible distance away to his frozen, leaden limbs. He was several yards from the longboat when he broke through the water and managed a weak 'Ahoy'.

'Grab the oar, Cap'n,' a sailor shouted.

The numbness which had overtaken Adam's body could no longer be vanquished. The shouts of the seamen and passengers receded. His limbs no longer obeyed his commands. Sea water gurgled into his lungs; his strength was gone. He began to sink further into the depths.

William Loveday was yelling at the sailors, his knuckles white as he gripped the ship's rail, staring at the last point where Adam had surfaced. 'Save your captain. Over there.'

In the uproar coming from the terrified passengers William feared his orders had not been heard. But Melthrop had jumped into the sea. Time hung suspended. A further boom of the cannon, and the ball again falling short of its target, were scarcely noticed.

'Get aboard. Hurry yourselves,' William shouted absently to the passengers. Only two men were left in the boats. He was filled with a sickening dread and could not drag his gaze from where Adam had disappeared.

Then two heads appeared, one dark-haired, the other bald. Adam's eyes were closed and as he was heaved over the side of the longboat a stream of sea water gushed from his mouth and he began to cough.

William swayed with relief. Melthrop looped a rope around Adam and signalled for their captain to be hauled unceremoniously aboard. Adam was laid on deck and after waving two members of his crew aside, staggered to his knees. The wound on his head was bleeding profusely, but he pushed any helping hands away from him and raised himself to his full height. He was pale, shivering, and his legs were barely able to support him. He turned to Melthrop, who was shivering beside him.

'What, no pipes to welcome your captain on deck?' Adam's words were slurred as he managed a grin.'

'Bain't no way for a cap'n to come aboard, more like an old woman,' Melthrop responded.

'Very true. I shall endeavour to be more correct in my arrival in future.' Adam swayed. 'I owe you my life, Melthrop.'

With his nephew safe, William continued his orders, 'Full sail, if you please, Mr Melthrop. Course north by north-west. Get those chests stowed and the decks cleared.'

Adam stood aside as a sailor heaved a chest to his shoulder. The man stumbled and the chest crashed to the deck. Its lid burst open and packages of various sizes wrapped in oiled paper slithered around the sailor's feet.

'Open that parcel,' Adam ordered.

A Frenchman shouted an angry protest. The sailor slit the wrapping with a dagger and two pounds of tobacco leaves spilled on to the deck.

'Open the others,' Adam persisted.

The Frenchman hit the sailor in the face and drew a pistol. 'No one touches my chest.'

There was a shot above Adam's head and the Frenchman dropped his pistol and clutched his arm where he had been hit. William Loveday was advancing on the *émigrés*, another loaded pistol pointing at the injured man. 'Throw all those parcels overboard. There will be no contraband on this ship. And check every chest before it is stowed below.'

'I give you a half-share,' two more Frenchmen offered. 'All our money is in that cargo. We were told we would make a fortune in England.'

'This ship is no smuggler,' Adam had recovered his

172

strength sufficiently to grate out. 'Another word from you and you'll be thrown off this ship together with your illicit cargo.'

'But how will we live in England without money?'

'You will live, is that not enough?' Adam countered.

'I am sure your countrymen will find you honest work,' William interceded, 'but you may return to French soil with your cargo, if you wish. By trying to trick us you would have placed the freedom of this crew at risk.'

'Are your crew so rich they would refuse this money?' the Frenchman jeered. 'Why do you not ask them? Or are they lily-livered?'

Melthrop grabbed the Frenchman by his collar. 'Give me the word, Cap'n, and I'll thrown this scum overboard.' Melthrop tightened his hold, causing his captive to choke. ''Appen there be enough dishonest men in England without scum like yourself adding to them. There's a Frenchie garrison trying to blow us out of the water for helping you – would you 'ave our navy turn on us for running contraband?'

A short Frenchman bowed to Adam, his voice cultured and his English perfect. 'Your pardon, Captain. We go to England to escape the tyranny here. This man shames us all. And this delay adds to our danger.'

William, who had been ordering the sailors to get the ship underway, turned to the passengers. 'One life has already been lost. There will be more if we do not get out of range of the fort's cannon.'

As if to emphasise his words a cannonball landed on one of the longboats. Splinters showered *Pegasus*'s deck, and while the longboat sank, two men screamed from their injuries. Their companions hauled them on to the remaining longboats and rowed hard towards the shore.

The Frenchman in Melthrop's hold shouted in fear. 'I

cannot return to France. Do what you must. But get us out of here before they sink us.'

Adam gritted his teeth to stop them chattering as he watched the *émigrés* being taken below.

William raged, 'Have we not risked enough this night to take them to safety, that such greed would see your ship confiscated by the excise men?' He turned to Adam. 'Get yourself into dry clothes or you'll take a fever. That was a brave thing you did, saving that woman's life. Foolish, but brave.'

'I entrust *Pegasus* into your capable hands, Captain Loveday,' Adam declared. 'Lucky for us those Frenchies in the fort never got our distance.'

A further boom from the cannon heralded their departure.

Adam grinned. 'Missed again.'

A shout came from the lookout in the rigging. 'Sail on larboard bow.'

'It's not over yet,' William cautioned. 'Pipe all hands on deck and clear for action, Mr Melthrop. Then get yourself into dry clothes.'

His clothes changed and with a tot of rum to warm him, Adam returned to the deck. His head ached from the deep cut to his temple and he was still shivering. The moon showed a silhouette of a French corvette in full sail, bearing down upon them.

'Our guns are no match for hers.' William looked bleak. 'She's bigger and carries more sail.'

'We outran her before. We'll do so again,' Adam declared.

'The fog saved us last time. Now *Pegasus* must really prove her paces.'

'The French will have a run for their money.' Adam sounded more optimistic than he felt. There was a lot of sea between here and England, and Squire Penwithick had warned him that the French had stepped up their patrols and would seize any English ship in French waters.

For three days Japhet had a dangerously high fever. On the fourth, despite Senara exercising all her skills, he lapsed into delirium. Fearful that such a fever could kill him, Senara broke her promise to Japhet to inform his father of his condition. She sent Bridie to the Rectory with a short note, explaining briefly that Japhet was ill after being attacked. She thought that would explain the bandages and, if Japhet recovered, it would be up to him how much he told his parents.

To explain Japhet's presence in the house to Carrie, Senara had told the maid that he collapsed with a fever of the lungs during a visit. The maid had been released from her duties while Leah and Bridie were in residence. Explanations were made easier as Edward was away from the yard, visiting a prospective customer in Falmouth.

'Why were we not told before that he was here?' Cecily remonstrated as soon as she entered Mariner's House. 'And why did he not come home? I would have nursed him.'

'Japhet did not want you to worry, and he did not think his wounds were as serious as they are. He neglected his injuries for some days, which is why they became infected. He made me promise I would not tell you he was here.'

'I have never heard such nonsense.' Cecily handed Senara her cloak and smoothed her grey gown over her ample bosom and waist. 'Where is he?'

'He is in the back room upstairs. His fever is high and he is delirious, which is why I broke my word to him and notified you.'

Cecily shot her a hostile glare, her fear for her son causing her to abandon the usual genial manner she extended to all parishioners. 'You take too much upon yourself. If Japhet is so ill, why was not Chegwidden summoned?'

175

'Japhet would not hear of it.'

'When was it your place to heed a sick man when common sense decrees a physician should be called?' Cecily hurried up the stairs.

When Joshua removed his broad-brimmed parson's hat and cloak and would have followed his wife, Senara delayed him. 'If the fever does not break by this evening then I fear the worst.'

'Then you should have sent for Chegwidden.' Joshua did not hide his annoyance. 'I know you did much for Adam when he was injured after he was attacked by footpads, but you cannot compare your skills with those of a real physician.'

Senara clutched the two cloaks close to her breast. She understood his anger but was hurt that she was being so harshly judged. 'I am aware of my limitations, sir. Japhet made me promise not to. He was conscious until an hour ago.' She hung the cloaks and hat on two pegs.

Joshua fixed her with a long assessing stare. Then he sighed. 'I took you for a sensible woman. There is more to this than you are saying. Out with it, Senara.'

'I cannot break my word to Japhet. I have already gone against his wishes to bring you here. You have the right to summon Dr Chegwidden as Japhet is your son.'

'I shall send for him at once.' Joshua moved away.

'I must tell you that Japhet's injuries are . . . well, difficult to explain.' Her voice was low and she hung her head, unwilling to continue.

'But you know what caused them?'

'Sir, Japhet bound me to secrecy.'

'And I release you from it. Have I not a right to know?'

She walked into the parlour and gestured for him to follow, then closed the door. 'Japhet will never forgive me if his mother was to find out.'

'It is that bad?' Joshua sighed and his expression softened. 'Nothing Japhet does will shock or surprise me, I fear.'

Senara picked up a pile of Nathan's clothing which had been drying by the fire and folded them. She could not look at Joshua Loveday. 'Japhet told me little of the incident. From the manner and extent of his wounds it is obvious that he has been whipped by a cat-o'-nine-tails. A sea-captain returned and caught Japhet with his wife. Japhet was in no position to defend himself when the attack started.'

She glanced at Joshua, saw the pain in his eyes, and added, 'Dr Simon Chegwidden is not known for his discretion. Japhet was ashamed and did not want his mother to know of the incident.'

'He should be ashamed.' Joshua gripped the edge of his black frock coat, the veins standing out in his hands. 'I might have known there would be a woman involved.'

'Do please send for Dr Chegwidden. I can do little more for Japhet than give him herbs to fight the infection and bring down the fever.'

'I will see my son and then make up my mind.' His manner gentled towards Senara but the tight set of his lips showed his anger at his son. 'I will not risk Japhet's life to avoid a scandal. At least he had the sense to come here, and did not hole himself up in some ungodly tavern where he would most certainly have died.'

Senara left Joshua and Cecily alone to sit by Japhet's bedside. Leah and Bridie were seated in the kitchen, unwilling to impose on the Lovedays' company. Scamp came in from the yard and whined for his food. Senara fed him and washed his muddy paws before settling him in the kitchen. She had delayed facing Cecily for as long as she could, and brewed tea for her visitors.

When she entered the bedchamber, Cecily held her son's

hand and there were tears streaming down her face. Joshua was kneeling in prayer.

Leah was behind Senara, carrying a bowl of cool water. Senara wet a cloth and wrung it out to place it on Japhet's brow. His skin burned to the touch.

'We must try to lower his temperature with cool cloths and get him to swallow as much of the tisane as we can. It will bring down the fever.'

'I will do that.' Cecily took charge. 'It is my right as a mother.'

Senara nodded. 'Do not hesitate to call me if you need anything.'

For the rest of the day she took refreshments to the room but Cecily had touched no food in her worry. Senara had been unable to perform any work she was so worried about Japhet. When Nathan fell asleep she again went upstairs. Japhet's hair was plastered to his head, which he kept tossing from side to side. The sheets were drenched with sweat. Joshua helped Senara to change the linen and the disturbance made Japhet cry out in pain and delirium.

'I think we must send for Chegwidden,' Joshua announced.

It was Cecily who shook her head. 'I have attended many sick beds. Senara is doing all that a physician would.' Cecily clutched Senara's hand as she passed. 'He is not going to die, is he?'

Senara lit a candle for it was rapidly getting dark, and studied her patient. 'His colour does not look so high. That he is sweating profusely is another good sign.'

Cecily wiped a tear from her cheek. 'Chegwidden is over-fond of opening veins and Japhet looks so weak. We will wait until morning. If by then he has not improved, Chegwidden must attend him.'

'You must eat, and Bridie has made up a bed for you in the

next room,' Senara said, her gaze watchful as Japhet tried to throw off the covers.

Cecily pulled up the blanket and replaced the cool compress on his brow. She looked at Senara. 'My dear, I was unforgivably rude to you when I arrived. I was worried about Japhet. I can see how well you have looked after my son.'

'Japhet has always shown me kindness. I pray he will recover.'

'Go and rest, Senara,' Joshua suggested. 'You look tired. Your mother said you had tended him all through last night. We will stay with him now.'

Senara nodded. 'If you could keep a cool compress on his brow and use the cloth by the cup to squeeze some of the tisane into his mouth, that will help.'

The family took it in turns to sit with Japhet through the night, though Cecily had to be persuaded to leave his bedside to sleep.

At first light Leah helped Senara to prepare breakfast. When Senara entered Japhet's room she found Cecily dozing by the bed and she started awake. Japhet was lying quietly.

'He has not called out for some while.' Cecily's eyes pleaded with Senara to confirm that Japhet was improving. 'Joshua said that Japhet had been set upon by ruffians and beaten after a gaming session. How did it happen?'

Senara placed the fresh tisane she had made for Japhet by the bed and put her hand on his brow. Joshua had followed her into the room. He looked as though he had not slept all night. She held the parson's stare, grateful that he had not spoken of the whipping. 'I do not know the details, Mrs Loveday. Japhet was in too much pain to talk.'

She checked the bandages on his chest. They were damp with sweat and smeared with a few watery yellow patches. 'He does not seem so hot. His fever is dropping. It will help if you can get some of the tisane into him. I will need to change some of the dressings soon.'

When she brought some balm and fresh bandages into the room, she looked at Joshua for help. If she removed the bandages in front of Japhet's mother, Cecily would see that her son had been whipped and would demand to know why. 'My mother has prepared breakfast for you downstairs.'

'That is kind but I could not eat,' Cecily answered.

Joshua put his hand on his wife's shoulder. 'But you must have something. And Senara will not want us getting in her way while she tends Japhet.'

'I can change a bandage. As his mother—'

Joshua shook his head. 'Japhet knows how much you dislike his fighting and gaming. And they were the cause of his injuries. He came here to avoid his injuries upsetting you. I think you should respect his wishes in that.'

When Cecily opened her mouth to protest, Joshua gently took her elbow, raised her to her feet and led her to the door. 'Senara broke her word to Japhet to bring us here. Spare him the indignity of knowing that you have seen how badly he was treated.'

'Very well,' Cecily was reluctant, 'since you will not tell me the full nature of his injuries. I can guess something of the reason behind them. It all sounds very unsavoury to me, but there are things a mother prefers not to know about her son's morals. I pray that he learns from this lesson. I will never turn my back on him, no matter how great a trial my fears for him become.' Cecily wiped the tears from her eyes. 'Surely he is not so wicked as to deserve this.'

'He is not wicked at all,' Senara comforted. 'He has a great love of life.'

'You are too charitable in your opinion of Japhet,' Joshua said without rancour after Cecily had gone downstairs. 'I pray daily that he will see the error of his ways. Otherwise I

180

fear he will end his days in gaol or, heaven forfend, swinging from a gibbet.' He too went down to breakfast, leaving Senara to her work.

Senara cut away the bandages and examined the wounds. It was only the ones on his shoulders and ribs which still needed tending, as the others were beginning to heal. She had brought a jar of leeches with her, but was relieved to find that the redness around the wounds had lost its harshness and they were no longer weeping pus.

Joshua returned without his wife. 'Cecily fell asleep rocking your son in her arms.'

Senara smiled. 'I think the worst is past.'

She deftly cleansed the wound and while Joshua supported Japhet in a sitting position, replaced the bandages. Japhet's father was not very complimentary in some of his comments as he voiced the fears which he had harboured over the years.

'The Good Lord knows I was no innocent before I took the cloth, but this wildness in Japhet, this recklessness and his roguery . . . it is reprehensible. I despair for him. Truly I do.' Joshua suddenly lost his temper. 'When I think of the worry he has caused his good mother, I regret Japhet is too big to put across my knee. Why can he not be more like Peter?'

As she worked, Japhet was very still, too still, and Senara suspected that he had been roused by his father's ire and was now feigning an unconscious state to avoid a confrontation with his parents. At this last remark she felt Japhet tense in her arms and she laid him down on the mattress.

'He does seem much calmer. The fever has gone. Perhaps we should allow him to sleep in peace and you return later.'

'I will not leave this room until I am assured that he is on the way to recovery.' Joshua sat on the chair Cecily had vacated and began to read aloud from the Bible.

181

Senara kept a covert eye on Japhet as she straightened the bed linen. When she stooped to tuck in the blanket, she whispered in Japhet's ear, 'He won't go until you show him the fever has gone.'

'Did you say something, my dear?' Joshua looked up from his reading.

There was a groan from Japhet and he opened his eyes, which were bright and focused. 'I'm not proud of myself, sir, and don't need a sermon.' He cast an accusing stare at Senara. 'Is this how you keep your word?'

Senara stepped back, hurt by his anger. 'Was I supposed to let you die and your parents not know how ill you were? You've been delirious since yesterday. If your fever had not broken you would have died.'

'Senara did what was right,' Joshua defended her. 'It is you who have fallen from grace, or does your memory fail you as to what deed brought you so close to your death? I doubt even this escapade will curb your wild and unholy ways.'

'I make no promises, sir.'

'I will tell Mrs Loveday that you are awake, Japhet.' Senara was suddenly ill at ease in their company.

'Let her sleep awhile and you should rest yourself,' Joshua replied.

Senara lay down on her bed but Joshua's conversation with his son soon became heated. She did not want to interfere but when it continued she needed to consider the welfare of her patient. Entering the sickroom, she cut across Joshua's remonstration. 'With respect, sir, Japhet needs to rest to recover his strength.'

Joshua turned to her. 'Do you defend his actions?'

'My concern is for his recovery, not his morals, sir. I would not have him risk a relapse. I must ask you to leave.'

The effort of defending himself to his father had taken its toll on Japhet. His eyes were sunken and, beneath the black

182

stubble on his jaw, his complexion was an unhealthy grey. Japhet's lids began to droop and his voice was weak: 'I beg you, sir, can this sermon not wait until another day?'

Cecily, who had been roused by the raised voices and torn between her husband's righteous anger and her son's weakness, sided with Senara. 'Joshua, you always said never to waste a sermon on deaf ears. Japhet is in no state to heed you, even if he had a mind to.'

She picked up her gloves and bonnet, which she had laid on a stool by the fire. 'Senara. I am beholden to you for saving Japhet's life.'

'He has always been kind and supportive of me,' she replied. 'It is little enough that I have done.'

Cecily unexpectedly kissed her cheek. 'Your knowledge of healing is a great gift. Plenty of our parishioners cannot afford medication for their ailments. You could ease so many of the discomforts and ills they must endure.'

'I would be happy to do so and would give my services freely but I fear to bring discredit to Adam.'

'How so?' Joshua looked puzzled. 'Many great and gracious ladies tend the poor of their manors. They would see it as their duty but their knowledge is sparse. But you must always protect yourself by having a maid present or, better still, a manservant, when visiting the sick, to be sure you are not taken advantage of.'

'You do not think that others of your family will view such work as undignified or a slur on the family name?'

'My mother did much work with the poor and needy,' Joshua added.

'But she was a lady.' Senara voiced her fears. 'She would be regarded with respect.'

Joshua took her hand and raised it to his lips. 'You belittle yourself if you think that you are not. You have natural grace and dignity, and in time the people will come to love and respect you. That is all any family hopes for.'

'I will see what Adam says. He is happy for me to help the families living at Trevowan Hard. I have always enjoyed working with herbs and plants. Time does hang heavily on my hands since Adam has been away. I would be happy to extend my work to the people of your parish.'

'Good. And we will be happy to welcome you to our services. Your absence has been commented upon.' Joshua laughed though there was reproval in his voice. 'We would not have our neighbours think you a heathen, would we?'

Senara dropped her gaze, alarmed at his proposal. She had been married at Trewenna church because Adam had been insistent that otherwise it would not be considered legal. She had been brought up to respect the old customs and rituals which honoured the old ancient gods and goddesses of nature. She did not believe in the all-vengeful god of hellfire preached from the pulpits. When she roamed the woods and moorlands she was in awe of their beauty. The god who created the perfection which was mother earth was a god of love and harmony.

Joshua was watching her closely. 'Surely that does not present a problem, Senara.'

She felt cornered. Her position and acceptance within Adam's family was so precarious, she did not wish to alienate this kindly couple. 'I have always been uneasy in small spaces where there are crowds. I feel that I am suffocating,' she prevaricated with a half-truth, for she *had* always felt stifled in confined spaces.

She was saved from offending them further by a cry of hunger from Nathan in his crib downstairs.

'Poor lamb, he should have been fed an hour ago. Excuse me.' She fled the room.

Chapter Ten

For three days the French corvette pursued *Pegasus*, always uncomfortably close but just out of cannon range. The heavy swell of the sea and crosswinds stripped away the Frenchman's advantage of speed. Adam had set a course to take them further out into the Atlantic to avoid other French ships coasting the inland waters. He then intended to sail north to the Scilly Isles and the protection of English waters. No sailing ship could combat a prevailing wind and, to avoid being blown further south, *Pegasus* rode into the wind, using it to take them further west. At least it was away from France.

On the fourth morning William ended his watch and reported to Adam in his cabin. Adam was studying a chart but sat close to the small brazier which heated his cabin. He sneezed several times and blew his nose.

'You look dreadful, Adam. I've told Melthrop to take over your watch.' William placed the sextant on the table and gave Adam his readings. 'The corvette is no closer, about five miles to larboard. Visibility is down to ten miles and overcast. Wind has veered two points to the east. No sign of any other ships.'

Adam replotted their course and rubbed his knuckles across his brow. His head ached abominably and his nose was streaming from the cold he had developed. 'The change of

185

wind could be to the corvette's advantage.'

'Melthrop will pipe all hands on deck if she comes within firing distance. You really should rest, Adam.'

The sound of running feet drew both captains' attention to the door of the cabin.

A young sailor with a circlet of boils around his neck and a thin, pale face rapped on the open door.

'Yes, Carter?' Adam said.

'A French frigate's been sighted directly ahead, Cap'n. Corvette is also gaining on us, sir.'

Adam rolled up the chart and replaced it carefully in a sea chest. He looked composed but a muscle was pulsing along his jaw. 'Order all *émigrés* to stay below. I shall join Mr Melthrop on deck.'

When the sailor left, William, who had been composed until now, looked anxiously at his nephew. 'We cannot survive an attack from two ships.'

'But if an engagement is inevitable they will feel the bite of English cannon,' Adam responded.

He was not surprised when his uncle followed him on deck. William would be as concerned as himself at this new danger. The closer proximity of the corvette sent a quiver of alarm through Adam. The French ship was larger than *Pegasus*, her three masts carrying both royals and top-gallants, and she would also be carrying more guns. His expression remained impassive. The raw soreness in his throat from his cold was now parched with something far more oppressive – dread that battle was inevitable. The wind was now in the corvette's favour. She could even be alongside them before nightfall, which was in an hour. All evasion tactics had so far failed. Their captain was evidently wily and experienced.

Adam turned his spyglass on what was as yet little more than a smudge on the horizon. The French frigate in full sail was bearing down upon them. Adam cursed silently. This was a powerful ship of the line and she was cutting off their escape to the west.

Adam passed the spyglass to William. His uncle scanned the horizon, and when he snapped it shut and returned it to Adam, his lips were set in a bleak line. 'Doesn't look too good. What action do you propose?'

'We have no choice but to head for the English Channel. There will be risk from encountering other French ships, but I see no alternative.'

William surveyed the sky, which was weighted with clouds. 'In an hour it will be dusk. There will be no moon tonight. It could be that the French will not expect us to make for Land's End but rather head for Guernsey and the protection of the harbour there.'

'St Peter Port is closer, but the risk of running into more French ships would be greater.'

'Instinct tells me to make for England,' William advised. 'Once in English waters there is the chance of protection from a naval frigate or a revenue ship.'

Shouts and orders from below drew his attention. The deck was a frenzy of activity. Each watch had been practising their paces. The crew were raw merchant seamen, unused to battle. On the outward voyage Adam had had them clearing the ship for action and manning the guns, preparing to load and fire until they worked as a smooth and efficient unit.

Now he stood to attention by the rail on the quarterdeck and watched his crew as Melthrop again ordered the ship cleared for action. The process of changing a ship from a floating home to a fighting vessel was a manoeuvre the men had still not mastered to Adam's requirements. They needed to take another two minutes off the time, precious minutes which would mean the difference between firing on the enemy or being blown from the sea if they came upon their foe unexpectedly. This time they would be prepared.

Feet pounded the decks as men picked for their poaching skills with a musket ran up the rigging to take up position to rake the enemy ship with gunfire. Below decks, the bangs and thuds of partitions being moved carried to Adam. He heard the creak of the gunports as they opened, while on deck sailors formed a line to pass cannonballs hand over hand to make a pile beside each swivel gun, which had been mounted and secured in position.

Mr Melthrop presented himself to Adam and saluted. 'Cleared for action, Cap'n.'

Adam checked his pocket timepiece. 'A minute faster than earlier. Keep the decks cleared and the men prepared for action until nightfall.'

William had not gone below decks to rest but had been studying the men's performance. 'You press the men hard, Adam. But they have improved remarkably in so short a time.'

'Unless we can lose those French ships tonight, they will be putting their training into action at first light. A pity we do not have enough spare cannonballs for them to have actually practised their aim. You will command the ship tomorrow, sir. I will be in charge of the gun crew.'

'Let us hope that it does not come to such drastic action.'

The milky haze of dawn brought with it a protective sea mist. The wind had dropped in the night and *Pegasus* had made little headway. William had changed course, making for Falmouth. Adam stared out of his cabin window, which ran the length of the stern. He could make out nothing through the mist. A fit of coughing tightened his chest and his head thudded as he blew his nose. He was hot and close to a fever, and his reflexes were leaden when he needed all his wits about him.

The familiar banging of screens being moved foretold the decks again being cleared for action. This was no practice manoeuvre. Every nerve screamed for him to race on deck and scan the horizon for sight of the French ships. He kept a tight rein on his composure, needing a cool head to survive the next hours if they were still being pursued.

Jamie Beckett, one of the youngest of the sailors and on his first voyage, hesitated by the open door of his cabin. He was barefoot and his homespun pantaloons hung loose to his calves, the baggy shirt and jerkin covering an immature body. His face was white and his eyes darted from side to side in fear. 'Cap'n Loveday's compliments, Cap'n Loveday. He requests you join him on deck.'

Adam picked up his sword belt and slid it across his shoulder. 'Anything else to report, Beckett?'

The young tar was breathing heavily and gulped before adding, 'Two ships closing, sir.'

'I will present myself to Captain Loveday directly.' Adam waited until the sailor had run back to his post. He placed his hands on each side of the chart spread out on his table. They were in mid-Channel, but the French ships had not backed off once they had left French waters. Now the odds were undoubtedly against them.

Another coughing fit racked his chest and his jaw was clenched as he arrived on deck. But nothing of his inner turmoil showed on his face nor in his manner as he strode to the quarterdeck. The mist had lifted enough to reveal the French frigate on a parallel course with them, and about five miles distant. In half an hour she could open fire on them. He did not let his step falter, noting with approval that the decks had been sanded to prevent the sailors' feet slipping during action. He glanced up at the pennant. Was he imagining it, or was it flapping more strongly and had it swung round two points? This could be the advantage they needed.

He nodded as he passed the crew standing in readiness against their guns, or perched up on the spars and yards, awaiting urgent orders. Adam could feel the men's stares on him, feel their fear. His stride was confident and his stare impassive, willing them to follow his example. Beside the two sixteen-pounder cannon, opposite each other amidships, were filled water buckets to douse the swabs or quench any fire breaking out during the attack. Four twelve-pounders were hidden behind the gunports on the lower decks. All was in readiness and to his satisfaction. Nothing had been missed.

Edward had complained at the expense of the new cannon but those guns were the greatest chance the *Pegasus* had of surviving an attack by the French.

'Remember all you have been taught,' Adam said as he passed each group. 'Hold your positions, obey each order without question, and we will win through. You are fine men, all of you.'

Adam struggled to overcome another coughing fit as he approached his uncle. William Loveday stood on the quarter-deck, hands clasped behind him and his expression set. 'They are both flying their colours, Adam. And they seem to have every intention of attacking. Our best course would be to tack about and get across the frigate's bows.'

Adam stared at the two tricolours, the only slashes of colour against a hazy sky. 'Our advantage would come from firing the first salvo, but we cannot afford to waste any ammunition, and our men are untested in battle. It would be better not to engage until we have to.'

'Damnable situation,' William answered. 'We have no choice but to await their first move and to keep out of their line of fire. You look terrible, lad.'

'Thanks,' Adam forced out through another bout of coughing.

William glanced up at the pennant. 'The wind has changed. If we can keep to windward of the frigate we could yet gain the advantage. And I pray that the wind will stiffen. Then in an hour we should sight land.'

Adam had been studying the frigate. It was now less than a mile away, though the corvette had lost ground. 'We will not have an hour, sir. The frigate is closing fast. Her gunports are open. Mr Melthrop, have the men stand by for action.'

'Come about,' William shouted.

Pegasus' sails were slackened and flapped wildly as she cut across the wind. There was a puff of smoke from the frigate, followed immediately by another. Behind that came the delayed thunder rumble of gunfire. One shot ploughed into the waves just short of *Pegasus*' stern. Ten yards closer and it would have crashed through the stern window, sending splinters exploding through the between-decks, turning it into a charnel house, with dead and mutilated *émigrés* and seamen. As it was, it set the children and women screaming.

'Keep the passengers quiet,' Adam ordered. 'The suspicion that we carry fleeing royalists is enough for the frigate to fire on us.'

The ship was responding to the rudder, spume splaying over her bowsprit as she began to turn and her hull keeled over from the strain of so much sail. A second shot ripped a hole in the mizzen mast topgallant and destroyed the crow's nest.

'Poor bastard,' William muttered, his expression stoic. The man aloft had been blown to pieces. Shrapnel rained down on the deck and three men were felled. 'If we hadn't come about that would have taken out the whole mast.'

There were screams of terror from the passengers below decks and Adam doubted any command could silence them. A third shot from the frigate fell fifty yards short of the larboard bow.

'We've got to try to demast her,' Adam shouted above the snapping of canvas filling with wind and the creak and whine of rigging. They had veered round towards the frigate, and Adam was relieved to discover that her larboard gunports were still closed. He ran down to the lower deck and checked the alignment of the sixteen-pounders. 'We may only have one chance, men.'

The frigate slid into his line of vision and Adam swallowed hard to force some saliva into his raw and aching throat. He waited, nerves straining. Then when the frigate was full broadside, he croaked hoarsely, 'Fire!'

The deck juddered beneath his feet as smoke spewed from the cannon and momentarily clouded his vision.

Melthrop yelled, 'Fire your muskets at will.'

William was shouting into a speaking-trumpet: 'Hard to larboard.'

Through the smoke Adam heard the shriek of splintered wood and cries from the wounded on the frigate. He was coughing, his vision further impaired by his eyes streaming from the smoke. Then the dun-coloured haze cleared.

'Look at that!' a gun captain yelled. 'Her foremast be gone. And it ripped through half the sails on the mainmast as she came down. That were some lucky shot.'

The frigate was far from beaten. Her larboard gunports were now open, the pale sun glinting off a dozen black muzzles which had been run out. *Pegasus* was veering past her, faster than the guns could be primed and fired. Even so, Adam held his breath. A full broadside would sink *Pegasus* for certain. He glanced at the quarterdeck, seeing William throwing his weight against the helm as he aided the helmsman to bring her about.

A glance to the east showed him that the corvette was now bearing down upon them. Their only chance was to take advantage of the freshening wind and make a run for it. The

English coast appeared as a grey line on the horizon. Could they make it? The frigate was crippled but still dangerous, and the corvette was as persistent as a terrier worrying a rat.

The spyglass showed him the white sails of another ship in mid-Channel. If it was French they were done for. He peered again through the spyglass and could just make out the British ensign. The ship's lines were indistinct as she was approaching bow first. From its size it was most likely to be a revenue ship rather than from the navy. But it was English and it could be armed.

Adam ordered the debris cleared from the deck and returned to the quarterdeck. Would the presence of this other vessel be enough to deter the French? And could it reach them in time? He began to breathe easier, confident that *Pegasus* could outrun the frigate.

A warning shot was fired from the English ship.

'They're going about,' William announced. 'The French have conceded.'

A cheer rose from the men on deck. Adam grinned at his uncle. 'That was closer than I cared for.'

'But we showed them, didn't we?' William laughed.

With the French abandoning the chase, Adam had expected the English ship to stand off. Instead it continued its course and was soon alongside. To Adam's amazement it was *Challenger*, the cutter built in their yard. Adam and William had both remained on deck supervising the clearing work.

'Ahoy there! Heave to, in the King's name,' the commander of *Challenger* shouted, 'and state your business.'

'We are *Pegasus* out of Fowey and are returning from France with passengers,' Adam replied to the uniformed officer standing at the ship's rail. The man was thin and of medium height, the peak of his bicorn hiding his features.

'Stand by for a boarding party,' the officer returned. A

longboat was being lowered and Adam was concerned to see several men armed with muskets climbing over the ship's side.

'Identify yourself and your reason for boarding,' Adam demanded.

'This is the excise cutter *Challenger*. We have reason to believe you have contraband on board and are possibly carrying French spies.'

Adam was feeling wretched. The exhilaration of besting the frigate had worn off and he was again light-headed and aching with fever. 'All we carry are passengers from Brittany. They have papers from His Majesty's Government granting them asylum.'

The officer stood in the prow, his hand upon the sword at his side. Four muskets were trained on *Pegasus*' crew. 'We are at war with France and any refugee must be interrogated.'

The arrogant tone stiffened Adam's spine. It was vaguely familiar but with the officer's face remaining in shadow, and Adam's head aching, he could not recognise it. He had not survived the encounter with the French to turn his ship over to a search by an upstart revenue officer.

'The devil you say, sir. With respect, we are on the King's business and have papers to prove it.' His rush of temper brought on another coughing fit.

'Heave to and allow us to board, or we shall be forced to fire on you.' The bullying arrogance in the voice which had so far eluded Adam, roused his anger. Belatedly, he recognised Lieutenant Francis Beaumont, the man responsible for getting Adam disgraced and serving a six-month sentence in a naval prison when the two of them had duelled. They were old adversaries. Beaumont was the worst kind of naval officer. Adam was younger, clever and idealistic. But Beaumont had been senior to Adam on their last naval voyage when they had clashed over Beaumont's brutality.

Beaumont had rescued his career because his grandfather was an admiral, but he had been relegated to revenue service. Adam had spent only a few weeks in prison before Squire Penwithick had offered him the chance to work for the Government in France, where Adam had later witnessed the fall of the Bastille. He had left the navy without regrets.

William moved closer to his nephew and whispered, 'Let me handle this, Adam. You are in no fit state. You should be in your bed.'

'I'll have no pompous upstart throw his weight round on my ship. I know that officer. We have been enemies in the past. He will stop at nothing to bring discredit to me.'

'We have nothing to hide, Adam. You are being stubborn.' William stepped to the ship's rail. 'I am Captain William Loveday of HMS *Neptune*, but currently in command of this brigantine. Identify yourself.'

'Lieutenant Beaumont, sir.'

'You have my permission to come aboard and inspect the passengers' papers. But your men will lay down their arms and only two may accompany you.'

'You have no jurisdiction over me, sir.'

'On the contrary, I am senior in rank and in a senior service. Do you wish me to report your conduct to your commanding officer, Mr Beaumont? I do not tolerate insubordination of any kind.'

Beaumont was glowering as he stepped over the ship's side. He picked his way as delicately as a tightrope walker over the broken mast spars and bloodied sawdust. The officer saluted William Loveday and when he turned to Adam his glare was hostile. 'I will see the papers of your passengers and then a half-dozen men will search this ship for contraband.'

'May it prove a valuable training exercise,' Adam returned. 'There is no contraband upon this ship, nor has there ever been. She is registered as a merchantman.'

Beaumont stepped closer, tipping back his head to peer down his long thin nose at Adam. Beaumont was immaculate in a gold-braided navy jacket and white breeches. A powdered wig with three rolls above his ears was tied in a plait at the back. Adam was aware that he had lost his hair ribbon during the action and his hair was hanging loose about his shoulders. His face was blackened by gunpowder, as were his tan leather jacket and breeches.

'Civilian life has done nothing for you, Loveday.' Beaumont's stare flickered disdainfully over Adam's figure. 'You look like a damned pirate. I mean to have you in chains and your ship confiscated.'

Adam hid his satisfaction when Beaumont examined Squire Penwithick's orders and papers. The man's face turned puce with anger on discovering that Adam had spoken the truth.

'Why do we not partake of some refreshment below decks, Mr Beaumont?' William was uncomfortably aware of the aggression between his nephew and this man. Beaumont was champing at the bit to find some evidence against Adam.

'I do not drink on duty, sir.' Beaumont was pompous in his declaration.

When his men returned on deck and reported they had found nothing, the glare he turned on Adam was murderous. Then a sly smile twisted his reptilian lips. 'There still remains the matter of letters of marque. You have these of course, or you would not have fired upon a foreign vessel. That would be piracy and a hanging offence.'

It took all Adam's control to master his rage. 'I have no letters of marque. We were forced to fire on the French frigate only after she fired first upon us.'

'But I saw you fire first,' Beaumont accused. 'I saw you come about and deliberately fire on her.'

'With respect, Lieutenant Beaumont, your eyes deceived

you.' There was a lethal calmness in Adam's voice. 'The French fired three shots before we retaliated. One blew away *Pegasus'* top mizzenmast and crow's nest. If I had been intent upon piracy I would have continued to fire on the frigate once she was demasted, not set course for home.'

The twist to Beaumont's lips was malicious. 'But you would have seen our sail. You would be concerned that you had been found out.' He turned to his escort. 'Arrest this man for piracy. This ship is seized in the King's name and is forfeited to the Admiralty. I alone now command her.'

'You exceed your duty, Mr Beaumont.' William stepped forward, his expression forbidding. 'Since I was in charge of this ship at the time of the attack and not my nephew, you have no case. As a captain in His Majesty's navy I am empowered to fire upon and engage any enemy vessel. I suggest you leave this ship now before I have no choice but to report your conduct to the Admiralty and Excise Office.'

'But this is not a naval ship, therefore you have no such jurisdiction.' Beaumont puffed out his chest, convinced that he had won.

William regarded Beaumont with scathing contempt. 'Any naval officer bearing government orders has the power to requisition a vessel in the performance of his duty. Do you dispute that Squire Penwithick is a Member of Parliament and privy to Mr Pitt's commands?'

Beaumont wavered, clearly unsure if William Loveday was bluffing or not.

'Sir, have you not the courtesy to answer a superior officer?' William barked out with such ferocity Beaumont flinched.

'Aye, aye, sir. I mean, I suppose that is the case,' he spluttered, and his nostrils flared as he battled to recover his composure. He scowled at Adam. 'This matter is not finished, Loveday. There's been an increase of smuggling between St Austell and Looe. Rumour is that it's being run by a gang in the Fowey area. The Sawle family are under suspicion but they have never been caught. You are related by your nephew's marriage to the Sawles. I hear St John Loveday has been seen spending money freely of late. And a ship like this could carry a handsome store of contraband.'

Adam started forward, his hand clasping his sword hilt at the implied insult. William put a hand on his arm.

'Do not play into his hands, Adam. He would like no better than for you to strike him. To strike a revenue officer is a criminal offence.'

Despite his uncle's wise caution, Adam retaliated. 'They say that Cornwall's most notorious smuggler has the excise men in his pay. Careful how you slur the name of my family. Your own reputation is far from savoury.'

The hatred sparked between the two men. Beaumont blanched. As the revenue officer's hand went to his sword, William stepped between the two antagonists. 'Lieutenant Beaumont, it seems that your duty is done aboard my ship. I would be obliged if you would vacate the deck. There are wounded to attend to and debris to be cleared before we get under way. Squire Penwithick will be informed that your prompt intervention prevented a further attack on us by the French. Your bravery is commendable.'

At the compliment Beaumont relaxed. He had been beaten by Adam in their duel and the security of his armed escort had prompted his bravado in front of his men. He saluted William Loveday. 'As you say, my duty here is done. Good day, Captain.' He ignored Adam and strode to the ship's side.

As the longboat pulled away, William rounded on his nephew. 'What the devil was that all about? And why did you antagonise him? You've made an enemy this day. I recognise his sort.'

'We've been enemies a long time. I got the better of Beaumont the last time and he will never forgive that.'

'Then take care,' William warned. 'He'll take what you prize most: *Pegasus*.'

Chapter Eleven

Eight days after Japhet arrived at Mariner's House he
appeared in the parlour as Senara was feeding Nathan.
Hastily she covered her exposed breast.

'My pardon, dear lady,' he apologised as he leaned against
the door frame. He was wearing his breeches and hose but his
chest was bare apart from a single bandage. 'I have imposed
too long upon your time. After you have changed this last
dressing I shall leave.'

'Your mother is expected this morning. Surely you will not
go before she arrives? Or are you returning to the Rectory?'
Senara put Nathan to her shoulder and rubbed his back until
he burped, then placed him in his crib.

Japhet sighed. 'Mama has doled out a lecture with every
visit. Much as I love her, I would avoid another. She upsets
herself so. I shall not go to the Rectory. Pious Peter will be
there. It would take only one of his sermons against sin, and
I vow I will ram his pontificating words down his throat. My
brother needs to be bedded by a lusty wench. Then he would
know why men are human and tempted to err.'

'So where will you go?' Senara noted that Japhet was
hunched, the wounds still too painful for him to stand
upright. She was worried about him. The fever had passed
and the cuts were no longer infected but he remained weak.

'Fowey is out of the question. And Truro is a long ride,

200

even if the roads are passable. If Adam had returned I would have asked to stay here. The Fetheringtons are having a ball soon, which is a welcome diversion.'

'It is not the liveliest of taverns but I am sure that Pru Jansen would put you up at the Ship kiddleywink.'

'Still too close not to have Mama fussing and lecturing.'

'Come into the kitchen and I will change those bandages and perhaps we will think of something.'

Japhet perched on the table and Senara examined the cuts on his back. As she worked she suggested one or two places for Japhet to stay, which he rejected.

'I will stay with Hannah. I can give her some help on the farm.'

Senara nodded. 'But will not Cecily pursue you there?'

Japhet grinned. 'Yes, but there is land enough for me to lose myself upon to avoid a confrontation.'

Senara hid a smile. Japhet had no fear of any man, but his small-framed mother was the one person he held in awe. Senara concentrated on her task. 'These last cuts are the deepest and are beginning to heal, though several of the whip marks will leave scars. I'm sorry.'

There was a shocked gasp from the doorway. 'Japhet, whatever has happened?'

'Gwen, I did not hear you come in.' Senara was agitated and cast an anxious glance at Japhet. He had pulled a towel across his shoulder to cover the whip lashes on his chest and ribs.

'So it's true,' Gwen rushed on, unaware of Japhet's discomfort. 'You *have* been in a fight.' She was staring at his torso, a vivid blush rising to her cheeks, then, shocked, she covered her mouth with her hand. 'But those wounds look as though you have been flogged.'

'I'm sorry you had to see them, Gwen.' Japhet's manner was guarded. 'And before you ask, I have no intention of telling you how I came by them.'

'But whoever did this should be brought to justice.' She was indignant. 'It is criminal. It is an outrage. It is—'

'It is no less than I deserved,' Japhet informed her, showing no sign of contrition.

'Gwendolyn, would you be so kind as to wait in the parlour so I can finish tending Japhet?' said Senara.

Gwen did not move and a tear trickled from her eye. Japhet could not meet her stare and Senara turned her back on Gwen to continue her work. When the last bandage was secured she stepped back to ask, 'Pleasant as it is to see you, was there a reason for your visit, Gwen? Or did you know Japhet was here?'

The woman's cheeks were awash with tears. 'I called at the Rectory. Mrs Loveday said Japhet had been hurt. I had already heard rumours that he had been in a fight in Fowey. I wanted to see that he was all right; if there was anything I could do . . .' She broke off rather lamely.

'I don't deserve your tears, Gwen.' Japhet spoke with unaccustomed harshness.

She trembled and stared dumbly at him. Senara could feel the tension building between the two of them. A clean shirt of Japhet's, which Cecily had brought on her last visit, was warming over the back of a chair by the kitchen fire. Senara threw it to him. When he had trouble pushing one arm through a sleeve, Gwen hurried to help.

'I can manage,' Japhet snapped.

Gwendolyn hugged her arms around her. 'I'm sorry. I only meant—'

'Ignore his rudeness, Gwen. He's been a terrible patient.' Senara picked up the pile of clothes she had been ironing before feeding Nathan. 'I have work to do.' She walked out, leaving them alone.

Exasperated at how easily he had wounded Gwendolyn,

Japhet said, 'So now you know the worst of me.' His hazel stare remained uncompromising.

'Do they hurt?'

'Like the devil. And what was the gossip you heard? Will I be able to hold my head up in society again?' His lips curled into a sardonic line.

Gwendolyn battled with her emotions. Japhet was defensive but clearly unrepentant. Their last conversation had ruined her sleep for nights. She should forget him. He was not for her.

Her gaze slid from his taunting stare to study a few drops of water which had dripped on the floor when Senara had been cleaning his wounds. 'I do not listen to the gossip, which is always grossly exaggerated, especially when a person has a certain reputation – people always want to make it blacker than it is.'

'Will the estimable matrons be locking up their daughters if I attend the Fetheringtons' hunt ball?'

She glanced up at him through her lashes. 'They do anyway where you are concerned. Or had you not noticed?'

Japhet chuckled. 'I do find a tedious number of dance cards already full when I attempt to make the acquaintance of a young lady of society.'

'Is that why you dance with me so often on those occasions?' There was a vulnerable slump to her shoulders and her stare darted everywhere but at him.

'Gwen, you do get the oddest notions. I dance with you because you are the most amusing woman present.' When she flinched as though he had struck her, he hastily amended, 'And one of the prettiest.'

'I'm not one of those silly women who have to be fed false flattery. And I hate it when you are so flippant about everything.'

He tilted his head on one side and regarded her thoughtfully. 'I don't deserve your friendship, Gwen.'

'Carry on being so pig-headed and flippant and you won't have it any more.' There was an overbrightness to her eyes. Then, to his astonishment, she turned on her heel and walked out of the kitchen.

'Any news of Adam?' he heard Gwen ask Senara. 'He should be home soon. I hope that now England is at war with France, it will not mean Adam takes up the life of a privateer, as once he had planned.'

Senara's answer was too low for Japhet to hear. He sauntered to the parlour door and leaned against it. Gwen was bent over Nathan's crib and her face softened as her finger gently brushed the sleeping baby's cheek. 'You're so lucky, Senara. You have everything you want. The man you love and a beautiful healthy child.'

'As you will have too, one day,' Senara replied.

There was such desperate hope in Gwen's eyes as she looked at the gypsy, Japhet felt an odd twinge. It was time Gwen got herself married and a family around her. It wasn't as though she was short of suitors. He turned away, strangely unsettled.

The emotion was fleeting. He found a jug of ale Senara had purchased for him from the kiddleywink and poured himself a tankard. When he entered the parlour, Gwen had gone. Senara was seated by the window, sewing a torn ruffle on one of Adam's shirts.

'I thought Gwen might stay and play a hand or two of cards to help pass the time,' Japhet said.

'I thought you had planned to leave here this morning,' Senara reminded him with a grin. 'You're very fond of Gwen, aren't you?'

'I'll get my things.' He paused by the door without answering her question. 'We never did find out why Gwen came.'

Senara raised a brow but did not reply. Why were men always so blind?

★ ★ ★

St John watched as Harry paid off the men who had finished stashing the landed kegs and packages in a disused mine shaft on the edge of the Bracewaites' land. His friend was unaware of the mine workings on his property, and there were three such shafts within a half-mile of each other, all perfect hiding places. The Bracewaites' gamekeeper and shepherd, both ex-smugglers, were each left a keg of brandy outside their lodge and hut for turning a blind eye to any noises in the night.

'A good haul.' St John grinned with satisfaction and pulled off his battered slouch hat. Rain dripped from it after a recent downpour. He was cold, his boots sodden and he could feel his shirt sticking damply to his shoulders where even his thick coat had not saved him.

Harry wiped the rain from his face with a coloured kerchief and swung back into the saddle. They rode abreast towards Penruan and, out of habit, scanned the country-side for sign of a riding officer overvigilant in his duty of patrolling the coast.

'Good profit to be made tonight,' Harry finally replied. 'I reckon such weather keeps the excise men roasting their toes by a fire. With France and England at war, it be easier to evade patrols. The navy will be busy elsewhere. War is always our most profitable time.'

'Let us hope so.' St John was concerned by Harry's words. His partner was always so restless, and no haul was ever enough.

'A pity the roads were so bad we couldn't get the goods away tonight by wagon.' Harry took a swig of brandy from his hip flask. His breath was already laden with fumes and he had been drinking steadily throughout the night. 'Are you sure Bracewaite can be trusted not to go sniffing round where he's not wanted?'

'These shafts are on a barren part of the estate. Since the mine closed, twenty years ago, it's only ever been good for grazing sheep. Bracewaite's only interest in his sheep is how much profit they bring at market.'

'Bracewaite be a mite friendly with Lanyon. Had him over at the house twice last week.'

The hostility in Harry's voice increased St John's unease. 'Lanyon approached him about a partnership in a new venture. Bracewaite is considering it. Lanyon is desperate to be accepted as respectable amongst the gentry.'

Harry hawked and spat on the ground. 'He bain't gonna live that long.'

'I thought Meriel had talked you out of that madness.' St John's heart clenched with fear. 'Everyone knows of the hatred between the Sawles and Lanyon. They expect something to happen since Reuban's accident.'

'That weren't no accident,' Harry flared. 'Once Lanyon is out of the way his men will work for us. We'll be the most influential free-traders along this coast. You'll be a rich man.'

'I want no part of his business or his death. If that's the way you're thinking then we end our partnership now.'

'You'll be the loser,' Harry jeered.

'Murder was never part of any plan of mine.'

'And what will Meriel say when she learns you no longer have the profits from smuggling?' Harry goaded.

'Her opinion is not of interest to me.'

Harry's lips curled back, his voice menacing. 'It bain't that easy to end our partnership, Loveday. You know too much. Free-trading bain't something you do when you feel like it. Once you're in, you stays in. That's the only way we knows who to trust.'

St John turned on him in outrage. 'I've no intention of betraying you, if that's what you fear. You have my word as a gentleman.'

Harry grinned. 'That don't mean nothing to me. Your word to another of your kind may be binding. You'd be shunned by your precious friends if you broke it. But to your kind I be less important than one of their sheep. You and me be partners, Loveday, and that's how it will stay.'

'You've served your purpose, Harry.' St John drew his pistol and pointed it at the smuggler. 'I will not be threatened. I've given my word and I will stand by it. But there would be no need for our partnership to end if you came to your senses over Lanyon.'

Harry stared at the pistol for a long moment. 'You bain't gonna use that?'

'A year ago I would not have done so. But now . . .' St John's eyes narrowed. 'You'll never get away with killing Lanyon. Come to your senses. We pay our men better than Lanyon. The Penruan men work for us now instead of him. That makes it harder for him to land his cargo. There are other ways of beating him.'

Harry's stare remained belligerent. 'I never thought you were ruthless enough for the trade, Loveday. Looks like I were wrong.' For a long moment he studied St John. He did not trust him for he trusted no man. No more than St John should trust him. Harry held out his hand to his partner. 'You be right. Lanyon deserves to die but he bain't worth swinging for.'

St John relaxed. Harry was difficult to control and he had not expected him to back down so easily. But Harry was also greedy. The smuggling was going well. Now that England was at war with France there would be a shortage of luxury goods from abroad. Those willing to take the risk in free-trading found their profits soared. They could be richer than they ever dreamed.

When the two riders parted on the edge of Trevowan land, Harry watched St John ride away. Despite his words to his partner he had no intention of allowing Lanyon to live. He would bide his time for a month or so. And he doubted that St John was now the right partner for him. Loveday could no longer be threatened and despite his new-found ruthlessness, he had shown that honour remained important to him. That made Harry uneasy. When Lanyon finally must die, St John could be a problem. The only way to ensure St John's silence would be to make him an accomplice to the murder.

'What will this war mean?' Amelia regarded her husband with fear in her eyes. 'I understand the implications of a war with France, but how will it affect the family? And Richard?' Her hand covered her mouth. 'He is still a child and that dreadful navy will pitch him into the thick of a battle. He'll be killed. I should never have agreed that he become a midshipman.'

She turned to William, who was seated with the rest of the family in the winter parlour of Trevowan. 'William, can you do nothing to save Richard? Could he not be transferred to a ship which will not be involved in this war?'

'Richard is safe for now. When I lost my command he was transferred to a ship transporting the convicts to Botany Bay. It will be a year before he returns and by then the war could be over.'

Amelia was not reassured. 'I did not allow my son to join the navy to be thrust amongst hardened criminals. And what hazards will he face in this new colony which is not even properly established?'

'Richard will see the world in his travels. It will be the making of him.' Edward refilled his wine glass from the decanter on the table beside his armchair.

'You must not worry about Richard.' Adam also added a word of comfort. 'He loves his life at sea.' He stood in front of a portrait of his great-grandfather. He was furious that he had been summoned to this meeting but that no invitation had been extended to Senara. He had at first refused to attend until Senara had finally persuaded him.

'I could not have come with you even if I had been invited. Nathan is suffering with croup,' she had said. 'I will not leave him, nor take him out in this cold weather. This meeting is important or your father would not have sent for you. There is no point in widening the rift between you and your family.'

'Father knows that I will not step foot in Trevowan while you are not welcome.'

'And he would not have summoned you if the matter was not important.'

Reluctantly Adam had come. Amelia had been restrained in her welcome, and had not mentioned the welfare of Senara or Nathan. At experiencing Amelia's coolness, Adam had an uncomfortable suspicion that Amelia's disapproval to his marriage was influencing his father. Until now he had always thought of Amelia as a compassionate woman. But because of his voyages and months away he had never got to know her well and knew little of her past.

Elspeth had nodded curtly at his greeting but the line of her mouth was disapproving.

St John was unusually affable. 'By all accounts you and Uncle William showed the French your buccaneering colours. I suppose you will now turn pirate and reap a fortune from French prizes in this war.'

'Once I would not have hesitated,' Adam replied, 'but it is hardly the life for a married man.'

'Tied to your wife's apron strings already, are you?' St John taunted, and Meriel, seated beside Elspeth, laughed.

Adam ignored them and would have joined William, but

Lisette had drawn his uncle on to the settle beside her and was talking to him in a low excited voice. William seemed to enjoy the attention she was giving him. Adam was relieved that his cousin appeared to have accepted his marriage, and had settled down to live quietly with his family.

Yet the atmosphere in the room remained tense. For the first time in his life Adam felt uncomfortable in the house he loved, aware that he was there on sufferance.

Edward addressed his family. 'This war could bring new prosperity to the yard, which is why I wanted us all together to review our future. Squire Penwithick has put the name of the yard forward for the navy to use the dry dock at Trevowan Hard for the refurbishment of one of its vessels which is no longer seaworthy. They need to increase the fleet as quickly as possible. And for that work they will guarantee a quarter of the cost in advance.'

'The navy are slow payers,' Adam observed, 'but we need any orders we can get.'

Edward rubbed the back of his neck. 'It will still be necessary to curb expenditure. I've written to Thomas. He has managed to repay another five hundred pounds of our money invested in his bank which was lost in his father's investments. That should be enough to cover most of the materials and wages for the yard. Unfortunately, even with the merger with Lascalles Bank on his marriage, Thomas cannot recover the debts against Amelia's property as they were tied up in a long-term loan.'

'Still you use any spare money we recuperate on the yard.' St John was furious. 'What about the stock which needs replenishing on the estate? We never replaced the prize bull that we were forced to sell. Is not improving our herd a priority?'

'Stud fees are cheaper. I have arranged with Sir Henry

Traherne that his bull, Gladiator, will cover our cows again this year.'

William broke off from his conversation with Lisette to cut across their angry words. 'I shall be leaving at the end of the week, having received orders to join the fleet at Plymouth. Let me know if I can be of help to the family before I go. Edward, you are welcome to what savings I have if the estate has need of them. I did not have all my money in Mercer's Bank as it was easier for me to deal with my Plymouth bankers. I only wish I could have helped you out last year when you were in such dire need.'

Edward nodded. 'That is generous of you, Will. Much of the estate stock was sold and should be replenished. If we buy more cows a bull would be a great asset. But any such money would be strictly as a loan until we are back on our feet again.'

'But were you not planning to buy a cottage in Plymouth, William?' Lisette declared. She looked displeased that she no longer had William's full attention.

William laughed. 'One day when I retire from the sea, but I have a good many years yet.'

'But you may meet a woman whom you wish to spend your life with.'

He patted her hand. 'I am too set in my ways for a woman to put up with me.'

'Then that woman would be a fool.' Lisette leaned forward to clasp his hand. 'You have already emerged the victor over two French ships. Though it saddens me it is my country you must fight, William, you are a hero.'

William disengaged her fingers and looked uncomfortable at her praise. She remained gazing at him with fervour.

St John gave a brittle laugh. 'How fickle is your loyalty,

dear cousin! You abandon your nationality as easily as an old gown.'

Lisette sprang up and hit his chest with her fan. 'My France is not this place of butchery ruled by Robespierre and the New Regime. I am a monarchist. They can cut off one king's head but we have another. Long live the King of France.'

Abruptly her mood changed and with a dramatic gesture she turned to William. 'I do not know how I shall bear it when you must leave us, William. If you have so short a time left with us, you must make the most of it to enjoy yourself.' She clapped her hands in excitement. 'And you promised you would take me to a horse fair so that I could buy myself a mare and not need to use one of Elspeth's. Will that not be a most enjoyable day?'

'You would do better to ask Japhet to find you a decent mount.'

Lisette pouted. 'But you promised that you would help me choose one. You cannot break such a promise.' Her eyes filled with tears and she lifted an anguished face to survey the family. 'Everything is more important than I. I am nothing. An orphan. An outcast. A foreigner.'

William sighed. 'I did promise to take Lisette to the horse fair, but there will not be one until the spring. I doubt I will be in England then. I shall contact Japhet. He will know if there is a suitable mare for sale.'

Lisette flung her arms around William's neck. 'You are so kind and wonderful.' She kissed his cheek and, with an embarrassed cough, he put her from him.

'Looks like you have an admirer, Uncle,' St John chuckled.

Edward groaned inwardly. He had been relieved that Lisette had stopped her wild behaviour after Adam's return, but he had not realised how much she had transferred her affection to his brother. Lisette had been spoiled and doted

212

upon by her parents; she was clearly missing such attention. He hoped her affection for William was a bid to replace a father's love and nothing more. Though William was clearly embarrassed by Lisette's ardour, it was obvious that he was also flattered and enjoying it. It was as well that he was leaving in a few days.

St John joined Adam by the portrait. He looked pleased with himself. 'Meriel is looking well, is she not? We are all praying that the baby will be a son, an heir to follow me to inherit Trevowan.'

Adam had not spoken to St John since the news of Meriel's expecting another child became common knowledge. Now he felt that he had been punched in the stomach. Trevowan was the home he loved. There was still a part of him which burned to possess it. He again cursed the fate which had robbed him of his birthright. 'You are to be congratulated.'

St John leaned closer. 'Papa is delighted at the news. He'll have no gypsy brat lording it over Trevowan. He has promised me a share in the profits yielded by the estate this year.'

'I am happy for you, St John.' Adam almost choked on the words. A son for his twin would mean the end of all his dreams to be master of Trevowan.

Lisette was distraught that William had received word from the Admiralty to rejoin his ship at Plymouth the following week. That he was also going to war and could be killed filled her with alarm. He was her only friend. He was the only man she could trust. So many she had loved had betrayed her. First her father by dying: he had said he would always love and protect her. Then Etienne, her brother, who had sworn that he cared only for her happiness, but he had starved and beaten her until she married a man she hated. Even her husband had avowed his love for her, and promised to lay the world at her feet if she wed him. Honeyed lies to trick her, for he had wanted only her innocence to corrupt and debase. Finally, Adam's betrayal had been the most bitter of all. Indeed all the Lovedays had betrayed her. They had shown her kindness on her arrival from France, then turned against her – allowing Adam to abandon her and seek out his whore.

She was wild-eyed as she paced her bedchamber. All she had ever wanted was to be loved and cherished. William alone had shown her affection and demanded nothing of her in return. William, who was so like her Papa – the only man to have truly loved her for herself. If William went away she would be lost. William kept the evil voices from her head which made her do wicked things. William calmed her horrors. William was never cross with her. He had become her saviour. How could she live, when he went away?

That night she did not sleep. Instead, she paced her room, her mind feverish with anxiety one moment, then ablaze with excitement the next. The next morning William and herself were leaving early, driving by carriage to an estate outside Bodmin where Japhet had arranged for them to look at a mare for sale. They would stay overnight in Bodmin and return the next day. She would have two whole days in William's company. Two days when no one would frown at something she did or said, or urge her to be decorous in her manner.

As soon as it was light, Lisette attempted to dress the dark wig she often wore to cover her shorn hair. The maid Jenna had been called away to light the fires as the other maid had been taken ill in the night. It was unfair to deny her the help of a servant, when she wanted to look her best for William. When the curls would not go right, she flung the hairbrush across the room and burst into tears.

'I must look my best. For William I must be pretty. I must be a good girl, then he will not go away.'

Close to despair, she tore off the travelling gown Jenna had earlier laced her into. Panting with frustration, Lisette dragged every gown from her wardrobe, discarding each one as unflattering or making her appear too young. For William she wanted to look elegant and beautiful. She had spent lavishly on clothes since her arrival in England, selling pieces of jewellery she had brought from France.

The maid tapped on her door. 'Breakfast is served, madam.'

'You must help me.' Lisette wrenched open the door and pulled Jenna Biddick inside. She was struggling to lace herself into a white gown embroidered with gold thread and seed pearls.

'But, madam, that is not suitable for travelling. It is for wearing at a soiree, or a dance.'

Lisette stamped her foot, her pretty face twisting with anger. 'This is the one I will wear. Help me.' She gave Jenna a vicious pinch on her arm, and the maid, used to her bullying tactics, helped her to change.

'Do I not look beautiful?' Lisette demanded as she twirled around and held out the full skirt. Her small breasts were pushed high by her corset and she had refused to wear a fichu to make the gown more suitable for day attire.

'Very lovely, madam,' Jenna said as she rubbed another bruise given to her by Lisette when she had not worked fast enough for her liking. 'Though what Miss Elspeth will say, or Mistress Amelia, I shudder to think. You have also missed breakfast. Captain William Loveday was most insistent that you leave early. He sent me to fetch you.'

'I am not hungry. Where is my cloak? The velvet one with the sable trim.'

'It will be ruined. And it was so expensive, madam. It could rain later.'

Lisette slapped Jenna's face. 'Do not answer back, you insolent slut. Fetch my cloak. I am the Marquise de Gramont; I had a dozen such cloaks in France. I am not a pauper. I will not be treated like one.' She swept regally from the chamber. It was time the Lovedays were reminded of her status, and of the life that she was used to as an aristocrat of France.

In her excitement her mind conjured the images of the days she had spent at Versailles, where she had been fêted as a beauty and courted by the highest nobles of France. It had been so long since she had been made love to by a real gentleman. The men she picked at random during her wild rides away from Trevowan were often pedlars or farm labourers: common men with no refinement. Twice rumours of her behaviour had got back to Edward Loveday, and he had locked her in her room and threatened to send her away. She had always denied the rumours, saying people were jealous of her. They suspected that she had been abused during the Terror and their sick minds made up evil lies about her. So far Edward had believed her and not the rumours, but she knew she must be careful in future. But how could she deny her nature? The English were so cold, so controlled in their emotions. How could they understand how passion could drive the terrors from her mind, make her feel alive again?

She had been furious at Adam's reaction to her advances. A man should be honoured that she had offered herself to him. But the English thought only of respectability and of what society would think of them. They were hypocrites, for if she was married they would turn a blind eye to her peccadilloes. She had decided that it was time she was married. Since Adam was no longer available, then why not

William Loveday? William was handsome, and he never condemned her conduct. He was like her Papa – her adored Papa, for whom she could do no wrong. And William would be away at sea, and who could blame her then if she occasionally strayed with her affections? Naturally she would be discreet. Yes, William would make a perfect husband.

Chapter Twelve

'Must you continue these hare-witted voyages to France?' Edward faced Adam across his office in the yard. The sparsely furnished room was smoky from the fire which was being blown back down the chimney by the strong wind.

'I have given my word to the squire. The voyages are profitable.'

'But they are extremely dangerous. The French will shoot you as a spy if you are caught.'

'You have made it clear that I have no future in the yard, sir. I will not spend my life working to build the yard's prestige if it will not go to my son.'

Edward rubbed his brow. 'Then sail and be damned! Do I not allow your wife to live at the yard?'

'A hollow gesture when Senara is not accepted at Trevowan. You accepted Meriel. What double standards do you now live by?'

Edward hooked his thumbs into the pockets of his waistcoat and seemed to be searching for words. Adam ground out, 'It's Amelia, is it not?'

Edward sighed. 'You have to understand her position. She was reared gently by devout parents; her sensibilities are offended. And I cannot say that I entirely blame her. You expect too much for women like Amelia to accept your wife.'

218

When Adam remained silent but mutinous, Edward blazed, 'It isn't done to marry your mistress and expect decent women to accept her.'

'Then my family will not embarrass you or your wife further. We shall leave Trevowan Hard.'

Edward sat down at his desk, suddenly looking weary. 'That is not what I want. I cannot say that this marriage has pleased me. And I have to consider the sensibilities of my wife.'

'Yet Amelia accepted Meriel. Is Senara less worthy than St John's wife?'

'Meriel was already part of our family when I married Amelia. Amelia gave up a life of comfort and luxury in London to come to Cornwall. She has not complained once over the economies she has had to bear in the last two years. Her manner over your marriage has surprised me, but I respect her feelings and would honour them.'

Adam hung his head, realising his father was in a difficult position. 'I love Senara. I do not regret my marriage, but I do regret the awkward position I have placed you in, sir. And Amelia.'

Edward relaxed. 'And about the yard. I spoke in haste. The yard will be yours. St John has no aptitude for shipbuilding. As for after your death, it will go either to Rafe or your son, Nathan, depending on which of them is the better ship-builder. That will be for you to decide.'

Adam relaxed. 'That means a great deal to me, sir.'

'However, I have not changed my mind over Trevowan. If St John does not have a son, Trevowan goes to Rafe.'

Adam gripped his hands tight behind his back but a muscle pumping in his jaw betrayed his emotion. Trevowan was the home he adored. Every room of the house, every acre of land was imprinted in his heart. No other place could ever match it. It was too much a part of him. He had never accepted that it was St John's birthright but now Edward's tone was final. His sacrifice in marrying Senara had been greater than he imagined.

His head tilted back with stubborn pride. But to choose between Senara and Trevowan would have been impossible. He had never believed until now that his father would be so ruthless in protecting his lineage. He had thought that his father would accept his marriage, as he had St John's.

'I will never be ashamed of my wife or my son. I shall build them a house and estate worthy of a Loveday.' He spoke out of pain, but when the words were said he found it was not bravado. He really meant it.

Edward studied Adam and for the first time since his marriage his father's expression was approving. 'I would have expected nothing less from you, Adam. Your great-grandfather achieved as much, though he had the advantage of marrying a Penhaligan.'

'My land and home will be gained by my own achievements. I will not rise upon a woman's dowry.'

'Which are admirable sentiments, but what if you were to die in France? Or *Pegasus* is sunk? What provisions then for your wife and son?'

'I would trust the welfare of my wife and my son to your honour, sir. I do not believe you would see them homeless or starve. In such circumstances Senara would be content to live simply. She has no wish for grandeur and riches.'

'Yet you would build her a mansion?' Edward queried.

Adam resented his father's reasoning and ignored the logic behind Edward's statement. 'Can I rely on your honour, sir, to provide for my wife and child, if the need should arise?'

'They carry the Loveday name, do they not? I will never turn my back on any person I am responsible for.'

Adam felt some of his antagonism subside. There was a weariness about his father's stance which had not been present before their financial crisis. His hair was greyer and deeper lines scored his jaw. Adam had always thought of his father as invincible, and now he acknowledged that his own conduct of the last year had added to his father's worries.

'You have always done what is right, sir. I regret the pain I have caused you. If you need me at the yard I will find a way of repaying Penwithick's loan to arm my ship, and inform him that I am no longer able to honour my agreement with him.'

Edward nodded. 'Our family strength is in our unity, as was proved with your cousin Thomas's problems with the bank last year. Stick by your agreement with Penwithick. We cannot afford for *Pegasus* to lie idle, and she will bring you a good income. All my spare cash is tied up in the yard. For me to provide even the modest living expenses for your family would be impossible at this time. The house is, of course, yours.'

There remained a stiffness to Edward's manner so Adam knew he had not been entirely forgiven. And he was still angry that Amelia had taken a stand against Senara. It was an uneasy truce.

The Loveday coach bumped along the rutted frost-hardened track, jolting William's bones and his forbearance. The morning mist veiled the landscape and the cold wind channelled through the valley to penetrate the coach. Even his greatcoat and muffler, over a waistcoat and thick jacket, did not fully protect him. His mind was absorbed with the prospect of rejoining his ship, and Lisette's constant chatter gave him no peace. The excursion to buy her a mare had been an impulse to please her which was now testing his patience. He was not used to a woman's chatter and the constant flow of it bombarded him. He scarcely heeded her words, nodding occasionally or answering in a monosyllable at what seemed an appropriate moment.

'William, I despair that you have not heard a word I have said,' Lisette pouted. 'Are you unwell?'

'Your pardon, my dear. My mind is on joining my ship and the preparations I must make. I am poor company.'

She extracted her hand from the fur muff and clasped his hand to press it to her face. 'You are so good to me, my very dear William. You are an important man, a captain in His Majesty's navy, and I drag you from your duties. How thoughtless I am.'

He shifted in his seat and gently withdrew his hand. Her lovely face was framed by the fur-trimmed hood of her cloak, and her eyes were bright with concern as she studied him. Her feet rested on hot bricks wrapped in a tapestry foot-warmer and, as she moved, her knees brushed against his leg. When she leaned forward, her cloak gaped to reveal the swell of her breasts above the neckline of her gown. The smooth touch of her skin and the smell of her perfume seemed to be overpowering his senses. Her delicate beauty had always moved him, but now such close proximity to Lisette was acutely disturbing.

To cover his confusion, William folded his arms across his chest and sat further back in the seat. She chatted on, one moment enthusing about the prospect of the new mare, the next unable to contain her excitement about the ball Lord Fetherington was holding at Easter. Seeing her so animated and exuding a childlike innocence in her pleasure was enchanting. How bravely she had put her terrifying experiences in France behind her. He admired that courage – and in one so petite and beautiful, he found it hard to resist.

Her excited chatter subsided and her eyes became sad. 'I shall miss you, William. And fear for your safety. I will not sleep once you sail for worrying that you will be in danger.'

'You must enjoy yourself at the hunt ball and meet more young men.'

She threw up her hands as though in alarm. 'I have never cared for young men, except Adam, because I thought he was different. Young men will fall in love at the glimpse of a well-turned ankle. They are fickle and a new love steals their hearts with each new encounter. They fall in love with a pretty face before they fall in love with the woman.'

William laughed. 'You are too hard on them. All men admire beauty.'

'But do not older men have more discernment? All young men do is talk of themselves, boasting and bragging, to try to impress a woman. Their experience of life is driven by their own selfish needs. An older man, however, is confident and assured. He has no need to boast, for his reputation speaks for him. Like you, William.'

'I do not deserve such praise.' William experienced a strange constriction in his chest at her words and cursed the kippers which he had eaten for breakfast. 'But older men are creatures of routine. We become set in our ways and do not like change.'

'Some older men, but not you, William. The hunger for life and adventure is in your blood. Are you not excited at the prospect of war? Of conquering the seas and the enemy of your country?' She reached for his hands and held them tight. 'I owe you so much. You have been a great influence upon me since you came to Trevowan. You have been patient, never judging me or lecturing, but guiding me with understanding. You have shown me that I can be happy.'

The carriage lurched and she was thrown forward. The touch of her hands burned through his clothing as she struggled to right herself. As he held her shoulders to steady her, the carriage lurched again, and Lisette was thrown on to his lap.

She threw her arms around his neck and giggled. 'This is much better. I was being tossed about like a pea in a whistle.' She nestled her head on his shoulder, her body pressed against his. She tilted her head to smile at him and the carriage swayed. Then her parted lips were on his, their softness and warmth rousing a desire so sudden and fierce it was impossible to quell. He kissed her with passion.

The ardour of her response set William's blood on fire, his need overshadowing reason. There was a shout from Jasper Fraddon, who hauled the horses to a standstill, jostling the occupants within the carriage.

'Woah there! Good day to you, Master Japhet and Master Peter.'

William set Lisette on the seat beside him. His hand shook as he eased a finger around the tight line of his cravat. The door was wrenched open and Japhet climbed inside, followed by his brother.

'How kind of Japhet to go to so much trouble on my behalf.' Lisette resented the intrusion and it showed in her eyes.

William smiled at his nephew. 'It is most appreciated.' He looked back at Lisette and continued, 'There are two mares for sale that we should consider on the Kellow estate outside Bodmin. They were to be sold as two-year-olds at the Spring Horse Fair. Japhet believes we could have either one at a good price. I am no expert on horseflesh and shall respect his judgement on which is more suitable for you.' William was still unsettled by the ardour Lisette had roused in him. Usually a man of few words, he rattled on: 'As we are to stay overnight in Bodmin, it would not have been proper for just the two of us to stay at an inn, would it, Lisette?'

'But we are uncle and niece, are we not?' Her glance upon

William was provocative. 'You English are so staid in your ways.'

'Appearances are everything,' William continued. 'Your reputation must be protected. Amelia could not spare a maid from her work to accompany you as would have been more appropriate.'

'Oh, fiddle-de-dee!' She laughed and turned to Peter. 'Do you chaperon your brother who has such a wicked reputation?'

She regarded the two brothers sitting opposite. Peter, at twenty-one, was eight years younger than Japhet. His face in repose was serious while Japhet's sharper features always seemed to be amused or mocking.

Japhet grinned. 'Peter would like nothing better than to be the custodian of my morals. He decided to join us when he learned that we would be of service to our beautiful French cousin.'

'I have business in Bodmin.' Peter, who had been staring at Lisette, dropped his gaze when she looked at him. 'Philip Henwood, whose mother lives at Trewenna, was arrested for begging and vagrancy in the town. His mother asked Father to speak for him and to pay any fines due and bring him home. Papa has taken a chill and I offered to go in his place.'

'You must be a great help and comfort to your father, Peter,' William said.

'And how is the fair Lisette?' Japhet was studying her closely and also his uncle. 'For a cold day you both look rather flushed.'

'Lisette is naturally excited about purchasing a mare,' William countered. 'She has not been to Bodmin before.'

William was annoyed at the knowing sparkle in Japhet's eyes. He also did not care for the way Peter could not take his eyes from Lisette.

Lisette declared she was tired and rested her head against

the velvet upholstery of the coach and closed her eyes. It surprised William that she did not want to join in the conversation of the younger men. Peter took his Bible from inside his jacket and began to read, though his gaze lifted every few minutes to watch Lisette.

Japhet spoke of the war with France and what it would mean for William, and soon William was deep in conversation with his nephew. Lisette dozed and her head nodded to the side and rested on his shoulder, which earned William a wink from his older nephew.

Japhet lowered his voice. 'You have certainly tamed the wench. Edward was near despair.'

'Nonsense. With all the family problems Lisette had been ignored.' William was dismissive. 'She was lonely. I trust the family will be more aware of her needs once I leave.'

Japhet nudged his brother's ribs. 'A lonely heart is the easiest to capture. And Lisette is not without a sizeable dowry. Now Adam has wed elsewhere, this is your chance to win a wealthy bride, Peter. I am sure Uncle Edward would welcome the match.'

'The state of matrimony is a holy commitment and should not be mocked.' Peter did not lift his eyes from the Bible but there was a deeper colour to his cheeks.

William bit down on a rush of anger. Clearly Peter was infatuated with Lisette. Had it been any other woman, William would have been amused. But Peter would be the wrong husband for Lisette. He was too young and inexperienced to handle Lisette's temperament and would make her unhappy.

William was relieved to discover that the town of Bodmin crowned the hill to their left. He changed the subject to talk of the mares they were to see and the best price which Lisette could expect to pay.

'Kellow is an honest man and his stock has a good

pedigree,' Japhet elaborated as they turned off the main Bodmin road towards a farmhouse on the next rise.

'It is a bleak place, this moor.' Lisette awoke to stare out of the window. The mist had lifted and the weak sunlight played over the dark heather, the scattered trees twisted and gnarled as gargoyles.

'A dangerous place indeed,' William observed. 'Only a desperate man or a fool would cross it at night. It is the haunt of highwaymen and to deviate from the track a man could flounder in the bogs.'

Two hours later Lisette disregarded Japhet's advice when he recommended one of the two-year-old mares. Instead she chose a dappled palfrey with a pure white mane and tail, which was in the next stall.

Mr Kellow led her out for Lisette's inspection. He was a short bandy-legged man with a gruff manner. 'She be the finest mare I've bred in a long year, but she be not cheap. Properly trained she be to take a lady. I had reckoned to sell her to Lady Jane Pensilva or to one of the Rashleighs.'

'I do not care how much she costs. I must have her,' Lisette declared with passion.

'My dear, are you sure you can afford her?' William cautioned. 'She is double the cost of the other mares.'

'It is my money. I shall spend it as I see fit. She is so beautiful I cannot resist her. I love her already.'

William looked disapproving at her extravagance and she smiled at him. 'I will call her Antoinette after our ill-fated Queen. She is so beautiful, she will make me forget all the horrors I have witnessed.' She giggled as the palfrey nuzzled her hand. 'See, does she not also love me already?' Lisette threw her arms around the mare's neck. 'I must have her. She will be someone I can love when I have lost so much.'

After such an emotional outburst William did not have the heart to refuse her. 'Have you enough money, Lisette?'

She held up a diamond bracelet. 'I will sell this in Bodmin. And I shall order oats and bedding for her. Antoinette will never be a burden on Uncle Edward's finances.'

'That is very commendable of you, my dear.' William smiled indulgently.

'And it pleases you, William, that I do this?' Her eyes sparkled as she kissed the nose of the mare. It was a deliberate provocative gesture and Lisette was openly flirting with him.

William cleared his throat and on recalling the passion he had experienced in the coach was captivated by her charm. 'Yes, it pleases me. It shows your true sweet and generous nature.'

Lisette hugged the mare again. 'Then it is settled. I have made a good bargain, Japhet, yes?'

'She is a fine palfrey but she is not a bargain,' Japhet commented drily. 'Had you not been so obviously eager I could have beaten the price down by another twenty-five guineas.'

'I grow weary of all these lectures on penny-pinching. I am the Marquise de Gramont. I am no pauper.'

Peter pursed his lips, his expression disapproving. 'She is a horse of pride and vanity, named after a frivolous woman who brought her country to its knees. What need you of such a horse, Lisette?'

There was a flash of anger in Lisette's eyes as she regarded Peter. Then her mood changed and she became coquettish. 'But am I not proud and vain and also frivolous? You have told me this on more than one occasion, Cousin Peter. Perhaps I need instruction on these matters. Yet are you not also proud and vain? You pride and vanity is in your self-righteousness.'

Japhet laughed. 'Lisette has you there, Brother.'

Peter paled and turned on his heel to march from the

courtyard and climb back into the coach.

'Have I upset him?' Lisette was wide-eyed with innocence.

William shook his head. 'Peter can hand it out but he cannot take criticism.'

Japhet stooped to whisper in Lisette's ear, 'But then my brother is much smitten. He has met his match in you, Lisette.'

William frowned at overhearing the remark. He glanced at Lisette and was discomfited at her secretive smile. He made the final agreement with Mr Kellow for the mare to be delivered to Trevowan in two days, when payment would be made.

It was dusk when they arrived at the inn where they were to stay in Bodmin. A thick mist was masking the town and the temperature had dropped to almost freezing. The inn was full. The three men were forced to share a room and Lisette had no choice but to share with another gentlewoman.

Lisette was not pleased. The day had started so well when they had set out from Trevowan. William's kiss had proved that he desired her. Yet once they were joined by Japhet and Peter, William had become withdrawn, his manner cool though courteous. Lisette smiled. It was the English way for a man to hide his emotions. Tonight could have held such possibilities if she could have been alone with William.

The next day Lisette was delighted to find both Japhet and Peter had business within Bodmin and she had William's company all to herself. She was in a merry mood as she held his arm when they walked to a reputable jeweller to sell her bracelet. Another day of mist blurred the rooftops and chimneys, and the smell of smoke was heavy in the air. Lisette held a silver pomander of dried rose petals and lemon to her nose, to mask the less savoury smells of rotting vegetation in the gutters and the press of unwashed bodies in the streets.

'Are you sure you would not have preferred I call a sedan chair for you, my dear?' William guided her round a muddy puddle. 'Even wearing pattens, I fear your shoes will be ruined.'

'But in a sedan I must sit alone. I enjoy your conversation too much to deny myself a moment of your company.'

They sold the bracelet for four times the price of the mare, and Lisette talked excitedly of her palfrey.

'Is there a decent saddlery in this town? Antoinette must have the best. I would have a bridle and reins of red leather and a saddle with silver stirrups.'

'You will soon have no money left if you spend so lavishly.' William was taken aback at her extravagance, for he had never been ostentatious.

Lisette shrugged. 'I am a rich woman. Why should I not have all that I want? In France I had three Arab mares and all their harnesses were embossed with silver.'

'To flaunt your wealth when there is so much poverty is not always wise, my dear. And though you have many pieces of jewellery, if you continue to spend in this manner, you will soon deplete your fortune. The jewels are your dowry. They will ensure that you make a suitable match. You are too young and beautiful to remain a widow for long.'

She wrenched her hand from his arm and turned to stare into a shop window. 'You think I am as Peter said: vain and frivolous. A foolish woman who only cares for her pleasures. I have had so little pleasure since Papa died.'

To William's concern her shoulders were shaking. He put his hands on them to turn her to face him. She was crying. 'I am not saying you should not have pleasure. But these are uncertain times. Your jewels are your security for your future.'

'As always you are so wise, William. I am frivolous and foolish. I will make do with an ordinary saddle for Antoinette, even though I had set my heart on red leather.'

'Then you must have it.' It was impossible for William to resist the pleading in her eyes.

She quickly kissed his cheek and giggled when he blushed. 'I know I should not embarrass you by showing such affection in public. But how can I not? You give me such happiness, William. And to prove to you that I am not a silly goose over money, I will open an account with a banker here and deposit the remainder of the money from the bracelet.'

William smiled and patted her hand on his arm. 'That is very sensible. Edward will approve.'

They were approaching the town square and saw Peter preaching to a crowd, who had gathered around two women locked in the wooden embrace of the town stocks. The women had been in the stocks all morning, their heads were bent and lank hair straggled their shoulders. Their thin arms and bare feet were mottled with cold.

Peter paraded before his captive audience. 'Repent of your sins! Know that the Lord will forgive those who return to the fold.'

'Bring us a tot of warming brandy and I may think on it.' The eldest of the women squinted at him, then passed her tongue over cracked lips and revealed the rotting stumps of several teeth. 'Now there be a fine 'andsome preacher. I'll come to your rectory any day for a bit of preachifying. I do 'ave the sin of covetousness. And I could covet 'ee, me 'andsome buck, until 'ee do sing out the Good Lord's name in pleasure.' She let out a ribald cackle of laughter and was joined by her companion.

'Now, Betty, thou shall not covet thy neighbour's preacher. I saw 'im first.' The younger, cross-eyed woman blew a kiss to Peter.

Peter turned his back on the stocks and addressed the crowd. 'Cast out your sins and know the glory of the Lord. Repent and the Kingdom of Heaven is yours.'

'Pay no mind to those old hags, preacher man.' Another woman sauntered to Peter's side. She had once been pretty, but her skin was grey from long absence of the use of soap, and three lice crawled along a tress of matted blonde hair. 'My 'andsome buck, 'ee come along with Peggy 'ere. 'Ee gotta sin afore 'ee can cast it out. And I bain't sinned in an age.'

'Mock the Lord's wrath and you will burn in the fires of hell.' Peter ignored the taunts and turned his eyes heavenwards, the Bible clutched against his chest. He was dressed in black as befitted his chosen calling, his tall, slim figure filled with the majesty of his master. A glow of passion enhanced his dark, handsome features as he cried out, 'Dear Lord, forgive these lost souls.'

A group of eight apprentices in their leather aprons raised their fists and jeered at Peter. Their muscular build and the grey dust which layered their hair and clothing proclaimed them as stonemasons. 'Can't be much of a preacher if he bain't got no church or Methody chapel in which to sermonise.'

The tallest of the apprentices was thickset and in his late teens. 'Why, this preacher bain't much older than I be! What do 'e know about the rights and wrongs of sin? Do 'e think 'e be better than we?'

The others jostled and egged each other on, eager for a fight.

One of them moved forward. ''E bain't no proper preacher. At 'im, lads. Time 'e learned to mind 'is manners. Calling us sinners bain't sociable to my mind.' They advanced towards Peter. 'A dunkin' in the 'orse trough will teach 'im ter mind 'is manners.'

232

They came at Peter in a rush and his stomach churned with nausea. Apprentices were the scourge of many towns, and often gangs would hunt down a rival group, looking for a fight. An unruly gang would run through the streets shoving aside or mocking and molesting decent citizens. They respected no one, and barged into carts of costers or pedlars to steal what they could. They would smash a pieman's tray of wares just to see urchins scrabbling for the food and the pieman bellowing in anger.

A rotten turnip, which had earlier been thrown at the women in the stocks, splattered against Peter's ear and a stone whizzed past his head. Fear pumped through his veins. He searched the crowd for assistance. Any decent citizen had disappeared, and the dozen or so onlookers were rough characters eager for any diversion.

Peter backed away. He did not believe in violence, but would have stood and defended himself against a single attacker. But to his cost he knew gangs of this type would not stop at throwing him in the horse trough. That humiliation would not satisfy them. Their blood lust would drive them on, kicking and punching him until he was unconscious. It had happened to him before.

The apprentices spread out to block his escape.

'Where be those fine words now, preacher?' their leader scoffed, and made a grab for Peter's collar.

Peter sidestepped and hit out at the apprentice, only to receive a blow to his head which made his ears ring. Another apprentice flung his arms round Peter's torso from behind and trapped his arms at his sides. The leader's face loomed before him, and he smashed his fist into Peter's nose.

'Step back or I'll slit your gizzard!' Japhet's voice rang out and Peter saw the tip of his brother's sword pressed to his assailant's throat. 'And tell your friend to release the preacher, if you value your life.'

The leading apprentice's heavy features twisted with fear. 'Let 'im go.'

Peter was released and he staggered to his brother's side, blood streaming from his nose. Japhet waited until the other apprentices had backed away before he withdrew his sword. A breathless constable, summoned by William, arrived on the scene.

'What's going on here? Disturbing the King's peace and threatening others with a sword is an offence for the Magistrate to decide.'

'Don't be a fool, man,' Japhet snapped. 'These apprentices were accosting my brother. How else was I to stop them?'

William stepped forward to intervene. 'It is as my nephew says. The apprentices were spoiling for a fight.'

The constable did not attempt to follow the fleeing apprentices. His stare was accusing upon Peter. 'You lay preachers get the crowds more riled than an 'anging. These troublemakers be your nephews then?' The constable scowled at William, unimpressed by the expensive cloth of his clothes. 'Jus' 'cos they be gentlemen don't mean they bain't broke the law. They be disturbin' the King's peace.'

'I am sure it is all a misunderstanding.' William pressed a silver crown into the constable's hand. 'You have my word that my nephew will not preach in Bodmin again.'

The constable tapped his cudgel against Japhet's chest and Japhet had to bite down the desire to retaliate. 'This bain't the first disturbance you've caused. There were some dispute over a card game if I remember last winter. Caused 'alf the furniture in a tavern to get broken. The landlord put in a complaint.'

'I was in Truro all last winter,' Japhet responded. 'You must be mistaken. I acted today to save my brother from a beating, knowing that my uncle had already gone to call for the watch.'

'Clearly you are diligent in your duties, constable,' William declared. 'We have but stayed in Bodmin overnight and are about to continue our journey. I must rejoin my ship in a few days. Captain William Loveday of Trevowan at your service, sir. My nephews will give you no further trouble. We leave within the hour.'

The constable's gaze flickered over Peter, and William feared his nephew may yet be arrested.

'The place for sermons be in a church,' the constable stated. 'Decent folk don't take kindly to being condemned as sinners and the like when they be going about their business. I want your word there'll be no more preaching in this town.'

'I cannot deny people the salvation of the Lord.'

'Peter!' William warned.

'Let him enjoy the comforts of the prison and a day in the stocks.' Japhet rounded on his brother. 'It might bring him to his senses.'

'The same could be said of you, Japhet.' William lost his patience. 'Though what your poor mother will make of this I shudder to think.' He fixed both his nephews with a stare which would have frozen the blood of any dissenting officer or sailor on a vessel he commanded.

The constable glared at the two brothers. 'I got 'ee two marked. I never forget a face. If there be any more trouble in Bodmin from either of you, it will be prison, and this incident will also be brought against you.'

Japhet shifted uncomfortably. He *had* been in the fight last winter mentioned by the constable and was now eager to be gone before the constable decided to arrest him. 'Uncle William is right, Peter.' Japhet tipped his hat to the constable. 'I had no intention of creating a disturbance, but clearly I could not allow my brother to be beaten by the apprentices.'

Peter continued to look as though he would martyr himself for his beliefs. Lisette had watched the events from the

235

safety of a shop doorway and ran across the street to proclaim, 'It is all my fault. If we had not come to Bodmin to buy a mare, none of this would have happened. I should never have come to England. I bring nothing but trouble and shame to those who would help me.' She burst into tears.

'Are you happy now, Peter?' William raged. 'Has not Lisette suffered enough?'

'I never intended that Lisette would feel responsible.' Peter was appalled. 'Dear lady, your pardon.' He turned to the constable. 'I will not preach in Bodmin again.'

'Then get on your way,' the constable grunted, but continued to regard Japhet. 'I know your face well an' truly now. Next time you cause trouble in this town, you'll be up before the Magistrate, and it will take the King himself to stop your imprisonment.'

'I should have let them throw you in the horse trough, brother.' Japhet watched the constable strut away, slapping his cudgel against the palm of his hand in a gesture of self-importance and intimidation. 'It's time you learned to defend yourself. At least carry a dagger. How can any Loveday not know how to use a sword?'

'The Lord will protect me,' Peter replied.

'The Lord has better things to do than protect fools,' William declared. 'I would never have allowed you to join our party if I thought you would act in this manner. It is not the conduct of a gentleman, especially when a lady is present.'

Lisette was enjoying the attention of the men and, aware of Peter's interest in her, could not help defending him. 'I am sure Peter intended no harm, William. It was those dreadful young men. And Japhet was so brave to go to his aid. A man who knows how to wield a sword is so dashing.'

William glared at Peter. 'Japhet is right in that. You should learn how to defend yourself. Next time you may not escape so lightly. Now if you would escort Lisette back to the inn where we are staying. I have some business of my own to attend upon.'

Lisette pouted. 'Could I not come with you?'

'It would not be appropriate. I learned last night that a naval officer and friend whom I served with for many years is dying. He retired to Bodmin.' William smiled indulgently. 'Peter will take care of you. I shall return to the inn in an hour or so.'

'I am at your service.' Peter blushed, and bowed to Lisette.

She had been happy with William, and again Japhet and Peter had ruined it. Why had William abandoned her to the company of this pompous and callow man? It was too vexing. She thought herself accomplished at gauging men's moods, and William had not been unsusceptible to her guile. Yet he could distance himself from her just when she believed he was finding her irresistible. Was it because of the difference in their ages? Despite the kiss, did William see himself as her protector, and a family member? A man with such ethics would not be easy to seduce.

She smiled at Peter. It would be amusing to flirt with him when he had shown an interest in her. Peter was naïve where women were concerned and so different from his rakehell brother.

'You and Japhet are not alike. God's work is clearly important to you.'

'I would be like my father.'

He could be so pompous she could not resist taunting him. 'But was not Joshua like Japhet in his younger days? Should not a man experience life before he can guide others away from sin?'

'Temptation is offered to us by the devil. Godlessness results in anarchy. As is happening in France today.'

'I do not wish to speak of my country.' Lisette pulled her

arm from his and walked briskly ahead.

Peter groaned and ran after her. 'Your pardon, Lisette. I have offended you. I am a clod – an imbecile. I forgot how much you suffered.'

'Do not speak of it. I forbid it.' She covered her face with her hands and turned away from him.

'Of course. How can I make amends?' He did not attempt to touch her, but there was anguish in his voice.

She glanced over her shoulder. 'You must devise a way to entertain me until William returns. Does nothing of interest happen in this town?'

'If I had my guitar I could play for you.'

'I did not know you were so talented. I adore music.' She again took his arm and smiled up at him. 'I am happy that you do not regard it as a sin.'

'The guitar was given to Japhet and myself one Christmas by Uncle Edward and he paid for a tutor for us both. Japhet had no patience to learn. He preferred to strut about practising his swordplay. I used to enjoy playing, though in recent years I have not done so. It is a frivolous pursuit.'

'If you have a talent for such music, is that not a gift from God?' she taunted.

Peter hesitated, his eyes bright with adoration when he finally added, 'Perhaps that is so. I could play for you at Trevowan, if you permit it.'

'That would be most pleasant.' He was a handsome man and it would be entertaining to encourage his attentions. With William at sea, she would be bored at Trevowan without someone to admire her.

Chapter Thirteen

The first week of April was mild and the spring sunshine turned the hills to emerald. The Lovedays were cramped into two coaches as they travelled to Lord Fetherington's home, Pengarth. The hedgerows were coloured with the first leaf buds and around their roots early violets were emerging. Above them yellow lamb's tails danced on hazel branches, and rooks circled and bickered in treetops as they inspected last year's nests.

Elspeth leaned forward to peer up at the sky, which was clear except for a few wispy clouds. 'It will be a fine day's hunting tomorrow if the weather holds. Lord Fetherington's pack is the finest in the county and I will be able to put Eglantine through her paces. She seems in fine form; the Rashleighs treated her well.'

She rapped Edward on the knee with her cane. He had dozed through most of the journey. 'You do not do enough hunting, Brother.'

Edward frowned. He had worries at the yard and this visit was ill-timed. 'For some of us there is more to life than the hunt, Elspeth.'

Amelia said, 'You work too hard, Edward. Our friends have been neglected this winter. Though of course Adam's wedding has put us in an awkward position.'

Edward did not like the recrimination in his wife's voice.

239

'Our friends will have to accept my son's marriage – as I have done.'

Amelia sat tight-lipped. Her love for Edward had been tested in the last six months and she found herself on guard against the next unseemly conduct which would rock her sensibilities.

'I look forward most to the dancing.' Lisette hugged herself with pleasure. 'Such a pity that Meriel could not attend.' She glanced at St John, who sat opposite her and who showed no sign of displeasure that his wife was absent.

Amelia nodded. 'One cannot be too careful at such a time. I hope that Meriel was not too disappointed, St John.'

'Dr Chegwidden is adamant that she must take no exertion or she could lose the child.' St John shrugged. Meriel had been furious at missing the weekend, protesting she would take every care not to tire herself.

Elspeth gave a deprecating sniff. 'It surprises me that a woman from such hardy stock has such a delicate constitution. She could have lost Rowena, coming to term at eight months.'

'That was due to an accident,' Amelia reminded her. 'The poor woman fell down the stairs.'

'Then for once that bumbling fool Chegwidden is right.' Elspeth looked over the top of her pince-nez at St John. 'If her constitution is so fragile that she finds it impossible to tend the fowls, a jolting coach ride could see her lose the baby.'

'That is exactly what I told her.' St John leaned his elbow on the window sill and covered his mouth with his fingers to hide his satisfaction. Meriel could have lost fifty or a hundred guineas in her passion for gaming this weekend. He could put that stake money to better use. And since the pregnancy her moods had been more irascible than ever. He avoided her company in the Dower House because each time they saw each other they quarrelled. The freedom from her complaints and demands this weekend would bring was a welcome respite.

Their pace slowed as they entered the elm-lined drive to Pengarth. Coaches pulled by four horses in sparkling harnesses paraded sedately towards Lord Fetherington's country home. Before the grey stone house was reached the drive divided and the barking from his Lordship's pack of hounds proclaimed the direction of the kennels and stables.

When the coaches turned beneath the stone arch of the gatehouse into the flagstoned courtyard, excited passengers shouted greetings to other arrivals. Mud-splattered coachmen clung to horses' bridles. The animals sweated and snorted with impatience after travelling across half the county, and were eager to bury their muzzles in nosebags of oats. Liveried footmen staggered bow-legged under the weight of their masters' valises, and harassed maids fussed around their mistresses' trailing skirts to ensure that they were lifted clear of lingering puddles.

Pengarth had been built three hundred years ago as a fortified manor. It was dominated by the central great hall and its vaulted church-style roof and turreted watchtower. A wing with tall mullioned windows had been added in Elizabethan times and in the last year of Queen Anne's reign nearly eighty years ago, Lord Fetherington's grandfather had added a three-gabled wing with casement windows, the date 1714 inscribed below the central eaves. The house enclosed the courtyard on three sides, the gatehouse and wall forming a square.

The first Loveday coach halted before the jutting porch, the roof of which, supported by four columns, protected travellers from the weather. Joshua and his family, including Hannah and Oswald, were behind them.

Lisette was excited, calling and waving to acquaintances in other vehicles.

Elspeth frowned at her. 'I do hope you will act with decorum, Lisette. We do not want a return to your past behaviour.'

Lisette smiled sweetly, ignoring Elspeth and Amelia, her gaze upon William, Edward and St John seated opposite. 'But am I not a changed woman?'

When no one answered, William smiled at her. 'Your manners and conduct have been exquisite.'

'Exemplary conduct for one week does not make up for the trials we have endured in the past,' Elspeth returned, but her manner had mellowed towards the Frenchwoman since Eglantine had been restored to her. She amended, 'However, we are delighted that Lisette now feels settled and happier within our family. And, yes, her conduct has improved.'

'Praise indeed, Sister.' Edward glanced at Amelia, concerned that she was looking pale. She had spoken little during the journey.

William had alighted and held up his hand to assist Lisette and Elspeth from the coach. St John alighted from the far side and hailed the Hon. Percy Fetherington, who was talking to another friend outside the porch.

Edward touched his wife's hand. 'You have been very quiet. You are not sickening for something, my love?'

'I am well.' There was a tension in Amelia which had been growing in recent weeks.

'This weekend will do you good. Lisette's conduct must have been a strain on you.'

There was the glitter of pain in her eyes. 'Can you so easily dismiss that this is the first time that we shall meet many of our neighbours since Adam's wedding? Neighbours who did not attend because they did not approve of his bride. How are we to face them?'

'Adam is not here. Our neighbours are our friends.' He

squeezed her hand. 'You will meet them with your usual charm and fortitude.'

She drew her hand away. 'I feel deeply shamed by Adam's marriage. It condones a morality I was not brought up to accept.'

Edward was shocked. Troubles in the shipyard and the worry of meeting outstanding loans had absorbed all his attention in recent weeks. He had not realised how deeply Amelia felt. He was still angry at Adam's marriage but the deed was done and the best must be made of it. This was a side of Amelia he had not realised she possessed, and he was annoyed by her attitude. He expected her support, not her condemnation.

'You voiced no such concern when I explained the circumstances of St John's marriage before we were wed.'

'It was a matter I had to consider, but they had been married for some time and Meriel had been accepted by your friends after Rowena's birth. This time it is different. I have to face the censure of people who have become my friends.'

'If they are true friends they should understand your feelings,' Edward reasoned.

Her eyes flashed with anger. 'How little you know how women will gossip in society. Some will gloat at my discomfort. Others will judge that I have failed as your wife, unable to instil in your sons any respect for decency.'

'I'd like to hear them say it to my face,' Edward snapped.

'You will not be the one to hear it. It will be done behind raised fans and with sly looks and whispers.' Amelia's voice trembled. 'You were one of Cornwall's most eligible widowers. There was many a matron put out that you brought a foreigner from London into your home, and had not considered their widowed sister, niece or daughter.'

'And having been surrounded by matchmaking mamas for twenty years, why do you think I fell in love with and married you? It was your humour and courage I admired. You have always been my abiding strength. This outburst is unlike you, Amelia. And unworthy of you.'

'Unworthy of me!'

He cut across her words before she could go on. 'Yes, unworthy. The Lovedays remain united no matter what befalls us. I can understand that a woman as gently reared as yourself would be shocked by my sons' behaviour. They are strong-willed men. In the country these things happen and are accepted more than in society in London.' He hoped his words would placate her to ensure a peaceful weekend.

Amelia hung her head but there was a harsh edge to her voice. 'You think I am being foolish, but I cannot help how I feel. And I fear that Richard and Rafe's morals will be endangered.'

Edward was outraged by her words. 'Are you suffering from some malady? Clearly the strain of the last year has become too much. Rafe is but a toddler.' Edward was unprepared for the fury in her eyes.

'But Richard is not. He will soon be fourteen. It is an impressionable age. And he dotes on Adam. He is a midshipman because of Adam's influence. And now there is a war with France. What if he is killed?'

She alighted from the coach without waiting for Edward's assistance and, after greeting their host, went straight to their room. When Amelia did not appear after an hour Edward lost patience with her. He had never suspected her of being a prude for she was a passionate woman. Her attitude disturbed him.

When Edward entered their bedchamber he found Amelia sitting on the window seat staring down at the formal knot garden. She had been crying and held a crumpled lace handkerchief to her brow. He sighed. He loved her too much to see her so hurt.

244

'Amelia, your outburst surprised me. My family has always been a troublesome one. I did try to warn you before we wed.' He put his arms around her, feeling the tension in her figure. 'The Lovedays weathered the scandal of Meriel and we have survived near ruin and the rumours which could have destroyed us. All that you took in your stride.' He kissed her hair. 'Do not let this spoil the weekend. I have been neglecting you. Perhaps later in the year we can go to London to visit your old friend. We will attend the play and the opera, visit a dressmaker to buy you new gowns in the latest fashion. We will do all the things you miss by living in Cornwall.'

'I would like that,' Amelia leaned back against him, 'especially to visit your sister Margaret. She was a good friend to me.'

Edward laughed. 'Without Margaret's incessant matchmaking, we would not have met. And you have brought so much happiness into my life, my darling.'

Amelia returned his kiss. She loved Edward. He was a passionate man, but he had brought up the twins without a mother. Many a man would have married to provide a mother for his sons and a comfort for himself. Edward had loved his first wife, Marie, and wanted no other to replace her until he had met Amelia. That made him special. Edward could not be responsible for his sons' and nephew's lack of morality when he was such a moral man himself. That was what she loved most about him.

St John endured the hour of Mozart's music played by the string quartet. He was eager for the gaming to begin after supper. Twice a young blonde woman in front turned and smiled. Japhet, seated beside him, nudged his arm.

'You have an admirer. A pretty young thing. If she were not so obviously taken with you, I would pursue her myself.'

'Then you have no interest in Gwendolyn Druce? I notice you've barely spoken to her.' St John allowed his gaze to travel over the slender form of the woman.

'Gwen is dangerously unattached.' Japhet stroked his upper lip. 'It will do her reputation no good to be linked with me.'

'It is unlike you to show such consideration where women are concerned.'

Japhet glared at him, then chuckled and winked when the blonde woman again turned to observe St John over the top of her fan. 'That is Mistress Purity Newbold, wife to Major Newbold, currently garrisoned in Scotland. She is visiting her mother living in St Blazey. Apparently Mrs Newbold cannot abide the cold weather. Now that is an invitation to warm her bed.'

'And what of the mother?' St John was sceptical. Purity Newbold was pretty, with a soft feminine manner, unlike Meriel with her temper tantrums and harsh demands.

'She slipped on the flagstones on their arrival. She's sprained her ankle and has taken to her bed.'

The music ended and supper was announced by the liveried major-domo. Purity Newbold appeared at St John's side and he offered her his arm to escort her in to dine.

'You have a kind and friendly face.' She spoke in a breathless whisper. 'With Mama taken so poorly, I know no one here except the Fetheringtons, and they are busy with so many guests.'

'Then allow me to be of service in any way that I can,' St John offered, delighted that Meriel was not present to hinder his interest in this lovely woman.

'I would like that very much indeed.' The invitation in her eyes was blatant as they conversed whilst dining.

When the card tables had been set out, St John was nevertheless reluctant to miss an opportunity of playing for high stakes with his friends. Yet Purity was entrancing and he suggested, 'Shall we partner each other at whist?'

She hesitated. 'People will talk as I have spent so long in your company over supper. Perhaps later . . .' Her gaze locked with his, and the corner of her mouth lifted in an inviting smile. 'I trust I can count on your discretion. I am a married woman.'

'And I a married man.'

'Then we understand each other, Mr Loveday. My room is at the end of the corridor on the second floor of the Elizabethan wing. Shall we say a quarter to midnight. We will not meet again until then.'

He raised her fingers to his lips and he felt his blood quicken in expectancy of two nights in her bed. When he entered the anteroom set aside for the men intent on serious gambling, Japhet winked at St John.

'From your satisfied smile I would say you have made a conquest. Time you broke those chains Meriel cast upon you. You married too young to confine yourself to one woman for the rest of your life.'

St John laughed. 'And if my luck holds at cards, I will know that fortune is smiling on me.'

St John's evening met all his expectations. The next morning the weather was dry and sunny for the hunt. The party of riders were in high spirits as they partook of the stirrup cup. St John exchanged secret smiles with Purity but diplomatically devoted his time to Hannah as Oswald was not hunting. Japhet and Gwen were laughing together, but Lady Anne Druce, who would be following the hunt with some of the older ladies in a carriage, repeatedly called Gwendolyn to her side. She was determined to keep her daughter and Japhet apart.

Japhet then flirted with Barbara Keyne, a vivacious young brunette who had been virtually ignored by her husband of two years, Sir Arthur Keyne. Sir Arthur, short and portly, though only a few years older than his wife, already had the jaded air of a reprobate. He also had a reputation for cornering any unattended woman and forcing his attentions on them. He was a lecher without thought or feelings for his victim and Japhet despised him.

Lady Keyne, however, Japhet found captivating. Sir Arthur had inherited his title from his father who had died a year ago and they lived ten miles from the Rectory.

Japhet caught sight of Peter astride the bay mare he had recently purchased. Unlike the other Lovedays, Peter was only an average horseman. He had been content until last summer to walk the highways as a lay preacher. The mare had meant he could journey further afield. Usually, he scorned the pleasures of the hunt as a sin of bloodlust and idle pursuit. This morning he was smiling, his mare close to Lisette on her grey palfrey.

Japhet grinned at seeing Lisette flirting with his younger brother. Twice Peter laughed, his dour manner discarded in her company. Lisette was the last woman Japhet thought would have attracted Peter. It was obvious to Japhet that beneath her innocent façade there was a wanton streak, though Peter would only see the innocence, and her suffering in France would make her appear vulnerable and fragile. Japhet nearly laughed aloud. Lisette may appear delicate as a will-o'-the-wisp, but she was artful and deceptive. There was pure iron running through her. It seemed she had finally learned that tantrums would not serve her with his family. Instead she had resorted to guile.

Yet even as Lisette encouraged Peter with her fluttering lashes and the way she leaned in closer towards him, Japhet did not miss the covert glances she cast towards William Loveday. His uncle, who was surrounded by his brothers and other men of his own age, was laughing and enjoying himself.

Yet twice William's gaze was drawn towards Lisette. Was that sadness or regret in his eyes?

Japhet was amused. That minx had also snared his uncle's heart, Japhet would place a hundred guineas on it. His eyes narrowed, no longer amused. Lisette was encouraging the attention of both his brother and uncle. Peter was saintly and innocent. William was bold and courageous in battle but, despite his years, still naïve where women were concerned. What mischief was she up to?

The huntsman sounded his horn. The hounds milling around as the horses' hoofs moved in unison away from Pengarth, their noses already dredging the ground for scent of a fox.

Japhet edged his Arab mare towards Lady Keyne but found Edward Loveday was now talking to her. As Japhet drew near, his uncle raised his high-crowned beaver to Barbara, saying, 'I am sorry to hear that your mother-in-law is ill. Do give her my regards and wishes for a rapid recovery.' There was the faintest furrowing to Edward's brow as he wheeled Rex to ride beside Amelia.

Gwen clattered past without looking in Japhet's direction to join the lead riders, and Elspeth was behind her. The first fox was drawn in a cover a mile from Pengarth. Already the riders had spread out. St John and Purity Newbold were galloping neck and neck amongst the first dozen riders. Peter and Lisette were falling towards the rear, and both had declined to jump a hedgerow and steep bank. The palfrey, for all its showiness, was not bred as a hunter. Lisette looked intent on catching up with William, and Peter was struggling to keep up with her gallop.

Japhet was an accomplished horseman but an indifferent hunter. Though his injuries from the whip had healed, some of the deeper wounds ached if he rode for too long. He had made a wager of ten guineas with Percy that the first fox would not be killed within an hour. He decided against an impulse to catch up with Gwen and adjusted his pace to stay beside Barbara Keyne. She responded to his flirting and they were falling further behind the other riders, with her husband a half-mile ahead of them.

'I do believe your horse looks to be coming up lame.' Japhet reached across to hold her bridle and they halted.

'She does not appear lame.' Lady Keyne was smiling and did not pull away. The horses moved closer together and Japhet leaned across to kiss her.

The kiss did not end until their horses moved apart. Barbara sighed and her eyes were heavy-lidded with desire. 'But it would be ill-conceived to continue if my mare is showing sign of lameness.'

He dismounted and examined the foreleg. When he looked up at her his eyes glittered and his voice was low and suggestive. 'There is no swelling but in my opinion it would be wise to return to Pengarth. Permit me to escort you, Lady Keyne.'

'How inconsiderate of me to deprive you of a day's sport. The house will be all but deserted. Only one or two of the guests remained behind.'

Japhet grinned. 'Then I must offer my services to ensure you are entertained. The hunt will not return for another four hours.'

'Four hours alone in your company.' Barbara laughed and wheeled her mare around. 'You have a certain reputation, Japhet Loveday.'

'Which I always aim to live up to, Lady Keyne.'

'Then I shall have high expectations of being most thoroughly entertained.'

After four hours in the field and the successful killing of a fox, St John was looking forward to another evening of gaming and the pleasure Purity Newbold had again promised him. The dancing did not attract him, but it would be uncivil not to partner at least three of the ladies. Another party of guests had just arrived and St John hoped that there would be some heavy gamblers amongst them. The stakes had been too low for his taste last evening and he had won only twenty guineas.

The dancing was in the old hall with its soaring hammer-beamed roof. Huge tapestries of ancient Greek battles brightened the walls, and the musicians played in the minstrels' gallery above their heads. Four wooden chandeliers, larger than cartwheels and each holding forty candles, were suspended on chains from the vaulted ceiling. They haloed the dancers in their silks and satins and cast long shadows into the furthest corners of the hall. The candle flames reflected like hundreds of cats' eyes in the women's diamonds. The hall was draughty and although at some time in its history two marble fireplaces and chimneys had been added to warm it, the burning logs gave off little heat.

Only a few of the older women continued to wear powdered wigs. Lady Fetherington wore a wig of horsehair and hemp wool covered in powdered paste which rose in a dome twelve inches above her brow. It wobbled precarious as aspic as she walked. Black silk patches still remained popular and one woman wore so many she looked stricken by an outbreak of the black death. And it seemed nothing could part Elspeth from her favourite headdress of a turban of gold cloth.

St John partnered Lady Traherne, Purity and Hannah before he felt it expedient to join the gaming. 'You cannot abandon the women yet,' Hannah admonished. 'You should ask Gwen to dance and rescue her from that dreadful man Lady Anne is blatantly encouraging.'

St John studied the couch where Lady Anne and Lady

Traherne were seated. Gwen was perched on the end beside her sister, looking bored, whilst a slight-framed man with a hooked nose expounded his views on some topic.

'Where's Japhet? He's usually Gwen's gallant knight in these matters.'

'Lady Anne is discouraging his attentions. And Japhet is wrong to have given so much of his time to Gwen. He is damaging her reputation. He should either offer for her, or not seek her out.'

St John guffawed. 'I can't see Lady Anne accepting Japhet as a son-in-law.'

'Gwen is old enough to wed without her mother's consent,' Hannah reminded him. 'She came into her inheritance from her grandmother last year. Personally, I think Gwen would make Japhet the perfect bride. She has a steadying influence on him. Mama had high hopes for the match a few months ago. Then Japhet took off on his travels. He cannot expect Gwen to wait for him for ever.'

'Where is my irrepressible cousin? I'm surprised he is not flirting with every available woman.'

Hannah raised a dark brow. 'Japhet is otherwise engaged. Mama was looking for him earlier. I learned that he returned from the hunt early with Barbara Keyne. Neither of them has appeared since.'

St John chuckled. 'The old devil. I should have guessed. He will not miss out on the gaming – no wench will keep him from that.'

'There he is.' Hannah sighed with relief. 'I have twice had to dissuade Mama from going to his room in case he was entertaining Lady Keyne there.'

Japhet was standing on the edge of the dancers, glaring across the room at the man who was conversing with Gwendolyn Druce. St John turned to Hannah. 'Who is that man with Gwen?'

Hannah shrugged. 'Some naval lieutenant, I believe. The grandson of Admiral Beaumont, who is a friend of Lord Fetherington.'

The lieutenant had bowed over Gwen's hand and, with a prod from her mother, Gwen rose to partner him in the next dance. To St John's amazement Japhet marched across the hall and cut between the lieutenant and Gwen. He took Gwen's hand and whisked her away before Lady Anne or the lieutenant could protest.

'What the devil are you doing talking to that pompous ass?' Japhet demanded.

'How dare you be so rude?' Gwen snapped. 'He has called several times on the family this winter.'

'Do you know who he is?' Japhet was incensed but had to keep his voice low as the dance progressed.

'Of course I know who he is. He is a lieutenant in the revenue service, the grandson of Admiral Beaumont and of impeccable lineage, according to Mama.'

'He is the man responsible for Adam being court-martialled.' They held hands and circled sedately before the dance took Gwen away from him. He continued to glare at her until she returned to his side in the set. 'Beaumont is the man Adam duelled with. He hates Adam. How can you encourage him?'

'That was some years ago, Japhet. And I do not encourage him.' Gwen was flushed with anger. Her chestnut hair was piled high in an attractive new style. The pale green silk of her gown, cut low and almost off her shoulder, revealed the creamy smoothness of her skin. The skirts were narrower this season and fewer petticoats worn, making her figure trim and provocative. 'He is pleasant enough company.'

'Then why were you looking so bored?' he challenged as the dance ended.

'Is this gentleman annoying you, Miss Druce?' Lieutenant

Beaumont hovered at her side.

Gwen smiled at her rescuer. 'Not any longer, Lieutenant Beaumont.' She turned her back on Japhet and walked away.

Hannah had also been watching the interchange and had seen Gwen's admirer head towards her brother. When Japhet spun on his heel to follow them, Hannah grabbed his arm. 'Japhet, let them go. You have no right to goad Gwen as you do.'

His eyes flashed as he stared down at her. 'How can she encourage that arrogant ass? That is the officer who boarded *Pegasus* on her return from France and wanted to confiscate her for carrying French spies and contraband. He hates Adam.'

William Loveday joined them. 'Japhet, your conduct is unbecoming. You have distressed your mother. You will make matters worse by antagonising Beaumont.'

Reluctantly Japhet agreed, but added with menace, 'I don't like the way Lady Anne pushes Gwen at every eligible man. She deserves better than someone like Beaumont.' He glared at the couple, who were now dancing together.

Hannah took Japhet's arm, seeking to diffuse his anger. 'Since my handsome brother does not see fit to ask his ageing sister to dance, it seems I must ask him. I am weary of keeping the matrons company. I observe many rakes here this evening, and would not dishonour Oswald by dancing with them. I rely on my kin to partner me and find they abandon me.'

Japhet led her to a line of dancers. 'I should not neglect you. It cannot be easy for you when Oswald has been so ill. You always loved to dance. Has Peter also neglected you?'

'When was Peter ever a dancer? He has two left feet and thinks I should be content to sit with the matrons since that is now my station in life.'

'I could never think of you as a matron. You are too full

of life.' Japhet dragged his gaze from Gwen and her partner and nodded across the room at another couple. 'Peter is dancing with Lisette. He is even smiling. I fear our brother is smitten.'

'Have you seen how Uncle William also watches Lisette?' Hannah arched her brows. 'Lisette has been pursued by admirers all weekend, though she would be wise to keep her distance from lechers such as Lord Fetherington and Sir Arthur Keyne. I thought two of Percy's friends would come to blows over her during the hunt. It was fortunate Uncle Edward or Amelia did not see the way Lisette encouraged them.'

'The woman is trouble. Adam should have left her in France.'

The dance ended and Japhet watched Gwen laugh at something her companion said. His expression darkened.

Hannah tapped her brother sharply on the arm with her fan. 'Japhet, if your intentions are not honourable towards Gwen, you must forget her. I would not like to see Gwen hurt. She is not another like Barbara Keyne.'

He stiffened with affront. 'Does nothing escape you? It is Beaumont who angers me. A man like that could never make her happy.' He led Hannah back to her seat and left the dancing to divert his anger by gambling. Several guests were gathered round the tables and Percy Fetherington beckoned him to join them.

An hour later he had lost heavily and threw down his cards to leave.

Percy laughed. 'The cards were not with you this night, Japhet. Or is your mind elsewhere? The lovely Gwen is much taken with Lieutenant Beaumont.'

'What is that supposed to mean?' Japhet scowled. 'Take care you do not sully the reputation of a pure and honourable lady.'

'One would think you were smitten to hear you talk so,' Percy grinned.

Japhet took a step towards Percy. 'I am a guest in your house, Percy, or I would take exception to your remark.' He shrugged, and his shirt tightened across the raised ridges of the scars on his back. It had not been the easiest of winters. He had never felt so discontented with his life.

Lisette was enjoying herself. She was admired and fêted by several gentlemen. Her gowns and jewels matched the splendour of any woman present and her title gave her precedence over most of them. Yet compared to many of the younger women, she was dressed demurely. Although she too had discarded the hoops from beneath her pink gown so that it settled more revealingly over her hips, her neckline was decorous, the sleeves tight and ending at the wrist in a frilled ruff. It was the dress of an adolescent and her dark hair was teased into soft curls around her face. In the candlelight she looked no more than fifteen.

The constant attention of Peter was beginning to annoy her. Whilst he was close William stayed away. William had not danced with her this evening. The only woman he had led on the dance floor was Amelia, and soon after he had retired to a smoking parlour with half a dozen of the older men. It took the edge from her pleasure. When he had not appeared after another half-hour, she slipped away from the dancers to waylay William when he left the smoking parlour. Surely he would not stay there all evening. Supper would be served soon and she would insist that he took her for refreshments.

Sir Arthur saw her leave unaccompanied. This was the chance for which he had been waiting. He had been interested in Lisette all weekend. Apart from a brief flirtation with her, when she had been distracted by Basil Bracewaite showering her with compliments, he had found no chance to get her alone.

Away from the vastness of the old hall, Pengarth was a warren of dimly lit passages. As he turned a corner, Lisette was ahead of him. Then a figure of a man stepped out from behind a pillar and took her hand to draw her into the shadows. Sir Arthur cursed the bad luck which had denied him his prey. He paused, listening to their whispers. The man's voice was pleading and this was answered by a soft giggle from Lisette.

Sir Arthur edged forward to observe the couple and was surprised to recognise the preacher Peter Loveday holding her in his arms before he kissed her with a tormented savagery.

Lisette did not protest. Sir Arthur moistened his lips with his tongue; voyeurism was a vice he could rarely indulge. The kiss was ardent, the preacher's hand hesitant before he finally captured her breast. Lisette's eyes were open and staring into the face of the young man. When the preacher finally broke apart, she slapped his cheek so hard that his head snapped back.

'How dare you use me so?' she hissed.

Peter Loveday hung his head but caught her hand to press it to his lips. 'Forgive me, sweet Lisette. I adore you. I cannot sleep for dreaming of you in my arms.'

'You would compromise me, Peter. That is unforgivable.'

'How can I regain your favour?' His voice rose in desperation. 'You cannot cast my affections aside. I shall be in torment.'

Her answer was so low Sir Arthur could not hear it. Peter Loveday stepped away from the column and disappeared into the passage leading to the Queen Anne wing. There was a rustle of silk as Lisette smoothed the folds of her skirts. Sir Arthur moved quickly to block her exit. He placed a hand against the pillar to bar her escape and the other slid around her waist.

'You did right, my beauty, to send away so callow a youth. I can show you so much more pleasure.'

His wet lips clamped down on hers. Lisette struggled, repelled by his touch. His large hands crushed her, bruising her breasts as they kneaded and pinched. She bit the offending lips and he drew back cursing, but still held her tight.

She cried out, 'Let me alone.'

'You'll not escape me.' He spat blood from his mouth and again ground his lips on to hers. She could feel the ridges of the pillar as it pressed painfully into her shoulders and hips and there was a rush of cold air as his hand hoisted her skirt.

Lisette was terrified. This was a return to the nightmare which haunted her. This man would make her a victim. She wriggled and managed to jerk up one knee into his groin. With a harsh cry he staggered back from her. At the same time there was the sound of a footfall and Lisette saw William approaching.

She ran into his arms, sobbing and nearly hysterical. It was several moments before William could calm her. In that time Sir Arthur slipped away unnoticed.

'I was attacked,' she finally calmed enough to say. 'Some dreadful man forced his attentions upon me. I was so frightened, William. If you had not come along . . .'

'Who is this man? Where did it happen?'

'There by the pillar. I do not know the man. There are so many new faces and it was dark.'

William put her from him to run to where she pointed. 'There is no one there.'

'You saved me, William. Always you are there when I need you.' She again threw her arms around him.

He could feel her trembling. It took all his willpower to

step back. 'Your hair is dishevelled and there is blood on your lip. I will get Amelia to tend you.'

'No. Amelia or Edward must not learn of this. They will blame me. They will say that I am bad.'

'It was not your fault.'

'They will not see that. They will see only that I have caused more trouble. I cannot go back to the guests. It was like those terrible days in France . . .' Tears splashed down her cheeks. 'I cannot face anyone. I must go to my room. Take me there, William. I am scared to go alone.'

'Lord Fetherington must be told of this outrage. His hospitality has been abused.'

Lisette shook her head. 'I am frightened but unharmed. I want no fuss. I want to forget the incident and forget the nightmare which was my life in France.' She swayed and fell to the floor in a faint.

William lifted her in his arms. She weighed so little that he carried her with ease. He was torn between summoning a maid or woman to help her, and allowing her to recover in peace without further inquisition. There were servants' stairs nearby which led to the rooms the Lovedays had been given on the second floor. Hopefully he could get Lisette to her room without anyone seeing them.

The stairs were clear but on the landing he was forced to duck behind a lacquered cabinet when there were footsteps from the main stairs and Peter appeared and walked to his room.

Lisette had not moved and William began to fear that something was more seriously wrong with her than having just fainted. The only light in her bedchamber came from the moon streaming through the open curtains. He laid her on the bed gently. He stood back and gazed at her loveliness. She was so frail, and so heart-rendingly young, with the innocence of a cherub. His fists bunched. If he learned who had attacked her, he would beat the man to a pulp. The violence of his feelings shocked him. William had not been in a fisticuff fight for seventeen years, though as a younger man he had fought frequently.

Lisette's eyes opened. She held up her hand for him to take. 'I am safe now. Thank you, William. Did I faint? How foolish of me!'

'You have been very brave, my dear.' He took her hand and sat on the edge of the bed. 'You have had a bad fright.'

'It brought back such terrible memories.' She began to shake and sat up. 'Hold me, William. Make the nightmares go away.'

'I should call a maid. I will tell her you fainted from the exertion of dancing.'

She clung to him when he would have stood up. 'Do not leave me, William. I am not brave. I am frightened. Make me forget my fears. Make me forget all that is brutal and horrid in this world.' Her hands spread each side of his face and she kissed him, soft and hesitant at first, then her lips parted with deepening passion. Her lips moved along his jaw and her siren's breath lured and entrapped him. 'Love me, William. Show me that a man can love with honour and respect. Only you can chase away my terrors with gentleness and love.'

William would rather have sailed into the teeth of a hurricane than dishonour her. But the urging of her voice was mesmerising, playing upon the fantasy of his dreams. Her eyes were large and pleading as she lay back on the mattress, her arms outstretched to welcome him. 'Love me, William. Make me whole again.'

It was many years since William had surrendered to the wildness and passion of his Loveday blood. He could no more deny Lisette than he could deny his heritage.

Chapter Fourteen

Adam had made two more voyages to France. It was now mid-May and, following Squire Penwithick's latest instructions, Adam had been in France a week and had joined a group of royalists. He was disguised as a carpenter in simple homespun clothes and a blue kerchief tied above the open neck of his shirt. His dark hair hung loose around his shoulders.

He sat astride the apex of the wooden roof he was rebuilding after the house had been destroyed by fire the previous winter. The house was the last in a row along one side of a market square and from his vantage point Adam overlooked the residence of the provost marshal. The two-storey building surrounded a square courtyard. Two sentries guarded an outer gateway and two patrolled the grounds inside. There was also a sentry on duty by the main entrance to the house, which faced the market cross.

Some thirty prisoners were crammed into the provost marshal's cells. One of those men, Sir Gregory Kilmarthen, was an English spy whom Adam had been ordered to rescue. Kilmarthen's mother was French and he had worked with Penwithick from the start of the revolution.

As he worked on the roof Adam had been studying the sentries' patrols and timing their change of duty. During the day the guard was changed hourly and at night it was every two hours. The local group of royalists Adam had joined was led by Emile Lecroix and several of his men were prisoners with Kilmarthen. They hoped for reinforcements from other royalists in the district to effect a rescue, but none had arrived and their band of men numbered only nine.

Yet they dared not delay. It would mean Sir Gregory's death and he was Squire Penwithick's most trusted agent, who co-ordinated the network of English spies in Paris and northern France. Kilmarthen had devised the escape routes and organised the safe houses for those wishing to flee France. Without him three-quarters of Penwithick's spy network in France would collapse, and it would take months to re-establish. In France Kilmarthen adopted the guise of a ragged pedlar known only as Long Tom.

To protect his own family and identity, Adam was now known as Black Jack. Adam had never met Long Tom, but had liaised with various of his agents on the coast and respected the man's courage and integrity. Long Tom had been taken in an ambush, when he had been visiting a royalist guerrilla camp. Adam feared that the royalists had been tortured. Long Tom would die before he would betray any within his organisation, but if one of his own men had betrayed him, how long could Sir Gregory Kilmarthen hold out?

There was a cry from the far end of town and Adam saw a troop of soldiers marching through the street led by an officer on a grey Arab mare. The officer, in his blue and white uniform and tricolour sash, sat stiff-backed in the saddle, his manner arrogant. Adam scarcely noticed him; it was the reason for the escort which clenched his intestines with fear. Amidst the riders, the tall timbers of a guillotine swayed as it was drawn through the town on a wagon.

The executions would begin tomorrow. He had no

choice but to act tonight, with or without the royalist reinforcements.

In the middle of May St John travelled on market day to St Austell. Uncle William had provided the money to purchase a prime bull, and from his smuggling profits St John could afford to introduce some fresh blood into the dairy herd. His father had been impressed at St John's offer, and with Adam's relationship with Edward still cool, St John wanted to gain his father's favour. He was prepared to buy eight heifers if the price was right. Buying the cattle was also the excuse he needed to get away from Trevowan for two days. Purity Newbold had sent word that she would be in St Austell overnight. They had not managed a clandestine meeting for two weeks.

Since the last two smuggling runs had shown a substantial profit, St John no longer needed to reinvest all the profits in a future cargo. After purchasing the heifers, he would deposit the rest with a bank his family had no previous connection with. It would give him a greater independence and enable him to use his smuggling profits for his own pleasure, and not continually to shore up his family's precarious finances.

The morning market was packed with farmers selling their livestock and wares. He haggled over the price of four heifers, and when the farmer refused to meet his price, he declined to buy them. There was always Liskeard or Truro cattle markets, and his search for new livestock would again provide the excuse to leave his home and Meriel's constant complaints. She had become unbearable since her pregnancy. Chegwidden had insisted that her whims must be met, for any upset could be detrimental to her and the child's health.

On leaving the market St John was forced to step aside to avoid four urchins fighting over a penny which they had found in the street. One bumped into St John, who immediately closed his hand over his money pouch, fearful the street fight was a ruse for one of the lads to steal his money.

'Sorry, sir.' The lad scowled up at him for his hand had encountered St John's covering the pouch. The stench coming from the urchin's rags all but made him gag, and through the rends of the boy's shirt his flesh was patched with weeping sores. 'Didn't see 'ee there, sir.'

St John was in a mellow mood with the prospect of meeting Purity, and instead of accusing him of being a pickpocket, he clipped the lad's ear. 'Look where you are going in future.'

St John strode away and was hailed by Sir Hugh Portman, who emerged from a tobacconists. Sir Hugh flipped open a gold snuff box and tipped some on to his wrist to inhale it with a loud sniff. His eyes watered. 'Inferior stuff. Can't beat London for quality. These yokels don't have the knack of mixing the more exotic blends.' He offered the box to St John, who declined. 'Didn't reckon to find you in St Austell, St John.'

Sir Hugh lived on an estate three miles outside the town. He was an old friend of Sir Henry Traherne and a frequent visitor to the Hall, encouraged by Lady Anne, who hoped for a match between him and Gwendolyn. Sir Hugh was a plain man and something of a buffoon, but he was extremely wealthy.

'I was looking to buy some heifers,' St John replied. 'No luck, though. I shall try Liskeard next week.'

'Are you staying overnight?'

'Yes, I've other business to attend upon.'

'Capital, my dear fellow. Then you must join us this evening. I am staying with the Wentworth brothers, Frank and Clive. Both being bachelors, they enjoy an evening of cards every market day. They will be delighted if you join us. The more the merrier.'

'I am not acquainted with the Wentworth brothers.' St John was eager to get away since Purity would be waiting for him, though the offer was tempting: Sir Hugh was a poor player and played for high stakes.

'The Wentworths moved here six months ago from Plymouth. Old army family. Both made major before they were invalided out after over thirty years' service. Frank lost his arm. Clive's sight is failing him. It does not curb his passion for gambling though. The brothers wager on anything. Join us at eight. Can't miss their house. The Billet it's called. Just off the main street.'

'I will join you if I am able,' St John evaded, and made a hasty departure.

Purity was at the inn waiting for him. She was upset that she could not stay the night as her mother was becoming suspicious of her daughter's frequent travelling. 'We will have but two hours together, my love. Mama insisted that I return home by evening. She has threatened to write her displeasure to my husband that I am not her constant companion.'

'Then we must waste not one minute of those precious two hours.' St John began to undress her. 'I shall be at Liskeard market in nine days. Will you be able to get away to meet me in the town?'

'It will not be easy, but I shall endeavour.' She pulled at his clothes with impatient ardour. 'I cannot bear the longing of wanting you. Our meetings are so few.'

When Purity had been forced to leave, St John was not displeased. Her passion had been inexhaustible and now he anticipated a pleasurable and profitable evening of cards with the Wentworths.

A scruffy servant with a shaved head and half of one ear missing admitted St John and announced him with a military click of his heels. The room he was shown into was gloomy except for a central light over the large card table. Seven men beside Sir Hugh were seated around it, smoking and drinking port and brandy.

Sir Hugh rose to introduce St John to his hosts. The brothers were thickset with wide white side-whiskers and wore short military wigs. 'Major Frank Wentworth and Major Clive Wentworth. Mr St John Loveday of Trevowan.'

'At your service, gentlemen.' St John inclined his head to them and the other guests.

'Any relation to General Boniface Loveday?' Major Clive Wentworth squinted at him across the table. 'I wager you five guineas, Frank, old boy, that he is.'

St John bowed to the brothers. 'Then I fear you have lost your wager, sir. We are a naval family.'

'Outflanked yet again by the senior service,' Major Frank Wentworth guffawed. 'You will know Beaumont here, another naval man. Grandson to Admiral Algernon Beaumont, don't you know.'

St John tensed at the name and inclined his head stiffly towards the man who had duelled with his twin. That Beaumont was now an excise officer increased his distrust. He had avoided the man's company at Pengarth and now found it forced upon him. He felt a perverse need to put the officer in his place and observed, 'Mr Beaumont was at Pengarth when we stayed with Lord Fetherington. My uncle has since rejoined his ship, HMS *Neptune*. Do you not have a command, Mr Beaumont?'

'It is Lieutenant Beaumont. My command is the revenue cutter *Challenger*.'

'Not out about your business tonight, though,' St John taunted. 'The weather is calm and the sky clear – ideal for an intrepid smuggler.'

The lieutenant's eyes narrowed. 'We have patrolled every

night for four weeks. My men have earned a night's rest, especially as two nights ago we boarded the lugger *Hope*. We arrested the crew and confiscated her cargo. It is locked in the customs house. I would wipe out the despicable trade which is cheating our government of taxes.'

'Did I not hear that the crew escaped on the way to the gaol?' St John had heard the story from Harry that morning. The *Hope* was not a ship they recognised and he had wondered who had been running the cargo. After a hard winter, often fishermen in any village along the coast would risk an occasional run to prevent their families from starving.

A well-dressed gentleman in a scarlet embroidered waistcoat raised his brandy glass and drank it down before smacking his lips with relish. 'Good French brandy this, Major. Good men have risked their lives to bring it to your table, I warrant.'

Major Clive Wentworth nodded. 'If they want to stamp out smuggling, the government should bring down the taxes on liquor.'

'Smuggling be a way of life for many, especially with so many mines closed,' Sir Hugh added. 'What is the use of issuing these new five-pound notes when most folk will never possess so large a sum all at one time?'

Major Frank Wentworth held up his hand. 'Now, gentlemen, no talk of politics or religion at our table. Nothing is more certain to ruin a good evening of cards than when politics and religion become involved.' He addressed St John and Beaumont. 'Is it right *Challenger* was built in the Trevowan shipyard?'

When Beaumont did not answer, St John responded with a deliberate barb. '*Challenger* was built by us. Thadeous Lanyon purchased her sister ship and we are currently building one for a merchant in Trenglos.'

St John watched Beaumont closely. There was a slight

narrowing of his eyes when Lanyon's name was mentioned. St John deliberately mentioned Lanyon, convinced that the smugglers' banker would have Beaumont in his pay. The officer's face was now blank of expression – one could say too blank, all expression masked to hide his guilt.

The man in the scarlet waistcoat leaned forward to introduce himself. 'Osborne Garrett, merchant of Falmouth. *Challenger* is gaining a reputation as one of the faster ships of her class. Would you agree with that, Lieutenant Beaumont?'

'It takes skill, as well as speed, to catch a smuggler. They are devious men,' Beaumont announced.

'Indeed,' Garrett raised his glass to St John, 'but speed will win in the end. I may just visit your yard, Loveday, and invest in such a ship myself.'

St John had heard of Garrett from Harry Sawle. He was their biggest customer in the county for silk and lace. St John did not believe the merchant intended to commission a ship, but was showing his solidarity for the free-traders.

The introductions over, the men settled to their cards. The stakes were high and the Wentworth brothers adept players, though on several occasions they were over-reckless and lost. Beaumont played with a concentrated doggedness. He had begun with a pile of guineas, which again made St John suspicious that he was in Lanyon's pay. Perhaps that was Lanyon's gold, and the smuggler was landing a cargo tonight knowing that he would be unmolested by excise men. It made St John more determined to win the money from Beaumont.

The cards smiled on him. In the first hour he won a hundred and fifty guineas, in the next two he lost a hundred of that. Then his luck again changed and his pile of guineas began to increase.

Outside the wind was beginning to buffet the window and

two men threw in their cards and decided to make for their homes.

'I trust my other guests will not be deserting us.' Major Clive Wentworth shuffled the cards, impatient to continue. 'The night is still young. That wind will blow itself out in an hour or so. Here's ten guineas which says the wind dies down before our mantel clock strikes eleven.' He put the money on the side table holding the brandy and port decanters.

Major Frank Wentworth placed ten guineas next to his brother's money. 'I'll add my ten guineas to that, Brother. Any of you gentlemen care to bet against us?'

Lieutenant Beaumont pushed ten more guineas towards the pile. 'I agree with our hosts. It is a squall, no more. Though to be caught in such a wind could be treacherous in these waters. The coast is notorious for shipwrecks.'

'You were wise not to be at sea this night,' Osborne Garrett observed. 'But I've lived in these parts most of my life. That wind is strong. I say it will not blow itself out until after midnight.' He placed ten guineas in a separate pile.

Out of perversity St John agreed with Garrett and placed his bet. As though to confirm his decision the wind hammered harder against the window and the brocade curtains shivered. Sir Hugh bet with St John but the other players declined the wager.

When the clock struck ten, the wind was still fierce. St John had lost another fifty guineas but was still seventy ahead of his original stake. Beaumont's original stake had halved, Garrett was also losing, as was Major Frank Wentworth. Although he squinted at each card he picked up, Major Clive Wentworth was still ahead.

Halfway through a hand the clock struck eleven and each man listened to the wind. All was quiet outside and Major Clive gave a triumphant hurrah. Then the wind crashed against the side of the house and a puff of smoke from the fire in the hearth set the men coughing.

'Looks like Loveday, Garrett and Sir Hugh have won our side wager.' Major Frank Wentworth made to pay the bet.

'I think not,' Beaumont interrupted. 'They stated that the wind would not die down until after midnight. If it does before that time then the wager is void.'

'That's splitting hairs,' Major Frank Wentworth stated. 'We lost. Simple as that.'

'I would agree with our hosts,' St John said, then could not resist the taunt, 'but I am not a man to be petty over a mere ten guineas. I think St Hugh and Mr Garrett will agree to be generous and wait an hour to prove our prediction was right. I'd even go as far as to wager another ten guineas that we will win.'

The brothers, Garrett and Sir Hugh readily agreed. Beaumont scowled and with ill-concealed reluctance added to the stake. Throughout the next hour he would listen to the wind and glare at St John. When the clock struck half after twelve, their hosts slapped St John on the back. 'That was a wily move of yours, Loveday. Now you've taken us for twenty guineas.'

'I'm a local man and know the weather. Though with Beaumont being a naval commander, I would have thought he would have read the conditions more accurately.'

'I read them well enough not to venture out of harbour this night.' The brandy Beaumont had drunk was making him belligerent.

Clearly Beaumont was a sour loser. That heartened St John. Beaumont was beginning to play more rashly and each time he lost, he refilled his brandy glass. St John drank sparsely, preferring to keep a clear head. It paid off. St John won more hands than he lost.

By two in the morning the tension in the room was palpable. The wind had finally died away, leaving an eerie silence as each man assessed their hand. There was a mound of five hundred guineas in the centre of the table. Only St John, Osborne Garrett, Beaumont and Frank Wentworth were left in the game.

Garrett was dealt two cards and with a groan he threw in his hand. 'That's me finished.'

Wentworth added another twenty guineas but in the next round also withdrew. Across the table from St John, Beaumont was breathing heavily. There were ten guineas left on the table in front of the lieutenant and he was sweating. St John had exceeded the limit he had set himself by fifty guineas, and there were twenty-five left in front of him. Beaumont drew a pouch from his coat and his eyes gloated as he threw it on the table.

'I wager fifty guineas, Loveday. It will cost you another fifty on top of that if you wish to continue.' He hooked one arm over the back of the chair and smirked. 'Looks like your luck has run out. No IOUs are accepted at this table, is that not so, Major Wentworth?'

'It is a rule which saves unnecessary embarrassment to my guests. A gentleman should always retire before he gets in too deep.'

St John's heart was pounding. He took a gulp of brandy and lifted his gaze to meet Beaumont's arrogant stare.

The officer smiled maliciously. 'Such a pity, Loveday, that you got in out of your depth.' He leaned forward to scoop the winnings towards him.

'I believe you are the one to overreach yourself. But then it takes a particular breed of man to be a revenue officer.' The scorn was heavy in St John's voice. 'All evening you have gambled that by raising the stakes high at the end of a game, your opponents would believe their hand was weaker than yours. Often they threw in their hands and you won.'

'You malign me, sir.' Beaumont dragged the guineas

towards him but could not control a smirk of pleasure. 'You're a poor loser, Loveday. Much like your brother. If it weren't for ferrying *émigrés* across the Channel, he and his ship would be languishing idle in dock.'

St John's hands slammed down over the lieutenant's. 'My brother is master of his own ship, and not some hired lackey harassing honest Cornish fishermen and merchant ships. But I have not conceded this game.'

He drew a money pouch from his jacket, which was the money he had been diverted from banking that afternoon by his tryst with Purity. 'There's two hundred guineas there. To win you must match my wager.'

Beaumont glared at him, then slumped back into his chair. His face was taut with fury.

Enjoying himself at the officer's expense, St John added, 'Whilst I was attending to business in the market this fore-noon, I did happen to overhear three men arranging to meet at Gorran Haven at high tide this night. That's not more than a few miles down the coast from here. While you've been losing your hard-earned money, I reckon some smuggler has landed a haul almost under your nose.'

Beaumont stood up. He was flushed and shaking. 'It was your duty to inform me at once if you had such suspicions.'

St John shrugged. 'Unfounded rumours are dangerous. I am a gentleman farmer – why should I interest myself in idle speculation of a possible landing of illicit cargo? Also I could speculate upon why a revenue officer was gambling vast sums of money, with his ship safely moored on a night of such a run.'

'Damn you, sir. What are you implying?' Beaumont spluttered.

'I imply nothing.' St John held the lieutenant's glare. 'We were talking of suspicion and supposition. I merely observed

272

how dangerous mere suspicions alone could be to a man's reputation.'

Major Clive Wentworth banged on the table with his open palm. 'Calm yourselves, gentlemen, if you please. Tempers can run high when so much money is at stake, but I will tolerate no incivility in my house. I've seen too many young, hotheads end their lives in duels over some imagined slight. Sit down, Lieutenant Beaumont. Mr Loveday implied no insult upon your character. I am surprised you should be so defensive. He merely made an observation.'

'Doesn't do to be too touchy in your line of work, Lieutenant.' Osborne Garrett poured Beaumont a glass of brandy. 'The hour is late and I shall return to the inn. I do believe you are lodging there as well, Mr Loveday. It may be beneficial for you if we walked together. With such a heavy pouch of winnings you may fall prey to footpads.'

'The hour is late,' St John agreed. He rose and bowed to Sir Hugh, his hosts and the other gentlemen present. 'Good evening to you, sirs.'

They had gone no more than fifty yards down the street when Beaumont ran to catch up with them. 'I will not forget this night, Loveday. *Challenger* will not always be moored on a night such as this. Too many gangs of smugglers make a mockery of our laws. That will change. And, unlike you, I do heed rumours. You've a brother-in-law, Harry Sawle, who would do well to stay indoors at night.'

He strode away and Garrett gave a low whistle. 'That's a man who carries a grudge. And a sore loser. You'd do well to stay clear of him. I'd hate to lose my best supplier of silk and lace.'

St John halted and Osborne Garrett laughed. 'Don't look so shocked. Your secret is safe with me. I run a reputable business with outlets in several towns. I would not risk dealing with free-traders, unless I had made enquiries and knew that they were trustworthy. Sawle has a reputation which could have proved unhealthy, but I reckoned a gentleman like yourself would keep such a partner in line.'

St John was flattered although he remained uneasy that his connection with Harry was becoming more widely known.

Garrett chuckled. 'With Beaumont safe in harbour, it was a pity *you* did not have a cargo coming ashore tonight. Or did you?'

'Not until next week. Should be plenty there which will be of interest to you.'

Adam cursed as his men crouched in waiting in the shadows opposite the provost marshal's residence. The arrival of the troop had changed their routine. The guard was now being changed every hour throughout the night. The appearance of the guillotine had heightened the tension within the town. Men and women parading in tricolour sashes or feathers in their hats were roistering in the taverns in anticipation of the entertainment Madame Guillotine would provide for them tomorrow.

Adam had tethered horses for himself, Emile Lecroix and Kilmarthen in the shadows beyond the market square. He could only trust that they would still be there when they needed them. Lecroix had drawn a rough map of the interior of the residence. He and Adam would deal with the guards outside the cells, while the rest of the men would be on guard to help them fight their way out should the alarm be raised.

It aided Adam's plan that the provost marshal was celebrating with the new officer. The cook had been busy all day, with smells of a roasted pig unsettling the hungry inhabitants of the village.

An upper window opened and a stout figure was silhouetted against the candlelight within. 'Where's those whores we sent for?'

There was a muttering from the sentry on duty as the door was opened and a man scurried out towards the town.

'Take him,' Adam ordered.

The man was quickly overpowered and Adam turned to Lecroix. The Frenchman was the youngest son of a count. His parents and all but one brother and sister, out of a family of ten, had been murdered by the revolutionists. 'I need four women's gowns at once. Can you obtain them?'

Lecroix grinned. 'A sister of one of my men who is a prisoner lives in the town. She will help us.'

He returned within minutes with two gowns, two shawls, a large mobcap and two hooded cloaks. He held up the dresses, made for a short, stout woman, and flung them at two of the men who had hair to their shoulders. 'Put them on, together with the shawls and mobcap.'

One man snarled and held the dress away from him in disgust. 'I'm not dressing as no woman.'

Lecroix chuckled. 'You'll be the prettiest of us all, Perrot.'

The other men laughed, easing the tension which had been building. Perrot scowled and pulled the dress over his head and jammed the mobcap over his long hair.

Adam swung a hooded cloak around himself and nodded to Lecroix, who had donned the other. Lecroix was three inches taller than Adam and his hair was cropped short. In the dark Adam hoped that their disguise would suffice to fool the guards.

Adam instructed, 'Remember you are ladies of the night. You may mince, sashay and giggle at will.' The whiteness of his teeth flashed as he showed his amusement at the command. 'Once through the door, deal with the guards. The others will follow us to the cells. Good luck. If we get back through the gate it will be every man for himself.'

Adam pulled the hood of his cloak over his face and led the men across the market square. He wriggled his shoulders and giggled in a high-pitched voice, and Lecroix was swinging his hips in a way any woman would have envied.

The sentry stepped forward to bar their way. 'I thought only two women were to come.'

Adam pitched his voice higher. 'The provost marshal is a man of vigour. He particularly requested that two women attend on both himself and his guest.'

'He gets all the fun and we do all the work,' the sentry grunted. As Adam walked through the door the sentry squeezed his buttocks. 'Very nice, my pretty.'

Adam giggled. 'I will have a special pleasure for you when I return, *mon ami.*' His fingers tightened on his sword hilt.

'How about a kiss?'

'I'll kiss you.' Lecroix sidled against the man and plunged his dagger into the sentry's side.

Perrot slit the other sentry's throat. 'That's another republican less.'

Adam had seen many men die in the Terror but he still found the brutality of it hard to stomach. Perrot's hatred he understood. The man's wife and twelve-year-old daughter had been raped before they were killed by a drink-crazed mob.

The sentries' jackets were taken and thrown to two of Lecroix's men to wear and stand guard.

Lecroix led the way to the cells down a stone spiral staircase. A sentry sprang forward with his musket raised. Lecroix threw his dagger at him, piercing the turnkey's heart. Before the second gaoler could leap from his seat by a table, Adam pressed his sword point to his throat. 'The keys.'

The terrified man nodded to a drawer in the table. Lecroix pulled it open and a ring of keys rattled in his hand. In a narrow corridor were six iron-studded doors, each with a small barred grille. 'Long Tom! Which cell are you in?'

'Over here.'

Lecroix opened the door and raised a pistol as several men pressed forward. 'Long Tom first.' A clamour of voices demanded release from the other cells, bony fingers thrust through the grilles in entreaty. 'Are any of my men present to take charge of this rabble if they want their freedom?'

Two men answered him.

'And keep the noise down, or none of us will get out of here,' Adam ordered, his glance eager upon the door where Long Tom would appear. A dwarf came out, his clothes filthy rags and smeared with dried blood from an open head wound. 'I said Long Tom was to come first.'

The dwarf grinned. 'Not what you were expecting, am I?'

Adam recovered his composure, but despaired that Long Tom could keep up if they had to run through the town to escape. 'Black Jack at your service, sir. Have you been badly hurt?'

'Nothing that will demand I need assistance in getting out of here. I am more agile than I appear.'

Adam felt himself reprimanded. Long Tom could not have survived so long helping others if he was not capable of defending himself.

The other prisoners had come out of the cell and Lecroix was holding them at pistol point. Perrot and his companions were armed with extra daggers and passed these to Lecroix's men who had been imprisoned. The bulk of the prisoners were criminals; there were also several men and a family of a wife and two children, who had been arrested for crimes against the new regime.

Adam ordered the turnkey gagged and locked in a cell.

'Why waste your time?' Lecroix demanded. 'Kill them!'

'Has there not been enough bloodshed in France?' Adam killed only in self-defence.

Lecroix shrugged. 'The family stay close to me and Perrot here. The rest of you must escape as best you can.'

Adam handed Long Tom a dagger and a spare pistol he was carrying, and ran up the stairs. Glancing back over his shoulder, he discovered that Long Tom was surprisingly fast and agile.

'Look to yourself, Black Jack. Do not concern yourself with me,' Long Tom declared as they reached the top of the stairs.

The courtyard was in darkness but the prisoners below were arguing and fighting in their haste to be the first up the stairs. Lecroix's men were immediately behind Long Tom. Adam drew his sword and cursed the commotion behind him which could betray their escape.

A door opened directly on to the courtyard and a soldier shouted, 'The prisoners are escaping!'

Adam darted into the shadows as musket balls whistled past their shoulders. There was an answering volley from Lecroix's men. The close fire momentarily deafened Adam, and a French soldier fell from a balcony inches from him. A uniformed figure loomed to Adam's right. Gripping his sword hilt in a palm slick with sweat, Adam lunged at the attacker. The blade encountered a soft, spongy resistance of fatty tissue as it slid into the man's gut.

There was no time for horror or emotion; the instinct for survival drove Adam. He would save these wretched prisoners from the lethal kiss of Madame Guillotine. He jerked the sword from the dying soldier's flesh and ran on. Ahead of him, Long Tom darted as effortlessly as a snake through grass as he weaved past the French soldiers, his dagger stabbing anyone who opposed him. Two soldiers collapsed holding their bellies, blood pumping through their fingers.

From the corner of his eye, Adam saw the steel of a bayonet flash towards him. He threw himself on the ground and rolled up on to his feet, the basketweave hilt of his sword smashing into the head of his attacker. He leaped over him, his boots skidding in a fresh pool of blood.

The royalists were through the outer door and into the street when running footsteps and angry shouts warned them of other soldiers tumbling from the front of the residence.

Adam whirled to block a sword thrust with his blade, and his fist came up to slam into his attacker's jaw. He sidestepped the groaning soldier and parried another blade a second before it would have entered his heart. As he spun on his heel to press his attack, his ankle was caught by a soldier lying on the ground and he stumbled. Years of running up the ratlines of naval ships and walking barefoot across the wooden spars had given him an expert sense of balance. He recovered his footing in time to block a second attack from an officer's sword.

There was no opportunity to recover his breath as he locked in a deadly sword fight. Adam's hair was streaked across his face, the breath harsh in his lungs. His opponent was an accomplished swordsman and Adam knew his life was in real danger. He sliced and thrust but his assailant parried each blow with alarming ease. Adam clenched his teeth as the officer's sword slammed down upon the hilt of his own, jarring Adam's wrist.

'Die, you royalist dog!' The man's breath was heavy with wine and garlic as it fanned across Adam's face.

Adam lunged and found his blade locked against the hilt of the officer's sword. The man's face was an inch from Adam's nose. Ebony eyes blazed at Adam. The surprise of an unexpected recognition was almost Adam's downfall as he found himself meeting the murderous glare of Etienne Riviere, Lisette's brother.

In that brief hesitation, Etienne twisted free and his sword sliced through Adam's thick jacket, nicking the flesh of his ribcage.

Rage at the way Etienne had abandoned his sister and mother intensified Adam's attack. His sword slashed with greater ferocity, but for the moment it seemed that Etienne had not recognised him. Adam bit back the abuse which screamed in his head. He needed to remain cool or he would die. Etienne was a fine swordsman but Adam had bested him before in a sword fight. On that occasion Etienne had conceded victory but as Adam walked away Etienne had slashed Adam's arm. It had happened a few days before Adam was to be betrothed to Lisette, and Etienne had vowed then that the marriage would never take place. Etienne had prevented the marriage by marrying Lisette against her will to the Marquis de Gramont. If that had not been infamy enough, when Etienne's mother had suffered an apoplexy from the shock of her son's behaviour, Etienne had shut his sick mother away in a convent.

Anger and loss of blood was making Adam light-headed. The blood from his wound turned cold in the night as it spread over his shirt, but the focus of his revenge channelled his reflexes and gave him a resurgence of energy. He executed a deft twist of the wrist. There was a grunt of pain as Adam sliced through to the bone of his opponent's forearm. Etienne's sword clattered to the ground. When Adam's sword came up, Etienne's dark eyes bulged with fear.

'Mercy!'

'Give me one reason why I should not kill you after what you did to Lisette.'

'Adam!' Etienne finally recognised him. 'Spare me. Am I not your cousin?'

Etienne Riviere deserved to die for the horror which had been inflicted upon Lisette. Adam crashed the sword hilt into Etienne's nose and heard the satisfying crunch of the bone breaking. 'That's for abandoning your mother.'

As he raised his arm to slit Etienne's throat an escaping

prisoner shoved Adam aside as he fled. Etienne slithered backwards on the ground. The French soldiers were now engaged in preventing the mass of prisoners rushing across the courtyard in a desperate attempt to escape. Lecroix had got the family through the gates.

'Black Jack, make haste,' Lecroix shouted, and disappeared from sight.

The bloody face of Etienne Riviere stared up at Adam from several yards away. Other fleeing prisoners pushed between their figures.

'Get out of there, Black Jack,' Long Tom shouted.

Another musket shot whizzed past his shoulder and felled the prisoner in front of him. Adam had no choice but to follow Long Tom. His cousin screamed, 'Damn you for an English spy, Loveday!'

Adam caught up with Long Tom as they ran to the horses. The revelry from the taverns had blocked the sound of the alarm being raised and no one challenged them. Long Tom did a curious leap to get his foot in the stirrup and straddle the mare. He kicked the animal into a gallop, his short legs clapping against the girth as he urged the horse faster. The pain across Adam's ribs intensified as he and Long Tom sped past the macabre silhouette of the guillotine which dominated the market square. The moonlight glinted off its evil blade. There were shouts and further shots behind them. Pain seared Adam's upper arm as a bullet grooved his flesh. For the second time that night he had escaped death from a fatal wound.

His mission was accomplished, Long Tom freed, but Adam knew it was not an end to the matter here. Etienne Riviere still had to be dealt with, and one day he would return to France to deal justice to his treacherous cousin. The enmity between them was too strong for it to be otherwise.

Chapter Fifteen

Work was progressing well at the shipyard. With a fine spell of weather the shipwrights were working extra hours and the vessels they were building were almost back on schedule. Edward was checking the yard's supplies. Stockpiles of timber and iron for the nails were abundant, paid for by the money given by Adam after his last voyage. The pressure of their debts were easing at last, unlike the atmosphere and tension which still pervaded relations within the family.

Edward frowned as he watched the carpenters in the shaping shed planing the edges of the timber smooth. Amelia still would not accept Adam's wife at Trevowan and Elspeth backed her. He remained angry at the marriage, but if it were not for Amelia's sensibilities, he would have accepted Senara into their family as he had Meriel. The rift with Adam sat ill with him. The compromising truce which had replaced the bonds of affection was a poor substitute. During his last leave Adam had spent all his time with Senara, and had not visited Trevowan. The constraint between Edward and Adam had been present even when they discussed the work and plans for the yard. The peace which Edward had enjoyed in the early months of his marriage to Amelia had dissipated amongst the problems which had since arisen.

At least some of the financial burdens had been lifted.

From the money earned by *Pegasus'* voyages Adam provided for the welfare of his wife and child. St John had finally proved himself in the management of the estate. Edward did not enquire about St John's personal income, which he suspected still came from smuggling. Since St John supported his family and the cost of running the Dower House, Edward no longer challenged him. St John knew the risks, and his son had been generous in restocking the farm. Both the twins' successes did not stop Edward from worrying that smuggling and privateering were dangerous occupations. The lives of his sons were more precious to him than the money they earned.

He went from the shaping sheds to the forge. After the bright sunlight, the stone building was gloomy and cloudy with smoke from the glowing coals of the furnace. Mike Fletcher, the blacksmith, was forging the heavy links of an anchor chain. The acrid smell of the red-hot metal stung Edward's nostrils and the high-pitched clink of the hammer on the metal made his ears ring. After the exchange of a few cursory words on progress Edward was glad to escape the inferno.

Edward next stopped by the wooden outhouse built beside Seth Wakeley's cottage. The carpenter stopped his lathe when Edward entered. His son, Timmy, and the two other apprentices Seth was training stopped chiselling the rough shapes of the ship's carved rails so that the men could hear each other speak.

'Good day to you, Mr Loveday,' Seth said. 'A fine morning, is it not? What can I do for you, sir?'

'I am just doing my rounds.' He nodded to a half-carved figurehead of a centaur for the brigantine they were currently building. 'You have an exceptional skill.'

Seth hobbled on his peg leg to a shelf holding a stack of drawings. 'I only be doing my job, sir. The Cap'n drew these for me afore he sailed.' He spread out detailed and accurate sketches of a dragon, an eagle resting on a globe of the world, and a beautiful woman, who looked remarkably like Senara, holding a spear. 'These be drawings of a sea dragon, striking eagle and lady of the sea. They be figureheads I bin asked to carve by various owners. I need you to send the customers a price, sir.'

'What has this to do with me? If you carve them in your own time, Seth, the profit should be yours. I can let you have the timber at a reasonable price.'

Seth shook his head. 'Cap'n Loveday did get me these commissions from men who've seen old Pegasus which I carved. My family would have starved when I lost my leg in the navy, if the Cap'n hadn't given me a job here. I don't want the responsibility of working for meself. You pay good wages, sir. I reckon it only be right, since Cap'n Loveday got the orders, that the yard gets the profit.' Seth took out a second sheet of paper with the names and addresses of the ship owners and handed it to him.

Edward thanked him, but as he walked back to his office he felt a growing sadness. Once Adam would have spoken of the orders and discussed this new project with him. The sound of laughter made him turn his head towards Mariner's House. Senara had come outside holding the baby, Nathan, and was bidding farewell to her mother and sister. Senara saw Edward watching them and inclined her head in acknowledgement of his presence. Lucy Mumford called her name and hurried over to Senara and was admitted to the house. Senara had won the respect of the shipwrights' wives by her remedies, but Edward hoped that she was not becoming too familiar with them. Senara had a position to maintain as Adam's wife.

He had promised Adam that he would ensure Senara and the child were safe and their needs catered for. He usually sent word for her to come to his office once a week to ensure that all was well with them. He decided now that he would call on her.

Carrie Jansen answered the door to his knock and looked flustered as she showed him into the parlour. 'I'll go fetch the mistress.'

Edward was surprised to see the baby sitting on the carpet with pillows propped around him to stop him from falling. He was in a white cotton gown and wispy black curls sprang out from around his muslin cap. Nathan studied Edward with open curiosity and waved the silver rattle in his hand. Edward was unsettled by encountering his grandson, who looked so like the twins when they were babies.

The laughter coming from the kitchen ended abruptly. Lucy Mumford hurried out of the house, dropping Edward a hasty curtsy as she passed. Senara appeared, rolling down the tight sleeves of her gown. She presented a neat and tidy figure; her green gown of fine wool was edged with a narrow band of velvet around the high square neckline and three rows of velvet decorated the skirts. A collar of creamy Brussels lace relieved the severity of the gown. She no longer wore her hair in a single thick plait, but dressed it elegantly in a simple chignon. Edward approved of her attire, which was serviceable whilst it showed a quality and style befitting his son's wife.

'Mr Loveday, you must forgive me for being otherwise engaged. I was not expecting you.' Suddenly her eyes shadowed. 'There is nothing amiss? Is there news of Adam? Has something happened?'

'Nothing has happened. I had no wish to alarm you by my visit.' When she visibly relaxed, he regretted that his manner was often harsh with her. He never quite knew how to treat this woman. Her origins may be lowly but she had a quiet dignity which could be disconcerting. He added more gently,

'I came to enquire that all was well with you and the child, and that you were in need of nothing.'

'We are well.' She gripped her hands in front of her waist. 'I do not expect you to trouble yourself on my account, sir.'

'I gave my word to Adam.'

She studied him intently before lowering her gaze. 'I forget my manners. Please be seated, sir. May I offer you some refreshment? Some tea? Or would you prefer claret?'

Edward had not intended to stay. Yet he was intrigued by her self-possession. There was no subservience in her manner, neither were there any false airs and graces.

'Some claret would be most acceptable.'

She rang a silver bell on the mantel shelf and the maid appeared. 'Mr Loveday will partake of some claret, Carrie. Remember to use the silver salver and bring the decanter and a glass.' There was a nervous tremor to her voice but her poise was unruffled.

Edward sat on the leather armchair by the fire and Senara sat opposite him on a high-backed rocking chair. The silence stretched between them as she waited for him to speak. Nathan lifted his arms to his mother. The rattle was waved enthusiastically and then he toppled over on to his side and lay laughing. Senara picked him up and held him in her lap.

'Perhaps you would prefer that I remove Nathan from the room,' she stated.

Edward shook his head, but continued to find the child's presence disturbing. This was his only grandson. The sight of him should fill him with pride. Yet he could not forget that Nathan was half-gypsy. Edward surveyed the room. Some changes had been made since Senara had taken possession – changes a woman would deem necessary to transform a house into a home. Curtains hung at the windows where once only the shutters served. A bunch of primroses were in a bowl on the table and a square red and blue Turkish rug took the starkness from the plain floorboards. There were also some sculptures of animals on the shelves which were realistically painted. He rose and picked up a unicorn. Underneath were the initials SL.

'Did you make these?'

'I used to be a potter, which I greatly enjoyed. My sister now uses my wheel to provide an income for her and my mother. I miss using the clay and it passes the time.'

'They are very beautiful. An unusual hobby. Have you ever considered painting with watercolours? Many women find that stimulating.'

Her head shot up. 'You mean watercolour would be more genteel. Adam is the artist. My skill has always been with clay. I like to work with my hands. I have also established a garden of herbs and flowers. That, too, you will no doubt consider unladylike. But it gives me pleasure.' There was a defiant tilt to her chin. 'And there are some who would say that it is ungentlemanly for a man to work with his hands. But Adam and yourself are skilled shipwrights.'

'I had not presumed to judge you,' Edward said with a light laugh, pleased that she had shown such spirit. He disliked meek women. 'But I am concerned that your skill with herbs may make the shipwrights' wives overfamiliar. They call on you often.'

'They accept me and none has yet overstepped her place.' Senara's eyes flashed. 'I receive few callers, but I am content in my solitude. It was a life I previously chose.'

Edward shifted uncomfortably and finished his claret. He felt that Senara was reprimanding him. 'You must come to me if there is anything you need. If there is some kind of emergency when you have need of my support it would be appropriate for you to send word to me at Trevowan.'

'Adam provides for all my needs. I have never expected

anything from your family. But I thank you for your offer, and I will remember it.'

Her calm dignity was something that Edward had not expected. He left, still unsure as to what had prompted his visit. With his emotions so tangled by Senara's serenity and poise, he had to force himself to remember that it was her gypsy blood which made it impossible for him to accept her as part of their family.

He was about to enter his office when a horseman hailed him. 'Letter for Mr Edward Loveday. I'm to give it to no one but he.'

'I am Edward Loveday.'

The man handed him the letter. 'My lady says to wait for a reply, sir.'

Puzzled, Edward broke the seal and his face grew pale as he scanned the contents. His hand shook as he put the letter inside his jacket. 'Inform her Ladyship that I will call on her tomorrow.'

He entered his office and poured himself a stiff brandy. A ghost had risen from his past and the matter must be of dire importance for him to have been contacted.

The morning after his card game at the Wentworth house St John had slept late at the inn. He was dressing when an excited voice in the innyard caught his attention.

'Ship's on the rocks at Black Head Point. Didn't hear there be any cargo washed ashore, but reckon it be worth goin' ter see. Could be fine pickings.'

When he left his room St John saw Osborne Garrett settling his account with the landlord.

'Did you hear of the shipwreck, Loveday?' the merchant declared. 'There's rumours it could have been a smuggler. No cargo, though, but then if there was danger it would have been jettisoned to avoid incrimination. And apparently only two lives were lost. One was the captain.'

'Nasty business, a shipwreck.' St John frowned. 'And if it was a smuggler then at least the owner won't be facing charges. It will be hard enough having lost his ship.' St John settled his own account and walked as far as the yard with Garrett, where the horses were already harnessed to the merchant's coach.

The sky was a brilliant blue and there was little wind. Garrett observed, 'Who would have thought after that wind yesterday it would be so pleasant abroad this morning? Glad you cut that revenue officer down a peg or two last night. Can't abide them, or the riding officers. Men like you, Loveday, have my admiration. Long may you outwit those vultures – unlike the poor man whose ship was lost, or the one who had his cargo confiscated. Rum do.' He shook hands with St John and climbed into the coach.

St John entered a bank and deposited seven hundred pounds into his new account. At so large a deposit, the bank owner had ushered him into his private office where he had been offered refreshments. The man fawned over him as an important and valued customer. St John enjoyed the feeling. Following as it did on Garrett's praise, he was proud of his status and achievements. For the first time St John was treated with respect for himself and not because he was his father's son.

In a generous mood, he kept back fifty guineas to buy a trinket for Meriel. While in the jewellers he picked out a more expensive brooch for Purity, as a token of his regard.

The visit to St Austell had been a success, even though he had not purchased the cattle. Yet that provided him with an excuse for another tryst with Purity. His step was light as he returned to the inn where he had stabled Prince.

Passing an alleyway, he recognised Lieutenant Beaumont's voice raised in anger.

'I can only do so much.' The revenue officer sounded as though he was pacifying someone.

St John drew back against the wall of the shop at the top of the alley and peered around the corner. Beaumont was in a doorway, and Thadeous Lanyon was accosting him, his fists clenched inches from the officer's face.

'Just make sure there's no guard on the customs house tonight. I know we agreed it would stay there for a week. My men will raid it tonight. I've got commitments to meet now that my ship ended on the rocks.'

So it was Lanyon's ship which had foundered and, by the sound of it, it was his cargo in the customs house. St John was delighted. Justice was at last catching up with Lanyon. His cargo had no doubt been confiscated as a ruse to persuade the authorities that Beaumont was doing his duty. It also gave Beaumont an excuse to be in harbour last night when a larger haul would have been landed. Lanyon now intended to steal his own cargo back at the first opportunity. It would not be the first time a customs house had been broken into and the cargo retaken by its owners. St John gave Lanyon his due: the old rogue knew all the tricks. The two men were still arguing as St John returned to the inn to collect his horse.

A half-hour later he was riding along the street, still digesting the information he had learned about Lanyon. Belatedly, he wondered if the wrecked ship could have been *Sea Sprite*. That may have repercussions for future orders for the yard.

'Loveday, curse you!' Lanyon appeared out of the crowd to grab Prince's bridle. His bulbous eyes were bloodshot, and his face was mottled with rage. 'That damned ship your father built capsized off Black Head in last night's storm. Call yourself shipbuilders? Your yard couldn't build a raft to stay afloat in a millpond!' He was shouting and gesticulating, and a crowd was gathering around them. Spittle sprayed from his mouth as he spat out his abuse. 'That ship weren't seaworthy. I'll see your yard ruined for this infamy.'

St John knew Lanyon was a mean and vengeful man and that he had a temper. That had been proved by the way he had beaten Hester so that she had lost a child. But St John had never seen Lanyon out of control in public. Anger gouged him. How dare the upstart defame the yard in such a manner! 'There was nothing wrong with the ship, though my uncle saw it some weeks ago and she was carrying too much sail. Sail not intended for the rigging we supplied.'

'Lies. That ship were unseaworthy. I never changed her rigging. Your family always had it in for me.' He was gibbering with rage. 'Families like yours can't abide it when a man betters himself. The Lovedays bain't getting away with this.'

St John was incensed. 'If *Sea Sprite* capsized, or failed to respond to her helm, it was because you had tampered with the rigging.'

'You cheated me. Hard cash I paid for her new design. Designed to sink in the first storm, that's what she be.'

'Your wits have gone begging, man.'

Lanyon waved a riding stick at St John. 'You stole my intended bride and you thought to see me ruined.' He struck St John across the thigh with the whip and then hit his horse. Prince reared and had to be controlled before St John could answer. 'You insult our honour. And since you have struck me, I demand satisfaction. Send your seconds to the Dower House. Pistols at dawn by the Druid stone on the moor.'

'I won't fight a stupid duel. I have justice on my side.' Lanyon struck Prince again. 'Your yard won't survive this scandal. It be you who'll be ruined, not I.'

Prince neighed and began to circle, endangering passers-by. St John was furious. He drew his pistol from the saddle holster and aimed it at Lanyon. 'Get your hands off my horse, or I'll kill you. You're too craven to face me in a duel, but you'd have an old crippled man run down by your carriage. Was that to pay back Reuban Sawle when Meriel chose to wed me? My family name and honour speaks for itself.'

The crowd were enjoying the spectacle and began to shout abuse at Lanyon. The smuggler backed away from St John. 'Do you hear how he threatened me? Loveday wants to silence me by a duel.'

'Not got your henchmen here to deal with him, Lanyon?' a man yelled from the crowd.

Lanyon spun round to regard the bystanders but ignored the heckler. 'What honest merchant is skilled with firearms? That proves the ship was never seaworthy.'

'When were you ever respectable, Lanyon? The Lovedays are an honourable family,' another man shouted. 'Can't say I've heard the same of you.'

Lanyon scowled at the crowd. 'I'll not be silenced!'

'Pull yourself together, man.' St John had tolerated enough. 'My family will not be threatened. We'll see you in hell first.' With Prince's bridle now free, St John touched his heels to his gelding's sides and set off at a brisk trot through the town. His temper was not improved by seeing Lieutenant Beaumont watching him, for the officer had clearly witnessed the interchange with Lanyon.

The lieutenant lifted his hat to St John in an ironic salute. There was an unsettling smirk on the man's narrow face.

St John was still cursing Lanyon when he rode into the shipyard to confront his father.

'Lanyon is declaring to all who will listen in St Austell that *Sea Sprite* was unseaworthy. That bastard is out to ruin us.'

Edward Loveday frowned. 'I learned of the shipwreck this morning. With Adam being at sea, Ben Mumford has gone to Black Head Point to see if it is apparent that the ship was wrongly rigged as William suspected.'

'Then you had better find some witnesses who would swear a statement that Sea Sprite's rigging had been altered.'

'The crew are the only ones who could swear to that. Lanyon would only use the extra sail on a smuggling run.' Edward rubbed the back of his neck, a sign that he was worried. 'Your Uncle William thought when he saw Sea Sprite that she was using an extended bowsprit to carry extra sail. But Lanyon would have insisted that it was retracted whenever they were in port.'

'Then it was a shame that the ship was not loaded with contraband. Lanyon would have then been labelled a smuggler and gaoled. The world would be well rid of such scum.'

Edward thrust his hands into the pocket of his jacket and stared out of the window at the shipwrights hammering planking into place over the ribs of a similar cutter to Sea Sprite. The second stage of payment on that vessel was due next month from the customer. If Lanyon continued to claim Sea Sprite had been unseaworthy, the customer could cancel his order or delay payment until further sea trials proved her stability. Edward could not afford to build a complete ship without advance money.

The strain on his father's face alarmed St John. Edward rarely discussed the financial circumstances of the yard with him. For him to look so worried, things must be far from stable. 'I challenged Lanyon to a duel, but the cur refused to meet me. A man like that has no honour.'

'You should not have challenged him.' Edward rounded on his son. 'Duelling is illegal. And how could it possibly help our reputation?'

'Would you have wanted me to let him get away with his accusations?' St John was aghast.

His father expelled a harsh breath and shook his head. 'In

the circumstances I may well have been tempted to do the same. But it was not wise to have threatened Lanyon.'

'The man was threatening to take us to court, and would drag our reputation as shipbuilders through the mire. Is competition not harsh enough without facing a court case to uphold our integrity?' St John marched to the door. 'I thought you would be pleased that I had defended your honour, sir.' He slammed the door shut behind him, furious that his father had disapproved of his conduct.

Edward rubbed the back of his neck to ease the tension cramping his neck and shoulders. Only yesterday he had begun to believe that their troubles were fading. Today more had sprung up, relentless as weeds in a seed bed, and they threatened to choke his peace of mind. Lanyon could be a problem. The man was vindictive and St John had made matters worse by threatening him in public.

Edward felt his responsibilities were as constraining as a yoke. He had so many problems to deal with. He should have left an hour ago to visit the Dowager Lady Keyne, an old and dear friend, who had sounded so desperate for his help in her letter.

An hour later he rode into the grounds of Beechwood Manor. It was the smaller of the two houses in Cornwall owned by the Keyne family. Most of the windows of the square, unimposing stone house were shuttered, the gardens and drive were unweeded and the once-immaculate lawns were peppered with daisies and dandelions.

An aged footman answered Edward's rap on the door and an equally old groom was summoned to attend Rex.

'Her Ladyship be expecting you, sir. She apologises for receiving you in her private chamber. Her Ladyship has not been well of late.'

Edward felt a twinge of misgiving. Lady Keyne had always

been a vibrant and energetic woman. She could dance all night, hunt all day and dance again through the next night.

He was shown up an oak-panelled staircase hung with ancestral portraits. The stairs were worn and creaked with age. The corridor was lighter, and crowded with suits of armour and painted battle shields. There were lobster-pot helmets and breastplates from the Civil War a century and a half ago. Rows of halberds and swords were hung on the wall, crisscrossed into patterns. The Keynes were an ancient, military family who more recently had gone into politics. Sir Robert Keyne had spent thirty years in Parliament. It was his widow, Eleanor, who had summoned Edward so mysteriously.

The room he was shown into was gloomy for the curtains were partially drawn. The air was stale and stuffy, and a large fire crackled in the grate despite the warmer weather.

'Mr Edward Loveday, my lady,' announced the footman.

There was the rustle of silk from a chaise longue and a thin pale arm was extended towards Edward. The woman's figure was in shadow while the sunlight fell upon Edward's face, making it harder to see her.

'My dear Edward, forgive me for prevailing upon you in such a manner.' The voice was husky, the memory of it sending a shiver of pleasure through him, but it sounded appallingly weak.

Edward raised the delicate fingers to his lips and was shocked at how transparent her flesh had become. Her wrist looked too frail to hold the weight of her hand. Once heavy diamond bracelets would have danced and sparkled upon it as she waved it tirelessly in her ceaseless gaiety. 'Eleanor, I am, as ever, your servant to command.'

'You are ever the gallant, Edward! No man ever commanded you, let alone a woman. But I thank you for coming so swiftly.' She paused and drew a laboured breath. 'How handsome you still are. You have scarcely changed. There is a touch of grey at the temples which becomes you. It has been too many years.'

'A decade or so, I fear. You have spent much time in London.'

'It has been fifteen years since last we met. Fifteen long years. I was exiled in London. Robert banished me from Cornwall. He knew my heart remained here.'

'He knew of us? We were discreet.' Edward had chaffed at the pains they had taken to protect Eleanor's reputation when he had yearned to spend more time in her company. Their affair had lasted two years before she had left for London.

'Some things were impossible to hide. My love for you overshadowed my marriage. Robert never forgave me. He punished me by keeping me close in a loveless marriage.'

Edward kneeled at her side and was struck afresh by her beauty, yet it was a beauty now touched by the angels. The corn-gold hair was piled high and fell in ringlets about her shoulders, but what had once been her natural glory was now a wig. The high cheekbones and large blue eyes showed no sign of ageing, but at forty the cheeks were too thin, the eye sockets too sunken, and she constantly gasped, snatching air to sustain her. With horrifying realisation Edward knew that Eleanor Keyne was dying.

'Has it really been so long? There were so many empty years after you left.' He gazed into her eyes and swallowed against the knot of pain in his throat.

'But your first love was always Marie. I knew that.' She stroked the side of his face.

'Marie gave her life bearing the twins and we had been married just a year. That sacrifice is forever carved in a man's heart. But you showed me that life still held joy for me: that I could love again, even if that love too must be lost. You were married and must one day return to your husband.'

'We had two wonderful years, did we not?'

'Two magnificent years, which I treasure. Sir Robert was a fool to put his career before you and stay in London, which you loathed. It must have been hard that he kept you a prisoner there. Could you not have returned to Cornwall?'

'Not without placing another in danger, who was more precious to me than my own happiness. Oh, Edward, I do not know how to tell you this without you despising me for a weak and foolish woman.'

'You were never weak and foolish. And I could never despise you.' He smiled. The love of their two-year affair had never entirely died, but it had been pushed to a dark corner of his heart as he strove to forget the woman who could never be his.

'And if I were to tell you that we have a child? A daughter. Whom I was forbidden to tell you of by Robert. My husband threatened I would never be able to see her again if anyone learned the truth.' She clutched his hand and tears spilled down her face.

Edward rocked back on his heels. 'I have a daughter!'

'The dearest, sweetest child. A little headstrong, but she has needed that to cope with the difficulties which life has presented to her. Her life has not been as I would have wished it. I was powerless to do otherwise.'

'Why did you not tell me of her last year when your husband died?'

'I had just become ill and I feared how you would take the news after so many years. I thought I would get better – that all would be well and I could now somehow help Tamasine.'

Eleanor was forced to rest and as she struggled to drag in more breath, Edward raised a glass of cordial to her lips. She lay back and closed her eyes, her voice weaker as she continued, 'Robert refused to acknowledge Tamasine. She was taken from me at her birth and sent to a wet nurse. Then when she was old enough, she was sent away for schooling. I was allowed to see her only twice a year. That time was so precious. It was all I came to live for. Robert forbade me to tell her that I was her mother. She was known as my ward – the daughter of a cousin who had borne her out of wedlock, and who had died at birth.'

'That is inhuman.' Edward's mind was reeling that he had a child who must be fourteen by now. 'Where is this child? Here?'

'Tamasine would never be allowed here. My son and four daughters are as spiteful as their father. They would use her as a servant, revile her, and make her life wretched. They must never learn of Tamasine's existence. The money for her schooling and upbringing came from that left to me by my mother. That legacy passes to my eldest daughter, Glynis, when I die. I could not mention Tamasine in my will, or they would find her . . . hound her . . . persecute her.' A sob was muffled by her hand against her mouth. 'I could not bear that. Tamasine is so beautiful – so spirited and intelligent.'

Eleanor lay on the pillow, her eyes closed and tears streaming down her cheeks. 'Edward, promise me that Tamasine will be cared for. That you will become her guardian. She is at a ladies' academy in Salisbury. Robert wanted her far away so that she would not contaminate his family. You will care for her, Edward? You will not fail her? Fail me?'

'It is no little surprise to learn of her existence,' he reassured, but held himself stiffly from the shock. 'I will instruct my lawyer that the girl be given an adequate allowance.'

Eleanor reached out to him. 'But you must go to her, meet her. I will not live much longer. I need to know that she will be safe. When I die, assure her that she will not be alone in the world.'

'I cannot assume direct responsibility for her.' Edward was

cautious. 'I have remarried. It would be unacceptable for my wife to take my illegitimate daughter into our home.'

'I do not expect that.' Eleanor rose on to her elbow, her eyes large and pleading. 'Edward, if you loved me at all, you must promise me you will visit Tamasine after I am gone. And give her this.' She drew a velvet pouch from the side of the day bed. 'Open it.'

He tipped into his palm a heart-shaped ruby pendant, with matching brooch and earrings. He had given these to Eleanor as a token of his devotion when she had left on her last visit to London. They had expected to be reunited in four months.

'I never came back because I was carrying Tamasine, who was born six months after I left. Obviously, Robert realised the child was not his. Tamasine should have the jewellery as security for her future as her dowry. I want you to give it to her, with my love. Promise me. And that as her guardian you will find a suitable husband for our daughter. She deserves better than life has so far given her. Yet I love her so very much.'

Edward could not refuse. Eleanor was weak and the meeting had taxed her strength. But as he raised her hand to his lips, her fingers closed tightly over his. 'I never forgot you, Edward. I never loved another man as I did you. Our love lived on through Tamasine. I knew you would not fail me.'

Edward rode home in a sombre mood. The meeting now seemed like a dream, the consequences overwhelming. Only the pressure of the jewellery pouch in his pocket told him that it was real. It was no light responsibility he had taken on. And in view of Amelia's recent condemnation of his family's questionable morals, the knowledge that he had fathered an illegitimate child would put a severe strain upon their marriage. He even wondered if she would forgive him, were he to tell her.

He did not like secrets, but Tamasine Loveday Keyne – as

he had learned, to his dismay, was his daughter's full name – had to be kept very much a secret. At least Loveday was not an uncommon name for women in Cornwall, and no one would discover the truth. If they did he was certain that the consequences would be unpleasant.

Chapter Sixteen

Furious with Lanyon, St John went to Penruan to find Harry Sawle. His lugger was in the harbour and St John found Harry in the Dolphin Inn. Reuban was on his stool, peering over the open hatch of the cellar. There was a blanket covering his wasted leg stumps and another around his shoulders.

'Make sure that brandy be hid good and proper and the casks of brewed ale put in front of them.'

'I know what I be doing, Pa,' Harry yelled back.

'You be putting my livelihood in danger,' Reuban snarled, but there was a whining to his voice where once there would have been menace. He was skeletal thin and his skin taut over his skull. The once-lively eyes were sunken and narrowed by pain. 'The excise men searched the cellar last week. And me an honest tavern-keeper.'

'You have never been honest, Reuban,' St John said by way of greeting.

'Loveday, what you doing 'ere? Got some baccy for your old father-in-law?'

'I've business with Harry.'

Harry came up from the cellar and beckoned St John to follow him into the kitchen. When Reuban would have followed, he rounded on the old man. 'This be business, Pa.

301

And of late you've got a loose tongue in your head when the drink's in you.'

'I would'na say a word against my own. What you take me for? If I had me legs I'd take a swing at you for that.'

'It's not what you say against me but your bragging as to how no one gets one over on the Sawles. Last night you declared there's men hereabout should keep an eye on their backs – and their women.'

'Lanyon made a cripple of me. When you gonna make him pay?'

'Soon . . . if your blabbering don't get me hanged first.'

'Show the world the Sawles won't be made fools of. I'd have turned Lanyon off and dumped him in the sea long afore now if I were just half the man I used to be. That stupid wench Lanyon wed 'as got you dancing to her tune.'

Harry thrust his bunched fist under his father's nose. 'I'm warning you, Pa. One more word and, legs or no legs, you'll feel the weight of this.'

Reuban hawked and spat towards the spittoon on the floor. The phlegm missed. 'Get yer ma to have this place cleaned up, it be not fit for pigs.'

'But there's a pig wallowing in it,' Harry said as he marched through to the kitchen and slammed the door behind him.

Sal paused in plucking a chicken, the brown feathers stuffed into a sack to be saved to fill a pillow or mattress. 'Must you always rile your pa? Don't he suffer enough?'

'And he makes damned sure everyone else suffers with 'im,' Harry glowered. 'He asked for the brandy. There just bain't no pleasing 'im.'

Sal eyed St John wearily. 'How be Meriel?'

'She is bored. You know you are welcome to visit her whilst she is confined to her bed,' St John offered.

'We bain't never been welcome at Trevowan and that be

right and proper. But I've missed seeing Rowena.' She concentrated on her work as she added with tartness, 'Real little Loveday, that young minx.'

St John smiled at mention of his daughter. 'I'll have Rachel bring her to you when next she comes to the village.'

Sal gave him an odd look which was disconcertingly pitying. 'My Meriel bain't always done right by you. I hope she gives you the son you want this time.'

At the sound of angry voices in the taproom, Sal dropped the chicken on the table and left the kitchen to intervene in the argument between Reuban and a customer.

St John spoke heatedly to Harry about his encounter with Lanyon. 'Reuban is right. Lanyon needs teaching a lesson,' he concluded.

'So you reckon it could be his cargo in the customs house?' Harry looked pleased. 'I was sure that Beaumont was in his pay.'

'From the conversation I overheard it sounded like Lanyon intended to steal back the cargo.'

'Then we shall relieve him of the trouble and get to it first,' Harry grinned. 'If Lanyon is in league with Beaumont, the customs house will not be heavily guarded. I reckon it be worth the risk.'

St John returned to Trevowan and wondered if he had not been too rash in agreeing to Harry's plan. Meriel was resting on the day bed with a plate of sweetmeats on her lap. He confided his misgivings.

'You can't let Harry down. It will not be without its dangers, but think of the rewards. Once the baby is born we could have a season in London without worry about the expense. You have always promised to take me.'

'Your love for money and pleasure is greater than your concern for me. I could get killed.'

Meriel was scathing in her contempt. 'That's why I admire

Harry. He never reneges on a plan. This is your chance to teach Lanyon that you are the better man and you have not the courage to see it through. Stay at home tonight, let Harry do your dirty work, and that makes you no better than Lanyon – rising on the risks made by others.'

St John stormed out of the Dower House but her goading had caused his anger to return and against his better judgement he decided he would join Harry tonight. Not only would they beat Lanyon at his own game but they would make the arrogant Lieutenant Beaumont look foolish.

Two evenings after the shipwreck a heavily veiled Hester Lanyon sought refuge in Keziah Sawle's house. It was an hour after dark and Keziah was surprised that anyone would call at such an hour.

She took Hester through to the kitchen where her maid, Gilly, was bathing her own daughter, Nancy, in the sink. Keziah had been in the middle of drying her son, Zacky, after his bath when Hester had knocked at the door and the child was balanced on her hip in a towel. The two children were a year old.

Keziah sat in a rocker by the range and continued to dry Zacky and gestured for Hester to sit on the wooden settle opposite. 'Bain't often you leave the shop or your house these days, Hester. Villagers be saying you be a rare recluse. Your sister, Annie, were here t'other day buying some of my goat's cheese. Said she bain't seen you in weeks; that you weren't at home when last she called.' Keziah tried to peer through the veil to the woman's face. Hester's pregnancy was beginning to show. She was stooped and groped towards a chair and sat down. Then she burst into tears.

Keziah exclaimed, 'Oh, my lovely, what be wrong? Don't take on so.'

Hester looked at Gilly, who was now pulling on Nancy's

bedgown. 'I should not have come.' She tried to stand but fell back into the chair.

Keziah nodded to Gilly, a slim girl of sixteen who had been abandoned by her lover when she became pregnant. She had come to Blackthorn Cottage as wet nurse for Zack. 'Take the children upstairs to bed, Gilly.'

Once Gilly had made the two journeys up the stairs and she could be heard singing as she settled the children in their cots, Keziah said, 'This bain't no social visit, so what be wrong, Hester?'

'I can't go back there. I must see Harry. He'll have to take me away.'

'That's rash talk, my lovely.' Keziah flicked back a strand of her wiry amber hair. She knew that Harry was Hester's lover, and that probably the child she carried was his also. She thought Hester was a fool. Lanyon was not a man to be cuckolded. She'd seen women stripped half naked and whipped through the streets after being dragged to the courts by an irate husband. No one punished the man who had fornicated with the woman. Often as not those women were then cast out, and the only life left to them was to work in a bordello. Harry had a roving eye, and Hester wasn't the only lass he'd bedded this winter. Clem was always chuckling over his brother's amorous adventures. Keziah thanked God that her husband was faithful, though she had threatened to leave him and take Zack with her if he ever strayed.

'I can't stay with that monster another day,' Hester sobbed. 'Thadeous has left Penruan to go to Truro. He'll be gone a day or so. I have to get away afore he returns.' Her sobs became louder. 'Why bain't Harry here? I need him.'

Keziah put her hand on Hester's shoulder to comfort her and the woman winced. Keziah lifted the veil and could not control a shudder. The candlelight flickered over the woman's face. Hester's nose was bloodied and broken, and one eye was black and swollen. There was also a jagged piece of flesh at her neck where she looked like she had been bitten.

Keziah groaned. 'Lanyon did this?'

Hester nodded. 'He returned from St Austell in a foul mood yesterday. His ship were wrecked and he's lost a fortune in cargo. I thought he were going to kill me. If I hadn't pleaded for the baby I think he would have.' She grabbed Keziah's hand. 'Where be my Harry? His lugger bain't in the harbour. He's got to get me away.'

'As far as I know Harry bain't back in Penruan until late tomorrow.'

Hester cradled her stomach and rocked to and fro. 'I can't go back. Thadeous will kill me, I know he will. The man's a devil.'

Keziah rose to fasten the shutters over the kitchen window. Their house was high on the ridge with a steep climb down to the village below them. But she did not want to risk prying eyes taking an interest this night.

'I'll not hear of you going back, my lovely. I'll hide you here in the back bedroom. I'd not see the child endangered. If your husband dares shows his face here, I'll threaten him with summoning Chegwidden. Are you sure the beating you took is superficial? He didn't try and harm the child?'

Hester shook her head. 'He wants a son more than he wants me. He's said enough times that a wife be easily replaced.' She rubbed her stomach. 'The child be moving. Thadeous did not touch my body.'

'That be something. But no wife can be replaced while she still be alive.' Keziah shook her head. 'Why ever did you wed him?'

'I was a fool,' Hester wailed. 'I can't stay here. What about Gilly?'

'She bain't one for gossip. And in a way she be part of our family. Zacky would never have survived without her and I

306

gave her a home when she needed it most. She would never betray me or mine.'

'How good you are to everyone.' Hester sniffed back her tears. 'It's true Gilly has never spoken a word about your business when she's been in the shop and questioned by the villagers. How do you win such loyalty?'

Keziah shrugged. 'Treat folks decent and often as not they'll do right by you.'

There was a scrabbling sound by the door leading to the yard. It burst open and Baltasar trotted in. The billy goat prodded Keziah gently with his horns and pushed himself between her and Hester.

Hester screamed and the chair toppled over as she stood up in a rush and backed away from the goat. 'Get him away.'

'Hush, your nerves are all shot to pieces. Baltasar bain't gonna hurt you, my lovely. He be house-trained.' Keziah chuckled. 'Well, almost. He had to be with young Zacky around. He knows any nonsense from him and he's out in the yard with the nannies.'

Hester eyed the goat distrustfully. 'I don't know how you can bear him around you.'

'He were the child I could never have.' Keziah ruffled the goat's ears. 'When my first husband died, I did not get much company on the farm. Baltasar got spoiled. I'd be lost without him around me.' She had always treated the goat as others would a dog and was rarely seen without him trotting at her side. She did not care if she made a strange sight striding through the village with Zacky strapped to her back with a thick shawl and Baltasar trotting on a rope. Keziah had no interest in other people's opinions of her. From the curious glances she received when Zacky was with her, Keziah knew many of the villagers suspected the child was a by-blow of Clem's and did not come from an orphanage as they had stated. Zacky was Clem's child all right, the mother dead, from all accounts. Yet from the moment Keziah had seen him left on her doorstep she had known Zacky was a blessing from God.

Hester dabbed at her swollen nose. She had come here out of desperation when she had found that Harry's lugger was not in the harbour. She had felt she could trust Keziah.

'Since Harry is not here, would you feel more comfortable at your father's house?' Keziah asked.

Hester shook her head. 'Pa would never stand up to Thadeous's bullying. He'd tell me that my place was with my husband. Sides, it would be the first place Thadeous would look for me.'

'Unfortunately Lanyon has the law on his side. But that don't mean you have to stand for his ill treatment. I doubt your husband will think of looking here. He don't suspect you've been seeing Harry, does he?'

'He'd have killed me if he had.' Hester was adamant. 'What will Clem say if he finds me here?' Hester kept a nervous eye on the goat. Baltasar was chewing at a bunch of carrots Keziah had been preparing on the table.

'Clem has no love for Lanyon.' Keziah kept her opinion to herself that it was Harry's reaction she was less optimistic about. If Harry had been stringing Hester along to pay back Lanyon for stealing the woman he had intended to wed, he would not be pleased to have Hester foisted upon him. But if the woman was carrying his child, he had a responsibility to safeguard the mother. That was what mattered to Keziah. She pitied Hester. She could not see Harry leaving Penruan or Cornwall. He was making too much money at his smuggling for that. Keziah feared that Harry and Lanyon would come to blows – and it would be an unholy clash of wills.

When Baltasar began to nose the rabbit pie Keziah had not long taken out of the range to cool, she shooed him out of the kitchen. 'Get away, you daft bugger. Clem will have your hide if you eat his supper again.' She realised her phrasing had been unfortunate and filled a beaker of goat's milk for Hester to drink. 'This will build up your strength, my lovely. Would you like a slice of the pie?'

'I couldn't eat.'

'Then I'll get you to your bed. Rest awhile until Clem comes home, but you must eat. If not for you, then for the child.'

'Do you be sure Clem won't mind me staying here?' Hester had always been in awe of the burly fisherman. She blamed Clem for encouraging Harry's wild streak, but Clem had changed since his marriage. He rarely got into fights, and Harry scoffed that marriage had made an honest fisherman of his brother. Which meant that Clem no longer worked with the free-traders. She wished Harry would give up the trade. She would make him change his ways once he took her away from Penruan.

'The jowters were at the harbour today, buying up the fish in the smoking sheds. Clem will have spent the rest of the day in the Dolphin drinking. As long as his supper is hot and ready for him, he'll not send you away.' Keziah frowned. 'Did anyone see you come here?'

'That's why I waited until it were dark. I passed no one.' Hester had finally discarded her veil. She held her head on one side and her eyes closed as pain pummelled through her.

Gilly returned to the kitchen and gasped as she saw Hester's injuries.

'Hester is going to stay with us until Harry returns,' Keziah informed her maid. 'You might as well know that Hester is carrying Harry's child. That makes her family. You can see how her husband treats her. No one must know Hester is here.'

Gilly nodded. 'I got no reason to speak against her. Any

man treats a woman that way don't deserve a wife. Pa used to beat my ma and me. We spat on his grave the day they buried him. Poor Ma died within six months. Plain wore out she were.'

Keziah led Hester to the bedroom. 'There bain't no fire in this room but it be right above the kitchen and it don't get that cold.'

Hester rolled on to her side on the bed and drew up her legs, her hand resting protectively across her stomach. 'I shall never forget your kindness, Keziah. You must think I be a whore for carrying on with Harry, but I do love him. I've always loved only him. He is all that makes my life bearable.'

'It bain't my way to judge folks. What about your maid, Phyllis? Would she guess you've come here?'

Hester shook her head. 'Harry and I were careful no one saw us together. She did not even know I had left the house. Thadeous also gave her a beating. She took to her bed with a bottle of his brandy. I daren't send for Chegwidden. Lanyon said he'd kill us both if the doctor set foot in the house.'

'Do the poor woman need help? Was she badly beaten?' Keziah was incensed at the man's cruelty. Though she understood Hester's plight, she was shocked that Hester had abandoned Phyllis when the woman had been hurt.

'Phyllis were more drunk than hurt. She'll take to her bed for as long as she can get away with it. She were always a lazy slut. Thadeous got her for himself, more than to help with the work.'

'When do you expect Lanyon to return?' Keziah decided that tomorrow she would make discreet enquiries to learn if the maid had been unduly harmed.

'He never tells me much of his comings and goings. When he were in a rage he did say he would see a lawyer. I think he means trouble for the Lovedays.'

Keziah left Hester to sleep.

When Clem returned from the Dolphin he wanted Hester sent back to her home. 'It bain't our affair, Kezzy.'

'He'll end up by killing the child. She's already miscarried once because of Lanyon's brutality. That be your niece or nephew she be carrying. What do you think Harry would say if you put her out and anything happens to the child?'

'This be Harry's business, not mine.' Clem remained belligerent.

Keziah served his supper and gave him a large tankard of ale. Then she put her arms round him and kissed him. 'Let her stay until Harry gets back tomorrow. Let him decide.'

Clem stabbed the pie with his fork and swallowed a mouthful. He ate in silence, his expression bleak. When he had downed the tankard of ale, he handed it to Keziah to refill. As she put it back on the table, he affectionately slapped her buttocks. 'The wench can stay until tomorrow. If Harry wants to beat Lanyon senseless, then I'd be happy to help him. But otherwise I bain't getting caught up in no business between a man and his wife.'

In the middle of the night Phyllis Tamblin dragged herself out of bed. Every muscle ached and it hurt her to breathe. She could not go on like this. That bastard would end up killing her one day. She limped along the corridor to check that the mistress was sleeping. The door was shut and locked and no sound came from within. Lanyon had gone to Truro and would not be back until late tomorrow. Hester would be licking her own wounds and often kept to her room when she had been beaten.

Phyllis straightened with a grimace. The pain was bad but she had suffered worse. She could bear the agony if it meant she could gain her freedom. Phyllis had thought of running away often in the last months as the beatings got worse, but she was terrified of getting caught. She had used that time to

311

watch Lanyon, and she had discovered his secret hiding place for money in the cellar. Even Hester did not know of that.

Phyllis lit a candle and climbed down the steep steps of the cellar. Apart from some wine and brandy bottles stored in a rack, nothing was here but some broken wooden chairs and an old mattress with horsehair innards sticking out through holes. Lanyon was too wily to risk using his own cellar for contraband.

Such was the fear which Lanyon instilled in her, she glanced nervously over her shoulder as she approached the far wall, and again as she lifted out the two bricks to reveal a hole. Several pouches of money were piled inside. Her heart thudded so hard it hurt her chest as she slipped three of the pouches inside her bodice. They were too heavy to carry any more and held more than two hundred pounds: more money than Phyllis could earn in a lifetime and enough to get her to London and set herself up running a lodging house.

A person could lose herself in London. She daren't risk any of the towns round here. Even Plymouth or Bristol would not be safe, for Lanyon visited them on occasion. It did not matter how long it took to get there. Once out of Cornwall she would buy herself a decent dress and take the mail coach to London.

Phyllis was trembling with fear as she left the house. She had never been alone before. And if she was caught with Lanyon's money on her, they'd hang her for sure. And if Lanyon caught her first . . .

A rush of nausea made her vomit in the gutter. Hanging would be a merciful end compared to what Lanyon could do to her.

She hesitated and looked back at the house where she had known only suffering and pain. What was there to lose? She'd be dead soon enough if she stayed with that monster.

Chapter Seventeen

H arry Sawle lowered the sail of his fishing lugger and allowed the vessel to glide towards the quay. The tide was low and the keel of the boat grazed the mud but did not run aground. The quay wall loomed high above the men as they moored by an iron ladder. Fortunately, the quarter-moon would provide sufficient light for them to keep their bearings, whilst still providing deep shadows for protection. There were few clouds which would hinder their vision. It was a perfect night for a raid.

'There be the customs house.' Harry pointed out the building to St John, who was crouched beside him. The single-storey building stood alone, which would make their raid easier.

Another two vessels came alongside and Harry nodded to Barney Rundle, who had been briefed of their plans. There were eighteen men in three boats. It had been dark for two hours, and lights spilled from the windows of taverns on to the streets, but did not reach the water. The fishing fleet was still moored. It was three hours to high tide and Harry reckoned that it would be an hour before any fisherman arrived to prepare his vessel for a night's fishing.

Timing had been critical in organising this raid. Harry had guessed that Lanyon's men would strike once the inhabitants of the port were asleep. To strike first made their own raid more dangerous. There was still movement and lights within the houses. They had to be finished and away before Lanyon's men arrived or there would be a fight between the gangs. An hour was time enough to be away from the quay, avoiding any fishermen and a confrontation with Lanyon's men.

Harry signalled for his companions to remain hidden as he scanned the quayside. There was no sentry patrolling outside the customs house, though a single guard was seated on a barrel, sheltering from the wind. Harry saw his musket propped against the wall of the building. Apart from a fiddler playing in a tavern the town was quiet.

If Lanyon was in league with Beaumont, the officer would have put only a token guard on duty. There would be at least one other inside and it was probable that the door would be locked. Harry had brought Snatcher with him, a skilled picklock.

Harry nodded to Barney Rundle, a fairground fighter who had returned to Penruan for the winter. Rundle silently climbed the ladder and stepped into the shadows. Harry lost sight of him as a cloud covered the moon. The faintest thud told him that Rundle had dealt with the sentry. The moon reappeared to show Rundle dragging the unconscious sentry to the back of the building where he tied and gagged him. Each man had been given orders not to kill unless his own life was threatened. Harry did not want a hanging offence on their hands. If any man was caught, they knew to stay silent and not implicate their associates, otherwise their families would suffer. Though his orders were harsh, the men were paid more money than their fishing had earned them during the last hard winter.

St John crouched in the shadows and his stomach clenched with fear. What had his fury against Lanyon got him involved in? This was the most dangerous undertaking of his

314

life. He wore shabby work clothes and a mask over his lower face. Two pistols were stuck into his waistband, and a dagger inside the leg of his boot.

They crept stealthily through the shadows and Snatcher bent over the lock of the only door to the customs house. When Snatcher straightened, Harry gave the signal for the men to burst in. Surprise was with them. Two guards were huddled around a burning brazier playing dice.

Harry pointed a pistol at them. 'Get over by the wall and don't make any foolish moves if you want to live.'

Fear twisted the men's faces. They were both in their late teens. Obviously, Beaumont had not chosen them for their valour. 'We bain't gonna do nothing.'

'Tie 'em up and gag 'em,' Harry ordered.

Fifty kegs of brandy and geneva were piled along the back wall. Harry ran across the room and prised up a trapdoor. 'The cellar is where the most expensive stuff will be. You four men get down there and throw the parcels up. Take care with the packets of lace and silk. I don't want them dropped and ruined.'

Some of the men had started to heave the brandy kegs on their shoulders. St John stopped them. 'Leave the brandy until last. We will not have time to clear it all.'

They worked swiftly, making several journeys along the quay, but as the tide was so low, they were slowed by having to throw down each parcel or keg to the two men waiting in each lugger to stow it safely. As St John was returning to the customs house for another parcel, he heard movement from the guard behind the building. The man was again conscious.

Harry ran past him, his arms laden. 'See to the guard. He'll raise the alarm.'

St John hesitated as he stood over the prone figure. He balked at hitting an unarmed man. The guard, who was no more than a lad, had wriggled into the moonlight. He

315

stopped moving as St John approached. Above the gag around his mouth, his eyes were round with terror. He shook his head, clearly fearing death. St John brought his pistol butt down on the back of his head. The sickening thud clenched St John's gut with nausea but the excise man had slumped. St John could not prevent himself feeling for a pulse. Thank God he had not killed him.

Harry was running back as St John straightened. 'This bain't no bloody duelling ground. If he'd raised the alarm we'd all swing.'

The cellar was empty and the men were tiring and staggered under the weight of the geneva kegs. St John was worried at the time they were taking. 'Leave the rest and let's get out of here, Harry.'

'No.'

'Don't be a fool. We've taught Lanyon a lesson. Let's go before we are seen.'

Harry hesitated but St John grabbed his arm. 'There's only a dozen or so casks left. Are they worth getting killed for?'

Even as he spoke there was a shout from a group of men who had emerged from the nearest tavern and walked down to the quay. 'Eh, what you lot about? We're supposed to be in on this.'

Eight men lumbered towards them. 'Thought you'd cut us out, did 'ee.' They began to punch the nearest smuggler.

Another of the attackers grunted, ''Ere, these bain't our men. They be stealing our cargo.'

'Get on the boats,' St John shouted. 'Forget the barrels.'

The kegs were dropped and one smashed open, the brandy gushing out on to the flagstones. A fight broke out as the two gangs merged. Harry drew his pistol and ran to help his men.

St John did the same, shouting, 'Get on the boats.' He pressed his pistol against the head of one of their attackers.

'The rest of you back off or your friend dies. Our men, get out of here.'

'Do as he says or I'll kill this bastard as well.' Harry had his gun pointed at the man who had challenged them.

'That be our cargo. You be the ones who ambushed us that time on the moor. I recognise your voices. We got no money for that night's work.'

'There's enough geneva and brandy left in there for two kegs apiece,' St John shouted. 'Take it and run for it. If you stash it your master will never know. He'll think we took the lot.'

When the man hesitated, Harry added, 'I reward men who be loyal to me. Unlike your present master. And unlike him, I don't send men to do a job I bain't gonna risk my own life and freedom over. Ever met this master you're working for tonight? Do you even know his name?'

'He be the most important smuggler on this coast.'

'And he stays cosy by his fire whilst you risk your necks.' Harry sneered. 'He bain't never done a run himself – never risked his life, nor felt the fear when the dragoons or excise men appear on the clifftop. Do you reckon such a man is worth your loyalty? He bain't there protecting your back in a fight, is he?'

'Never saw it that way afore. We've always been tubmen. It bain't usual for those who pay us to be on the beach.'

'They be rich, fat bastards.' Harry spat on the ground. 'They risk their money and reap fortunes from every run. You put your life on the line for a few guineas.'

'You be right,' the man still sounded wary, 'but our master bain't a man to cross.'

'Neither be I.' Harry's mood changed. 'You're either for me or agin me. I know your faces. I'll kill to protect me men just as I'll kill any man who goes against me. And I pay better. What d'ye say? Give us your names and you'll be contacted. I need more men.'

'Name's Snape.' The man he held capitulated.

'Taplin,' another offered.

'Williams.' 'Bellows.' 'Monk.' The others reeled off their names.

'Then, Snape, I hold you responsible for the loyalty of your friends here. Just make sure you don't get caught with the goods tonight.' Harry ran back to the lugger with St John behind him. The other two vessels had already cast off.

'Can we trust them not to talk?' St John stepped down into the prow as the lugger moved away from the quay.

'If they know what's good for them, they won't.'

As the luggers slid further into the harbour a fisherman hailed them. St John's blood froze that they were about to be discovered.

'Ahoy there! That you, Charlie and Joe? You be eager to freeze your balls off!' The fisherman laughed. 'Your old woman nagging you again, Charlie, for spending too much time in Ma Yeo's kiddley?'

Another fisherman on the same smack joined in. 'More like nagging him for spending too much time in that whore Biddy's bed, if I know Charlie.'

St John's nerves stretched taut. Snape and his men coming out of the customs house could betray them. He glanced back to the quay. The customs house looked quiet enough, though he did see one shadow slinking towards the town.

'That be the way of it, lads.' Harry answered the fishermen as the sail caught the full wind and the lugger picked up speed.

'That weren't Charlie,' the first man shouted. 'Who you be?'

Harry did not respond. The fishermen had yet to raise their sails and would never catch them. They slid through the harbour entrance and his whisper scythed the air. 'That could've been a close call.'

'We're not in the clear yet.' St John scanned the water for any sign of pursuit.

It was not long before Harry nudged St John's knee. Three fishing smacks were heading towards the quay, keeping close to the shore. Harry grinned. 'They'll be Lanyon's men. Won't they be in for a surprise.'

'What if they see us?' St John was sweating.

'They'll think we be fishing boats sailing on the tide. They won't suspect nothing, not until they find their cargo gone. Then we'll be safely away.'

St John was still anxious. 'Where are we going to stash this cargo?'

'How about the cave in Trevowan Cove?'

'Are you out of your mind?'

Harry laughed. 'Only jesting. The tubmen are waiting five miles down the coast. It will be taken across the moor tonight on pack ponies and out of the district. The dragoons will be all out in force tomorrow searching for it. By then it will be loaded on a dozen wagons going in several different directions to our customers. I've had to pay each man double for this night's work. This will teach Lanyon he bain't cock of the roost.'

Harry was in high spirits when they reached the place where the tubmen waited. 'Your friend Mr Osborne Garrett will be receiving an ample share of this haul, St John.' He jumped on to the beach to join the tubmen. 'I'll stay with the men. Once this is unloaded I'll sail to Plymouth. I've business with an agent and will be away a week. The Guernsey suppliers be getting nervous now we be at war with France. They be demanding more money in advance.'

He threw some parcels on shore for the tubmen to carry to the waiting pack horses, then added, 'Keep out of Lanyon's way, Loveday. It might be a good time for you to attend any business you have away from Penruan or Trevowan.'

319

'If both of us are out of the district, it will look suspicious.' St John was still nervous that they would be discovered. 'There's too much work to be tackled on the estate for me to be absent. And one of us should be on hand to brazen it out if Lanyon starts his accusations.'

Harry laughed. 'They can make all the accusations they want but without any cargo there bain't no evidence. This lot will be safely hidden by morning.'

After beating his wife and servant, Thadeous Lanyon had left Penruan for Truro. His savage anger remained with him throughout the next day. He visited a lawyer to begin proceedings against the Loveday yard, but the lawyer was a fool and did not think Thadeous had a case.

'I'll break them if it takes the last penny I have,' the merchant raged.

He went down to the waterfront and prowled the area. The whores were lank-haired, ravage-faced women, which in his present mood did not appeal to him. Years ago this was the only type of woman he could afford. His pride now demanded better. He wanted a pretty, young woman who was free from disease, clean and sweet-smelling. It was time he hired a new servant, for Phyllis's dubious charms had paled.

His discontent deepened. Frustration fed his earlier anger; the craving building within had to be satisfied. It was growing dark and as the respectable citizens of the town cleared the streets, he felt isolated. The anger fed old demons. All his life he had been an outcast.

He had been brought up in a dilapidated cottage on the moor with a leaking roof, and broken shutters over the paneless windows. Abandoned by his mother when he was a child, he had lived in fear of Mose Lanyon, his brutal father. Mose Lanyon was a smuggler, rustler and wrecker who beat him when he was sober and beat him harder when he was drunk. Neighbours, who were few, shunned the Lanyon cottage and as a child Thadeous had no friends. Twice he had run away from home but his father had found him and dragged him back. The third time was after a cattle raid. Thadeous had reported his father to the authorities for stealing three cows, which were still in the byre by the cottage. Mose Lanyon was arrested and hanged at Bodmin, and finally, at the age of twelve, Thadeous was free of his brutality. He survived by stealing and had killed his first man at fourteen when he came across a drunken pedlar on the moor. Stealing the pedlar's mare and covered wagon, he travelled the country selling wares. Slowly he prospered and he made extra money as a tubman. At seventeen he married his first wife – a young woman who was an orphan and who had inherited a rundown farm. When the farm did not provide them with a living he sold it and sold her favours to any man with a shilling. He also began to look with longing at the homes and dress of the gentry. That was the life he wanted. He was tired of living alone and travelling the roads. He wanted to become respectable.

It had been a long journey. Yet still Thadeous was not accepted. The villagers of Penruan were polite, but that was because most of them owed him money. The gentry he craved to emulate continued to look down their noses at him. He had hoped to marry to win status. His first wife he had sold to a brothel when he was nineteen, and he assumed her long dead. Two other wives he had married for their money. One had died from an overdose of laudanum. She had been a stupid, weak woman, always snivelling. Her dowry had enabled him to buy the shop and drying sheds in Penruan. His third wife had died of a fever after a beating he had given her when she had denied him his marital rights. Her dowry had provided the investment for his early smuggling runs which had eventually made his fortune. Yet for all the wealth he had acquired, the gentry still did not accept him.

Thadeous glowered into the darkness of an alley and leaned back against a wall. It had been a mistake to wed Hester Moyle, who was no more than a chandler's daughter. He had chosen her to spite Harry Sawle. The revenge had backfired. Hester was another disappointing bride. But at least she could yet provide him with an heir – something his other wives had been incapable of. But it did not solve his need for acceptance. For that he would have to marry into a family of ancient lineage. There were plenty of those who were impoverished. With such a wife the gentry and nobility would have to accept him.

Unfortunately the loss of the *Sea Sprite* had depleted his income. He would need a year or two to replenish that. In the meantime Hester would have served her usefulness and been disposed of.

Frustration ground through him and refuelled his anger. He was not by nature a patient man. He had waited too long and striven too hard to have his ambitions slip through his fingers.

The sound of light, hurried footsteps caught his attention. A woman hesitated at the top of the alley he was walking through. He ducked into the shadows to study her. She was carrying a basket over her arm and was too well dressed to be a servant. The alley was now dark and wound in a dogleg towards the next street. The woman started forward to continue on her way. Then, with an impatient tut, she paused again at the entrance to the alley before entering it.

'My poor little Patrick is so sick, this will save me several minutes,' she muttered to herself as she looked nervously from side to side.

Lanyon stepped out in front of her. Before she could scream, his hand covered her mouth, and he dragged her behind some empty wooden crates. The basket fell to the ground and she began to struggle. She smelled of lemon soap and the wool of her gown and cloak were expensive. As she fought to escape his hold, her breasts and hips moved against him and his lust ignited. He could not live without a woman, although he hated them, as he had hated the mother who had abandoned him.

He slammed her head back against the wall and, stunned from the blow, she sagged in his arms. Then he pushed her to the ground and hoisted her petticoats to her waist. Her flesh was firm, inflaming his desire.

'Spare me.' Her voice was muffled against his hand. 'I am a married woman. My child is sick.'

Thadeous did not look at her face. He did not care if she was pretty or ugly. He wanted to punish her for the mother who had abandoned him, all the people who shunned him, and for the loss of his ship. Someone had to pay. It did not matter who.

He had spread her legs and was about to enter her when she recovered enough from her dazed state to struggle in earnest. 'Stop. I beg you. No. Dear God. No!'

As he rammed into her, the iron fingers of one hand pressed into her throat to silence her cries. She fought hard and his fingers tightened. Her movements became weaker as she gasped for air. A frenzy of desire blinded him to everything but his need. Finally satiated, he drew away. She lay unmoving, her basket upturned and the bottles of physic from the apothecary broken around her. Her skirts were about her waist, exposing shapely white thighs. Her head lay in the gutter, the lace cap muddied and torn, and her blonde hair floated in a puddle. She had been pretty but now her tongue lolled obscenely from her mouth, and her eyes were staring in death.

As Thadeous heaved himself to his feet and adjusted his

clothing, there were voices in the street. He ran to the far end of the alley and did not stop until he reached the inn where he was staying. He paused a moment outside to regain his breath, then ambled into the taproom and demanded a large brandy and an eel pie for his supper.

The next morning when he entered the taproom to break his fast, two merchants awaiting the London coach were discussing the rape and murder of the wife of the head clerk of a bank.

'Mrs Blake was a most estimable woman,' one declared. 'She collected old clothes for the orphans. And left five children and not one more than eight years old. Her husband is inconsolable, they say. She'd gone to an apothecary for physic for her sick son.'

'I blame the anarchy in France,' his companion announced. 'It's setting a precedent for lawlessness and sedition everywhere.'

The first man shook his head. 'Our town is not safe for a decent woman. The waterside brothels encourage the base lusts of men. We are plagued by gangs of drunken, brawling sailors, and now decent women are accosted. The constables have no control over law and order, it would seem.'

Lanyon ate his roast beef and ham with scarcely a twinge to his conscience. Yet he found the beef and ham had lost its flavour. His rage at losing *Sea Sprite* still seared him. He would not rest until he had been avenged for its loss. At least there were the goods in the customs house which his men would have reclaimed.

His thin lips twitched at his cunning. Beaumont had been restless that so many cargoes were being landed. By capturing those goods the officer would get his credit, and would receive none of the blame when the customs house was robbed.

Lanyon left Truro to return to Penruan in his coach. As

the vehicle lumbered over the rutted road, his mood was sour that the lawyer he had seen the previous day doubted he could win a case against the Loveday yard. His hatred for the Lovedays increased with each painful jolt of the coach.

It was almost dusk as he approached Penruan. Sheltering from a rain shower a figure detached itself from the split trunk of an oak which had been struck by lightning. The man called out for the coach to stop.

Lanyon stuck his head out of the window. A scruffy beggar with a staff held out a folded piece of paper. 'You be Lanyon? I were told your coach would pass this way. I were to give 'ee this. The man said 'ee'd give me a shilling for me trouble. I bin waitin' fer hours.'

Lanyon snatched the note, his face turning puce with fury as he read it. 'Drive on,' he shouted.

'What about me shilling?' The beggar held on to the door of the coach.

Lanyon slammed his fist into the man's nose and heard the bone break. The beggar fell back and the coach lurched as the back wheel ran over his ankle. When the man began to scream in agony, Lanyon ordered the coach to halt and yelled up to the driver. 'See to him.'

He watched as Guy Mabbley walked back to the figure on the ground. The driver had been Lanyon's henchman for years, and knew what Lanyon expected of him. He was heavily muscled and used his brawn to persuade anyone in debt to Lanyon to part with their money.

'Me ankle be broke,' the beggar groaned.

Mabbley kicked the beggar, his boots slamming into the man's ribs and head. The beggar yelled as his body jerked under the blows, curling into a ball to protect his head with his hands. Finally the beggar lay still. A final kick sent the ragged figure into a water-filled ditch. If he was not already dead, he would be by morning.

Lanyon acknowledged Mabbley's return with a nod, and the coach rocked as he climbed back on board and whistled to the horses to move forward. A red mist filled Lanyon's mind. The letter was from Beaumont telling him that the cargo had already been stolen before his men got to the customs house. He also mentioned that St John Loveday had been in St Austell and knew about the cargo being confiscated.

The streets of Penruan were dark and deserted as Lanyon alighted outside his house. He snapped at Guy Mabbley, 'I want St John Loveday taught a lesson – a lesson he bain't likely to recover from. There'll be twenty guineas for you if the job's done right.'

The deaths of the woman and beggar were forgotten by the time Lanyon entered his house. His thoughts were focused on getting revenge on the Lovedays. He was hungry and cold and his anger erupted to find the house in darkness and no fires lit.

'Hester! Where the devil are you, slut?' He stamped through the rooms, banging open the doors and shouting. 'Hester, get your miserable hide out here. Phyllis, you lazy whore, get me food and brandy.'

The only sound was the echo of his voice around the rooms. The house was deserted. With a howl of fury, he stamped through the house in search of his wife and servant. Banging open the door to Phyllis's room he saw the empty hooks where she hung her clothes. He threw back the lid of a wooden coffer and found that also empty. The maid had run away. His wife would pay for this. Was she cringing in her bed, hoping to avoid his wrath?

When he discovered Hester's room also deserted, he could not believe that his wife had had the courage to leave him. There were clothes hanging in her closet but then he noticed that her cloak was missing. He snatched off his wig and stamped on it in his rage. The women were in league together.

'You'll not get far, madam. No one walks out on me. And you be carrying my son. I'll find you. And once my child be born, you'll rot in hell for this.'

He stumbled to the cellar and removed the two bricks from the wall. Half the money was gone. He whirled round, apoplectic with rage. 'You bitches will pay! I'll hunt you down! You'll never escape me!'

Tomorrow he would pay a dozen men to hunt for his wife and servant. Phyllis could rot in a ditch like the beggar. But Hester would have to be locked in the cellar and kept alive until after his child was born.

Chapter Eighteen

The heat of the sun beat upon Japhet's back as he swung the mallet down on to the fence post until it stood secure. Oswald Rabson straightened from holding the post and lent upon it. He was sweating heavily and lines of weariness were grooved each side of his mouth.

'I don't know how we would have managed without you this spring, Japhet.' He coughed and absently rubbed at the tightness which invaded his chest. He picked up a cross-rail to span the last two posts Japhet had erected. Even that effort made him gasp for breath. 'I worry that you would rather be elsewhere. Life can hold little pleasure for you on the farm. You have always been a man at ease in the town. We are stopping you earning a living.'

'I would not be here if I did not want to be.' Japhet hammered two nails into the fence rail and moved to the far post to fasten the other end. 'I've had a winning streak at the card tables and sold four mares at the horse fair for a good profit. I have money enough for my needs. And town life can have its drawbacks. I have overstayed my welcome too often in Bodmin, Truro and Bristol.'

'You mean there are irate husbands looking out for you?' Oswald laughed.

'An occasional husband mayhap, but not every gentleman is a good loser at cards.' Japhet squinted against the sun. His conscience did not rest as easy as once it had. When financially straitened, he had picked too many pockets, and on several occasions played the High Toby and held up a coach – although he never stole from men who looked as though they could not afford to lose a purse. He had used his quick wits to play upon the gullible and too often escaped the retribution or capture by a whisker. Such a life no longer held the excitement it once had. He was twenty-nine and had begun to realise that there was more to living than the pursuit of pleasure. He needed some purpose – but what that purpose was still eluded him.

He shrugged. 'It is years since I spent spring in the country and I am enjoying working on the farm. It is time I put my days to better use.'

'Your father would welcome such words,' Oswald replied. 'But you are staying because Hannah asked you. She fusses too much about my health. I have always suffered with my chest in the spring and summer.'

'And the last two winters you've had a lung fever.'

Oswald frowned. 'So it *is* because of Hannah. I do not want you to stay because you feel you have to.'

Japhet grinned and pushed back his hair which hung in sable waves about his broad shoulders. He had taken to wearing it unbound about the farm. Already his skin was a dusky gold from the sun and there was a day's growth of beard on his jaw beneath the long side-whiskers. He had not shaved this morning as he had been up since four helping Oswald with the difficult birth of a foal. 'I am here because, for the moment, this is where I am content.'

Japhet heaved another fence post into position and felt the surge of energy pulse through his arm and shoulders as the mallet swung down. Strangely, he was content. His encounter with Kitty Veryan's husband had tempered his appetite for womanising. The beating he had received and given the captain did not trouble him. It was the knowledge that he may have had to take the captain's life to save his own which disturbed him. He had been in countless fights and even duels, his skill with a pistol and sword preserving his life and ensuring that his opponent was wounded but never fatally. He would kill in self-defence but never over a point of honour.

The incident over Kitty had made him re-evaluate his life. He had been shocked at how easily he could have ruined her life by his own selfish pursuit of pleasure. Japhet had made discreet enquiries and learned that Kitty remained in her husband's home. Captain Veryan no longer sailed on long voyages. Japhet hoped that Kitty was happy.

The long hours of work on the farm took the edge from his wilder desires. He was invited by Barbara Keyne to attend their weekly card parties. Sir Arthur had selected his lady companion for the night before nine in the evening and, as the guests were expected to stay over, Lady Keyne came to Japhet's room once they retired. The cards had also smiled on Japhet and he should have been content. Yet there remained a restlessness in Japhet which he could not dissipate or find the answer to.

Another two posts were in place when Japhet saw Oswald sway. He tossed down the mallet and walked back to the stone bottle of cider propped under the shade of a gorse bush. He drank deeply before handing it to Oswald who was now resting on the grass. Japhet walked back to the wagon and heaved two more fence posts over his shoulder, placed them in position and went back to collect the rails. Two riders appeared over the rise in the next meadow. He smiled at seeing Gwen, but his smile faded as he recognised her companion, Lieutenant Francis Beaumont.

Gwen waved. She was wearing a military-style red riding habit and a hussar hat with a black plume. It should have clashed with her russet ringlets but instead it enhanced their fire and lustre.

'We have just come from the farmhouse and Hannah asked us to bring you these. Luke is teething and fretful so I said I would save her the ride over here.' She drew up to Japhet and handed him a basket. The smell of warm pasties was appetising.

'You are looking lovely today, Gwen. That habit becomes you. What brings you to the farm?'

'I promised Hannah a pattern book of the latest fashions some weeks ago but have been too busy to call.'

When he lifted his hands to assist her to alight, Gwen shook her head. 'I cannot stay. Mama has invited Lieutenant Beaumont for luncheon.'

Puzzled at her cool manner, Japhet resorted to teasing. 'Pray, extend my compliments to your dear mama. I hope she has recovered from a fit of the spleen. Lady Anne had difficulty breathing when I was dancing with you at Pengarth. I have been remiss not to call more often.'

Gwen looked away. 'We have come not to expect you.'

Oswald bowed to Gwen. 'It is our fault that Japhet pays so few social visits. He has been a tremendous help on the farm.'

'Did you see the foal?' Japhet reclaimed her attention.

Gwendolyn laughed and relaxed. 'Davey insisted I saw it. There was a time when you spoke of breeding from your own mares.'

Japhet returned her smile. 'One day I hope to. But that will take a large investment to be done well. I would also need my own farm.'

'And it would also mean commitment and settling down. Things you prefer to avoid.' Her voice sharpened. She turned to Oswald who had asked her a question about her mother.

Puzzled by her tone, Japhet turned to the excise officer.

'Your occupation gives you much leisure time. Are there no dastardly smugglers to hunt down, or their secret caches of contraband to uncover?'

'The riding officers work on the land: I patrol the seas.'

Beaumont peered down at Japhet from his horse and his thin lips twisted in a sneer. His stare was critical.

Japhet stood with his hands on his hips. His boots were covered in dust and his black breeches were indecently snug. His hair was unbound and he was unshaven as no gentleman would appear in public. With his shirt open to the waist, his chest was exposed, showing a gold cross which caught the sunlight. His sleeves were rolled up disclosing browned forearms and he looked like a common brigand. There was a flash of white teeth when Japhet grinned up at Gwendolyn Druce in an insufferable manner which made Beaumont's blood boil.

Beaumont dabbed at his brow; his cutaway coat, waistcoat and high-necked cravat were deplorably hot. He had not visited Traherne Hall to jaunt further across the countryside on a hot day, but to sit in cool elegance and pay court to Miss Druce. He had arrived as she had been about to ride and Lady Anne had insisted that he accompany her daughter. Gwendolyn had set off at a furious pace which he had been hard put to keep up with. She had not spoken to him the entire ride and to be forced to watch Japhet Loveday flirting with her in such a familiar fashion was galling.

Japhet showed no sign of abating with his compliments. 'I've never seen you look so well, Gwen. How is life treating you? I see so little of you these days. And I have visited Traherne Hall. Or does the Lady Anne spirit you away as soon as I am seen approaching?'

'I no longer allow Mama to dictate my life, as well you know,' she parried, and tossed back her hair with a proud defiance.

Japhet laughed. 'And rightly so, but does your estimable mother know that?'

Anger sparked in Gwendolyn's eyes. 'It is time Mama and others realised that I am capable of making my own decisions about my companions.'

At the barbed challenge in her words, Japhet bowed to Gwendolyn and raised a dark brow in teasing enquiry. 'May it always be so. You have impeccable taste . . . usually.' He glanced at her escort, who was glaring at him. 'Let me not delay you further. Mr Beaumont looks flushed and uncomfortable from your ride.'

'I believe we shall be late to dine if we do not hurry, Miss Druce,' Lieutenant Beaumont interrupted.

Japhet picked up a fence post and sauntered along the field.

'That man is insufferably rude,' Beaumont declared. 'He deserves to be called out for the way he spoke to you.'

'Japhet is an old and dear friend.' Gwendolyn watched him walk away and there was longing in her eyes.

'You must take care which men you bestow your friendship upon, Gwendolyn. That man has an unsavoury reputation where women are concerned. I doubt his intentions are ever honourable.'

She turned on him. 'It is Miss Druce, if you please, Mr Beaumont. I have not given you permission to be overfamiliar with my name. Perhaps it is your intentions which should be questioned. I did not invite you to accompany me, nor have I encouraged you to call at the Hall. Japhet has never been less than honest with me. And I do not care to hear my friends maligned.'

She dug in her heels and her Arab mare sped across the field, leaving Lieutenant Beaumont struggling to keep up with her. He was furious. He had chosen to honour Gwendolyn Druce by calling on her and she treated him no better than a churl. It was clear that she was enamoured of that rogue Japhet Loveday. The Lovedays were the bane of his life. First Adam had cost him a career in the navy, then St John had made a fool of him. Now this impertinent knave Japhet seemed to hold the affection of the woman he had chosen to marry. Indeed, needed to marry and very soon. Gwendolyn was heiress to a sizeable fortune and he was living beyond his means. His grandfather had cut off his allowance at the beginning of the year, declaring it would not be reinstated until he married a woman of notable family, and settled down to provide an heir. Francis was the last of his line. His grandfather had threatened to leave everything to his married niece, Venetia, if she produced a son before Francis had wed. And Venetia had recently announced that she was with child.

Francis Beaumont had also seen the way Japhet Loveday had looked at Gwendolyn Druce. The man cared for her – probably more deeply than the philanderer would admit. Loveday was a fool. That made Gwendolyn Druce even more desirable to Francis. He would win her from Japhet. That would spike the Lovedays' pride and deprive them of ever winning Gwen's fortune.

Japhet glanced up and saw Gwen speeding away from her companion and laughed. 'He won't stand a chance and, of course, he's after her money.'

'Hannah says Gwen is in love with you.' Oswald handed Japhet a nail.

'Hannah, like my mama, wants to see me shackled to a wife.'

'Love does not bind you by physical bonds but by devotion,' Oswald replied.

Japhet looked at him in surprise. Oswald was a close-mouthed man for such an emotional outburst. 'Hannah is happy. Is that not what matters? I would make Gwen miserable.

334

I doubt I could be faithful. We are friends and I suppose there is a bond between us which I have experienced with no other woman, but she deserves better than I could give her.'

There was pain in Oswald's eyes as he held Japhet's gaze. 'And does not Hannah deserve more than I can give her? My health is failing and she works harder with each year. She is a Loveday and deserves a life of ease. My family may be an old one, but we lost our money in my grandfather's time.'

'Hannah loves you. She would not change her life,' Japhet defended his sister.

Oswald grinned. 'Then how is Gwen different? The likes of that pompous oaf escorting her today will never make her happy.' Japhet was striking the fence post with unwarranted force, prompting Oswald to add. 'Are you so sure that you do not love her?'

Japhet hit his thumb with the mallet and cursed roundly.

'You have not answered my question,' Oswald persisted.

Japhet glowered at him as he sucked his throbbing thumb. 'I have been in love many times. What I feel for Gwen is different. It is a comfortable affection. Love is a pain – a kind of frenzy.'

'No, Japhet, that is lust. Can you truly say you have never desired Gwen?'

'Now you impugn my manhood.' He laughed. 'Any red-blooded man would want to bed her. But she is pure – untarnished. I would not dishonour her.'

'It has not troubled you with other women's reputations.'

Japhet lifted the linen cloth from the basket Gwen had brought to them, handed a pasty to Oswald, and hoped that eating would silence this inquisition. He lay back on the grass propped on one elbow. 'Is that how everyone sees me, as a despicable cad?'

'I cannot answer for those you may have crossed in your life, but most of us regard you as an irrepressible rogue. And how you manage to keep so many ex-mistresses regarding you with fondness defeats most men's imagination.' Oswald laughed. It made his chest wheeze and he continued in a laboured breath, 'And those men envy you your successes with women. But is that all you want from life?'

Japhet bit into the pasty and chewed it thoughtfully. 'In honesty, I do not know what I want. I know what I do not want: boredom, poverty, loss of freedom, and the constant responsibility of another person. All the things that would make me fail to make a wife happy.'

'Then you would underestimate your wife, if she truly loved you.'

Japhet threw back his head and laughed, although Oswald's honesty made him uncomfortable. Seeing Gwen with Beaumont had unsettled him. The feeling made him restless. Perhaps it was time to leave Cornwall for a while. He wanted the conversation changed. 'Now even you lecture me. I know the perils of love. It is Pious Peter who is heading for disaster.'

'Is he still infatuated with Lisette? Hannah thinks it would be a good match.' Oswald looked serious. 'Lisette will open Peter's eyes to the real world. Lisette will make him forget his bigotry. For all his repressed desires Peter is a passionate man.'

'That shows how little Hannah knows. Lisette would be a disastrous match for Peter, or anyone. She's self-centred and a natural wanton. I know that look in a woman's eyes. She would devour Peter and spit him out for breakfast.'

'Edward and Amelia seem to be encouraging him.'

'Uncle Edward wants shot of Lisette. But Peter could never handle her. She will run rings round him and make him profoundly miserable.' Japhet chuckled. 'Though that might be what he wants and deserves. When Peter is not bigoted and patronising, he has a strong streak of martyrdom in him.'

336

★ ★ ★

Peter Loveday did not see himself as others saw him. All around him were souls who had lost their way to the Lord. He wanted to guide them to redemption, allow them to see the error of their sins, and save them from hellfire. All the passion of his natural desires was repressed so that he could serve his god with true piety. His brother and cousins must be made to see the error of their ways. They were his cross to bear. Though they mocked him, he had resolved never to abandon their souls to the devil.

And there was no more deserving soul who needed saving than Lisette. The horrors she had suffered in France had at first disgusted him. Then he had seen her beauty, the innocence she radiated, and knew that she could be saved. Lisette was his Mary Magdalene. Until now Peter had never understood how Jesus not only forgave such a debauched woman, but allowed her to follow him.

Meeting Lisette had shown Peter the power of compassion which Christ had preached. That Lisette was a Papist should doubly have condemned her to Peter, for he had no tolerance for idolatry. As he became more enamoured of Lisette, he reasoned that she had never had the right man to guide her religious teachings. Also she had been married against her will to a monster. When fate had released her from that marriage, Adam should have done the honourable thing and married her. Instead he had been seduced by a gypsy, a heathen who did not attend church. Also Senara had an unholy knowledge of herbs which made Peter suspect her of witchcraft. That Adam had abandoned Lisette, his former betrothed, to marry his gypsy were the actions of a man bewitched.

Peter had agonised at the humiliation Lisette had suffered by Adam's marriage. She was so frail and delicate. Was it any wonder that temporarily her wits had been unhinged? Pain and suffering had driven Lisette to wild and unacceptable behaviour. He had seen the devil wrestling to win her soul. When Adam first abandoned Lisette to search for his gypsy, Peter had taken Lisette a Bible for comfort. She had tossed it aside. When he gently remonstrated and guided her towards the wisdom of the Lord, she had stared blankly at the wall. Every day he offered up prayers for her and his prayers had been heard. Lisette had changed. The wildness had left her eyes and she appeared to enjoy his company, though her conversation remained more frivolous than Peter would have wished, and when he tried to bring her to God, she sent him away.

She had been kinder to him since they had travelled to Bodmin. He visited Trevowan twice a week, and played the guitar to entertain her. At first he had been shocked at the bold way she flirted with him. He reasoned that in France they had a different outlook upon such matters. Unused to flirting, he believed her when she complimented him, or told him his company brightened her days. With each meeting his feelings turned from infatuation to adoration and then to a love which bordered on obsession. He wanted to marry her, cherish her and bring her into the embrace of the Lord who would wash away her sins.

His step was jaunty as he arrived at Trevowan for his second visit that week.

'Peter, you are here again.' Amelia hid a smile at the frequency of his visits, their reason all too obvious. She was arranging flowers in a vase in the winter parlour. 'It is a lovely afternoon and Lisette has gone for a walk in the cove. Why do you not join her?'

'I think I will, Aunt.' Peter bowed. His exit was so indecently fast that he almost collided with Elspeth, who was limping across the hall after returning from her daily ride.

'What is the hurry?' she snapped as Peter sped past her.

Amelia laughed. 'He is eager to see Lisette. He is in love.'

Elspeth frowned. 'You should not encourage him. Much as I would have Lisette off our hands, she's too wilful for Peter. It would be a disastrous match.'

'Peter needs a wife and preferably one with a dowry. I think you wrong Peter. Lisette has been more malleable since Peter has been calling upon her.'

'If anyone had any influence over that young minx, it was William,' Elspeth snorted. 'Thank God for this war which has kept him away from her clutches. I began to fear there would be an understanding between them.'

'William and Lisette, surely not?' Amelia laughed. 'He is too old for her. Peter is the same age as Lisette. Edward would approve of the match.'

Lisette had taken off her shoes and stockings and was walking through the waves as they lapped against the sand of the cove. Her toe stubbed against a large granite pebble and with a cry of rage she picked it up and hurled it into the sea. She waded to the beach and sat down to rub her foot.

'Everything in this land is against me.' Lisette pouted as she stared at the deserted beach. She was bored and lonely. She missed the clamour and bustle of her château in the Auvergne, and the extravagant ballets and balls she had attended at Versailles. Why could not the Lovedays live in London?

Discontented, she kicked at the sand. There would be endless diversions and entertainments to amuse her in London. Here there was only hunting, which she endured rather than relished, or the occasional dining with friends. It had been weeks since she had seen William. After their night of passion he had left her before daybreak and returned to his ship. Expecting his adoration, she had clung to him, declaring her love. He had kissed her with tenderness, but his manner had become withdrawn. She had not believed him to be a man to so use a woman and discard her. Lisette had expected a proposal and that he would set her up in a charming house, which she would insist was in a fashionable part of Truro. There she could have escaped the vigilance of the Lovedays and, while William was at sea, entertain new friends. But while William spoke of their future he had not wanted to announce their betrothal until he knew what plans the navy had for him and he returned from Plymouth.

The single letter he had written to her had asked after her welfare and said that he regretted his sudden departure. His ship had developed some problem, which had prevented him from sailing with the fleet, and he hoped to visit Trevowan before he sailed. It was an unemotional letter when she had ached for words of love and devotion. Lisette had burned the letter and her temper had been mutinous ever since.

'Did William have anything to say to us in his letter?' Amelia had asked at breakfast the next day.

Lisette had shrugged. 'Why should he? It was addressed to me. He asked how I was faring and that he hoped that I was becoming more accustomed to the English way of manners and conduct.' She had thrown up her hands in pique. 'When will you understand that I am not English? I am French. It is natural for the French, who have a great passion for life, to show what we feel – unlike you English who keep your feelings wrapped up in wet blankets.'

'It is not that we do not take pleasure in life, Lisette,' Amelia had rebuked. 'It is that we are more decorous in the way we express our feelings.'

'Except men like Lord Fetherington or that terrible lecher Sir Arthur Keyne. They are so coarse. In France if a man pursues a woman he does it with flair and delicacy.'

'I dare say the intentions are the same – to destroy the woman's virtue. I could condone neither behaviour.' Amelia had been affronted. 'But you are singularly honoured that William has written to you. I doubt Edward has received more than half a dozen letters in all the years William has been at sea.'

Lisette did not understand the significance of Amelia's words, she was too angry with William for not complying with her plans.

'Lisette, are you hurt?' Peter Loveday called now. She was jerked from her reverie and stopped rubbing her foot to watch him approach.

'Peter, you are a knight come to rescue me from the ennui which plagues me.' Her skirts had been lifted to her knees to reveal bare slender calves and she saw Peter's gaze drawn to them. She lifted her foot. 'I hurt my foot in the water. It is so painful, I fear I may have broken my toe.'

Peter kneeled on the sand and cupped her foot in his palm. He gently moved her toes. 'Does this hurt?'

She sucked in her breath. 'A little.'

'I do not think it is broken. It looks bruised.' He continued to hold her foot.

Lisette studied him with her head on one side. His hair was longer than he used to wear it and it now reached his shoulders. She touched it, remembering that she had said that she disliked his cropped hair. 'You have grown your hair. How handsome it makes you look. Not so stern like those dour Methodists and Quakers.'

A blush spread upwards from his plain stock.

'Did you grow your hair to please me, Peter?' She enjoyed teasing Peter, who was so naïve where women were concerned. Yet he was handsome, and she had seen many women try to capture his interest. She had overheard Japhet joking, saying that he despaired for his brother, who was still a virgin. Was that true? Surely not, but there was an innocence about him.

341

He swallowed several times as he massaged her foot and she hid her smile. His face was taut as he repressed his emotions. Peter desired her. It would be amusing to seduce him.

'I think you did grow your hair to please me, Peter. A woman is always flattered when a man does something special like that for her.'

'Do you want to put your foot on the ground to see if it will take your weight?' He glanced uncertainly at her.

Lisette shook her head. 'My foot is sore. And your hands are so gentle. They are easing the pain. Will you rub the instep and my calf? The muscle is strained.'

His fingers ran lightly across her skin and around her ankle and the length of her calf. Lisette lay back on the sand. 'That feels wonderful. The pain is easing, but you must not stop.'

She closed her eyes and enjoyed the pleasure of his hand caressing her flesh. With a sigh she flung her arm back over her head and waited for him to kiss her. The movement on her leg ceased. There was the lightest touch of his lips on her instep and she heard his breathing change. Her foot was placed on the sand and her soft sigh should have encouraged him to become bolder. Nothing happened. When she opened her eyes, she saw him clutching his hands together and his lips moved in silent prayer. It took all her willpower not to laugh.

She sat up and put her hand on his thigh. 'You pray over me as though I were mortally wounded.'

'I pray to avert sin.' His voice cracked as she ran her hand along his thigh. And as his darkened eyes locked with hers, she leaned forward to kiss him and draw him down on to the sand.

After the briefest hesitancy, he kissed her with an ardour which made her breathless. Peter may not have been the most

342

accomplished of lovers, but if he took her with haste, it was with an energy and thoroughness which made her cry out in pleasure.

When they lay in each other's arms, she insisted, 'Next time we meet, we must be more circumspect and use the cave as our trysting place.'

Peter groaned and swayed to his feet. His stare was distraught as he scanned the cliffs and beach lest someone had seen them. 'There can be no next time, not like this. We must wait until we are married. But there is no need for us to wait long. My father will post the banns on Sunday.'

Lisette scrambled to her feet, her petite figure shaking with fury. 'What is this talk of marriage? I never said I would marry you.'

'Of course we must marry. I have dishonoured you. The devil got into my blood and I was tempted, but I will not see you shamed. I intend to stand by you and we shall be wed in a month.'

Lisette stamped her foot, too angry to notice the pain. 'We will not be wed in a month, a year, or even a lifetime. I am to marry William.'

'William who?'

'How many Williams are there in your family?' She flung up her arms in exasperation. 'But you must say nothing of our betrothal. It is a secret until he comes home on his next leave.' She retraced her steps along the beach to where she had left her shoes.

Peter ran after her and spun her round. 'How can you consider marrying Uncle William. He is old. And you have just given yourself to me. I am your husband in all but name.'

Lisette laughed and poured out her scorn. 'Peter, you are so naïve. I have also slept with William. But him I love.'

'That is a lie. You cannot have given yourself to Uncle William. Why are you playing this cruel game?' He grabbed her arms and shook her. 'I love you, Lisette.'

Her expression was haughty as she demanded, 'Take your hands off me. I am the Marquise de Gramont. Why should I marry a penniless preacher? Certainly not because we have enjoyed each other's body. I was lonely and needed comfort. I love William.'

He thrust her from him so hard that she sat down with a jolt on the beach. Lisette beat the sand with her fists as rage consumed her. 'Go away. You are unpleasant and insufferable. I thought we could pass our afternoons enjoyably together, but not now—'

Peter stumbled back from her in horror. 'Jezebel! My Uncle William and Uncle Edward must be told that you are a whore. You shame our family.'

Lisette sprang to her feet and slapped his face. 'You will say nothing. I have given you a great gift and you would abuse it. I will say that you forced me. That you went crazy and, after years of piety and frustration, your desires got the better of you. I will denounce you for a hypocrite. Go away. I do not want you to visit me again. I thought you were kind, but you are like the others. Only William is different.'

'Others! Dear God, how many others have there been?' Peter backed from her in disgust.

'Enough to know that William is who I wish to marry. You are a boy – you are not a man. You should be grateful for what I have taught you.' Her angelic face was twisted with anger. 'You cannot preach about the redemption of sin until you have experienced sin. You have lain with your uncle's betrothed. It is you who have violated your family honour. Crawl on your knees to your God and beg His forgiveness.'

Peter was shocked by her invective. Could this frail, petite beauty be so evil? 'I did not know of this betrothal. The evil is yours. I cannot let you deceive Uncle William. He may forgive the shame you endured in France, but not this.'

The malice in her eyes made him clasp the cross hanging round his neck.

'Speak and I shall tell your mother every intimate detail of what happened today. Indeed, I shall tell her so much more than what happened that she will never be able to look on you again and not be horrified at the debauched creature she gave birth to.'

'It is you who are debauched – unclean.' Peter was tortured by her confession and her virulence.

His accusation left Lisette unmoved. 'You can ruin my reputation if you wish. And I will ruin yours. Then who will listen to a preacher who has scandalised society by raping his own uncle's future wife, and that uncle a brave captain who is risking his life at sea against the enemies of his country.' She smiled as venom continued to drip from each word. 'If you are wise, you will say nothing, Peter. There are souls more worthy than I who need you to save them. I was past redemption, the day Adam and your family abandoned me to the lechery of my husband.'

She walked away and Peter fell to the sand and prayed. Tears streamed down his cheeks and his heart was sealed in granite. He prayed until the sun disappeared over the horizon. The red and orange clouds rose like the flames of hell awaiting to devour him. He could not abandon the Lord's work. Uncle William was no innocent. Today Lisette had seduced him for her own amusement, but Uncle William would not have allowed that to happen. If he had slept with Lisette then he was no better than she.

He continued to pray. Lisette had shown him the ease with which sensuality and passion could destroy a man's resolve. He was no better than his brother Japhet, whom he reviled for his loose morals. Women were the handmaidens of the devil to drive a man beyond his limits. But he acknowledged to his shame that he could no longer live without the comfort and pleasure their bodies could afford him.

Meriel, now four months pregnant, reclined on the chaise longue in the Dower House parlour. By refusing to risk the child by continuing her duties on the estate and about the house, she was often bored. The family were too busy with their own work to visit her, though Amelia would call in for half an hour every day. Even Rowena did not relieve her boredom; the child irritated her with her ceaseless chatter and questions. Rowena would demand stories to be read to her and Meriel had been too lazy to learn to read when the family had insisted at the start of her marriage. Also, Rowena demanded that Meriel entertain her, while Meriel craved the company of her friends to hear the latest gossip and talk of new fashions.

When Rachel Glasson announced the Hon. Percy Fetherington and Basil Bracewaite, Meriel sent Rowena away to play with her hobbyhorse in the garden. Meriel had been eating marchpane and brushed the crumbs from her rose taffeta gown, which had been tightly laced to hide her swelling figure. A third man was with her visitors.

Percy bowed over Meriel's hand and raised it to his lips. 'May I present the Earl of Wycham, a nephew of my mother, whose country seat is in Devonshire though he sensibly lives most of the year in London.'

'Your servant, ma'am.' Lord Wycham barely touched her hand with his fingers and his manner was aloof.

Meriel ordered Rachel Glasson to bring a tray of tea and some Madeira for the men. The Earl of Wycham was an attractive man of similar age to his companions, with dark blond hair, slim of build and above average height. He gave the parlour a sweeping appraisal and flicked a lace-edged handkerchief over the seat of a chair before he sat down.

'I thought we were to visit the main house,' the earl stated.

'I was interested in meeting Japhet Loveday again. The scoundrel took a hundred guineas off me at a card game at Lady Christow's last summer.'

'Japhet does not live at Trevowan,' Percy replied. 'I explained that. He's staying with his sister at the moment. 'Meriel is St John Loveday's wife. You met him at the races last week when Japhet won on his Arab mare.'

Lord Wycham favoured Meriel with a longer stare. 'So this is the beauty Bracewaite has been praising all week. And rightly so. An English rose amongst the wild briars. Is your husband a jealous man that he hides you away in the country? You would be the toast of London were you to visit during the Season.'

His words were no more than the compliments she had come to expect from Percy's friends, but unaccountably they sent a delicious shiver through her. She had never met an earl before and he was young as well as handsome.

'I have never been to London, my lord. Are you often at Court?'

'Court is a dreary place in recent years. Prinny's set is far more stimulating.'

'You are an intimate of the Prince of Wales!' Meriel regarded the earl with greater interest. His hair was cut short and the collar of his cutaway coat was so high it was in danger of blinkering him like a horse. The sleek fit of his breeches and elegant knot of his cravat also impressed her. He carried a walking cane with a large sapphire set in a silver orb. 'I had heard the Prince's set described as rather fast and quite notorious. Are you notorious, my lord?'

'Notoriety is not something I aspire to.' He regarded her with amusement.

Meriel was curious to know more. 'Is the King truly mad?'

'His Majesty has often been considered eccentric by many,

and by others unstable. His health is uncertain.' Lord Wycham studied his nails as though they were of more interest than the conversation. 'This war disturbs him, whereas the Prince and his advisers would crush the rebellion in France and restore its monarchy.'

'Would that not be difficult since they have cut off the King's head?' Meriel had no understanding of the implications of the revolution in France. If the French were all as volatile as Lisette, then it was not surprising the country was in such a state of unrest. Lisette was always causing problems which disturbed the peace of Trevowan.

'Unfortunately, the Dauphin is still a child, but he would be guided by wise advisers,' his Lordship replied.

When Basil and Percy began to discuss the situation in France, Meriel pouted. 'I am not entertained by talk of politics. How dreary you men can be sometimes. Basil, you always know all the latest gossip.'

Basil Bracewaite obliged her, but Lord Wycham did not join in their conversation. For most of the time he stared out of the window to where the cliffs curved round to the headland of Trevowan Cove. Unused to being ignored in such a fashion, Meriel flirted outrageously with Basil and Percy, and twice caught his Lordship's stare upon her. Each time she felt her pulse race faster. Percy and Basil were fools compared to this courtier. It was him she wanted to impress. Yet he seemed immune to her charms.

Abruptly he stood up and announced, 'Your pardon, Mistress Loveday, but we are engaged to dine with the Rashleighs in Fowey.'

While Basil and Percy begged her forgiveness for deserting her after so short a visit, and effusively kissed her hand, his Lordship remained aloof. He allowed the others to lead the way from the parlour, then bowed to Meriel. 'It has been a pleasure to make your acquaintance.'

'You are polite, my lord, but not sincere. I believe you have been bored.' She was ruffled that he appeared unaffected by her beauty, when she had found him so fascinating and wished to impress him.

His mouth lifted into a ghost of a smile as he raised her fingers to his lips. 'On the contrary. Until we meet again in more favourable circumstances.'

With that enigmatic remark he left. Meriel gazed wistfully through the window to watch him mount his horse and ride away. He cut a handsome and regal figure.

Rachel Glasson cleared the tea tray and wine glasses. 'Fancy a grand earl be visiting us. And he such a handsome man. Don't reckon I shall see the likes of such a grand man again.'

'Who can say?' Meriel dismissed Rachel. For a moment she cursed her pregnancy which had ruined her figure, but with tight lacing she barely showed. She had a feeling that they may well be honoured with the earl visiting them again.

Keziah Sawle spent hours consoling Hester Lanyon until her patience was strained past its limits. Hester did nothing but cry and bemoan her fate. Keziah had never believed that feeling sorry for oneself solved any problems.

'If you don't stop this crying you will harm the child.' Keziah laid a bowl of chicken broth by the bedside. Hester had been with them a week. Her bruises had faded but she refused to leave her bed, bleating in terror that Lanyon would find her.

'That monster you married bain't in Penruan. Gone to Truro again, I heard. The house be locked up and there bain't no sign of Phyllis Tamblin so he must have taken her with him. Villagers think that you are with them.'

'What of Pa and my sister, Annie? Don't they think it strange I never told them I were leaving Penruan?' She sobbed louder. 'Pa's too scared to stand up to Thadeous. Thadeous said he'd ruin him if I told Pa how I was treated. He would too.'

'Gossip is that your pa and sister bain't got much time for you since you been wed. Reckon you think yourself above them.'

'I never did.' Hester rubbed at her tear-streaked cheeks. 'Thadeous would never let me visit. He kept me a virtual prisoner in the house or the shop. I weren't allowed to go nowhere, even with Phyllis to accompany me.'

'You managed to meet Harry.' Keziah folded her arms across her large breasts. 'Look at the trouble that will cause.'

'Harry was the only reason I did not kill myself to escape my misery.' A flash of the old Hester's spirit emerged. 'I lived for a meeting with him, however brief.' The tears fell faster and she stumbled over her words. 'Where's . . . H-Harry? Why bain't he . . . c-come?'

Keziah sat on the bed and pulled the patchwork quilt up to cover Hester's swollen belly. The woman was hollow-eyed, her sleep broken by nights of weeping.

'Harry is about his business. I reckon it took longer than usual. Or he decided to stay out of Penruan for a week or so. It were Lanyon's cargo he stole from the customs house. He would be covering his tracks.'

'No doubt with some whore,' Hester sobbed. 'Can't Clem find him? I need Harry. I can't stay in Penruan. Thadeous will find me.'

'Clem don't know where Harry be. I doubt Lanyon would've left the village if he thought you'd be nearby. He be looking for you, but not in Penruan. And knowing our Harry's hot temper, it be better he bain't here. Once he learns what Lanyon did to you, there'll be the devil to pay.'

'I need Harry. I can't go on without him.'

Keziah picked up the broth and lifted the spoon to

Hester's mouth. 'You must eat. What use will you be to Harry if you be weak from lack of food? And think of the babe. 'Tis as well Harry bain't here to see you in this state. You're so pale you look like you've just risen from your coffin. Your hair be all matted. If Harry is gonna take you away you will need your strength. Now eat!' Keziah pushed the spoon against Hester's teeth and her expression was fierce. 'Harry bain't gonna want you looking like a ghoul.'

Hester drank the broth. Keziah smiled to lessen the harshness of her words. She needed to shock Hester out of her moping. 'That's better. Weeping ravages your looks. We'll get your hair washed and you all prettied up. Harry fell in love with your spirit as well as your beauty. This bain't the time to disappoint 'im, is it?'

Hester clasped Keziah's wrist. 'I don't know what I would have done if you hadn't taken me in. Thadeous will have sent out men to search for me. He bain't gonna risk losing the child he thinks is his.'

'Clem has gone over to Launceston market with some of the billy kids to sell. He thinks Harry might be there. It be best if you and Harry be gone from Penruan afore Lanyon returns.'

'Harry won't leave. He's said that all along.' Hester struggled not to cry. 'He wants Lanyon dead and then they'll hang him. What will I do then?'

'Happen you should have thought of that afore all this went so far,' Keziah said under her breath as she tidied the room. Hester had fallen into a doze and Keziah shook her head. Her fear was growing for this woman and for Harry. Harry would not rest until Lanyon was dead. Then God have mercy upon them all for the consequences that would reap.

Chapter Nineteen

Adam was dining in his cabin on *Pegasus* with Sir Gregory Kilmarthen, who had returned to England with him. Tomorrow they would dock in Falmouth. Three of the people they had rescued from the prison had asked for passage to England. Sir Gregory would also disembark, wanting to buy some respectable attire before he reported to Squire Penwithick.

'Will you be glad to be back in England?' Adam asked his companion. 'You have been away for several years.'

Sir Gregory stared into his glass of claret and shook his head. 'I enjoyed the subterfuge and was useful in France. Here I am an outcast.' He shrugged. 'I have been away for fifteen years. My family regarded me as some kind of circus freak. Once I was sixteen, my father was happy to provide me with a large allowance providing I spent my time abroad.'

He refilled his glass, sat back in his chair and continued, 'I travelled to many European cities, but never found a place to fit in amongst those of my class. At twenty-two I joined a group of travelling players in France.' His eyes gleamed with fond remembrance. 'They accepted me in a way my peers had never done. During the next seven years I made many acquaintances: aristocrats, revolutionists, royalists. No one saw me as a threat and many revolutionists in the early days spoke openly in my company.'

'Did you approach Penwithick, or did he recruit you? I can see how useful you could be to him.' Adam leaned forward with his elbows on the table, fascinated by the story.

'Fate stepped in as she so often does,' Sir Gregory chuckled. 'One of Penwithick's agents had been wounded and I chanced upon him dying in a wood. I was still with the players at the time and the shortage of food was sowing the seeds of revolution. The man was delirious from a stomach wound and was speaking English. I gave him some water and spoke to him to ease his passing. In his last hour he became lucid and, realising that I was English, he gave me a verbal message which he said was vital that Penwithick received. He died minutes later.'

Adam was surprised that Sir Gregory was little more than thirty. His square, line-scored face had made Adam assess his age to be at least a decade older. 'And you have been working for Penwithick ever since?'

'One thing led to another. I had to leave my friends in the troupe as I needed to move freely about the country when I set up the network of spies. My disguise as a pedlar stood me in good stead. But no longer.'

Adam felt a twinge of guilt that he was to blame. 'It was ill fortune that Etienne Riviere recognised me. He will investigate the lives of the men who escaped that night.'

'A dwarf is only invisible until there is a reward on his head.' Sir Gregory spread his arms in resignation. 'Life moves on.'

'What will you do?' Adam sensed his new friend's despondency.

'Since I inherited my title on my father's death, the estate has been sadly neglected. Seeing so much death and destruction in France has made me nostalgic for my home.' His tone was falsely optimistic. 'My mother and sister live alone at Athel Grange. They will no doubt resent the intrusion of my arrival into their lives, as I shall resent theirs. Such are families.'

'Now we are at war with France, our government will have need of a man of your experience. I am sure a post will be found for you.'

Sir Gregory laughed. 'And there was I waiting for you to offer me a position as second officer when you sail the seven seas, my buccaneering friend.'

'I would be honoured to have you on board.' Adam returned Kilmarthen's laugh. 'There will always be a berth for you if you hunger for adventure, Sir Gregory.'

'I may take you up on that offer, Adam. I cannot see me finding life on my country seat, or even buried away in some government office, stimulating for long. And none of this Sir Gregory nonsense between us. To men whose friendship I value, I shall always be Long Tom.'

They docked at Falmouth on the early tide and Adam was eager to reach Trevowan Hard that afternoon as the wind and tide would be with him. He escorted Long Tom to the gangplank. 'I hope we meet again.'

'I am sure we will. I've a mind to see this pretty wife of yours after I have given my report to Penwithick. I shall be staying there a day or so before I travel to Athel Grange in Somerset. I shall insist that the squire invites Senara to his home. I will not have those doughty matrons snubbing the wife of my friend.'

'I thank you, but I am not sure that Senara will. She has no wish to mix with those who think themselves better than her.'

'And from what you have told me of Senara, she sounds as though she is worth a dozen of any of them.'

Adam watched his friend disappear amongst the crowd. There was a swagger to the small man's step and, despite his ragged clothes, a confidence which made several hardened sailors move aside when they blocked his path. Adam shook his head and chuckled. He had never met a man quite like Long Tom.

Some of the crew had also left the ship since Adam had no clear sailing date for his next voyage. As the anchor was being raised, there was a shout from one of the crew who had gone ashore.

'Cap'n, you better see this afore you sail.' The sailor waved a piece of paper in the air.

The gangplank was lowered and Adam's temper soared as he read the pamphlet. 'Where did you get this?'

'They be circulated in the taverns and around the town. A man said he'd seen one in Truro four days past. Reckon someone be out to ruin your family, Cap'n.'

'Thank you for bringing me this. There is an evil hand behind it, and I shall find out who. But why would someone so attack us?' The pamphlet was entitled 'A ship wrecked by the incompetence of its builders. The true and most shocking facts of unseaworthy ships built at T—v—n H—d by E—d L—v—y.'

The sailor informed him, 'While we were at sea, *Sea Sprite* were wrecked off Black Head. She broke up in the storm.'

'Then I doubt I shall have far to look from Penruan for the culprit. I told the owner *Sea Sprite* would flounder if he continued to load her with extra foresails. He'll not get away with this.'

Two hours later *Pegasus* entered the Fowey inlet. Adam remained angry and wondered if his father had learned of the pamphlet's circulation. The sky was clear and the day was exceptionally hot for early June. Ducks were nesting in the river reeds and two herons were feeding by the bank. At the rattle of the anchor chain there was a flapping of wings as the ducks and herons took to the air to fly over the trees.

Adam stood by the ship's rail as the longboat was lowered

to row the shore party to the jetty. The sun burnished the fresh timbers of the two partly built ships in their cradles. Even from this distance Adam could see that work had progressed while he was away. Several of the shipwrights paused in their hammering to raise a hand in greeting to Adam. Some of his anger dissipated as Timmy Wakeley ran towards Mariner's House to tell Senara of his arrival, but she was already at the door and hurrying to the jetty.

The joy on her face momentarily pushed aside his anger and he regretted that their meeting would be under such public gaze. He absently rubbed his throbbing arm and felt the dried blood tug the bandage and fresh blood well to spread warmly across its surface. Adam grimaced. He had hoped that his wound would have healed before he met Senara. She would fuss and worry that he had been shot.

He was impatient to step ashore as the longboat bumped against the jetty. When his father appeared from the office, Senara hesitated at the edge of the jetty. At her uncertainty, Adam cursed his father's stubbornness towards her. He ran to Senara and lifted her in his arms to swing her round and kiss her. A cheer greeted him from the shipwrights and Senara laughed and beat his shoulder with her fist.

'Put me down, whatever will people say?' she blushed.

Adam held her tight and grinned at her. 'They will say that Adam Loveday is bewitched by an enchantress.'

'Your father will not approve,' Senara reminded him. 'He is waiting to greet you.'

'My wife comes first. The joy of seeing you on the jetty is one I shall always hold dear. How is Nathan?'

'Growing more like his father every day.'

Adam continued to study her. 'How have things been while I am away? You look pale. You have not been upset by anything?'

'I have been busy helping with the sick here or in your

356

uncle's parish and preparing simples and balms for their ills. I will tell you everything later; your father is waiting. But I have missed you.'

Adam kissed her cheek and left her to join his father.

'How was the voyage?' Edward asked as they entered the office.

'Fine.' Adam dismissed his adventures at the more pressing news. 'Have you seen these? I was given one at Falmouth. They are also being distributed in Truro and no doubt every town in Cornwall.'

'I was given one two days ago and have today received a letter from Mr Tregurrian, the Inspector of Sloops and Boats. He will visit at the end of next week to inspect the yard.'

'But he passed the original plans for the cutter. I sent him a report on her sea trials. The revenue service would never have taken possession of *Challenger* if they had not been satisfied with the sea trials.'

'Let us hope it is but a formality. Unfortunately, the revenue service have suspended their order for the second cutter pending his judgement. Another two orders have been cancelled from new customers in the last week. They must have read the pamphlets.'

'Then they must be invited to attend with Mr Tregurrian. He will prove our ships are not only seaworthy but the fastest in their class.'

'I have extended to them such an invitation. Whether they will attend is another matter. Competition is fierce and we are still a small yard compared to many. Unfortunately the bow of *Sea Sprite* was smashed on the rocks. There is no evidence that she had been re-rigged and was carrying extra sail.'

'But Uncle William said that he had seen her bowsprit extended. Others must have seen it.'

357

Edward rubbed the back of his neck as he paced the small office. 'The bowsprit would have been retracted and the larger sails removed whenever *Sea Sprite* was in port. It will be their word against Lanyon's, and Lanyon is capable of bribing witnesses.'

Adam went to a sea chest and pulled out a leather-bound sketchbook. 'I have my drawings as proof. Every ship we have launched has been sketched either by myself or an artist.' He laid two drawings side by side. The only difference between them was the name on their bows. '*Challenger* will be the proof that Lanyon is lying.'

'Except that Mr Tregurrian will rely on the report from her captain. Unfortunately Lieutenant Beaumont has no reason to help the Lovedays. We have cost him too much, and not just his commission in the navy. A customs house was robbed of cargo which probably belonged to Lanyon. When I questioned St John, he admitted that Harry Sawle was involved.'

'Which means St John had a hand in it as well.'

Edward shrugged but his expression was tense. 'St John denies it. He has promised to end his association with the smugglers. He knows I disapprove. But he did admit to winning a large sum of money from Beaumont at cards.'

Adam bit back a retort. St John was making too much money to give up his partnership with Harry Sawle. 'Beaumont is a bad loser. But even he cannot dispute that *Challenger* is the finest in her class.'

'He already has. He professes that she is difficult to sail in heavy seas and only his skill saved her from capsizing on one occasion.'

Adam banged the desk with his fist. 'He's lying. I'll take Tregurrian out in *Challenger* in a storm if I have to, and will prove how seaworthy she is. Tregurrian is no fool. He was a naval captain himself until he lost an arm in an encounter with Barbary pirates.'

Edward closed the sketchbook with a snap. 'He will respect the word of Lieutenant Beaumont, for Tregurrian served under Admiral Beaumont.'

Adam felt the hopelessness of so much evidence weighing against them. 'We are not going to let them ruin us, are we?' He held his father's weary stare.

Edward sighed. 'I thought our trials were over when some of our fortune was restored by your cousin Thomas's bank. They could well be just beginning.'

'But we weathered the threat of financial ruin last year and this time we have right on our side. Uncle William will give evidence that he saw the *Sea Sprite* with an extended bowsprit. Surely Tregurrian will respect the words of a serving naval captain against a court-martialled naval lieutenant.'

'It would be better if any talk of courts martial were kept out of it,' Edward cautioned. '*Sea Sprite* and *Challenger* were designed by a court-martialled naval lieutenant. Tregurrian is a man who does everything by the book. He will be aware of both your and Beaumont's naval records. I doubt he will view either favourably.'

The happiness of his homecoming was marred for Adam. The injustice of Lanyon's accusations about the yard angered him. He returned to Mariner's House, his mood troubled and abstracted.

Senara showed him the herb garden she had planted. 'Bridie helps me to gather other herbs from the woods and hedgerows in the mornings. She has also become an adept potter. She enjoys making the pots so much that Leah has trouble persuading her that she must still attend the school here.'

She frowned as they returned to the house and Adam remained distracted. Nathan was asleep in his crib and

Senara dismissed Carrie for the day. The evening meal was cooking in the range and Senara put her arms around her husband's neck when he slumped in a chair. He pulled her round to sit on his lap and though he kissed her, his attention was elsewhere.

'I can feel your anger. Have you quarrelled with your father again?'

'Nothing escapes you, does it?' He smiled but his eyes remained troubled. 'I did not quarrel with Father. It is Thadeous Lanyon.' He told her of the pamphlet and his conversation with his father.

'The yard's reputation speaks for itself. *Pegasus* and *Challenger* are fine examples of your expertise.'

'Not if Lieutenant Beaumont is in Lanyon's pay. And he hates me. He will see this as means to avenge himself on me for beating him in a duel.'

'You were the better man then, and you are the better man now. The ship will prove her own worth and this Lieutenant Beaumont will be made to look a fool.'

Adam kissed Senara again. 'You make it all sound so simple.'

'I have faith in what is right.'

Adam saw her pallor and feared that she had not been truthful about her health. 'I talk of my problems but how have you been? You look pale and you are always so robust.'

She cupped his face in her hands and kissed him with passion. 'I am happy with my work with the sick. Your uncle's approval protects me from wagging tongues. Some of the nearby villagers have begun to seek my remedies.'

'I am not so sure I want you subjected to so much sickness. You could fall ill yourself. The physicians are paid to tend the sick.'

'Only when the sick have money for their services. Adam, I cannot allow people to suffer for lack of a shilling to pay for the doctor.' She valiantly tried to suppress a yawn, overcome with sudden tiredness.

'But you look so tired, my love. My first concern is for you.'

She bit her lip and there was a sparkle in her eyes. 'I am as strong as an ox, but there is a reason why I am tired. Whilst I carried Nathan I found I fell asleep every time I sat in a chair.'

It took some moments for her meaning to sink in. His eyes widened with astonishment. 'Are you telling me you are again with child?'

She grinned. 'It is early days but I suspect so.'

Adam hugged her. 'My love, that is wonderful news. But I shall have to spend more months at sea if I do not want my wife's belly to swell each year with a child.' He laughed, his passion flaring as he kissed her.

When she breathlessly drew back from him, she taunted, 'And do I have no say in the matter? I would prefer a large family rather than be deprived of your company. But I would not change the life you have chosen.' She pulled his shirt from the waistband of his breeches and pushed the arms of his jacket from his shoulders.

Adam shrugged off the jacket and twisted round so that Senara was cradled in his lap. As her hands moved down his arm she gasped and drew away from him. 'You've been hurt. There is fresh blood on your sleeve. Adam, why did you not say?'

'It is but a scratch and I did not want to worry you.'

She ran to fetch her box of bandages and a bowl of water. 'Take that shirt off and let me look at it.'

He sighed and pulled his shirt over his head.

Senara cried out, 'Adam, there is a deep cut along your ribs.'

'A nick from a sword, nothing more, my love.'

361

Senara peeled back the bandage on his arm. 'And from the looks of it this was caused by a bullet.' Her hand shook as she cleaned the wounds and her voice was strained. 'How easily you dismiss a bullet and sword wound. An inch deeper or to one side and you could have been mortally wounded. The cut on your ribs is infected. On your previous voyage you sustained a head wound and nearly drowned. Must you lead so dangerous a life?'

'I am serving my country.' Adam lay back with his eyes closed as she pressed pus from the cut on his ribs and twice his flesh twitched and his jaw clenched.

Senara was angry. 'You serve your own lust for adventure.' Adam grabbed her waist and rolled with her on the floor. 'You fuss too much! Neither is serious. I have been home two hours and still have not made love to my wife. Woman, you must learn to get your priorities right.'

Phyllis Tamblin had travelled for ten days, mostly on foot. Whenever a horseman or wagon approached she left the road to hide in the hedgerow. Lanyon would have his spies looking for her and she dared not risk discovery. She slept under hedgerows, shivering from cold and fear, her sleep broken by terrors and nightmares. She had never been alone before.

The girls' dormitory of the orphanage where she had been raised had been crowded, with scarcely room for a person to stand between the meagrely stuffed straw pallet beds. At twelve she had been turned out of the orphanage and found work in a laundry where the girls were huddled in an attic at night. She had hated it and did not like the skeletal manager who took his turn with all the girls and beat them if they refused. He never rewarded them as the beadle in the orphanage had done. Phyllis had left there to work in a busy tavern, willing to sell her body to supplement her poor pay. The customers were often too drunk to pay for her services. When she had taken a shilling from a customer, he had raised the alarm, declaring he had been robbed, and she had fled in terror of arrest. Phyllis had drifted from farm to farm during the year before Thadeous Lanyon had employed her at the hiring fair. On the farms she was with a group of milkmaids, or a work force harvesting a crop.

Now the vast openness of the countryside frightened her. Any rustle in the undergrowth made her fear that Lanyon's spies had found her, or footpads would rob her. The money bags stolen from Thadeous Lanyon were heavy and made her progress slow. To avoid discovery she had skirted villages and was constantly hungry. When she saw the houses and church towers of Liskeard ahead, Phyllis hoped that she was far enough away from Penruan to be safe. She needed food. From the carts heading towards the town, today was market day. It would be more crowded than usual. She had to take the risk or she would have no strength to continue.

The money pouches were tied with twine around her waist and hung down under her petticoats. She had taken two pieces of silver from them and wrapped them in a kerchief in her skirt pocket.

A mile from the town the road became busier, and she blended with the farmers with their wagons loaded with milk churns or produce. One farmer led two horses with two panniers on each of their backs: four pink snouts of tiny piglets poked out of one pannier, and three black-and-white-faced sheepdog puppies from another. A goose girl chivvied her flock, with their tarred feet and waddling bodies, along the road. Phyllis passed a woman and child carrying baskets of eggs and another leading a donkey laden with wicker baskets for sale. Another woman was bent double carrying bundles of faggots which were lashed to her back.

Phyllis pulled the hood of her cloak to shadow her face and kept her head bowed as she walked through the narrow streets leading to the market square. She stopped a pieman and gorged herself on two pasties. Her strength and confidence returned. She also bought two loaves, a blood sausage, a large wedge of cheese and another six pasties. That food would sustain her for another week of walking.

Before she left the town, a farmer's wife's stall drew her. There were bottles of elderberry, rosehip and dandelion wine amongst the eggs and cheeses. Phyllis licked her lips. She had been forced to drink water from streams. Since her work in a tavern she had always favoured intoxicating brews. If she purchased a basket to hold her goods, she could carry a bottle or two of elderberry wine. It would give her comfort when she lay alone in the hedgerow tonight.

The wine was more potent than she expected and she had drunk half a bottle before she left the town. As she walked, she began to sing and her step became uncertain. In a few days she would be in Plymouth and there it would be safe to join the stage for London.

Phyllis stumbled several times as the sun began to set and she was disgruntled to discover that the first bottle of wine was empty. She tossed it away with a snarl. The laden basket was growing heavy. She should have brought fewer pasties and another bottle of the wine instead. The pouches of money jingled faintly and satisfyingly against her thigh as she clambered over a stile. Long shadows snaked across a fallow field where the grass grew in soft tussocks.

Phyllis giggled. 'I got the better of you, Lanyon. You thought you could use me like a cheap whore. Well, I knew I had but to bide my time. Now I'm rich. I bain't gonna be no man's whore ever again.' Her foot caught the top bar of the stile and she pitched forward and cursed. She straightened with an effort and found her red skirt had caught on a nail and she tugged it free, ripping the material. She staggered through the knee-high grass until she fell headlong over a thick tussock. Her head spun crazily with the effort to rise and with a groan she sank down again. Within minutes she was in a drunken stupor.

Grimley and Fisher were two of the dozen men Lanyon had sent in search of his wife and servant. They had worked as tubmen for Lanyon for years. Grimley was of middle height and slim, with a long loping stride, and the younger by a dozen years though neither had any idea of his age. Grimley reckoned he was getting on for thirty but he'd been saying that for the six years that Fisher had known him. Fisher was shorter than his companion by two handspan. To make up for his inches he was one of Lanyon's most vicious bullies.

They were losing hope of finding the two women and that meant the loss of the gold coin Lanyon had promised the men who found them. All day they had strolled through the press of people haggling for wares in Liskeard market. There were no two women together matching the descriptions they had been given.

'Looks like we be out of luck again,' Fisher scowled.

'Market don't close for another two hours. Time yet.' Grimley leaned back against an empty cattle pen and sucked on his empty clay pipe. His gaze never stopped scanning the crowd. He lived at Polmasryn but had twice been in Lanyon's shop in Penruan when Phyllis Tamblin was serving. There had been a knowing look in the woman's eye when she had served him with tobacco. He had waited for her to leave the shop that night, hoping to waylay her. To his annoyance she had left at the same time as Lanyon's wife, and he had no chance to approach the younger woman. That night he had been needed as a tubman over at a cove three miles away and he had not returned to Penruan since. But he had remembered the pretty servant, and absently rubbed his groin as he visualised the pleasure of finding her and spending an hour in her company.

An hour later Fisher was irate. He picked his nose and wiped his finger down the front of his filthy jerkin. 'They bain't here. I'm going for a jug of ale. I reckon they be out of the county by now, or one of the others 'ave found 'em.'

Grimley had been watching the figure of a cloaked woman. For a warm day the hood was suspiciously covering most of her face. She was carrying a basket of loaves and wine bottles. The woman slid into an alley opposite and took out a wine bottle to drink from. As she did so her hood slid back. From this distance Grimley could not be sure, but it looked like Phyllis Tamblin. He nudged Fisher. 'I think that be the serving wench. We'll follow her and see if she leads us to the wife.'

They pushed through the crowd but before they reached the edge of town a cowherd herding eight heifers from the pens blocked their way. There was a scuffle as they pushed past him. The men hopped in pain when their feet were trampled by the cows' hoofs, as the stubborn beasts refused to move out of their way. They had lost precious minutes and when they were finally free of the cows, there was no sight of the cloaked woman.

'We've lost her.' Fisher hawked and spat on the ground.

Grimley scratched the stubble on his chin. 'This street takes us out of town. What if she met up with her mistress and they be travelling on?'

Fisher picked his nose for several moments before answering. 'If that were Lanyon's servant I reckon they be somewhere in town. Lanyon's wife be with child. She bain't fit to go trudging the highway. It be dark soon. We'll look again tomorrow. I want some ale.'

'I'll join you later.' Grimley continued to stare along the road which curved towards the open countryside. The cloak of the woman he had seen had been dusty and bits of grass had clung to its hem. If the women had any sense they'd know Lanyon would be looking for them. It could be the mistress had sent her servant into town for food and was waiting for her out of sight along the road. It was worth a look. He headed back to the stable where he had left his nag.

The road was disappointingly empty and the light was fast fading. Grimley was about to end his search and join Fisher for an ale when he saw a ribbon of scarlet flapping on a nail of a stile. He had glimpsed the servant wearing a dress of that colour. He surveyed the field. In the twilight he caught a glimmer of white petticoat lift in the breeze from a bed of grass. His eyes narrowed with cunning and he tethered his nag to the stile and climbed over. The woman was sleeping so heavily he was able to bind her wrists and ankles without even waking her.

He heaved her over his saddle and, at her groan, he slapped her face to bring her to consciousness. 'Where's your mistress?'

'No mistress,' Phyllis moaned, still groggy. She couldn't move and her face hurt. Another slap knocked her head against what felt like a horse. It even smelled like a horse. Panic speared through her drunken stupor. She was trussed like a hog to be roasted.

'Where be your mistress, Lanyon's wife?' A dagger blade was pressed against her throat.

'I be alone. My mistress be at home. I don't know what you be talking of.' The blade pressed harder and she cried, 'I got his money. Take it. But I don't know nothing about Hester. She were sick abed when I ran away.'

'Where's this money.'

'Under my petticoats.'

He threw her skirt and petticoats over her head, exposing her bare thighs and buttocks. Phyllis was sobbing in terror. 'Don't hurt me, sir. Take his money. But don't hurt me.'

Grimley grabbed the money and felt its weight in his hand. He whistled as he gauged the contents of the pouches. He believed the servant when she said her mistress was not with her. Lanyon would not pay for the return of a servant. It was his wife he wanted. He ran his hand over the ivory buttock exposed by the moonlight. The servant whimpered.

'Please, don't hurt me. I'll be good to you, real good to you, sir.'

The temptation was great: he could have the woman, then kill her and run off with the money. But there was Fisher. If the servant's body was found, he'd tell Lanyon, and what if Lanyon knew that the servant had his money? Lanyon was not a man you stole from.

Grimley knew he would never be able to walk down a street without looking over his shoulder and expecting an assassin's blade in his back. Lanyon would cast his net wide. There was no escaping him or his henchmen. Lanyon's instructions had been clear. The servant was to die, and his wife left unharmed as she was carrying his child. But the servant's body was to be disposed of. Lanyon wanted no one recognising the servant and linking her to him.

Grimley mounted his nag and headed towards Bodmin Moor. He had no intention of sharing the reward money or the woman with Fisher. Grimley had lived on the edge of the moor as a child and knew some of its secrets. There was a place where the bog was treacherous, and if a body was weighted with stones it would be sucked under the mud without trace. But first he would have his sport with the wench.

The next evening Grimley visited Lanyon at a property the smuggler owned near Lostwithiel. It was a rundown farm tenanted by the Renfrews and their three sons. The family were part of the team who distributed Lanyon's contraband in their farm wagons. Lanyon had decided not to return to

Penruan or be seen in public until Hester was with him. He would thus avoid any unpleasant gossip or later speculation about Phyllis's non-appearance on their eventual return. He would arrive in Penruan with his wife and a new servant. He had been confident that Hester would be returned to him within a few days. As the days progressed his anger mounted at the delay.

Grimley was shown into the musty-smelling parlour of the farmhouse. The furniture was covered in a green layer of mould except for the chair by the fire where Lanyon was seated. He was eating, and ripped pieces from a cooked chicken with his hands. Grimley dropped the money pouches on the floor by Lanyon's boots.

'The maid stole 'em. Before I killed her, she swore your wife were still in the house when she ran away.'

'The wench was lying. Where would Hester go? Her family wouldn't take her in. They know I'd not stand for it.' Lanyon's face was mottled in fury and he pushed aside the chicken.

Grimley became uneasy. 'The servant bain't lying. I made sure of that. Maybe your wife had a lover. Harry Sawle's got reason to—' Without warning Grimley found himself staring down the muzzle of Lanyon's pistol. His throat dried with fear. There was murder in Lanyon's eyes. He shook his head and began to back away. 'There were no sign of Hester with the servant.'

'You've got a big mouth, Grimley. I don't trust you.' Lanyon fired and stepped over Grimley's body as he lay twitching in his death throes. The bullet had gone through his throat.

The pistol shot had brought three of the Renfrew men to the door. Lanyon scowled at them. 'Bury the scum, and you bain't seen nor heard nothing of what passed here.'

Martha Renfrew appeared and watched dispassionately as

two of her sons dragged the still twitching body of Grimley outside. A scrawny farm dog, with its backbone and haunches visible beneath its mangy coat, crept forward on its belly and its long pink tongue scooped hungrily at the bloody trail.

Martha Renfrew was a blowsy drab. Her blouse of indeterminate colour was stretched tight across her large, sagging breasts. 'Don't Harry Sawle run a rival gang of smugglers? Also he bain't no friend of yours. Him and Hester were mighty close afore you wed her. The Sawles never were a family to cross.'

'You listen to too much gossip.' Lanyon waved the pistol at her. 'Take care.'

'You'd not kill me with me 'usband and sons to witness it. I'm jus' stating facts which be plain for all.'

'Sawle weren't in Penruan for two days before Hester disappeared. I checked,' Lanyon snapped. He kicked out at the dog, which cowered and slunk from the room.

'Get me some more food, and cease your blathering, or you and your family will end the same way as Grimley.'

'Do you never fear for your own back, Mr Lanyon?' Martha said as she ambled to her kitchen.

He had been responsible for four deaths in as many weeks. A few more would not trouble him. The Renfrews were useful to him, but not Harry Sawle. He and St John Loveday were proving too much of a menace to his free-trading.

Chapter Twenty

The death of Eleanor Keyne was a shock to everyone and it seemed the whole county turned out for her funeral in the parish church. All the older Lovedays were to attend. Adam would not go without Senara and declared he had never mixed socially with the Keynes because of his years in the navy. After so many weeks of good deeds, Japhet had left Hannah's farm and no one knew where he had gone. Peter had also left the district, declaring that he would stay within a seminary until he was ordained into the Anglican faith.

Edward was surprised when St John and Meriel joined him as he prepared to leave Trevowan.

'I would pay my condolences to the family,' St John announced.

'It is good to see Meriel taking some air,' Elspeth observed. 'She spends too long lying indoors. The woman looks hale enough to me to perform some of her lighter duties.'

'I am feeling much better, Aunt,' Meriel replied. 'A gentle carriage ride is far from exertion.'

Meriel had insisted that she accompany St John when he announced that he was attending the funeral. 'It has been months since I mixed with our neighbours. The Keynes are an important family. I am surprised that Edward does not cultivate their company more.'

'They spend most of their time in London.' St John bore

Meriel's company with ill grace.

The day proved disappointing to Meriel. She abhorred funerals, which were so dreary, but she had put on her prettiest dress and made Rachel Glasson lace her tightly so that her condition would not be too apparent. She had hoped that Lord Wycham would attend. Her heart leaped when she saw him surrounded by the most eminent families of Cornwall. She hovered close by, hoping that he would join her. He raised his hat to Meriel but made no attempt to converse with her.

St John had left her side once the funeral was over and was now talking to a pretty woman, as they walked back to the house.

Lord Fetherington sidled up to Meriel and his hand slid behind her waist to move over her buttocks and squeeze them. 'I missed you at our ball. How unfortunate that your health did not permit you to attend. I had anticipated a weekend of pleasure for us both.' There was a strange clicking to his words and she realised that where there had been several gaps in his teeth, he now was wearing a set of false wooden ones. They were garish, reminding her of the crocodile she had once seen at a Punch and Judy show at Redruth Fair. His pock-marked face, with its drooping eye-lid, had always repelled her. She wished she had never encouraged him, but it had been a heady experience to have a lord eager to bed her, and his Lordship had not been ungenerous. Now she moved away to avoid his touch. 'My lord, I do not care to be mauled in public like a common doxy. A funeral is not the place.'

'With everyone taking their refreshments on the terrace as the weather is so warm, come into the house. I will find us a room where we can be alone. I have long awaited for you to honour your promise to me, my dear.'

She struck his hand with her fan. 'You presume too much,

my lord. I remember no promise.'

'When you accepted my jewels,' he leered at her, his breath hot against her ear, 'there was an agreement between us.'

'I am with child, my lord. And in delicate health.' She marched away and waved frantically to Basil Bracewaite to join her.

Basil was attentive to Meriel, but as usual too opinionated for her liking and she quickly tired of his company. Her stare was sullen as it passed between Lord Wycham and St John, who was still conversing with the pretty woman.

'Basil, who is St John speaking to?' She could no longer contain her anger that her husband had abandoned her. She was discomfited that at such times few of their neighbours, except for the men, sought her company.

'Mrs Newbold. Her husband is in the army and garrisoned in the north. The colder climate did not agree with her health.'

'The weather has been warmer this last month. I would have thought it mild enough for her to rejoin her husband.'

Basil shrugged. 'She seems content in Cornwall.'

'Has St John known her long?' Meriel did not like the way St John laughed constantly at what Mrs Newbold was saying.

'They met at Lord Fetherington's ball. Such a pity you missed it, my dear. It was a splendid occasion.'

'So everyone keeps telling me.' She fumed inwardly. Of late St John was often away from Trevowan overnight. They could not all be smuggling runs. 'Is that woman my husband's mistress?'

Basil choked and controlled his coughing fit. 'What a suggestion!' he finally blustered.

Meriel smiled at him though a chill of dread gouged through her. If St John was enamoured of another woman, her power over her husband would wane. On many occasions

St John had used her pregnancy to prevent her accompanying him when he visited their neighbours. 'Men and their little peccadilloes.' She forced a light laugh. 'It would not be the done thing at all for a man to appear in love with his wife. Adam is quite a laughing stock I hear, the way he fawns over Senara.'

'I doubt anyone would laugh at Adam Loveday, unless they were prepared to cross swords with him. Though any man who marries his mistress shows a singular lack of imagination in my opinion.'

'Why is that, Basil?' There was a hard edge to her voice.

'Is he not taking into his home goods he has already sampled?' Basil had been drinking from his hip flask ever since he arrived and his eyes were glazed from the alcohol. Never the most discreet of men, when in his cups, he was often patronising and opinionated. He was impervious to Meriel's angry glare as he blundered on. 'And if you've bedded the wench, who is to say others have not before you. A man should take a wife only of impeccable reputation.'

'And what of the mistress? The woman he has used for his own pleasure without thought of her reputation?' Meriel accused. 'What if that woman was tricked by false promises, to give her virtue to a man who is no better than a cad?'

She walked away from him with an angry swish of her skirts. Belatedly, Basil remembered the circumstances of Meriel's marriage to St John Loveday. He had not been living in Cornwall at the time and cursed his tongue. It would take more than a box of comfits or some petty gewgaw to get back into her favour. He had spent the best part of a year trying unsuccessfully to bed her. Only an expensive trinket would erase the crassness of his words.

Meriel meandered through the mourners. When she caught the eye of a gentlewoman watching her, she smiled condescendingly and moved on. She would not give them the opportunity of snubbing her if she stopped to speak. She paused at the edge of the terrace close to where Lord Wycham was conversing with two men. This time he excused himself to his companions and bowed to her.

'You look ravishing, Mrs Loveday. I am delighted that you are well enough to attend.'

'My health is not as indelicate as my physician would impose upon me.' She smiled sweetly.

'With such a beautiful wife, a husband would be a fool not to take the greatest care of her.'

Meriel glanced towards St John and Mrs Newbold. 'My husband is often occupied with other matters. I am left to my own devices to find ways of passing the time.'

Lord Fetherington was descending upon them. 'Wycham, my dear fellow, Lord Falmouth was hoping for a word with you.'

Lord Wycham bowed to Meriel and there was a silent promise in his eyes. 'Until I have the pleasure of your company again, Mrs Loveday. Your servant, ma'am.'

Lord Fetherington guided the earl away, to Meriel's annoyance.

'You want to stay clear of that little minx,' Fetherington warned. 'A tease and a fortune-huntress. She was the daughter of a tavern-keeper before she snared Loveday.'

'A woman of such beauty can be forgiven much. Were you not flirting with her earlier, Fetherington?'

Again Meriel was left on her own and decided to break up St John's cosy tête-à-tête with Mrs Newbold.

Her husband frowned as she approached. 'Will you not introduce me, St John?'

'Mrs Purity Newbold.'

'Purity.' Meriel gave a scathing laugh. 'Why do I feel it was an ill-conceived choice of name by your parents? I am feeling tired, St John. I wish to leave.'

'I will escort you to our carriage where you may rest. We will not leave until Father is ready. He is engrossed in conversation at this moment.'

'Does your father know how often you neglect your wife in favour of your whore?' Meriel enjoyed Purity Newbold's shocked gasp. The woman was pale and ill at ease.

'My pardon, Mrs Newbold. My wife forgets her manners.' St John grabbed Meriel's arm and marched her to the carriage. 'How dare you shame us in public? You act like a fishwife. Have you learned nothing as to how decent society conducts itself?'

'You neglect your wife for your whore, sir. What gentleman would do that? It is you who have shamed me before our friends. Whatever sordid affairs you conduct in private, I will not be shamed in public.'

Edward had seen the exchange between Meriel and his son and now the couple looked to be quarrelling. He sighed. Would the woman never learn her place and how to behave? St John was a fool to ignore her and spend so long talking to Mrs Newbold. People were bound to talk. He wondered if his son was having an affair with the major's pretty wife. If so, he hoped that Amelia did not suspect.

Being here had been trial enough for Edward. Since he had visited Eleanor when she was dying, he had been plagued by guilt for the child born of their love, and for which Eleanor had paid so high a price in her marriage. Now that Eleanor was dead, he must honour his vow to her and visit their daughter. There was a week until the inspection at the yard. He would set out to Salisbury tomorrow. He disliked having to lie to Amelia about the journey, yet how could he tell her the truth, when she had so condemned the lax morals of his sons?

The sun was high over the headland when Harry rode

through the narrow streets of Penruan. He was soon aware of the fixed stares upon him. If he looked a fisherman in the eye, the man would lower his gaze and walk away. A greeting from him was met with a nod and the man disinclined to loiter. Harry's enemies may fear him, but he had always been popular amongst the men of Penruan.

Ginny Rundle was leaning against her open doorway. 'Ye be back then, Harry Sawle.'

Harry glared at the stout midwife. 'What do that suppose to mean?'

Ginny's wrinkled face did not flinch, neither did she look away. 'You'll find out soon enough, Harry lad. That's if it bain't all bin your doing.'

He entered the Dolphin Inn and demanded, 'What be going on whilst I been away? There bain't a man can look me in the eye.'

Reuban was perched on his wheeled stool behind the bar. His eyes were bleary with drink and he grinned, showing three yellowed teeth in an otherwise toothless mouth. 'Reckon you done ruffled Lanyon's feathers proper. I knew you'd make the bastard pay for what he did to me. But I didn't think you'd show your face again so soon.'

Sal shuffled into the taproom and glared at the dozen fishermen supping their ale. 'Shut your blathering, Reuban. Our Harry bain't done nothing. And if you men know what be good for you, you'll not go gossiping about what you've heard.'

Harry lost patience. 'What you defending me for, Ma? I bain't done nothing. I've been away on business, that be all.'

Reuban chuckled. 'He's been putting things right between us and Lanyon. I knew my son wouldn'a let that bastard think he'd won.' Reuban poured a large brandy and held it out to Harry. 'I'm proud of you, son. You showed that no-good—'

'Reuban, have your wits gone begging? Harry bain't done nothing,' Sal cut in to halt Reuban's indiscretion, and then rounded on her son. 'You bain't done nothing foolish, have you, son? Lanyon shut up his shop and house. He left Penruan the day after you took off. He be acting like a man possessed since his cutter were wrecked. You heed your old ma, Harry, and keep out of his way.' Sal shambled out to the kitchen, conscious that too many inquisitive ears were listening.

Harry followed her. 'Did Lanyon take Hester? He must have if the house be closed. Where'd they go?'

'No one knows.'

'Lanyon never shuts the shop.' Harry was worried. Had Lanyon found out about him and Hester and this was a new way of punishing her?

Sal saw his expression and sighed. 'Forget her, Harry. Hester be another man's wife now. She bain't worth you tangling with Lanyon over.'

'You know nothing, Ma,' Harry seethed. 'If Lanyon has shut his shop, he's up to something.'

'Let it be, Harry.'

Harry punched a dead rabbit hanging on the wall waiting to be skinned. The bones crunched and a smear of blood stained the wall. 'It's time Lanyon got what's coming to him.'

Sal grabbed his arm, her body quivering with fear for her son. 'Don't do nothing rash. Talk to Clem. He says for you to go up to the cottage as soon as you return. I hope you bain't got our Clem involved with the smuggling again. I thought Clem were done with it. If you had any sense you would too.'

Her lecture washed over him. From the taproom he could hear Reuban cursing a customer.

Sal groaned. 'There he goes again. Our takings be down. Reuban's cursing is sending our customers to drink at The

Gun. At this rate we'll end up in the workhouse. Lanyon gets richer as we get poorer.'

'Not any more he won't.'

Sal shook her head and sank down on to the chair by the Cornish range. She held her head with her hands and rocked to and fro. She was worn out with work and worry. Reuban was ruining their business. Clem had been acting strange all week. She had thought that at least her eldest son had begun to lead a respectable life since he had wed Keziah. Now Harry had that gleam in his eye which always spelled trouble. She did not think she could bear any more.

Golden dust motes sparkled like glow worms in the shaft of afternoon sunlight as it slanted from the window and across the bare wooden floorboards of Clem and Keziah's parlour. The two upholstered chairs were worn on the seats and arms from age, and the front of the dresser was scored from Baltasar's horns. The goat had taken a dislike to the piece of furniture.

Oak beams ran across the ceiling and formed an arc shape across one of the walls. Two little watercolours hung each side of it: one of Keziah's mother, stern-faced in lace cap and collar, and another of a wooden sloop her grandfather had captained.

Harry paced the parlour and listened with growing fury to Hester's story. By the time she had finished he was shaking with rage. 'This has been put off too long. I'll find Lanyon and he'll regret he were ever born. Hester had better stay here in case Lanyon returns afore I deal with him.'

'But I still don't understand why the house and shop have been shut up?' Hester twisted the wedding ring on her finger.

'It be obvious,' Harry snapped. 'That slut Phyllis Tamblin must have run off. She's obviously had enough, the same as you.'

'Can't you stay a few days, Harry?' Hester moaned. 'I bain't seen you for so long. I'm scared at what could happen. I want shot of Thadeous, but not if it puts you in danger. What good would that do me? I love you, Harry. Let's forget Thadeous and run away somewhere he bain't ever gonna find us.'

Harry shook his head. 'There bain't no such place. I bain't gonna run from the likes of him. It has to be this way. I want you as my wife, Hester. The only way that can happen be with Lanyon dead.' He turned to Clem. 'You with me on this, Clem? Lanyon's got it coming for what he did to Pa.'

Clem stared into the flames of the fire. Keziah sat in a rocking chair nursing Zack on her lap. The chair creaked as it moved back and forth and Keziah watched her husband with a fixed intensity, but she did not speak.

'You're my brother and what Lanyon done to Hester bain't right. Nor what happened to Pa. But I got Kezzie and Zacky to consider.'

Harry spat in the fire and glared at Keziah. 'That be you speaking; it bain't our Clem.'

Clem rose to confront his brother. 'Kezzie don't deserve that. She were the one who insisted Hester stay here when she came to us for help. You bain't no better than Lanyon the way you be talking. I've done with that way of life. You beat Lanyon at the smuggling and his wife be carrying your child. Bain't that enough?'

'You think it right the way he beats Hester?'

Clem glared at Harry. 'He don't treat her worse than Pa treated Ma before we were old enough to stop him. There bain't no law about a man beating his wife. And some would say that by carrying another man's child she do deserve it.'

Harry lashed out and caught Clem in the eye. His brother crashed back against the stone fireplace and he swung back at Harry, hitting his chin and sending him sprawling across a spindle-backed chair which broke under his weight. Zack started to scream and cry.

'That's enough, the both of you.' Keziah clutched Zack to her shoulder. 'I will not have brawling in my house. You be frightening the child.'

'I don't want to fight you, Harry,' Clem held out his hand to help his brother to his feet, 'but Lanyon bain't worth swinging for.'

'I never thought you'd let Lanyon get away with what he did to Pa. You bain't no brother of mine. Keziah took your manhood from you when you wed her.'

He slammed out of the house without even saying goodbye to Hester, who burst into tears.

Keziah lost her temper with the woman. 'Stop feeling sorry for yourself. If you've any sense you'll go after Harry and stop this madness. Do you want to wed Harry with Lanyon's blood on your hands?'

Hester sobbed louder. 'He won't listen to me. He never has.'

Clem went out of the room and came back with his jacket. 'I've got to stop Harry.'

'You won't do no good, Clem.' Keziah handed Zack to a terrified-looking Gilly, who clutched the child tight to her chest. She dropped her voice to a whisper. Hester's sobs prevented others hearing. 'Harry wants Lanyon dead because he'll be rich when he marries the man's widow. Is that worth risking your life for? Think of your son. He needs a father.'

'Harry be my brother.' Clem patted her shoulder. 'I can't desert him. He'd be there for us if we needed him.'

Keziah hung her head. She knew of Clem's brutal reputation before they wed and was proud of him for the way he had changed. But she understood family loyalty. She could not condone what he was doing, but in this she would stand by him.

Chapter Twenty-One

Adam was checking the repairs to a topsail, the canvas spread out over the deck of *Pegasus*, when he was hailed from the jetty by Ben Mumford. Adam shielded his eyes against the glare of the sun as he studied the man at Mumford's side.

'Inspector of Sloops and Boats to see you, Cap'n,' Mumford shouted.

Adam groaned. Mr Tregurrian was not expected for another week. Edward had gone away to an important business appointment and was to return the day before the inspector's visit. Nothing had been prepared to show him. Adam climbed over the ship's side to the longboat and rowed himself to the jetty. He was in scuffed leather work breeches and an old shirt, which were hardly suitable attire to present an efficient image to a government official.

When he stepped on to the jetty Adam saw that Tregurrian had walked away to look at one of the ships. It was a cutter which was having its planks nailed to the hull. Tregurrian was talking to two of the shipwrights. Ben Mumford looked anxious and scratched his bald head as Adam approached.

'Inspector said he'd speak with you after he'd had a look round the yard. I thought he weren't expected until next week.'

'He wasn't, but I suppose we should have anticipated that

the inspector would want to catch us unawares. This way we have not had time to hide anything that could be incriminating.'

'He bain't gonna find nothing like that in this yard.' Ben hitched up his breeches over his rounded stomach and tightened his belt a notch. There was a battle gleam in his eyes.

'I've time to change and make myself presentable. Have two men row out to *Pegasus* and stow away the sail. I shall likely be engaged with the inspector for most of the day.'

On his return to Mariner's House he found Senara bandaging the knee of a shipwright's daughter who had fallen over in the school yard. 'Surely her mother could deal with that.' Adam suspected that Senara was being taken advantage of.

The girl's eyes started with fear as she stared at Adam and, muttering a hasty 'thank you', she hobbled out of the door.

Senara shook her head. 'The cut was deep and the child was in pain. You frightened the poor thing. How am I to win the trust of my patients if you terrify them?' She frowned. 'Something is wrong, or you would not have been so short with the girl.'

'Tregurrian is here. The matter was for Father to deal with. Now I will have to. I need to change my clothes – and I shall have to ask him to dine with us. Is that all right with you?'

Senara forced a smile and nodded. It was the first time she would act as hostess for Adam and she was nervous. 'It is a duty I must face sometime. I shall prepare a special meal, though it will not be up to Winnie Fraddon's standards at Trevowan.'

'You will be the perfect hostess.' Adam kissed her cheek, aware that Senara was being put in an awkward situation, but seeing no other resolution.

'You deal with Mr Tregurrian and do not worry about me. I shall cope.'

He ran up the stairs to change. Senara put a hand to her head and sighed. She turned to Carrie Jansen, who was coaxing Nathan to eat some chicken broth. The soup dribbled down his chin and Carrie scooped it back into his mouth. 'I'll finish feeding Nathan, Carrie. If your mother is not too busy at the kiddley, would you ask her to help me today? The Inspector of Sloops and Boats is here. We need to impress him in every way we can.'

'Ma will be happy to help.' Carrie hurried away.

Senara lifted her son above her head and shook him gently so that he laughed, showing his first tooth, which had just broken through his gum. She could not wait to tell Adam but it must wait until much later as there was so much to do. Panic momentarily engulfed her. Everything had to be perfect. She did not want to shame Adam by in anyway forgetting her manners. Etiquette unnerved her. There were so many pitfalls she could fall into which could embarrass her in front of Adam's guest.

Adam was leaving the house when Pru Jansen and Myra Wakeley, the wife of Seth, arrived.

Myra said, 'I were at the kiddley when Carrie came in. The more help Senara can have, the better this day.'

Pru nodded. 'Cap'n, while you show this inspector that this be the finest yard in all Cornwall, we'll cook him a meal he'll remember with pleasure. My ma always said that the way to win a man is through his stomach.'

'I appreciate your help, ladies.' He looked over their heads and winked at Senara, who was wiping a tear from her eye. He had no doubt that she would cope splendidly, but for her sake he was glad of the women's support.

Once back in his father's office, Adam took the ships' plans and his latest sketchbook from their coffers, also the scale model of the cutter from the shelf, and placed them on the table. He then went out to find Mr Tregurrian who, despite the loss of an arm at sea, was climbing over the scaffolding and inspecting the half-built cutter in detail. He was a slender man in his early fifties. He wore no wig and his thick grey hair was cut short above his collar. Tregurrian had a reputation for thoroughness. Although he had purchased the post as a means to provide an income, he was an ex-naval commander with an accomplished career behind him. He would be thorough, but he would also be fair.

But for now he was giving nothing away and Adam remained on edge. He had faith in their workmen but mistakes could sometimes be made and overlooked. The weekly check on all work carried out had been due today. Without his father's presence, the weight of the yard's reputation was on Adam's shoulders.

In view of the coolness between him and Edward since his marriage, Adam was annoyed that his father was not here. He had not told Adam what business was so urgent that it had taken him away at this crucial time, nor where he had gone. It was another sign of the distance which had grown between them.

'You have a large number of craftsmen working for you, Captain Loveday,' Tregurrian observed. 'The yard is busy. Sometimes that leads to corners being cut and work rushed.'

'You will not find evidence of that here, Mr Tregurrian.'

Tregurrian remained expressionless. 'I would make my own inspection of the yard in my own time. The accusations against the yard are grievous.'

'They are malignant and false, sir.' Adam hotly defended the honour of his workers. 'You are free to go where you will and speak with anyone you wish. We have nothing to hide. I have the plans and the model of the cutter ready for you in the office when you are ready.'

'I saw the plans and model when I passed the design.' Mr Tregurrian placed his hand across his chest, his manner stiff.

'It is the finished vessel which is my concern.'

Adam did not want to appear to be watching Mr Tregurrian's inspection of the yard, or allow his presence to intimidate any of the shipwrights when the inspector was questioning them. He tried looking through the ledgers of listed stock, but the figures ran together in a jumble and he could not concentrate. Sketching had passed many hours on ship when time hung heavily, but when he picked up his charcoal and pad, he was too restless to sit still. A glance through the window showed Tregurrian emerging from the blacksmith's forge to enter the shaping sheds where carpenters were tracing from standard patterns the sections of ribs. He was momentarily diverted by the appearance of Scamp running across the yard from the woodpile with a dead rat in his mouth.

After an hour the strain of being cooped in the office was too much, and Adam sauntered over to the cradle holding a cargo ship. A dozen men were working on her. Her keel was laid, the curved ends supported by wooden platforms. Groups of men worked in twos or threes around her to assemble the rib sections. Each rib was made of three parts. The central curved floor sat directly on the keel and, once the futtocks were secured at each end, the ribs would support the sides of the vessel. The tenth rib was being hoisted into place by the pulley rising from the ship's centre. Two men heaved on the ropes and another two were at each end of the rib, guiding it into place. Adam had witnessed the scene hundreds of times, but seeing each ship take form, even at this early stage of the construction, was a marvellous sight.

A saw had been left beside a pile of wood shavings, the blade at a dangerous angle should anyone step on it, and a wooden box of nails had been kicked over. Adam shouted to an apprentice, 'Pick up that saw and nails. You should know by now to look after your tools.'

'You keep a shipshape yard, Captain Loveday.' Mr Tregurrian joined him.

'There are accidents enough which cannot be avoided, without carelessness causing them. The nails are too expensive to be lost.' Adam led the way to the office.

'Not all yards are so fastidious. Some lose at least one worker a month through hazardous conditions. Have there been many accidents this year?'

'Fortunately no fatalities. Only one man has died here in the last four years.'

'That is a good record, Captain Loveday.'

'Minor incidents cannot be avoided. An apprentice broke his arm when he fell from the scaffolding in the rain. A carpenter was knocked unconscious when an apprentice dropped some deck planking from the cradle.'

'The men speak highly of your wife's healing skills. She saved the apprentice's arm. Many a physician has lost a patient through gangrene.'

Adam opened the door to the office and offered Mr Tregurrian the leather chair behind the desk. A tray containing a flagon of claret, a jug of cider, the appropriate glasses and a plate of cold meats and cheese had been brought to the office whilst he had been out. When Mr Tregurrian accepted the cider and cheese, Adam blessed Senara for her foresight. The atmosphere between them relaxed.

'So what is your verdict on Thadeous Lanyon's accusation, Mr Tregurrian?'

'I find his accusation hard to believe but I have yet to assimilate the facts, which are not in your favour.'

'And they are?'

'*Sea Sprite* capsized. The winds were strong but not exceptional that night.'

'But her rigging had been tampered with. I am convinced

that Lanyon fitted a running bowsprit and extended the foresails.'

'Why would he do that? I understand she was a fast ship for her class.'

Adam hesitated briefly. It was unethical to denounce Lanyon as a smuggler when they had known the purpose behind the cutter being purchased. Yet the yard's reputation was at stake. 'What if Lanyon needed to be able to outrun a revenue vessel?'

Tregurrian coughed and shifted uncomfortably in his chair. 'That is a serious accusation.'

'And so are Lanyon's lies.' Adam lost his temper. 'It was greed which made Lanyon alter the design. Running bowsprits are not unusual in such cases. We do not fit them, but another yard could have done so. As I am sure that you know, the bowsprit is made like a telescope to extend when extra sail is needed. When the vessel is in port, the bowsprit would be retracted and appear as normal.'

'With *Sea Sprite* so badly smashed on the rocks that would be difficult to prove. And no contraband was found near the wreck.'

'How long was it before any official reached the site? Two days I would guess. Time enough for any incriminating evidence to be disposed of or carried away by locals scavenging on the beach.'

'Lanyon declares the ship was always difficult to handle. He is backed up in that by Lieutenant Beaumont. *Challenger* is built to the same lines.'

'I was in the navy with Beaumont. He is incompetent. If it wasn't that his grandfather is Admiral Algernon Beaumont, he would never have lasted as an officer on any ship.'

Tregurrian frowned. 'Beaumont left the navy under a cloud, as did you yourself, Captain Loveday. The two of you were court-martialled for duelling. You were both lucky to get off so lightly.'

'Beaumont and I had differences of opinions on several occasions.' Adam was disinclined to explain further.

Tregurrian pinned him with a fierce stare. 'Beaumont claims you constantly challenged his orders. In short, that you were insubordinate to a more senior officer.'

Adam stood to attention, his hands clasped behind his back. It took all his willpower to answer with civility. 'I challenged only an order which would endanger the ship, or his excessive bullying.'

'Bullying is part of the character-forming for our young officers in the navy,' Tregurrian defended.

'There are men who carry it to excess and it shows their vindictive nature. That is not the issue here.'

'Is it not?' Tregurrian leaned forward, his eyes narrowing. 'These accusations are serious. You say the cutters are seaworthy. Lieutenant Beaumont disputes it.'

Adam struggled to master his anger at the turn of questioning. 'Then I would again question his competence to command her. When *Challenger* and *Sea Sprite* both left this yard they were identical except for one point of design.'

'They differed in the bowsprit that is the whole issue.' Tregurrian still showed no emotion, but there was a harsher line to his mouth.

'I am not referring to the bowsprit.' Adam lifted the scale model on the deck and pulled the two halves apart so that Tregurrian could see the interior. 'Here in the aft of the lower deck a partition was put in at Lanyon's request. The door was concealed. It was to hold the most expensive items of cargo, which would remain undetected should he be boarded and the ship searched.'

'Are you accusing Mr Lanyon of being a free-trader?'

'I am merely stating that he insisted that the partition was kept secret. There was no other difference in the design of the two ships.'

'Why is this partition not on the plans?' Tregurrian peered at the unrolled parchment.

'Lanyon insisted that it be kept secret. I was the only man who worked on the partition.'

'Then it is still down to your word against Lanyon.' Tregurrian stood up and glared at Adam. 'And if you made this change without it being recorded, you could have easily altered the bowsprit.'

'But we did not.'

Tregurrian's head snapped up, his glare haughty and condemning. 'Once a design has been approved by an inspector, no deviation from that design should be put into effect without authority.'

'With respect, sir, a partition would not affect her seaworthiness.' He barely controlled his action to pound the desk with his fist as his anger rose at the prejudice he now felt himself facing. Such pedantic bureaucracy had always stifled him in the navy.

'No, but it shows that you have not been entirely honest with me. How far would you go to protect the reputation of this yard and a ship you designed?' The last words were spoken with scorn.

Adam felt a wave of fear crash through him. He was handling this interview all wrong. He should never have lost his temper. 'I would go as far as it takes to vindicate our honour. But I would not lie. No extended bowsprit has ever been built in this yard, sir. You have my word on it.'

The remark changed the inspector's manner. 'Squire Penwithick informs me that you are a man of your word. He speaks highly of you.'

Was there no part of his life which Tregurrian had not already investigated? Adam tensed.

Tregurrian laughed softly. 'Do not take my thoroughness amiss. Beaumont has been subjected to equal scrutiny. I am inclined to favour your opinion of the man. As to the bowsprit . . . I need proof, Captain Loveday. And at the moment with the lack of evidence to prove otherwise I cannot discount that Lanyon has a case against you.'

Adam had been searching his mind and crossed the office to rummage through a tall drawer chest. 'There could be something.' After searching through three drawers he pulled out several small sketchbooks and flipped through them. 'There is this. Is this proof enough of the partition? They are the notes I made for myself.' It was a rough sketch with the dimensions stated and the contours of the position within the lower deck.

He also flicked over the pages of a larger sketchbook which recorded a drawing of the completed vessel with its name and date. 'I was at sea when *Sea Sprite* left the yard but an artist was engaged. There is a picture of every ship and how she looked on her completion. It is a practice of the yard.'

Tregurrian sat down and pulled some paper from his pocket. 'But this only proves that the bowsprit was retracted at the time. How do I know Lanyon did not want that kept secret? Perhaps you did that work yourself so that no other shipwright was aware of the change.'

Adam stood in silence as Tregurrian flicked through the notebooks.

'Your notes are precise, Captain. I also note that you date each entry.'

'Rather like entering a ship's log, it has become a habit.' Adam nodded to another dozen of the notebooks in the drawer. 'Within them is a record of all my design ideas over the last five years. I constantly keep a book close to me to jot down any ideas I may have, or sketch a new design of ship seen at sea. Here is the latest. Since I have kept such a record of the partition, which was against Lanyon's instructions, would I not have done so for the bowsprit?'

'Lack of evidence is unfortunately no proof in a court of law. That your drawings are dated does point in your favour.' Tregurrian frowned and rubbed his eyes. 'The Loveday yard has always had an impeccable reputation. But until recently you built smaller ships.'

'*Pegasus* is moored in mid-channel.' Adam played his last card and hoped he did not sound desperate. 'Inspect her. We have built two others and their owners are pleased with their speed and handling in storms.'

Tregurrian held up his hand. 'Your integrity speaks for itself, but I cannot dismiss Lieutenant Beaumont's statement. For now I must reserve judgement. May I use your inkwell? I need to write some notes.'

Adam gestured for him to do so. Grudgingly, Adam acknowledged to himself that Tregurrian was being thorough in his duty.

The room seemed hot and airless and Adam opened a window, but the ring of hammers and din of voices made him shut it. The sight of the empty dry dock increased his exasperation. A ship had been due to come in for a refit but the owner had cancelled. Already Lanyon's persecution had cost the yard a customer.

'Mr Tregurrian, I assure you that it would be impossible to make and fit a bowsprit without anyone in the yard being aware of it. And Ben Mumford did know of the partition to the ship though my father did not. He was in London that summer.'

Adam ran his fingers through his hair. He was making matters worse. Now Tregurrian would believe they were dishonest in their dealings. 'I built the partition for Lanyon in confidence and in secret, because that was what Lanyon insisted upon. I would never have agreed to fit a running bowsprit on a vessel I had designed. I believed her speed would speak for itself. We needed *Sea Sprite* to attract new orders for the yard. How would it have served our purposes to make her unsafe?'

'That is all part of this investigation, Captain Loveday.' Mr Tregurrian replaced the quill in its stand and closed the lid on the inkwell. He shook sand over the parchment, then carefully folded it and put it in his jacket.

'But my uncle saw the bowsprit extended on *Sea Sprite*. He is captain of HMS *Neptune*. *Sea Sprite* passed him in the English Channel. He is at Plymouth awaiting orders to sail, if you wish a statement from him.'

Tregurrian had been studying the sketchbook of completed ships. 'This is a most irregular case. It would still be Captain William Loveday's word against Mr Lanyon's and he is your uncle. He is bound to speak for you.'

'He would not lie for us, neither would my father expect him to.' Adam was incensed at the implication.

'Your pardon, Captain Loveday, but you must realise how difficult it is to obtain facts and evidence in these circumstances.' He closed the sketchbook and Adam stared at the leather cover. 'If the bowsprit had not been smashed on the rocks, we would have had the evidence we needed.'

'But surely you can ascertain the seaworthiness of *Sea Sprite* by putting *Challenger* through any sea trials.'

'I doubt the revenue service would release her.'

'Then put one of your men on board her.' Adam lost his temper at Tregurrian's intransigence. He immediately held up his hands. 'Your pardon, that outburst was inexcusable.' So much depended on this meeting that the strain was getting to him. He took out his pocket watch. 'I am sure you are hungry, Mr Tregurrian. My wife and I would be honoured if you dined with us.'

393

Tregurrian nodded. 'That would be most pleasant. The inn where I am staying in Penruan served an unpalatable supper, and an equally unappetising breakfast. I have had the most damnable indigestion all day.'

'At what inn are you staying?'

'The Gun.'

Adam could not quite suppress his grin of amusement. 'The Gun is owned by Thadeous Lanyon. My wife has a sovereign remedy for all stomach complaints.'

As they walked to the house Tregurrian informed Adam, 'I have approached Lieutenant Beaumont about spending some time at sea on *Challenger*. He was against it, but I shall insist. I do not believe that you would risk damaging the reputation of your shipyard by fitting an unsuitable bowsprit to a newly designed hull.'

Adam dared not hope that the interview had gone well. Too much depended on it.

Chapter Twenty-Two

S t John was losing interest in his affair with Purity New-bold. It was difficult for her to get away from her ailing mother. Each time he was from home for more than a few hours Meriel would scream at him and work herself into a frenzy. The last time it had happened she had collapsed on the floor with pains in her stomach and St John had feared that she would lose the child.

Meriel was advised by Dr Simon Chegwidden to remain in bed for a week. This she did with bad grace and the physician called every day. At the end of the week he pronounced that on no account must Meriel be upset. A little gentle exercise might be beneficial to her. This St John suspected had been at Meriel's instigation for the physician was known to be susceptible to a pretty face.

Once Meriel had recovered, she nagged St John at every opportunity to take her to Truro.

'It is not fitting that you be seen in public in your condition,' St John reminded her.

'My condition barely shows. I will not be kept a prisoner here. Are you not going to the races outside Truro with Japhet next week? Basil said it was all planned. I will not be left here on my own.'

St John cursed Basil for his indiscretion. He had intended this trip to Truro and its cattle market as an excuse to see

Purity. Although he had purchased some cattle, he needed at least another four heifers to improve the herd. Purity's mother had declared herself well enough for a shopping trip to Truro. It was arranged that he and Purity would spend an evening at the assembly rooms and he would go back to her rooms that night. He had decided that it would be the last time he would see Purity. One of the new milkmaids recently engaged at Trevowan and who lodged with the tenant farmers had caught his eye.

Perhaps it would be as well to pander to Meriel's whim and allow her to visit Truro. It did not mean that he would have to forgo a tryst with Purity. If Meriel were to attend the afternoon races, watching them from their coach, he would insist that for her health she rest in the evening. That would leave him free to do as he pleased.

The Mertle Moxon Academy for Young Ladies was a dour, grey stone, gabled building, set in formal grounds. The surrounding high hedge was symmetrically trimmed and rectangular rose beds lined the drive with regimental precision. There was not a weed or dead flower in sight, and the lawn edges looked as though they had been cut with a razor. Edward shivered as he alighted from his coach. The rigid formality of everything was cold and unwelcoming.

Mrs Mertle Moxon, when he was admitted to her study, was dressed in widow's weeds. A black straw bonnet covered her hair and the veil was draped over her face. She was rake-thin. Her black gown was buttoned to the neck with a high stiff collar; black lace, fingerless gloves encased her bony fingers, and her only jewellery was a thin gold wedding band. She was seated behind a leather-topped mahogany desk which was cleared of papers and held only an inkwell and a silver candlestick.

'Sit down if you please, Mr Loveday. I dislike people

towering over me.' Her voice was as harsh as a sergeant at arms.

Edward sat down, momentarily feeling like a schoolboy dragged before his own formidable headmaster. That he could not see her face was equally disconcerting. He glanced around the office. The room was north facing, the gloom accentuated by dark oak panelling. A glass-fronted bookcase stood in one recess. There were no ornaments apart from a carriage clock on the mantel shelf. The lack of lace covers or adornments favoured by a woman was singularly unsettling. A regimental barracks had more warmth and comfort.

'I have sent for your niece, Mr Loveday.'

'She is not my niece. I am her guardian,' he corrected and felt the intense burrowing of her stare through the opaque veil.

'Indeed!' Her voice sounded like cracking ice. 'The family resemblance is unmistakable. Then, her case is most unfortunate . . . as are those of all my girls. Her other guardian, Lady Keyne, professed to be a distant cousin.'

Edward stiffened. He did not like the woman's tone or innuendo. Mrs Moxon gave a dry, unpleasant laugh. 'You need not fear, Mr Loveday. We are most discreet here. That is why our fees are so high. All our girls are from families of prominence. Though, of course, like Miss Keyne, they have all been born the wrong side of the blanket. They are taught genteel manners and are trained to become governesses. Some have become companions to elderly gentlewomen.'

Edward disliked Mrs Moxon more with each sentence she uttered. If she was condescending and sneering to him, what miserable lives were the girls in her charge subjected to? 'Is no attempt made to find them suitable husbands, madam?'

'Occasionally, but for a man to dismiss the matter of their birth a substantial dowry is needed. We had not yet reached

397

agreement over this with Lady Keyne. Do you intend to pay the girl's fees?'

'As her guardian they are my responsibility. If a suitable husband can be found, a dowry will be provided.'

'There is a fee involved in such a transaction, unless you have some husband in mind, Mr Loveday.'

'Tamasine is but fourteen – a little young to become a bride.'

'She will be fifteen in September,' she corrected with a sniff of disapproval that he was not aware of his ward's exact age. 'It is never too soon to consider such a matter. We keep girls here only until they reach sixteen. If a dowry is not provided, a post will be found for her next September when she reaches that age. That is where our responsibility ends, Mr Loveday.'

There was a tap on the door and Mrs Moxon barked out an order to enter. Edward kept his back to the door, inexplicably nervous at encountering the daughter he had not known existed until two months ago.

'I did the best I could, ma'am, but she were in the grounds as usual.' A woman's voice was high and nervous.

Edward saw Mrs Moxon's hands clench. 'How dare you present yourself here in this manner, Miss Keyne. It is most unacceptable. Leave at once and return when you are suitably attired to greet a visitor. This is your new guardian, Mr Loveday. Lady Keyne is dead.'

Edward was appalled at Mrs Moxon's brutality. Eleanor was probably the only kindly person Tamasine would have known outside of this dreary place.

He stood up quickly to prevent the girl from leaving. She was already at the door. Her black hair was loose about her shoulders and the dull grey gown was ill fitting on her slender figure. There was a thin line of dew on the hem of her dress but the young woman looked impeccably dressed to Edward. The woman who accompanied her hung back with her head bowed and wrung her hands in agitation.

'Please do not leave, Miss Keyne. I am sure that you are perfectly presentable,' he said.

Mrs Moxon sucked in her breath. 'I will not have my authority undermined, Mr Loveday.'

'I would rather meet my ward as she sees fit to present herself to the world, than as you deem is necessary. It will show me more of her true character. I acknowledge that her attire is not of the standard you require of your young ladies. Such a meeting has no detriment to your discipline, Mrs Moxon.'

Tamasine turned and her head tilted back with all the Loveday defiance. When she turned he was shocked to find himself staring into a face which, apart from a feminine softness, was a striking likeness to himself when he was her age. Even their eyes were the same blue. For some reason he had expected her to look like Eleanor. She was clutching a plain linen cap in her hand and he noticed the two top buttons of her high-necked bodice were unfastened.

'Would you leave us, Mrs Moxon?'

'I cannot leave one of the girls in my charge unchaperoned. We do not know you, Mr Loveday.'

'Then Miss Keyne and I will stroll in the garden and you may have someone watch over us, though I expect our conversation to be private.'

'Very well.' Mrs Moxon nodded to the nervous woman hanging behind Tamasine. 'Miss Pinchett, you will chaperone Miss Keyne.' She then turned back to Edward. 'Kindly do not walk upon the grass. It is out of bounds to our staff and pupils.'

'Fortunately, I fit neither of those roles. Any damage which we may do to your lawn will be adequately compensated for by Tamasine's fees.' He experienced a perverse need to overrule this obnoxious woman. He despised petty rules and was heartened to see that his comment had won a smile from the girl.

'Our gardener, Digby, is very diligent in removing from our grounds those who break our rules. He used to ride postillion on the London mail coach and once killed a highwayman with his bare hands.'

Edward was not prepared to tolerate the woman's rudeness. 'He is welcome to try to remove me, Mrs Moxon. But, one must enquire whether such a notorious character is suitable in such close proximity to your charges.'

'These are dangerous times, Mr Loveday.' Mrs Moxon would not back down. 'Digby is here to ensure the protection of us all.'

'And act as gaoler given half a chance,' Tamasine whispered as they left the study. She studied Edward with a disconcerting intensity. 'I knew Lady Keyne was dying. She wrote to tell me.' The brightness in her eyes showed that she was upset but she controlled her tears. 'Lady Keyne was always very kind to me.'

They walked in silence through the school, Tamasine's step brisk with suppressed impatience. Edward was aware that the young woman was studying him.

Unexpectedly, she said, 'I had expected some wizened lawyer to act on her behalf, not someone so bold and dashing. You certainly put the Crow in her place.'

Edward could not stop a soft laugh. 'Dashing is not a phrase which sits well upon a man of my venerable years, Miss Keyne.'

'And you have a sense of humour. I like that. I will never forget Lady Keyne but I think I will like having you as my guardian, Mr Loveday.' Her openness was refreshing but not at all what Edward had expected.

She went on with equal candour, 'The last time I walked across the Crow's precious grass I was locked in the cellar and given bread and water for five days.'

'Rules are made to be obeyed, Miss Keyne. I should not have set you such a bad example.'

'Poppycock. You were wonderful. Everyone is too terrified of the Crow to cross her. Are you my father, Mr Loveday?'

They had reached the entrance and Edward faltered in his stride. 'I am your guardian, Miss Keyne.'

Tamasine shrugged. 'If you say so, Mr Loveday. You look like you could be my father. I would have hated it if my father had turned out to be Sir Robert Keyne. He sounded such an ogre. Lady Keyne was my mother, wasn't she? A guardian would not have become so emotional each time she visited.'

They stepped on to the grass and heard Miss Pinchett behind them making strange strangling noises, her hand fluttering as though she thought she should detain them but did not have the courage. Edward did not know how to answer Tamasine's forthright questions and decided to ignore them. 'Lady Keyne requested that I be your guardian. We were friends of long standing. She instructed that I was to give you this.' He passed the jewellery pouch to her.

Tamasine tipped the ruby pendant, brooch and earrings into her hand. 'Lady Keyne always wore these on her visits. I shall treasure them because she was the sweetest woman I have ever known.' She put them away, unimpressed by the wealth they presented.

'They are worth a great deal of money. They will be part of your dowry.'

'So I am to be married off.' She bristled with indignation and increased her pace across the forbidden grass, so that Edward had to lengthen his stride to keep up. 'I will not be parcelled up with a few trinkets to some old man, so that I can be conveniently forgotten. I have no wish for such a marriage.'

'You prefer to be a governess?'

'Teaching snivelling spoiled brats? I think not.' She spun round, her face flushed with displeasure. There was a stubborn tilt to her chin Edward had seen too many times from Adam not to be warned that this was a serious confrontation. He had to remind himself that the girl was only fourteen. 'I intend to be my own woman. If I marry it will be to someone I can love and respect, someone who wants me for myself and not for any dowry.' She spoke with a passion all too familiar to Edward.

He sighed inwardly. He had anticipated meeting a meek young girl willing to comply with the arrangements he made for her future. 'You are already an attractive young woman. Many a man will be honoured if you chose him as your husband.'

Her blue eyes flared with anger. 'But I will have no choice. I have seen it happen too often. Once we are sixteen, the pretty ones get sold off to some ageing, pot-bellied man who cannot stop pawing them. Our chosen spouses are no paupers – they want a young and pretty wife. That's how the Crow makes her money – by pocketing half the dowry as her fee.'

At Edward's shocked expression, Tamasine laughed, and seemed to be enjoying herself although her tale was outrageous. 'That is not the half of it. The girls who are not pretty but have a dowry will be paraded like servants at a hiring fair before suitors, who will marry them to escape their creditors. Only the ugly and poor ones become governesses.'

'That is scandalous!' Edward was horrified.

Tamasine shrugged. 'Most of the girls accept it as their lot. Our guardians are usually embarrassed by our existence – we are by-blows after all.'

'The devil! What language is that for a young lady?'

Edward had heard enough for one day.

Tamasine's eyes widened with injured pride. 'I speak the truth, sir. And what language is that of yours to use before one of my tender years?'

Despite his chagrin at her audacity, Edward found it hard not to smile at her outburst. There was no doubting that she was a Loveday. She was irrepressible and there was no halting her speech.

'Why would I be hidden away here and brought up as a gentlewoman if I was not born outside of marriage? Though I prefer the term love child. It has a less sordid ring to it, do you not think?'

Edward cleared his throat, aware that he was out of his depth in dealing with this young woman. 'I think you are far too forward,' he reprimanded, no longer amused at her lack of decorum. 'Mrs Moxon has been sadly lacking in your education. No gentlewoman would speak as you do.'

'I despise women who are weak and subservient.' Her head tilted back as she declared, 'Then it is as well I intend to be an actress when I leave here.' Tamasine opened her arms wide as though to embrace the world. 'Apart from Lady Keyne the only other woman to visit here was Clarinda Derwent, the actress. Cassie Derwent left last year to follow her mother on to the stage. She was my best friend. Clarinda told me all about the theatre. She is the mistress of a duke. Of course, Cassie was not his daughter; her father was another actor.'

'Miss Keyne, I have heard quite enough.' Edward was taken aback by her confession; a part of him remained shocked at such worldly talk and another part admired her candour. Her face was animated when she spoke of those she cared for. Even the theatrical gestures showed a woman hungry to experience life. Such traits did not bode well for the future.

'I could not permit a ward of mine to entertain the notion

of appearing on the stage. You have another year in which to improve your manners and schooling. I will visit you again before your sixteenth birthday. If you are to be married it will be to a man who has my approval, and one whom I believe will make you happy. I will have no arguments upon the matter.'

'How did my mother die? What was she like?'

The mercurial change of subject just as Edward thought he had brought the conversation under control startled him. 'Are you referring to your guardian, Lady Keyne?' he corrected.

They had reached a stone seat on the far side of the lawn. Tamasine sat down and folded her hands demurely in her lap. 'Please, tell me about her. If she was not my mother, then she was the closest to a parent I have ever known. I was very fond of her Ladyship. Yet there was a great sadness about her.'

Edward scanned the garden and saw Miss Pinchett skirting the lawn to walk on the gravel path. She kept glancing nervously from them back to the house where a movement at a window showed Mrs Moxon also watching them. Assured that Miss Pinchett was too far away to hear what they were saying, Edward sat down beside his daughter. 'Lady Keyne was a remarkable and spirited woman. She was beautiful, witty and charming, but this you know. I had not seen her for many years as her life was in London with her husband.'

He edited much of what he knew of Eleanor, selecting only facts about her personality not her personal life.

'You have told me little, Mr Loveday,' Tamasine accused.

'If Lady Keyne had wanted you to know of her personal life she would have informed you.'

'Where do you live, Mr Loveday?'

'In Cornwall.'

'And you have children?'

'I have three sons.'

'Did you ever want a daughter, Mr Loveday.'

Her questioning was unsettling. There was no place in his life for this daughter. He would ensure that she was provided with an ample dowry to marry a man of family and position, and he would honour his promise to ensure that the marriage was suitable. He stood up. 'Your chaperone is beckoning to us. It must be time for your lessons.'

She looked at the bleak exterior of the school and there was a defiant tilt to her chin which was very characteristic of Adam. Edward had to swallow against a lump of emotion in his throat.

Tamasine stood up with her hands clasped in front of her. She took a steadying breath and asked breathlessly, 'If you are not my father, why am I called Tamasine Loveday Keyne?'

Edward could no longer hold that forthright stare. He watched a squirrel run across the grass and up the trunk of a tree. 'Loveday is a common woman's name in Cornwall. You must make no more of it than that.'

She blinked rapidly and he could almost feel that she was fighting an inner battle. Her expressive eyes portrayed her feelings of hope, uncertainty, fear, sadness and eventually resignation.

She smiled tremulously. 'I have not had a visitor for over a year. It is time for our daily promenade, though I long to run headlong through the woods, not walk in a sedate file through Salisbury with my head kept bowed. But I forget my manners.' She held out her hand to him. 'I thank you for your time and the trouble you have taken to come here, Mr Loveday. It has been a long journey for you.'

He took her hand and, feeling her trembling, he clasped it firmly. She had bravely accepted Eleanor's death though her eyes were sad. His admiration for the young woman increased. He found himself moved to say, 'I will never fail you as your guardian. I will visit whenever I have business in London and must pass this way. Mr Melchett is my lawyer in Truro. If you have urgent need of me on any matter, a message will reach me through him.'

'You are very kind, sir.' Her voice broke and without warning she threw her arms about his shoulders and kissed his cheek. 'I shall never forget you, sir.' Then, with a sob, she ran across the lawn.

Miss Pinchett cried out in alarm. From out of the shrubbery a thickset man appeared who proceeded to shout at Tamasine. He sped across the lawn and grabbed her arm, almost pulling her off her feet as he shook her.

'That is enough.' Edward ran to protect Tamasine. 'How dare you lay hands on my ward in such unseemly manner?'

The man thrust his bull neck forward, his eyes yellowed and rheumy. 'She knows the rules.'

'It is I who insisted that we walk across the lawn. What rule did I break, other than that of petty tyranny over girls whose lives are bleak enough?'

A line of girls filed out of the main entrance to the school. They walked ranging in height with the smallest of about seven years at the front and the elder girls at the rear. They all wore the same shapeless grey gowns, with plain unattractive linen bonnets tied under their chins and black capes. None of them was speaking. Obviously that was another rule stripping any pleasure from the daily walk.

Four teachers carrying riding whips walked outside the column. Any girl who raised her eyes to look at Edward was rapped sharply across the elbow with a whip. Edward was incensed at the inhumanity. Yet he could do nothing unless he was prepared to take Tamasine out of the school. Then where would she go? Eleanor must have deemed the Academy suitable. In a little over a year Tamasine would leave here. Having glimpsed something of the fire within his daughter, perhaps the restraints imposed by the school curbed the wilder of her Loveday traits.

On his journey home Edward found himself thinking about Tamasine constantly. She had courage and spirit and would be a beautiful woman – a woman any man would be proud to own as his daughter.

After the departure of Edward Loveday, Tamasine had to face a list of misdemeanours read out in front of the assembled pupils. As punishment for not wearing her cap when she presented herself in Mrs Moxon's study, Tamasine was forbidden to leave the house for a month. To be restricted from access to the grounds was torture for her. Whilst the other girls took their afternoon walk, Tamasine was made to stand on a stool in the corner of the Crow's study.

They were punishments she had borne many times, but with each year rebellion to escape the school she hated became stronger. She had nourished a hope that her new guardian would take her away. To alleviate the boredom of her punishment she retraced every word Edward Loveday had spoken to her. His image was carved in her mind. He was the father she had dreamed of: self-assured yet not arrogant, handsome and not without humanity. She did not believe him when he had denied being her father. Their looks were too similar, especially the colour of their eyes. There were no mirrors available to the girls in the school, but Tamasine had seen her reflection in windows and rain puddles. Edward Loveday was an honest man but when he answered he had not been able to hold her gaze.

She knew an illegitimate child had no rights. Mrs Moxon would tell them often enough. But Tamasine clung to the image of freedom which Edward Loveday represented and each day her faith in him strengthened. He must have been very handsome when he was younger and Eleanor Keyne would have found him irresistible. Tamasine was convinced that Edward Loveday was her father and that her mother had been Lady Keyne. It made her more determined than ever to break away from an enforced marriage arranged by the Crow.

The jewellery given to her by Edward Loveday had been hidden in a hollow tree trunk. If the Crow found it, it was likely Tamasine would not see it again. The jewellery could secure her freedom. Someday, somehow, she would escape from here and take control of her own destiny.

Chapter Twenty-Three

Halfway through the journey by coach to Truro, St John regretted allowing Meriel to accompany him. Her list of demands was endless. She clearly intended to make up for the months of enforced inactivity.

'I shall need some silk for a new gown. The seamstresses in Truro are more skilled than the local women.'

'I gave you a roll of mulberry silk from our last run,' St John protested. 'The seamstress has yet to make that up for you.'

Meriel pouted. 'Mulberry is an old woman's colour.'

'How ungracious you always are.' St John lost his patience. 'We cannot afford such a purchase. Be content that you are to visit Truro.'

'You are such a clutchfist. There's been enough money to provide for your needs. Would you have your wife appear a dowd amongst Truro society?' She was working herself into a fury, her shrill voice as monotonous as a woodpecker drilling into a tree. 'And I need shoes. My satin slippers are beyond repair and my walking shoes pinch. And hair is worn more naturally now, but Rachel is useless as a lady's maid. I must attend a wigmaker and obtain the exact match of colour. It is quite the thing for false ringlets and curls to add height and thickness to one's own hair.'

To ignore her, St John closed his eyes but she repeatedly

struck his knee with her fan whenever she wanted to reclaim his attention.

'I shall need at least fifty guineas to spend at the gaming tables,' she demanded as the coach rattled past the shadow of St Mary's church and entered King Street. She brought the fan down hard on his knuckles.

St John snatched it from her and threw it out of the window. 'You will get nothing by carrying on in such a fashion, madam. And you will certainly not be gambling. You have no head for cards and always lose.'

'That was my best fan,' she shouted. 'You're going to have to replace that now. And you cannot stop me gambling. All our friends will be at the tables.'

'You have recovered your strength with remarkable ease,' St John retorted. 'Chegwidden agreed that the trip would be beneficial to you, only if you continued to rest. If you stop acting like a fishwife I may agree for you to purchase a few necessities and sit with the matrons of an evening. Dr Chegwidden was adamant that you must avoid too much exertion or excitement.'

Meriel glared at him and suspected that he had seen through her ruse to evade her household duties. When Meriel was about to protest St John nailed her with an uncompromising stare.

'Do not take advantage of my generosity in permitting you this excursion.' There was no tenderness in his tone and Meriel knew she had overplayed her hand. St John no longer loved her and she had lost her power over him. If she could not get the riches she wanted from him, she would find another way.

Her expression was sullen as she stared out of the window at the people crowding the streets. The clang of the town crier's bell followed them but his bellowing announcement was too distant for them to hear his words. They passed the elegant façade of Lord Fetherington's house and Meriel scowled.

'I do not see why we do not stay with the Fetheringtons. His Lordship knew you were to attend the races, did he not?'

'His Lordship did not extend an invitation. I saw him talking to you at Lady Keyne's funeral. He looked displeased when he left your side. I assumed that you had upset his Lordship in some way.'

'I refused his Lordship's lecherous advances.'

'He does not usually take insult over that, but would see it as making the pursuit more enjoyable.'

Meriel refused to acknowledge that his Lordship would snub them over the jewels he had given her. She hated to stay at an inn with the smell of cooking, tobacco smoke and stale ale, which reminded her of the origins she chose to forget.

'It is too bad of Percy not to invite us.'

'He and Basil are staying with Lord Wycham, who has taken a house in town for the races.'

If Lord Wycham was in town, Meriel was determined that she would again meet him. The memory of her encounters with the handsome Earl of Wycham brought a warm glow to her body. There was a man who could give her all that she desired in status and wealth, but the child she carried could ruin her chances to win his affection. She feared he would leave Cornwall soon. It could be months before she met the likes of him again.

After the coach journey to Truro St John insisted that Meriel rested that evening. She protested although the jolting coach ride, followed by a rich meal of lampreys in oyster sauce and several slices of beef running with meat juices, had given her a dull nagging stomach ache. It had not completely eased when she awoke in the early morning. The bed was empty beside her.

Meriel thumped the unused pillow, angered that St John had spent the evening carousing and gaming whilst she had been confined to their room. She hated the restrictions of her pregnancy, especially as she may have missed an opportunity to see Lord Wycham.

Outside her window was the sound of trudging footsteps. 'Five of the clock and all's well,' the watchman shouted.

Meriel groaned and turned on her side. A peel of church bells disturbed her sleep. How could anyone consider going to church at this unearthly hour? There were increased stirrings in the streets, making sleep impossible as the town began its day. Apprentices were noisy as they opened the shutters of their workrooms or shops. Hammering had started further along the street at a furniture maker's shop. A pieman was abroad announcing his wares, hoofs pounded the street, and the wheels of laden carts creaked past her window. Meriel had forgotten how noisy Truro could be.

An hour later the door to her room opened and she sat up with a gasp of fright and yanked aside the bed hangings.

'Where have you been all night?' she demanded of St John. In the pale sunlight St John looked dishevelled. Strands of his hair had fallen loose from its ribbon and his cravat was tied at an odd angle. There was a lingering smell of perfume as he discarded his jacket.

'You've been with a whore!' Meriel raged. 'I can smell her on you.'

'She was no whore. I mean there was no whore.' He had spent the night with Purity Newbold and she had been tearful when he told her their relationship was over.

'Do not think you are coming into my bed, stinking of your woman.' Meriel hurled a pillow at St John. She winced at the nagging pain in her stomach.

He caught it to his chest with an inane grin. 'Since for appearances' sake we are forced to share a room, I will not be banned from my own bed. I am deuced tired.' He hiccuped and opened a money pouch over the counterpane, the gold coins spilling around Meriel. 'This should silence your complaints. I won two hundred guineas at cards. You may take fifty and purchase your gown and fripperies, madam. I am feeling generous. You may either take a shopping trip or join me at the races.'

'If I forgo the races and rest all afternoon, will you take me to the assembly rooms this evening?' It was a difficult choice, for Wycham was more likely to be at the races, but to look her best for him she wanted her new purchases. There would be another race meeting tomorrow.

St John fell on to the bed without removing his clothes. 'Providing that you do not spend more than I have stipulated, I will consider the matter.' His words slurred as he fell asleep.

She counted out the money. There was enough for a gown, slippers and to visit the wigmaker and have her hair dressed. If she met Lord Wycham she intended to outshine any other woman present.

It was unfashionably early when Meriel ventured abroad from the inn. She was too impatient to await until St John rose from his slumber. She wanted to shop with leisure, intending to hunt out bargains and make the money stretch as far as possible. She had glimpsed a bonnet in a milliner's window which she could not resist. St John was always so impatient in shops and would find a way to curtail her pleasure.

She spent two hours with a seamstress, having chosen cream dimity embroidered with red rosebuds and the gown to be edged with scarlet ribbons. Another hour was spent at the wigmaker's, who had matched her blonde hair to perfection and showed her how to insert the false hair and instruct her maid to dress it in a becoming fashion.

Her feet throbbed as she peered into a shop window where pink satin shoes with diamanté buckles tempted her. Could she beat the price down on them and the bonnet she craved? She was five guineas short. The milliner lowered her price and with her hat box swinging on her arm and her step light, Meriel returned to haggle with the shoemaker. How could Lord Wycham resist her with her new hairstyle and clothes?

Suddenly her arm was roughly grabbed and she was propelled past the shop front and into a narrow passage. Something hard was jabbed into her ribs as she was about to scream.

'There be a pistol at your back. Cry out and I fire,' Thadeous Lanyon snarled in her ear.

He pushed her forward to the end of the passage, which was blocked off by a tall warehouse. 'Don't call out, or you be dead. Where's Hester?'

'How should I know? Have you lost her in Truro?' Meriel's heart pounded with fright. The alley was gloomy and stank of urine where drunks had used it as a privy in the night.

He slapped her face. 'Don't play games. Where's that no-good brother of yours taken her?'

Meriel lashed out at him with her hat box. It hit the side of his head but the lid came off and her pretty hat fell into the slime of the gutter. She cried out and turned to retrieve it, but was jerked upright by her hair. The scalding pain of the pins and hairpiece being wrenched from her scalp brought tears to her eyes. 'My hair! You've ruined it!' She stamped on Lanyon's foot but his hold did not lessen. 'I haven't seen Harry for weeks.'

'Lying bitch. Do you think I don't know that St John Loveday is Sawle's partner? No doubt urged on by your greed.' The hairpiece was thrown on the ground and Lanyon twisted his hands through her hair to pull her head back. Through her pain she saw his ugly face inches from her own.

His eyes bulged and glittered with hatred. 'No one takes what be mine.' His spittle splashed her cheek and ran down her face.

Meriel had suffered Reuban Sawles' beatings for years and her anger at the way Lanyon was treating her gave her the strength to retaliate. Her fingers sought to gouge his cheek but her gloves made her attack ineffectual. He twisted her round and slammed her body against the wall of a warehouse. Pain shot through her stomach and the baby kicked in protest. Meriel lashed backwards with her foot, her shoe grazing down Lanyon's shin. 'I know nothing. Now get your vile hands off me.'

Lanyon grunted in agony but did not slacken his hold. The pain in her side was building, as she writhed and twisted to be free. 'I'm not Hester who you can beat and the law will do nothing. Harm me and my husband will see you rot in gaol.'

'Still the Miss Hoity-Toity, thinking herself better than me.' He punched her, catching the side of her stomach. The baby juddered inside her and Meriel began to tremble as fear turned her legs to jelly and she doubled over. Lanyon raged in her ear, 'You're to blame for this. You started it when you refused to wed me.'

Lanyon hit her twice more as he mouthed obscenities and threats. 'I've waited a long time to punish you for the insults you heaped on me. Did you really think you could escape my anger?'

Meriel was sobbing with pain, the sounds from the street seemed a long way away and the passage was deserted. 'You won't get away with this,' she gasped. 'St John . . . Harry will . . .'

Lanyon laughed. 'Loveday be weak. He be no threat to me. And Harry . . . I took Hester from him and he did nothing. He bain't as tough as he brags.'

Fear for herself and the child swirled in swathes around

Meriel. The pain was crippling her ability to fight. He hit her again in the stomach.

'Please no, I am with child. You'll harm it.'

A kneading palm pressed into her abdomen. 'Aye, you're bloated as a whale. Hester's gone and she be carrying my child. But you're at my mercy, bitch. I've waited a long time to see you beg.' He hit her again and she sank to her knees. She vomited and tried to protect her child with her arms.

The madman above her was panting and she could smell his sweat as he ground out, 'This be a lesson for your husband not to take what be mine. He can lose something he prizes.' His boot slammed into her stomach. 'With luck you and the brat will die . . .'

Meriel screamed as she saw his foot raised to aim at her head.

'Who is there?' a man's voice shouted. 'Thief! Get your foul hands off that woman.'

Lanyon kicked her head and Meriel lost consciousness. To escape, Lanyon opened a door leading out to the passage. He ran through the deserted storeroom at the back of a shop and sprang out through an open window on the far side. He was in a labyrinth of alleys snaking through this quarter of town and no one would find him.

The man who had raised the alarm shouted, 'Someone get after that thief. There's a guinea for the man who catches him.'

Only two men ran into the shop. The others backed away, unwilling to apprehend a violent man.

Her rescuer bent over. 'Good God, it *is* Meriel Loveday!' Lord Wycham thought he was looking at a corpse; the woman was so pale and unmoving. Her dress was filthy from the gutter, her hair was a tangled mess and there were bruises on her face. He touched her throat and felt the faint beat of a pulse.

Lord Wycham had thought he had recognised Meriel as she came out of a milliner's, but then had lost her in the crowd. A glimpse of a woman in the same coloured blue gown as she had been wearing, being accosted and dragged into this passage, had made him investigate, but he had been some distance away.

His shouts had drawn several spectators and he turned to a printer's apprentice in an ink-stained apron. 'Run to the best physician in town and tell him a woman has been beaten and is near to death. He is to come to the Red Lion Inn.'

'Do you mean to say you know this woman?' Lord Wycham's companion, a gentleman in his late thirties, was looking at him strangely. 'What sort of decent woman gets so molested in daylight?'

'She is no doxy, Mr Caversham.' The earl picked up Meriel to carry her. The Red Lion was a few minutes' walk away. 'It was fortunate that we were passing. We were playing cards with her husband last evening. St John Loveday.'

'I remember, the man was on a winning streak. It looks like luck has turned against him today.'

The sound of raised voices woke St John. He rolled on his side and grimaced at the pain stabbing through his head. He had drunk a substantial amount of brandy through the evening. The door to the room was opened and he peered blearily at the apparition of the Earl of Wycham carrying Meriel in his arms.

'Get out of the bed and let me lay her down,' Wycham ordered. 'Your wife was attacked and beaten by some madman. I've sent for a physician. What the devil were you about, allowing her to go about the town unescorted?'

'I didn't,' St John mumbled as he rose from the bed and stared with horror at Meriel's unconscious figure. There was a dark bruise and a lump forming at the side of her head. 'Who attacked her? She went out whilst I was asleep.'

'If her assailant had not been passably dressed, I would have said your wife was being set upon and robbed,' Lord Wycham replied. 'The man was short and barrel-chested, dressed like a gentleman but acted like a brigand. The attack was vicious. He seemed to be shouting abuse at her. I may have misheard, but I would swear the villain said something about teaching her husband not to take from him what was his. Bad lot. The man must be mad. Or a sore loser at cards, Loveday? Fellow like that needs to be called out in my book. Any idea who he is?'

St John was staring wordlessly at Meriel. Her face twisted with pain and she screamed. Her eyes opened, wide and staring, as her back arched in agony. He thrust his knuckle against his teeth in alarm. 'The child! Dear God, don't let the child be harmed.'

Meriel screamed. Lord Wycham made a hasty exit saying, 'Damnable business, Loveday. Hope they catch the cur who did this. If you know the man, I shall be happy to attend you should you call him out.'

'Who did this to you, Meriel?' St John gripped her arms to calm her when the screams subsided. Her eyes were wild and she gabbled incoherently.

The doctor arrived. 'Stand back from her. Your wife is delirious, sir.'

An hour later, St John's son was born four months early. He did not draw a single breath. The physician and midwife despaired of saving Meriel's life. Twice Meriel had screamed Lanyon's name in her pain and delirium. It was enough to confirm St John's suspicions about who had attacked her.

The doctor left the midwife to finish tending Meriel and took St John aside from the bed. 'Bad business. You must prepare yourself for the worst, Mr Loveday. Your wife has been brutally beaten and is haemorrhaging badly.'

418

St John turned red-rimmed eyes on the physician then slammed out of the room in search of Thadeous Lanyon.

The next day the body of Thadeous Lanyon was found floating in the River Kenwyn upstream from Truro's quay. He had died from a bullet wound to his temple. When officials brought his body back to Penruan, to inform his widow of his death, they found the shop and house deserted. No one appeared to know where Hester Lanyon or her maid had gone.

The first St John heard of Lanyon's murder was when a hand was clamped on his shoulder as he lay slumped over a table in the Red Lion taproom. He'd been drinking without stop since Meriel had lost the child.

Two burly constables stood each side of him. 'St John Loveday, I am taking you into custody for questioning concerning the murder of Thadeous Lanyon.'

St John shook himself and peered blearily into the bloated face of his accuser. As his vision focused he saw the constable was wearing a leather eye-patch. He looked more like a brigand than an officer of the law. 'What the devil do you mean? And who are you?'

'Name's Fogg. And this here's O'Connor.'

The second constable stepped forward to take St John's arm in a huge paw. He was tall and built like a bear with long shaggy hair. 'Thadeous Lanyon be dead and you have been heard threatening his life. Now on your feet. It's gaol for you.'

'I did not murder Lanyon.' St John lurched unsteadily to his feet. 'You can't arrest me. My wife is sick abed upstairs. She may not live.'

'I can't help your wife's condition.' Fogg spoke without sympathy. 'Will you come peaceful like, sir? Or do I call out the guard and have you marched through the town in chains?'

'Take your hands off me.' St John straightened but could not shake off O'Connor's bearlike grip. The taproom swayed around him and his head was pounding. 'This is outrageous. I have not seen Lanyon in weeks.'

'He's been in Truro for some days,' O'Connor rumbled from deep in his chest. 'He'd applied to the court for proceedings against your family shipyard citing them for incompetence. Reason enough for murder.'

Fogg searched St John for any weapons. 'The wound could have been from a duel. Lord Wycham were heard to offer to stand as your second.'

St John felt the stirrings of fear. 'I do not duel and certainly would not take a sword or pistol to Lanyon. It would be a horsewhip.'

Fogg pulled a dagger from inside St John's jacket. 'What would a respectable gentleman be doing with such a weapon, if he did not intend to use it?'

'I was set upon by footpads last January when I was in Fowey and two days ago my wife was brutally beaten in daylight. A man has a right to defend himself.' St John ran his tongue over his parched lips and reached for his tankard.

His hand was pushed away by Fogg. 'You need to sober up to regain your memory. There is also the matter of the attack upon your wife. You were heard to accuse Lanyon of that crime and declare you'd see him dead. The next day he is found shot through the head. Landlord said he saw you with a pistol. Where is it?'

St John put his hand inside his jacket, dimly remembering that he had taken to carrying his pistol. It was gone. So was his money pouch. He was finding it hard to take in the man's words through the haze of alcohol still engulfing him.

'I've been robbed. The pistol and my money are gone.'

'They didn't take the dagger. Selective pickpocket, weren't it?' O'Connor snapped.

'Where were you the night before last?' The question was fired at him by Fogg.

St John frowned and shook his head. 'I have no idea. I do not remember anything, but that my son died and I had several brandies here. Then I think I went out to find my cousin. I cannot remember anything after that.' He groaned and thrust his fingers through his hair. 'I couldn't have killed Lanyon, though I wish I had. He killed my son, the bastard.'

'And what cousin would that be you were looking for, Mr Loveday?' Fogg rapped out.

'Japhet. He is in town for the races. I needed to talk to him.'

'Or plan a murder. Japhet Loveday has a reputation for duelling.'

'How come you know so much about our family?' St John peered at him.

'A family as prominent as the Lovedays are well known everywhere. I arrested your cousin Japhet for disorderly conduct some years ago. Trouble has a habit of following him. The sheriff will likely want a word with him as well.'

'Japhet's never killed anyone either,' St John protested. He shook his head, fighting against the fuzziness which blurred his mind.

'Are you prepared to come peacefully, Mr Loveday?' Fogg lost patience and took some rope from his pocket. 'I will bind your arms if I have to.'

'I need to make arrangements for my wife with the landlord.' St John beckoned to the landlord, who was industriously wiping the bar top, whilst watching the proceedings. St John laid three pieces of gold, which he took from his waistcoat pocket, in the man's hand. 'That should settle my bill and pay the physician's fees when he calls again. Send

421

word to Lord Fetherington as to what has happened. And a messenger to my father at Trevowan. If my cousin Japhet—'

'You've made arrangements enough.' O'Connor pushed St John forward.

'Where are you taking me?' St John demanded.

'To the town lockup, pending the sheriff's arrival to question you tomorrow. If he decides there be evidence to prosecute, happen, since you be gentry, you'll be bound by your word not to leave the county until you've been called to trial.'

'Trial!' St John felt a great abyss open beneath his feet and cold fear trammelled him. He was shoved forward roughly and, as he stumbled, he called back over his shoulder, 'Get word to Japhet if you can, landlord. He's in town for the races. My father and cousin will reward you for your service.'

'Your cousin better have witnesses for where he was last night,' Fogg grunted as he marched St John to the door.

The landlord whistled for a potboy to attend him. He was not about to cross the Lovedays, who had important connections in the town.

Chapter Twenty-Four

A t the same time as the constables were arresting St John,
Edward was closeted with Adam in his office.

'We are not out of the woods then yet. You handled
Tregurrian well. I should have been here.'

'Senara also played her part. She provided an excellent meal
and charmed him as we dined.' Adam was quick to inform
Edward that his wife had helped him. 'Tregurrian was inclined
to believe us rather than Lanyon, but there are still the sea
trials with *Challenger* to undergo.' Adam had related all of his
interview but remained uneasy about the outcome. 'Beaumont
is being difficult. He has evaded two meetings with Tregurrian,
stating that he was unavoidably detained at sea.'

'And Lanyon has not retracted his statement?' Edward was
cross that he had not been here to deal with the Inspector of
Sloops and Boats himself.

'Lanyon has left Penruan on business. He's been gone over
two weeks, which is not like him.'

'Probably causing more trouble for us in Falmouth or
Truro. That man will not rest until he brings a case against
us.'

'We lost another order for a refit this week, sir. Looks like
the dry dock will be empty for at least a month.' Adam did
not want to add to his father's troubles but the matter could
not be avoided.

'Many more cancellations and Lanyon will see us ruined without even a court case. Word spreads fast. Once the reputation of the yard is lost it will take years to regain the trust of customers.'

'It would help if Beaumont caught more free-traders. Not that I like seeing the trade curbed, but it would mean that *Challenger*'s speed was shown to be difficult to match.'

Edward stared fiercely at Adam. 'Beaumont is not going to do us any favours. Why could you not have held your temper and not duelled with him? Of late our family has an unconscionable amount of conflicts waiting to ambush us.'

The remark perturbed Adam. His father was never defeatist. Was there more troubling Edward than he was saying? 'We have always triumphed over our adversaries in the past, sir. This time we have right on our side.'

There was a weariness to Edward's smile. He spread his hands with resignation. 'Right. Wrong. Justice. Injustice. Can all be coloured by public opinion? Mud sticks, or there is no smoke without fire, many would say. We have won through before and I trust we shall do so again.'

Japhet looked uneasy throughout his visit with St John in the lockup.

'This place gives me the shivers. I've been in it too often,' he attempted to jest. 'Deuced constables were all for arresting me. Fortunately, I was celebrating at Lord Fetherington's after winning my races so my alibi was impeccable. Sheba was on her best form. His Lordship was after buying her but that is one lady in my life I will never be parted from.'

'A pity I was not there with you,' St John groaned. He was squatting on the floor of his cell with his head bowed. The lockup stank of urine and the rats scurried across the filthy floor, showing no fear of the humans who shared their habitation.

'I've asked around but no one saw you that night.' Japhet took out a hip flask of brandy and passed it to St John.

'Someone must have seen me.' St John staggered to his feet. 'I'm not the only one who would have liked to see Lanyon dead. He's made dozens of enemies – Harry Sawle for one.'

Japhet stayed close to the door and kept his stare on the patch of sunlight visible through the tiny window. Any form of confinement made his flesh itch to get out. 'I saw Harry in town yesterday, but he's disappeared now. No one else who I've asked saw him.'

'Harry's wanted Lanyon dead for a long time.' St John held his throbbing head. 'Why can't I remember where I was?'

'We've all been that drunk at some time in our lives.' Japhet was feeling at a loss. 'I went to see Meriel. She seems to be on the mend. Looked dreadful – poor woman. Fetherington has offered that she convalesce at his home.'

St John leaned his head back against the wall and put his hand over his bloodshot eyes. 'Meriel will come out of this shining whatever happens. Damn her!' His laugh was caustic. 'Fetherington wants to get into her bed. Not much chance of that. Meriel doesn't like men.'

'She has enough dangling after her.' Japhet was not surprised. Meriel had never tempted him. There was a coldness and calculation in her eyes. 'Fetherington is not going to try to seduce her in her present condition.'

'He'd be welcome to her. The woman has cost me everything. I curse the day I met her. I gave up so much for her, and she cannot even give me a son.'

Japhet whistled through his teeth. 'That's the drink talking, Coz, though she can be a trial with her moods and tantrums. But she did give you Rowena.'

St John brightened. 'A man couldn't wish for a more wonderful daughter. But I need a son, Japhet. Trevowan will go to Rafe, or if Father changes his mind, to Adam. I don't intend to work all my life for Adam or his gypsy brats to inherit.'

Japhet waved aside the hip flask when St John would return it. 'You drink it. It may cheer you. And you are far from convicted. No witnesses saw you with Lanyon that night.'

The turnkey rattled his keys and Japhet was impatient to get out of the lockup. 'I'll keep asking around. We both know that you didn't kill Lanyon, no matter that the villain deserved it.'

St John sank back down on to the floor. He held his head in his hands. He would have been capable of the murder, his rage had been so great. He wished he could be absolutely certain that he had not found Lanyon and killed him.

Clem returned to Penruan. Harry had calmed down and declared that he had some contacts to make for a future run. Clem was worried that Lanyon would return to the fishing village and he did not want Keziah unprotected. He had made Harry promise he would not kill Lanyon. His brother's answer had been evasive – but then you could never pin Harry down to any commitment these days. Clem hoped that Harry had come to see reason.

When Clem sailed into the harbour after a day's fishing and heard the rumour that Lanyon had been killed, his first fears were for Harry. To discover what he could he sought out the two constables and found them in the Gun Inn sitting each side of a rickety table.

'I hear you be asking after Hester Lanyon. Do it be true that Lanyon be dead?'

The smell of fish was thick in the air as the Gun was situated close to the pilchard sheds. Clem was appraised in sombre fashion by the older of the two men, who was shaven-headed, with a bushy brown-and-ginger-streaked beard. 'Are you kin to Mr Lanyon, sir?'

'I asked if he were dead,' Clem countered. 'Word is that you be looking for his wife.'

'You know her whereabouts?' the older man asked. 'Name's Quirke – Jeremiah Quirke. This be Simms. And who may you be, sir?'

'First I want to know if Lanyon be dead or alive.' Clem scowled at Simms, who was short and slender with a jagged scar across his face. A pistol was stuck in the waistband of his breeches and a cudgel lay on the table between the two men. Clearly, they were used to dealing with trouble but that did not impress Clem. His only concern was that Harry had not been responsible.

Quirke's expression hardened. 'I'm the one asking the questions.' He had the manner of a bully, but Clem's size seemed to deter him from resorting to aggression.

Clem grabbed his stock. 'My question were simple enough.'

Clem saw Simms reach for the cudgel but his reactions were faster and he snatched it from the table. 'I didn't come here to start trouble.'

'We delivered his body to the Reverend Mr Snell an hour past.' Quirke's bluster subsided. 'Mr Lanyon was murdered. There be a reward of twenty pounds for any information as to his killer.' When Clem released him he swallowed and watched him warily. 'And now your name, sir?'

'Clem Sawle – fisherman.' The older man's small ferret eyes narrowed with speculation, and Clem added, 'I wouldn't be knowing nothing about a killer. Lanyon had many enemies.'

Quirke kept an apprehensive eye on the cudgel in Clem's hand. 'Some say Harry Sawle was one of them. You kin to him?'

'He be my brother. Lanyon's wife be staying with us, if you need to talk to her.'

The small eyes peering up at Clem were hard with suspicion and Quirke's lips compressed as he demanded, 'How be it that no one else knew where she was?'

Clem threw the cudgel on to the table and walked to the door. He was halfway down the street before the constables caught up with him. He informed them gruffly, 'There bain't no law against a man beating his wife half to death, more be the shame of it. Thadeous Lanyon did it regular. Last time Lanyon left Penruan, Hester came to my wife for help. Lanyon wouldn't let her visit Dr Chegwidden. The maid took off as well, from what we hear. She bain't been seen neither.'

'Why did Mrs Lanyon come to you and not seek help from her own family?' Quirke panted as he struggled to keep pace with Clem's long stride. 'They live in Penruan, do they not?'

'You'd do well to learn something about the man who were murdered. Behind his mask of respectability he were a violent, vengeful man, and few of his dealings were lawful. Hester were scared Lanyon would harm her family. She came to us because her and my wife be friends.' He did not hesitate with the lie. 'Mrs Lanyon's father be the chandler here. He bain't a fighting man.'

'And you are, Mr Sawle. Your family has a similar reputation to Lanyon's, from what I hear.'

Clem stopped walking and again grabbed Quirke's stock. 'You mind your speech. I used to be wild in my youth, but not now. My wife don't hold with fighting and the like – says it bain't decent. But most people knows better than to cross me.' He released Quirke and strode on.

Quirke was breathing hard and holding his side. 'Your brother's name were linked with Mrs Lanyon afore she wed.'

'Bain't no secret, Hester and Harry were courting for some years. Harry weren't the marrying kind. Hester weren't his

428

only woman. Mayhap Hester got tired of his womanising.'
Clem lengthened his stride as they began to climb the hill to
Blackthorn House. He avoided the front door and entered
through the kitchen.

'Kezzy, we got company,' he yelled. 'Some men here want
to talk to Hester. Lanyon's been found dead.'

'How did it happen?' Clem turned to Quirke, who was
leaning against the door post, fighting to regain his breath
and composure.

'He were shot in the head and the body dumped in the
River Kenwyn.'

There was a yell from outside and Simms ran in, clutching
his buttocks. Baltasar bounded after him. He greeted the
stranger in his customary fashion by butting him again in
the back, sending Simms sprawling on the floor. The constable gibbered in fear as the billy goat thrust his face into his
chest.

'One of Satan's demons has come to get me. Help me,
Quirke.'

'It's a damned goat,' Quirke snapped. 'Get up, Simms.'

Simms pulled out a pistol and brandished it at Baltasar
with a shaking hand. Clem kicked the man's wrist, sending
the pistol skidding across the floor.

Quirke pulled out his own pistol and shouted, 'I could
arrest you for attacking a sheriff's officer.'

'He were gonna shoot our prize goat.' Clem was incensed.
He did not hold with any form of the law, but had brought
the officers here for Hester to deal with, and to make sure
that Harry's name had not been connected with the murder.
'You should control your men better.'

'Who was going to shoot Baltasar?' Keziah appeared in
the inner doorway, pushing back unruly amber tresses from
her face. She clicked her fingers and the goat rubbed his nose
against her skirts and she gave him an apple from her apron

pocket. She grabbed the rope around his neck, which served as a collar, and pushed the goat towards the kitchen door. 'Outside. You bain't allowed in the house no more. And any more of your nonsense, you get tied up.'

'Beast like that should be locked up somewhere.' Simms got to his feet and edged away from the goat as it trotted past him.

'And who would you be, telling me what I should and should not do in my own home?' Keziah folded her arms across her chest.

'These men are here to talk to Hester. Lanyon be dead. Murdered they say. I reckon it be safe for Hester to return to her own home now.' He would be glad to get rid of Hester, whom he had never greatly cared for. She was too demanding and her constant wailing had driven him from his home every night this week. He supposed that Harry loved her in his way, but Harry was driven by the need to get his revenge on Lanyon – getting Hester pregnant was part of that revenge. And if he wed her now, Harry would be a very rich man.

Hester came into the room, the bruises on her face yellowed but still visible. Her gown was stretched taut across her swollen stomach and she was trembling so much Keziah had to help her to a chair. The officials questioned her about her husband's associates. But she shook her head. 'I know my husband was not well liked. He could be a violent man,' was all she would say.

'He had a good many enemies,' Keziah added. 'Have you any idea who murdered Mr Lanyon?'

When they walked to the door to leave, Quirke faced Clem. 'A man's been taken in for questioning. I'll be staying in Penruan until your brother shows his face. I want to question him. He were seen in Truro the day before Lanyon were murdered.'

'That don't surprise me. The races were on. Harry often attended them. Who you arrested?'

'St John Loveday. Bad blood between the Lovedays and Lanyon. Loveday has threatened Lanyon on more than one occasion,' Quirke sneered. 'Married to your sister, is he not? She were attacked in Truro and claimed it were Lanyon. She lost her child and Loveday went after Lanyon.'

'I never reckoned Loveday for a murderer,' Clem declared. 'How is my sister?'

'Her health weren't my concern. Lanyon's murder is. Harry Sawle has a reputation for dealing with people who cross him. He'd avenge the attack on his sister, wouldn't he?'

Clem did not answer but the fury in his eyes made Quirke take a step back from him. There was a thud and Hester had slid from her chair in a faint.

Simms gave an unpleasant laugh. 'Aye, it will be interesting to speak with your brother. The little lady here didn't look too upset to learn her husband were dead, but she took ill fast enough at the mention of your brother. Lanyon were a wealthy man for all he had few friends or graces. Makes you wonder why a pretty woman like her would take up with him.'

Clem grabbed Simms' collar and marched him to the door. 'Get out and take your filthy insinuations with you.'

Simms shrugged off Clem's hold and straightened his jacket. Quirke was watching the family through narrowed eyes. 'A respectable man don't end up with a bullet through the head. There's a lot that bain't right here. Lanyon may not have been popular, but he be a man of standing in the community. His death will be thoroughly investigated. Someone will swing for it.'

Clem went down to the harbour to prepare his lugger for the day's fishing. He was worried about Harry. He should have stayed with his brother. He had not heard from Harry and his lugger was still in the harbour. Had his brother killed Lanyon? Clem ground down a sick feeling of dread. Harry was more likely to be guilty than Loveday. But then both men had more than enough reason to want Lanyon dead.

Chapter Twenty-Five

L ord Wycham called at the Red Lion when he heard of St
John's arrest, concerned for Meriel's welfare.

'Dr Bell has attended the lady,' the landlord informed him.
'He left some drops to keep her sedated. Said not to let on
about her husband's arrest until she be stronger.'

Lord Wycham nodded. 'Most wise in the circumstances.
Lord Fetherington has requested that Mrs Loveday be transferred to his house in High Cross. My carriage is outside.'

The landlady heaved herself off a stool by the bar where
she had been talking to a customer. 'Dr Bell said that Mrs
Loveday can't be moved, your Lordship. It could risk
another haemorrhage.'

'Then I will see Mrs Loveday for myself.' Lord Wycham
strode to the stairs.

'I'll accompany you, my lord.' The landlady puffed and
wheezed as she followed him. 'This is a respectable inn and
Mr Loveday would expect us to observe the proprieties.'

'As is most proper,' Lord Wycham replied, and stood back
to allow the landlady to enter the bedchamber and announce
him.

'Mrs Loveday be sleeping,' she informed him.

The earl stared down at Meriel's pale face as she slept.
There were dark rings around her eyes and her cheeks were
hollowed. 'Is there no nurse to attend her?'

433

'I check on her from time to time. There be a bell by the bed for her to ring.' The landlady defended her lack of diligence.

'I shall send a suitable woman to be with her at all times. At my expense Mrs Loveday is to be given the very best of meats and wines to sustain her until her husband is free to attend to her needs himself.'

'Bad business this. For Mrs Loveday to lose her child and her husband to be arrested.'

'It is a bad business, as you say.' Lord Wycham replaced his high-crowned hat and was about to leave the room when Meriel stirred and opened her eyes.

They widened in shock at recognising him. 'My lord . . .' Then with a cry of distress she pulled the sheet across her face. 'No, you must not see me like this. I look terrible.'

'I see only your courage, Mrs Loveday.'

'They said it was you who found me and brought me here.' She kept her face hidden.

'I am sorry I did not come to your aid sooner. My condolences that you lost your child. You must think only of your recovery now.'

'I am beholden to you, my lord. But for you to see me like this is more than I can bear.'

He smiled at her vanity. 'Rest. Once you are strong enough to be moved, Lord Fetherington insists that you convalesce at his home.'

'Is my husband not with you?' She lowered the sheet to regard the room with her unmarked eye.

'He is helping with the search for your attacker.'

A bandaged hand, which had been grazed in her struggle, covered her face. 'My husband does not care what happens to me. It is the child he grieves for.'

There was a shocked gasp from the landlady. Lord Wycham bowed to Meriel. 'You are understandably overwrought. I will not leave Truro until I am assured that you are fully recovered.' He lifted the bandaged hand to his lips. 'Recover swiftly.'

The bruises to her face appalled him. Meriel had been one of the loveliest women he had met. Only the knowledge that she had been with child had prevented him from pursuing her.

The sheriff had interviewed many criminals from all walks of life. St John Loveday was brought to him in a dishevelled state, his breath reeking of brandy.

'I must get back to my wife,' St John had insisted. 'She is ill.'

'It grieves me that your wife was beaten so viciously in our town.' The sheriff had been furious over the incident. 'A respectable woman should be safe on our street in broad daylight. The description of the man given by Lord Wycham is very close to that of Thadeous Lanyon. Reason enough for your threats to kill him to have become reality.'

'I did not kill Lanyon. I went out and got drunk.' St John studied the sheriff with bloodshot eyes. 'My wife is near to death and whoever attacked her also killed my son.'

'Grief can make a man turn to thoughts of murder,' the sheriff persisted.

'I did not kill Lanyon.'

'Where were you the night after your wife's attack? The landlord of the Red Lion said you left the inn after drinking for an hour.'

St John held his head, which still ached abominably. 'I remember leaving the inn but nothing else. I wanted to drink to numb the pain of losing my son. I would still be drinking now if your constables had not arrested me.'

'You are the main suspect in the murder of Thadeous Lanyon. Because of the standing of your family in the county you will not be held in prison until your trial. I need your word that you will not leave the county and that you will attend trial at the assizes in Bodmin.'

'You mean that I am free to go?'

'For now, Mr Loveday. A case will be prepared for the assizes and unless a killer is found you will remain the chief suspect. I suggest you find some witnesses who saw you that night and will attest to your innocence. If not, a trial will prove whether you are innocent or guilty.'

Senara was grinding a mixture of fresh herbs with a pestle in a wooden mortar. The kitchen smelled of the lavender which she was boiling in a small cauldron over the range and reducing the liquid to a tincture. She was singing as she worked. Carrie was outside washing sheets in a wooden tub. As the weather was fine Nathan was on a rug making arduous attempts to crawl towards a bed of marigolds.

'Mrs Loveday, forgive my intrusion. I knocked but no one heard me. As I could hear someone was within the house, I took the liberty of entering. The door was open.'

Senara jumped at the shock of hearing a man's voice. The man standing in the doorway of the kitchen was no more than four feet high and was dressed in the latest fashion, his feet encased in the finest leather riding boots. He was looking at her with a nervous uncertainty.

'You must be Long Tom,' she said with delight. Then her mouth rounded in horror. 'Oh, your pardon, Sir Gregory. I did not mean to sound rude.' She curtsied in confusion. 'It is how Adam always speaks of you.'

Sir Gregory Kilmarthen laughed. 'Long Tom is less formal and far better between friends. You can only be Senara. Adam described you well. I feel I know you already. And I have caught you at a disadvantage. That is unchivalrous of me.'

The teasing light in his eyes charmed Senara. And there

was something more than polite interest in his eyes. They held a warmth of understanding, a compassion for people which was rare in an age of bigotry and prejudice. She spread her hands and shrugged. 'This is who and what I am.'

She pushed the mortar aside and lifted the cauldron from the range so that it did not burn dry. 'Adam is working on the cargo ship. I'll send Carric to fetch him. I am surprised he did not see you arrive.'

Long Tom grinned. 'He did. He was in the middle of supervising a complicated manoeuvre to fit some part of the ship. I insisted on meeting you this way. I must confess I was watching you for some moments before I spoke.'

The statement did not surprise Senara. 'In your duties in France it would be second nature to assess people before you approach them. I did not hear you approach. But then silence and stealth would also be important.'

He nodded and peered into the mortar she had been working on. 'What herbs are these?'

'Comfrey and feverfew.'

'What do they heal?'

'They reduce fever and heal infections, rheumaticky joint, swellings, gout, wounds. They are a good basic cure-all. No wise woman would be without a plentiful stock.'

'And these herbs here?' He proceeded to inspect bunches of herbs and lift the tops from pottery jars to sniff their contents, all the while enquiring of their purpose.

She answered him easily and as comprehensively as possible. When she brewed a pot of tea he refused to take it in the parlour. 'It is far more interesting in here. I have never been inside a wise woman's den, though I have visited a cunning man on occasion for a remedy for some ill. I have an aversion to physicians. As a child one fool of a quack suggested that I was suspended in a sort of cradle from a door lintel and weights put on my feet. My mother

437

was desperate that I grew to normal height.'

Senara shuddered at such ignorance and brutality. At that moment Adam appeared, having run from the cargo ship to the house. He grinned as he found them sitting across from each other at the kitchen table and a mass of Senara's unguents and potions spread between them.

'Ah, our estimable master shipwright has returned,' Long Tom quipped. 'I thought you would have turned pirate by now and be seeking your fortune at sea.'

'I have neglected my wife too much of late to sail on a lengthy voyage,' Adam returned. 'But I see Senara has kept you entertained. She has not been making you try any of her herb teas to test their taste and efficacy?' He laughed. 'She can be a terror with her purges.'

'Adam! What will Sir Gregory think of me? He insisted on staying in the kitchen when I offered him tea in the parlour.'

Long Tom chuckled. 'I like exploring new worlds. And this is Senara's home ground. I have been enthralled. You have a beautiful and delightful wife, Adam.'

'I was hoping to polish my manners as a hostess and he would not let me.' Her laugh was rueful. Their teasing had broken down any barriers and Senara was at ease in his company – unlike when Mr Tregurrian had dined and she had been tense and on edge all through his stay. Though Tregurrian had been polite, she had been aware that he was watching her and would judge any failing in her duties.

'You will stay to dine, will you not, Long Tom?' Adam invited.

'I have spent so long smelling the delicious aroma of your wife's cooking, I would have been affronted had you not asked me.'

Senara stood up and took Nathan from Carrie, who had come in from the garden and was staring at Sir Gregory. The maid was clearly shocked that Senara was entertaining in the kitchen. 'Then you men go off and talk. I've work to finish here, or there will be no pudding to accompany your meal.'

Adam winked at Senara as he led Long Tom through to the parlour. His friend was more interested in an inspection of the yard and Senara laughed as she heard Adam being subjected to the same degree of curious questions that she had been earlier.

The meal passed off with effortless ease for Senara and she could not remember when she had laughed so much. She adored Sir Gregory Kilmarthen.

The summer pudding and syllabub had been cleared away and the port brought in when there was an impatient rap on the door. Carrie had her hands full of plates so Adam went to answer it.

'Father. What on earth is amiss?'

Edward and Adam strode into the room and Adam hastily made the introductions. Edward hesitated, clearly unsettled by the presence of Sir Gregory.

'It is time I returned to Squire Penwithick.' Sir Gregory rose to leave.

'No, please stay.' Edward looked shaken and Adam offered him a seat. 'You will hear this news soon enough. Indeed, it will be the talk of the county. St John has been arrested and could face trial for the murder of Thadeous Lanyon.'

'That is absurd! St John has no love for Lanyon, but he would never kill him.' Adam was outraged.

'He had just cause. Apparently Lanyon attacked Meriel in Truro. She lost the child she was carrying. A son. St John was half-crazed with anger and grief.'

'How was Lanyon murdered?' Adam asked.

'Shot through the temple and thrown in the river.' Edward took a glass of brandy which Senara offered him.

'St John would not have done that. Not murder in cold

blood.' Adam was incensed. 'Did he have no witnesses as to his whereabouts?'

'All I have is a hastily scrawled missive from Japhet outlining the bare facts. Apparently St John got so drunk that he can remember nothing.'

'That sounds more like St John,' Adam replied.

'There is much more to this.' Sir Gregory studied the couple. 'I will find out what I can. I am not known in Truro.'

'We cannot expect so much of you.' Edward looked taken aback.

'Finding out such things is what I do best,' Sir Gregory explained. 'I will go to Truro at once and begin my investigation.' He bowed to Senara. 'I have not enjoyed such genuine warmth and hospitality for many years. I shall remember it always. I fear I could not prevail upon the squire's good wife to invite you to her home.'

Senara shrugged, aware that Edward was listening. 'That is her choice. It wounds Adam more than myself. I hope you find a witness to save St John.'

Sir Gregory left and Senara busied herself with Nathan so that Adam and his father could be alone.

'St John is innocent,' Adam reassured Edward. 'If anyone can root out the truth about Lanyon's murder Kilmarthen will. He's worked for Penwithick in France for years. At least, with Lanyon's death, the court case will be dropped against us.'

'As to that, the damage is done. The court case would have cleared our name. Now the matter will be made worse by St John being a suspect for Lanyon's murder. Speculation will increase that we wanted Lanyon silenced. The integrity of the yard and all our family has striven for will be at stake.'

'Then we must insist that Tregurrian continues with his investigation and a full report will be placed in the *Sherborne Mercury* to vindicate our reputation.'

Edward did not look convinced. 'Any sea trials will not be conclusive whilst the weather remains fine. This is not the season for storms. Tregurrian must be aboard *Challenger* in a gale for his report to convince customers that the cutter is without fault.'

When Harry returned to Penruan and saw that Clem's lugger was not in the harbour, he called on Keziah. She was in the byre milking the goats, and peered over the rump of one when he sidled into the shadows of the building.

'Where have you been, Harry?' Keziah was worried by his furtiveness. 'Constables be wanting to talk to you about Lanyon's death. Did you kill him?'

'Constables can find me if they want to talk to me.' His manner was gruff and he clearly resented her questions. 'I need you to talk with Hester. I'm gonna be at sea a lot in the next few months. It will look better if we bain't seen together. I'm gonna wed her but it will be after the child be born. Bain't wise to rush things now.'

There was a feigned nonchalance about Harry's manner which Keziah found false. She did not trust him. And he had accepted the news of Lanyon's death without question. She finished milking the goat and untied the nanny, which trotted back into the field. Keziah lifted the pail and studied Harry, who had kept his face in the shadows. 'You do not seem surprised at the news of Lanyon's death.'

'It be the fourth time I've heard it mentioned today. Where be Clem?'

'Out fishing. Did you do it, Harry? Kill Lanyon?'

Harry turned away so she could not see his face. 'I talk a lot of hot air sometimes. When I left here I was mad enough to. I couldn't find him and after a time I calmed down. I had other plans to make him pay.'

Keziah was not convinced. There was no emotion in his

voice, no sense of outrage at the accusation. 'Hester be frightened. She needs you near her, Harry.'

He glared at her. 'We both know that would be foolish. Is she working in the shop?' His voice was harsh.

'She has taken on two women to work there and a new maid to help at the house. Hester now be a wealthy woman. She has no need to work.'

'Servants gossip. I can't risk seeing her for a while yet. Has the funeral taken place?' Again no emotion. Just a flat question. But then Harry was never one to wear his emotions on his sleeve. He had too many secrets.

'Yesterday. Hester bore it well for a woman whose nerves are in tatters. There were plenty of vicious tongues a-wagging. I think you should speak with Hester.'

'If tongues be wagging now they'll wag more if we be seen together.'

Keziah folded her arms across her chest and her foot tapped on the flagstones as she strove to keep her temper. 'Hester is out of her mind with worry for you. She will not eat. It bain't good for her or the child. I'm taking the wagon over to Trevowan Hard with some of my cheeses for the kiddley. Hester has agreed to come with me to see Senara. She needs a tonic for her nerves. She bain't getting no sleep. Meet us in the wood by the crossroads at midday.'

Harry looked mutinous. He did not like being told what he should do, especially by a woman.

'One meeting so that you can tell her your intentions,' Keziah insisted. 'Hester deserves that from you.'

Harry nodded. 'I'm gonna be away more now – business matters. I don't intend another smuggling gang to think they can take over Lanyon's distribution. I need to know that you and Clem will keep an eye on Hester, especially when the baby comes.'

'We'll help Hester all we can.'

★ ★ ★

The next day Keziah stopped the wagon by the crossroads and Hester climbed down.

'I'll take the horse to the stream where there be some shade.' Keziah flipped the reins. 'If anyone passes, it will look like I be resting in this heat. Today be a regular scorcher.'

Harry came out of the denser trees as Hester approached. With a cry of delight, she ran into his arms. 'Oh, Harry, my love, I've bin so afeared.'

Harry could feel the bones of her ribcage through her gown. 'Kezzie said you bain't be eating or sleeping. You gotta look after yourself and the child.'

'I've been too worried – first dreading that Thadeous would return and then when you went after him . . .' Tears splashed down her cheeks. 'Harry, tell me you didn't kill him. Tell me they bain't gonna catch you and lock you away.'

'I'm here, bain't I?'

He kissed her absently to stem her questions. But when they drew apart, her eyes searched his. 'Did you kill him?'

He shook his head but there was a brittle glitter in his eyes as he stared over her shoulder.

She sagged against him in relief. 'I don't think I could have stood it. I wanted him dead, but how could we live together if his murder were always there between us?' She kissed him ardently. 'I love you, Harry. When we gonna get wed?'

'To avoid gossip you've got to be a decent time widowed. Have the child. We'll wed come spring. But I'm not gonna be able to see much of you. Our relationship has got to look like it started up again natural like.'

'The spring is so long away. This isn't another of your tricks to avoid marriage?'

Harry shook his head. 'I nearly lost you once. Do you think I'd risk it a second time? Come spring you'll be Mrs Harry Sawle. I promise.'

443

He walked to where the trees began to thin and kissed her again. 'Be patient, Hester. Everything is gonna work out.'

He watched as she went back to the wagon and hid behind a tree as a farmer rode by on a dun carthorse. The man tipped his battered felt hat to the women and plodded on. Harry smiled but it did not reach his eyes. No emotion seemed to touch him these days. His revenge on Lanyon would not be complete until everything the smugglers' banker owned became his.

Chapter Twenty-Six

After two weeks of hot weather the skies turned ominously black. A storm was about to break. Edward had gone to Truro to be with St John after receiving Japhet's missive. With the trials of both his brother and the seaworthiness of *Challenger* looming over the family, Adam had not returned to sea. Unfortunately, the family could not afford for *Pegasus* to lie idle for long. There was some good news: William Loveday had still not sailed from Plymouth. He had sent word to the yard that he had written a report for Tregurrian with a description of *Sea Sprite* and the extra sail she had carried.

Adam was restless and impatient. This was the weather they needed to test *Challenger*, but would Tregurrian be able to liaise with Beaumont in time to take her to sea in the bad weather? That morning Jasper Fraddon had ridden to the shipyard requesting that Adam call upon Amelia at Trevowan.

Adam spoke with Senara before leaving. 'After saying I would not step foot in Trevowan without you, I feel obliged to attend as Father and St John are in Truro.'

'Of course you must attend.' Senara did not hesitate. 'I never wanted any rift between you and your family. Amelia must be distraught with worry over St John. Go now before the storm breaks.'

When Adam arrived at Trevowan he found its peace disrupted. Amelia was in the hallway as he entered, having heard his approach. Her face was pale and strained with anguish. 'Thank you for coming. I am at my wits' end. As if our family does not have enough to contend with, Lisette has now gone missing.' Amelia lost her battle against her tears and broke down.

Adam put his arm around her and led her to the winter parlour. On hearing Adam's voice Elspeth called out and limped painfully down the stairs. 'The selfish baggage thinks of no one but herself. Edward is too good-hearted. He should have thrown her out when she caused so much trouble last year.'

'When did you last see Lisette?' Adam asked.

Amelia drew a shaky breath. 'Yesterday when we dined. We quarrelled and I lost my temper with her and sent her to her room.'

'No one can control the girl.' Elspeth sat stiff and accusing, her lips pursed. 'That showy horse of hers has gone. The stall was empty when Fraddon went to the stables this morning.'

'What caused the argument?' Adam hoped they would throw more light on the matter. The women were not being very clear. 'This is not just a ruse of hers to gain attention?'

Amelia dabbed at her face with a handkerchief and sighed. 'Ever since William left, Lisette has been getting worse. I thought for a time that Peter was taking an interest in her, but he went off to that seminary and there has been no word.'

Elspeth gave a deprecating snort, her tone scathing. 'The girl has been acting strangely for weeks and become more secretive. Yesterday she flew into a tantrum because William had written to Edward and not to her. Of all the nonsense.

Really, she expects too much of William, who has shown her nothing but kindness.'

'Do you think Lisette could be infatuated with William?' Adam frowned.

'He's old enough to be her father,' Elspeth snapped.

Amelia rose to walk agitatedly around the room. Her fists were clenched tight to her chest. 'She is very attached to William.'

Adam saw the strain showing on the two women. Amelia looked at the end of her strength. Lisette needed a good shaking at putting his family through so much. At times like these he regretted rescuing her from the French convent. 'Why do you think her disappearance is linked to William's letter to Father?'

'William mentioned that his ship would be sailing to join the fleet at the end of the month.' Amelia sank down into a chair and put her hand to her brow. 'Absurd as it sounds, I think she has gone to visit William in Plymouth. Last night she was ranting that only William understood her. She was hysterical that he was about to sail without returning to Trevowan.'

Adam remained puzzled. 'It does not make sense. Why would she go to Plymouth? William can do nothing for her.'

'Because the little madam has taken it into her head that William intends to wed her,' Elspeth informed him. 'I told her that she was making it up, as she had about her marriage to you, Adam. She ran upstairs screaming and locked herself in her room.'

'I should have checked on her when I retired for the night,' Amelia groaned. 'She had gone very quiet.'

Elspeth rolled her eyes to the ceiling. 'A welcome silence. The chit has made her bed, let her lie on it.'

Amelia looked imploringly at Adam. 'But we cannot allow Lisette to go off to Plymouth alone. What if William cannot see her because of his duties? And what could he do? He is in no position to escort her home.'

'This is no time for me to be leaving the yard.' Adam cursed Lisette's selfishness. 'She has done this knowing that there is no one to go after her. Fraddon has not the authority to bring her home if she proves difficult. Even if William orders her to return, do you think she will obey him?'

'If it suits her.' Elspeth shook her head. 'The young madam will do as she pleases and we can only be expected to do so much. She should be grateful that we have provided a roof over her head.'

'We cannot abandon her.' Amelia was appalled. 'A woman alone . . . the consequences are too dreadful to contemplate. She is our responsibility and we must bear it no matter how onerous her presence here has become. Why is it you feel that you cannot leave the yard, Adam? I can manage the estate until Edward returns.'

Adam felt he was floundering in a swamp. It did not appear that his father had told Amelia of the threat of losing everything which hung over the yard. 'There is a problem which I doubt Father would have wanted you to worry over. I must be on hand.'

'What has Edward not told me?' Amelia looked even more upset. When Adam hesitated, she snapped, 'This family and its secrets. Is it another scandal I shall have to live down? They are never-ending it seems.'

Adam resented the way his family was being judged, but he could see that Amelia was genuinely upset.

'You make too much of things, Amelia.' Elspeth was unsympathetic.

'Do I?' Amelia's hand was shaking as she rounded on her sister-in-law. 'I thought Edward had exaggerated when he spoke of the high-spiritedness of members of his family. I did not expect clandestine marriages, near bankruptcy, and a

448

half-mad woman foisted on me. I do not approve of convention being flouted. It should be the stability of our lives.'

Adam understood that a woman who had been governed by convention all her life would find the exploits of the Lovedays somewhat outrageous. 'Perhaps it is not convention which we flout, but prejudice, Amelia.'

'Adam is right. You are too sensitive, Amelia.' Elspeth turned to her nephew. 'We have ridden through many storms and emerged unscathed. Is the situation at the yard serious?'

He shrugged. 'There is too much at stake for me to leave and chase after Lisette. I will give Fraddon instructions to search for her in Plymouth. It should not be difficult to find her. She has money to stay at the best inn. If she is intent on seeing Uncle William, Fraddon will stay with her until Uncle William persuades her to return.'

'We can do no more.' Elspeth backed his decision. 'That baggage has brought on her own head any trouble which befalls her. It is time she learned to act like a gentlewoman. I trust William will give her a thorough dressing-down and send her home chastised and penitent.'

Adam pulled up the collar of his greatcoat as he rode back to the shipyard. The rain lashed him, lightning whiplashed against the black sky and the thunder boomed like cannon fire. Solomon was nervous, his head pulling to one side as they cantered home.

Between the grumbles of thunder, there was only the hiss of rain to be heard. The countryside was deserted of human or animal form. A jagged lance of lightning lit the sky. There was a sickening splintering of wood when ahead of him a beech tree was struck. Adam was forced to shield his eyes as momentarily the tree was outlined in a blue light. Then a sheet of flame shot up its trunk and a branch crashed to the ground. It lay blackened and smoking as Adam dug his heels into Solomon's sides to urge the horse to jump it. The gelding did so with a whinny and took off at a gallop with Adam crouched over his neck as he brought his mount back under control.

The stableboy emerged from the hayloft when Adam led Solomon into the stable. 'Rub him down and feed him well,' Adam ordered before sprinting across the puddles to Mariner's House.

All work outside in the yard had been stopped. Some tasks could be done in the shaping sheds but over half the men would have been sent back to their homes. He paused at his door to look back at the downpour. If Lisette was out in this, she was truly ripe for bedlam.

Harold Tregurrian wondered if he had not been too zealous by insisting that *Challenger* took to sea in the teeth of the storm. Lieutenant Beaumont had been sullen and uncooperative when the inspector had insisted on boarding his ship at Falmouth.

'I've told you the ship cannot be relied on in heavy seas, Mr Tregurrian. If she founders I will hold you responsible. Smugglers will not be about their work at this time of day, and I think it too dangerous to risk my ship.' Beaumont had stood on the gangplank, blocking his way.

'It is my reputation as well as the Loveday yard which is in question, Lieutenant. I approved the design. And if the ship is as uncertain in her response to the helm as you claim, the Revenue Service will wish her decommissioned and compensation paid to them by the Loveday yard. I want her put through her paces. Sail at once, if you please, sir. Take her along the coast to Lizard Point and we can see how she handles around Black Head where Mr Lanyon's ship foundered.'

'You are risking the ship and the lives of my men,' Beaumont responded.

'I will be the judge of that, Lieutenant. If I find the ship unseaworthy we will put in to the nearest harbour to wait out the storm.'

Beaumont complied with ill grace. Usually if the weather was bad he ordered his second officer to take control and he would stay below in his cabin. Tregurrian stood braced on the deck as *Challenger* ploughed through the seas, spume crashing over her bow. Beaumont was forced to stand tight-lipped beside him.

'The ship is handling perfectly, Lieutenant,' Tregurrian observed after two hours. 'Though I would have thought you'd be better trimming a sail or two. Minimum canvas will keep her more stable.'

'The extra sail would be used when pursuing a smuggling vessel.' Beaumont was quick to defend his actions.

'I would have thought that unnecessary. The ship's speed is superior, is it not?' Tregurrian corrected.

Beaumont was furious. His own career could be in jeopardy if he ran out too much sail to make the cutter handle badly. With Lanyon dead, there would be no payment of the generous incentive Lanyon had offered were the cutter to be proved unseaworthy. And with Lanyon's death, he had lost the monthly payments which allowed him to turn a blind eye to certain landing sites. Tregurrian had a sharp eye for detail. Beaumont could not afford to have his competence challenged. For another hour Beaumont kept the sail to a minimum.

'I cannot see where you find her difficult to handle, Lieutenant Beaumont,' Tregurrian stated as the storm abated and the rain eased. 'She has proved herself to me.'

'Every storm is different.' He did not see why the Lovedays should get off so easily. 'A particularly high swell with a north-westerly wind—'

'If her sails were trimmed I would foresee no problem. You

are ambitious, Lieutenant Beaumont. Rely on the dexterity of this vessel to overtake her prey, and I believe she will not fail you. The Revenue Office will be doing themselves a disservice if they do not place further orders with the Loveday yard. I shall inform them so in my report.'

Beaumont held his silence. Inwardly he was fuming. The Lovedays had won again. Without Lanyon's payments the pay of a revenue officer was poor and unsatisfactory. He needed the security of a marriage to an heiress behind him. Time enough had been wasted in his pursuit of Gwendolyn Druce. He had the approval of Lady Anne Druce and Sir Henry Traherne to the match. It was time the lady was brought to her senses and a date for their betrothal was arranged.

That prospect cheered him. There was more than one way to get back at the Lovedays. At least by his marriage to Gwendolyn Druce he would win out over Japhet Loveday. And then there was St John. He could swing for Lanyon's murder. Even if he did not and a witness was found to prove his innocence, there were other ways for Beaumont to wreak his revenge. He was certain now that St John was involved with the Sawle gang. He would patrol this part of the coast so diligently in future that should they escape arrest, they would be unable to land a cargo. And a smuggler could only escape arrest for so long. Especially as *Challenger* was so fast.

Beaumont controlled an urge to laugh aloud. To capture St John Loveday by the superior speed of *Challenger* would be a wry irony. Edward and Adam Loveday would not be so proud of their successful design then.

Edward arrived in Truro late in the evening. He had gone first to the Red Lion.

'Mr St John Loveday and Mr Japhet Loveday have left for the evening,' the landlord informed him. 'You be welcome to

452

wait, sir, but it be unlikely they'll return until the early hours.'

Edward was displeased. St John should be living soberly and creating a good impression amongst the townspeople, many of whom would attend the trial if it came to that. He should not be carousing until all hours. It was grossly irresponsible.

'I should like to see Mrs Loveday.'

Meriel was weeping into the pillow when Edward knocked on the door and was admitted by a middle-aged maid.

'How are you, my dear?'

Meriel wiped her eyes. 'Everyone has been so kind.' She told him about the attack and as she spoke of how she had been rescued by Lord Wycham, her mood brightened. 'His Lordship has insisted that I received the best of foods and care. Mrs Hogarth was engaged by him to be with me night and day.' She nodded to the maid who was sitting demurely in a rocking chair by the fire. A truckle bed had been made up at the side of Meriel's bed. 'Is St John not with you?'

Edward shook his head.

'He hates me now. The child was a boy.'

'I am sure you are mistaking his grief, my dear,' Edward consoled. 'The worry about your health and his arrest will have taken a toll on him.'

'Arrest! What talk is this?'

Edward realised that Meriel had not been told of her husband's arrest. He nodded to Mrs Hogarth to leave them before explaining, 'Lanyon has been murdered. St John is under suspicion.'

Meriel covered her face with her hands. 'No wonder he does not come near me. Lanyon deserved to die. But for St John to have killed him . . .'

'My son is innocent of this atrocity, madam,' Edward informed her curtly. 'Such talk could see him hanged.'

'I did not mean . . .' she faltered and broke into wild sobs.

Edward was at a loss as to how to calm her and hesitated to call the maid. Meriel had been indiscreet enough. Finally she stopped crying. He cleared his throat. 'You must be brave for St John's sake. We all regret the loss of the child. For now you must concentrate on regaining your strength.'

She nodded. 'I am to convalesce at Lord Fetherington's from tomorrow. It is so dreary here. Dr Bell, who has attended me, thinks I am strong enough for a sedan chair to convey me there. But he says the long journey to Trevowan would not be possible for another month.'

'That is generous of Lord Fetherington. You will be more comfortable there. And I am relieved to see that you have recovered so well from your ordeal.'

Edward left, having found the interview difficult. Meriel may have been weeping when he entered but she had sounded almost excited at the generosity Lord Wycham had shown her. She had not once mentioned her fears for her husband. But then Meriel had always struck him as having more care for her own welfare and interests than for those of others.

Edward took a room in Mrs Bridges' lodging house where he preferred to stay when in Truro. The beds were clean and free of bedbugs, the food always deliciously cooked, and the company more genteel than at an inn.

Mrs Bridges was a pretty, slim widow in her fifties and she was helped by her daughter whose family lived at the top of the house.

'I was surprised and upset to hear that your son had been arrested for the murder of that dreadful man Mr Lanyon,' Mrs Bridges said as she showed Edward to his room. 'Mr Lanyon stayed here once. His manners were so objectionable that I had to ask him to leave. The abuse which I was subjected to . . .' She shuddered. 'It was most unpleasant. I was fortunate that my daughter's husband, Nicholas, lives with us and showed him the door, though Nick was robbed

454

and beaten on his way home from work within a sennight of the incident. I did wonder if Lanyon were responsible. Is it true that he attacked your son's wife? They say Lanyon wanted to marry her once.'

'I do not have the full details, Mrs Bridges,' Edward evaded. The only drawback to the lodging house was that Mrs Bridges was too fond of gossip.

The next morning Edward called on the sheriff to learn more of the evidence against St John.

He listened in tight-lipped silence until the sheriff had finished, then stated, 'I am no lawyer but this evidence seems circumstantial to me. Is there any proof that Thadeous Lanyon was the one to attack Meriel?'

'Lord Wycham identified the corpse as the man he saw attacking Mrs Loveday. Such an attack is reason enough for a man to kill. And your son has uttered other threats against Mr Lanyon. Was not Lanyon also in the process of starting a court case against the Loveday yard? His death would silence accusations which, if true, could bring you to financial ruin. Men have been murdered for less.'

'The reputation of my shipyard speaks for itself. Lanyon had no case against us and he knew it.'

The sheriff leaned back in his chair and regarded Edward across his cluttered desk. 'I have my suspicions that Thadeous Lanyon was also a free-trader. And my information is that your son is also involved in the trade with another, Harry Sawle. Gangs have been known to murder a rival member, if it serves their purpose.'

'Why should my son be involved with free-traders? He is a gentleman and is occupied with the management of our estate.' Edward was indignant as he defended St John.

'My information is reliable, Mr Loveday. My constables are out looking for Mr Sawle, who could also be a suspect. Mrs Loveday is his sister, and Sawle has a reputation for fighting anyone who crosses him. But no one has seen Mr Sawle in Truro for months, except your nephew Japhet Loveday. He says he caught a glimpse of Harry Sawle in Truro, but it was from a distance and there are no other witnesses.'

'Why has Sawle not been questioned?'

'He is away from Penruan on business.'

'My son is not a murderer.' Edward was finding it difficult to hold back his despair that St John was so heavily implicated. 'If Lanyon was guilty of attacking St John's wife, he would rely on the law to deal justly with the crime.'

The sheriff stood up, indicating that the interview was at an end. 'Mr Loveday, your family is one of good standing in the community, but there have been incidents from some of its members which have been undesirable in the past. Your other son, Adam, was caught duelling in Falmouth and your nephew Japhet has disturbed the peace of this town on more than one occasion. Even from our more prominent families such conduct will not be tolerated. If St John can provide us with an alibi for the night that Thadeous Lanyon was murdered, there will be no trial.'

The meeting with the sheriff had done nothing to calm Edward's fears. His next call was upon Lord Fetherington to thank him for inviting Meriel to recover in the comfort of his home. The opulence of the Fetheringtons' townhouse with its gilded plasterwork was too ornate for Edward's taste.

Lord Fetherington took him into the library. 'More private here. We have a house full of guests.'

'While I appreciate your generosity to Meriel, will it not be too noisy here for her to have the rest she needs?' Edward was concerned.

Lord Fetherington waved aside his thanks. 'Little enough for us to do in the circumstances. And most of my guests will leave tomorrow now that the races are over.' His Lordship shook his head. 'Deuced confounded do, this matter with St John. The sheriff is a fool if he thinks St John is a murderer. Grant you, he may have killed the man in a duel. Not the same thing at all.'

'Lanyon would never fight a duel. But it was a clean shot to the temple which killed him. That is very much a duellist shot rather than some commoner taking a pot shot at him.' Edward stared forlornly into the glass of claret Lord Fetherington had given him. 'If St John had been with Percy or Basil Bracewaite when he got drunk that evening, there would be no problem. He cannot remember where he went, or who he saw after he left the Red Lion.'

'Given the circumstances, I would have shot that cur Lanyon myself. No jury will convict a man for killing the attacker who had beaten a respectable gentlewoman senseless.'

Edward took no comfort in the words. Juries could be fickle.

It was noon when Edward found St John and Japhet in the taproom of the Red Lion with other friends of Japhet's. Edward eyed his nephew's companions with reservation. They may dress as gentlemen but there was a harshness to their voices and shiftiness in their eyes which he did not trust.

St John rose from his chair at his father's approach. He looked subdued, his complexion pale and his eyes glazed from drink. It was not yet midday.

Edward stared at the sorry sight of his son with more anger than compassion. He drew St John away to sit in a -quiet corner by a window. The low beams of the room and gloomy interior of the inn were oppressive. 'Drinking will not solve your problems. Is it not the cause of this case being brought against you? Murder is no light matter. Sober up and get out there and try to retrace your steps for that night.

Something may trigger a memory of what passed, or who could have seen you.'

'You think I've not tried?' St John was in the depths of despair and could not hold his father's stare. 'Meriel was carrying a son. Lanyon attacked Meriel and she miscarried.'

Edward nodded in understanding but his glance was anxious as he scanned the room to note if anyone had overheard. 'Such talk will do you no good. Neither will drinking solve anything. You and Meriel are both young. There is time yet for you to have your son.'

St John stared down at the scarred surface of the table in front of him, his body slumped in dejection.

Edward resisted the urge to shake some sense into his son. 'You should be with her, comforting her, not indulging in self-pity with those ne'er-do-well friends of your cousin's.'

'They know how to enjoy life. What is wrong with that?'

Edward grabbed St John's chin and lifted his face so that his son had to meet his gaze. 'Where is the man I have been so proud of in the last two years? You have returned to sullen, dissolute ways. Where is your pride in your name?'

St John stood up, antagonism flaring his nostrils and narrowing his eyes. 'Have I not problems enough without enduring a lecture, sir?'

'Sit down! You will hear me out,' Edward ordered. 'The way you are acting will not help you. You must appear to be a pillar of society. You have been neglecting your wife, which many will find unsympathetic and inconsiderate.'

St John subsided on to the seat with ill grace. 'Meriel nagged to come to Truro against my wishes. She went out alone, more eager to buy fripperies than to preserve her reputation, or consider the health of the child. She brought this on herself and dragged me down with her.'

'She is your wife. And you will treat her with the respect that position deserves. You will show the world that you are a devoted husband, that your drunken lapse was caused through grief. You will stay in Truro until Meriel is well enough to return to Trevowan, and you will be seen to be lavishing attention on her.' Edward dropped his voice. 'And there will be no more free-trading. The sheriff has linked you with Sawle. Murders are committed between rival gangs and the sheriff knows that Lanyon was a smuggler. I expect you to live soberly and with the utmost propriety. Your reputation as a respectable citizen may be all that will save you if this matter comes to trial.'

He gave a similar lecture to Japhet before leaving Truro.

When the messenger of the Inspector of Sloops and Boats arrived at the yard with Mr Tregurrian's report, Adam opened it with shaking hands. When he read that Mr Tregurrian had found the cutter not only seaworthy, but that she handled supremely well in high seas, Adam gave a yell of delight. Mr Tregurrian had also sent copies of his report to the Revenue Service and the local papers to vindicate the Loveday name.

Adam returned to Mariner's House to tell Senara the news. Senara was seated at a table in the garden sculpturing a figure of the winged horse, Pegasus, from clay. She gave a moan as her husband approached and flung a damp towel over the figure.

'Was that Pegasus you are working on?' Adam could not contain his curiosity. He lifted the edge of the towel and his hand was slapped by Senara.

'You were not meant to see it. It was to be a surprise for your birthday. I thought he would bring us luck. Pegasus will always be special since you named your ship after him. You must not see it until it is finished.'

Adam put his arms around her waist and kissed the back of her neck. 'Pegasus has already brought us luck. Tregurrian has cleared the shipyard's name. Father should be here for such wonderful news. So much has gone wrong lately. I have sent word to Trevowan so he will receive the good news on his return from Truro.'

'And you have a meeting with Squire Penwithick this afternoon.' Senara smiled at him, but she had been uneasy since the summons for Adam to visit the squire had arrived. 'I suppose he wants you to go to France again. It is becoming so dangerous.'

Unaccountably, she shivered, her foreboding growing that this meeting would end the peace she had been enjoying with Adam at home.

The day was overcast but nothing could dim Lisette's pleasure as she walked from the church on William's arm. She wanted to sing out to the world that she was now Mrs William Loveday. Throughout the last week she had feared something would prevent the marriage by special licence. Only a silently disapproving Jasper Fraddon and William's second in command, Lieutenant Ashcroft, were in attendance. William was to sail in two days and there had been no time to inform the family.

With the problems at the yard and St John's trial troubling the family, William had been insistent that the wedding be a quiet one. That had not pleased Lisette, but her arrival in Plymouth had clearly put William in a difficult position – as she had intended. It had been his intention that they would wed on his return from sailing with the English fleet to fight the French, when a proper wedding could be arranged. She had wanted a large family wedding but not the wait. She would have more freedom as William's wife. Edward and Amelia would no longer be able to govern her life when she took up residence in the house that William would acquire for her.

After the ceremony the newlyweds dined at the inn where William had taken rooms on her arrival, for he had been living on his ship. The ship was noisy at night as fifteen men had been pressed into service and they were locked in the hold until they sailed. The men shouted for release until they were beaten into silence.

'This is not how I would have wished for us to be married, Lisette,' William said after they had dined and made love. 'You deserved a grander affair.'

'I married the Marquis de Gramont in Notre-Dame with half the royal court in attendance. The ceremony lasted two hours and the celebrations for three days. I was miserable and terrified throughout the service. I hated the man I was being forced to wed. I was never happy. The simplicity of this day is unimportant. Have I not married the man of my choice – the man who will make me happy?'

'And the man you love, I should hope,' William laughed as he kissed her.

'Of course, how can you doubt that I love you?' she countered as she surrendered to his kisses. 'Did I not risk my reputation to come to you? I must face the censure of your family. I think they will be cross that we have wed in such a manner. But I do not care. I shall have my own house. We will find one tomorrow.'

'My dear, you must return to Trevowan,' William shook his head and his smile was indulgent. 'I must know that you are safe. Edward will remain your protector. I may be at sea for months.'

'No, we look for a house tomorrow.' Lisette's voice was sharp. 'It is how we planned to begin our marriage.'

'But circumstances have changed, my dear. I had foreseen that we would wed next year, and I hoped that this war with France would by then be over. I would not place you in the danger of living alone. You will return to Trevowan.'

461

'This is intolerable. You have lied to me.' She pulled away from him and her lovely face was twisted with fury.

'You are mistaken, my love. How can you think that I would sail on so hazardous a voyage and not know that you were safe and protected by my family?'

'But I gave up my lovely title of Marquise to become a common Madame for you. I wanted my own home. Your family do not understand me. They do not want me at Trevowan.' She stamped her foot and began to hit William with her fists. 'I will buy my own house! I have my own money. Edward must release it.'

William was shocked at her conduct. 'From the moment that we married, your property became my responsibility. You have no money of your own now as such. I certainly will not condone you living away from Trevowan at this time. Control yourself, Lisette. I will not tolerate such behaviour.'

For answer she slapped his cheek. 'You are a monster. Where is the dear William who was so kind to me? Have I exchanged one gaoler for another?'

'Calm yourself, my dear. You are upset. Surely, you can see that I have only your best interests at heart.'

A stream of obscene invective was hurled at him which sickened William. This was not the sweet, frail angel who had so entranced and besotted him. The most depraved and coarsest harpy in the brothels of Plymouth would have learned a wider repertoire from her abuse. William backed away from his wife in horror.

'You will return to Trevowan with Jasper Fraddon tomorrow. He will carry a letter announcing our marriage to my family. You will never use such gutter language in my presence again, or I shall wash your mouth out with a soap made of mustard seed. It is a punishment which has stopped the most foul-mouthed of sailors under my command abusing their officers. Other captains would give them a hundred lashes.'

'I hate you. I hate you.' Lisette flung herself down on the mattress, her legs kicking wildly in her tantrum and her fists beating the pillow.

William turned away in disgust. His fascination for this beautiful woman had deafened him to all of his family's warnings about her conduct. He thought they had exaggerated.

'I shall sleep this night on my ship, madam.' He had already resolved to employ another two men to ensure that Fraddon returned Lisette to Trevowan.

As he was rowed out to his ship, he acknowledged that he had made the most disastrous mistake of his life.

Chapter Twenty-Seven

There was a dangerous calm to Lisette's manner when she returned to Trevowan. She affected a demure smile as she addressed Edward, Amelia and Elspeth, who were in the music salon.

Amelia stopped playing the harpsichord when Lisette entered the room, and gasped. 'Thank God you have returned safely. We have been witless with worry.'

'Your conduct is disgraceful.' Elspeth glared at her. 'What shame have you now brought down on our heads?'

Edward stood up, his tone blistering, 'Where the devil have you been?'

Lisette tossed back her head. 'I have been getting married. I am now Mrs William Loveday. Does that not please you, Uncle?' She laughed, enjoying their shocked expressions. 'What, no congratulations? No kisses to welcome me as a true member of your family? I am Lisette Loveday now.'

Jasper Fraddon passed to Edward the letter which William had written. It was short and to the point.

As Edward read, each word made him feel that again his world had been turned upside down. He did not understand how his brother could make so grave an error of judgement. Lisette would bring William nothing but trouble. He cleared his throat and attempted to make the best of what he believed was another catastrophe.

'William confirms the marriage took place two days ago in Plymouth. He sailed on yesterday's tide to join the English fleet, and bids that we continue to care for Lisette at Trevowan. He says that on his return he will buy them a house in Falmouth.'

Amelia looked stunned. 'This is a shock. I thought Peter and Lisette were . . .' She shook her head. 'It will mean yet more gossip. As if there has not been enough this year.' She rose shakily to kiss Lisette's cool cheek. 'Congratulations, Lisette. I would have wished that the marriage had not taken place in so clandestine a fashion. It seems to have become a disreputable habit of this family.'

'You forget, my dear, that we married in haste in London,' Edward was prompted to remind his wife, whose condemnation of his family was beginning to wear upon his patience. 'My family were not informed of our wedding until our arrival at Trevowan. You did not think that disreputable, or clandestine.'

'Our courtship was conducted in a perfectly respectable manner. And our wedding was so romantic, Edward. It was not the same at all.'

'How will others view it so differently?' Edward provoked. 'Many would say that Adam's marriage was romantic, for nothing would turn him from the woman he loved. He would have married Senara months earlier if I had given them my blessing. Lisette and William were driven by the need of him sailing to war – a war from which he may not return. I would describe that as extremely romantic, would you not?'

Amelia was taken aback at her husband's attitude. Primly, she defended her opinion. 'But I had no idea that William was interested in Lisette. He had shown her kindness, no more. It is so sudden. She simply takes off and returns as his wife.'

'You're not with child, are you?' Elspeth accused.

Lisette smiled. 'Definitely not. I am quite barren. I always have been.'

Elspeth's lips were sucked in with anger. She peered at Lisette over the top of her pince-nez. 'Which explains much of your amoral conduct. I hope you intend to mend your ways now that you are wed.'

'Whatever do you mean, Aunt?' Lisette was enjoying their discomfort. 'I had hoped that my marriage would free me from the constraints you see fit to impose upon me. But William was adamant that I remain here. Therefore we must continue to make the best of each other.' She blew Edward a kiss. 'And there will be no talk of shutting me away in an asylum. My husband alone has that authority now.'

Lisette looked insufferably pleased with herself as she swept from their presence. Her heels tapped ominously on the marble floor of the hall and to provoke them further, she sang a ribald song in French.

'Why did William not heed our warnings about her?' Amelia shuddered. 'When your sister visits us this July I was going to arrange that Lisette return with her to London. Margaret is a born matchmaker and would have found the perfect husband for Lisette.'

'The minx took William in.' Elspeth waved a finger. 'She was all false innocence around him. And sadly, there's no fool like an old fool. That little she-devil has run rings around him, as she would run rings around us all, though if William were here he could control her. Somehow I suspect that young madam prefers a husband who will be spending most of his time at sea.'

The stress of St John's forthcoming trial and the unexpectedness of Lisette and William's marriage had eased the tension between Adam and his father. They spent most mornings closeted together in the yard office where Edward again confided in Adam his fears for the family.

With her own wedding having caused such a furore, Senara did not want to judge Adam's uncle. Lisette had given Senara more reasons to dislike than to like her, but she hoped that William would be happy. All her instincts told her that it was improbable. She had come to shut her mind to the problems overshadowing St John – they were too dark and disturbing.

Senara could not sleep the night before Adam visited Squire Penwithick. The summer's heat was stifling and she tossed and turned.

In the month since St John's arrest, Adam had spent several periods away from the yard. Senara suspected that he was preparing to leave at short notice and the thought saddened her. She had hoped that he would not sail until after St John's trial. That was but two weeks away if Long Tom did not find a witness who could prove St John's innocence.

Adam had already left when she awoke on the morning of the meeting with Squire Penwithick. The emptiness of the bed was an omen which struck fear in her. She could not settle to work that morning. The child within her had quickened and its kicks were energetic and pronounced.

When Adam returned there was an air of suppressed excitement about him. She held up her hands before he could speak. 'I do not want to know where the squire will send you, for I shall not sleep with worry. Is it to be soon?'

'Not until after St John's trial. With the problems over the cutter I have neglected you these last weeks. Today we will ride together. Go and change into your riding habit.'

'I promised to visit Hannah. Cecily mentioned that Oswald has been ill. He finds it a battle to get his breath when they are harvesting. I've made a pomander of feverfew, lavender, rosemary and pine needles which will help him, but I need to collect some lungwort to make him a balm.'

'Then we shall pass by Hannah's during our ride.'

Senara did not query when they did not ride directly to the farm, but went along tracks which ran parallel to the River Fowey. After some time she became uneasy that this land was private. She was uncomfortable that they could be trespassing. Although the land looked fertile there was no livestock grazing or crops planted and the meadows were spangled with waist-high wild flowers.

'Where are we going? Are you sure this is not someone's land?'

Adam laughed and urged Solomon faster. 'Of course it is someone's land. The gypsy in you worries too much about such matters.'

'Trespass is a serious offence. Adam, please let us ride another route.' Senara, who was still not used to riding side-saddle, sighed as she gave her mare a fuller rein to catch up with her husband. She was breathless as they slowed to a canter. Adam halted on the high slope of the river bank which was covered in trees. There was the distant cry of a magpie and nearby a robin's call would normally have been a good omen to Senara.

Senara held her breath as a small herd of deer drank from the river's edge, then bounded back up the slope into the woods. There was a peaceful serenity to the place which was almost magical.

A track led away to the right and Adam trotted along it. When they passed between two tall stone pillars which were cracked and covered with moss, Senara felt her spine tingle in apprehension.

'Adam, please do not go on. This is someone's estate. It is not common land.'

'The fields and meadows we have ridden through belong to the house but no one lives here. St John and I often explored the woods as children. We used to try to scare each other with stories of ghosts, or marauding pirates sailing up the river.'

'I'm not sure I want to go on, Adam.' Senara could feel her stomach clenching with panic. Yet when she looked around her, the place had an enchanted feel about it. The trees which lined each side of the path interlocked their branches overhead, and were as imposing as the vaulted roof of a cathedral. Ahead of them on the overgrown track, dozens of rabbits and squirrels were feeding and a pheasant ran out of the bracken across their path.

'What do you think of this place?' Adam grinned.

'It has a special quality which is beautiful.'

Adam rode on, the track opened out and a grey stone house rose up from behind a ten-foot wall. The rusty iron gates were twisted and broken on their hinges. Inside the courtyard, Senara saw a dolphin fountain yellowed by lichen, and a dozen of the twenty or more latticework windows had broken panes. Ivy had grown over one end of the house, obscuring the windows completely.

'The house is something of a ruin,' Adam commented.

'Though once it must have been beautiful. It looks very old.'

'It is early Elizabethan. That makes it about two hundred and forty years old.'

Adam turned Solomon through the gates.

'No, Adam. It is not right to enter.'

'No one will see us. The place is deserted.'

Senara shivered. There was a haunting beauty about the place. In her mind she could hear the echo of children's laughter and the bustle of a once thriving household. 'It is a monument to a happy time which has passed. Curious onlookers do not belong here.'

Adam laughed. 'You and your fancies. Do you find the place unwelcoming?'

Senara became impatient. She had left Nathan on his own with Carrie for too long, and was eager to return to Mariner's House before he became fretful.

'Do you not like it, Senara?' Adam was watching her with a strange expression.

Again Senara shivered. 'We should return . . . Nathan . . .'

'Answer me, Senara.'

She gazed at the house and felt a deep sadness at its neglect. 'There was once much happiness here and there should be again. Houses have no soul without people to inhabit them.' Her mare moved forward but as she passed through the arch of the gateway, she felt the brush of something soft against her face. For a moment the scenery misted and beside her was the figure of a woman hanging from the arch of the gateway. The mist cleared and the image faded. It had not frightened her, for she had seen ghostly figures on occasions throughout her life.

'There is death here, Adam. Death through loyalty. And courage . . .' Her voice broke with the intensity of the emotion which she was experiencing. 'Such courage and remarkable pride. I feel quite humbled.'

Adam stared at her white face with amazement. Senara had backed her horse away from the entrance of the gateway. 'Lady Guinevere Polfennick was hanged at her own gate by Parliament deserters during the Civil War. She would not tell them where the family money was hidden. She was eighty-three and some say she was a witch who had laid a curse on any stranger who visited the property with ill intent.'

'And now you are about to tell me that there is some truth to this curse.' Senara laughed softly, adding, 'There's some lungwort on that beech tree. I must collect it.'

As she carefully cut the greyish leaves of the mossy plant with the small knife she always carried, Adam told her of the previous owners.

'There have been five owners of the house since the death of Lady Polfennick. Two or three died tragically – a drowning, a hunting accident – but that happens in many families. One entire family were wiped out by a cholera epidemic fifty years ago. Since then it was used more as a summer residence than a permanent family home. Twenty years ago the family moved away to live in other properties they own in Wales and northern England. The house fell into ruin and the estate became more neglected by the year. The estate has been forgotten. The undergrowth is like a jungle on most of the acres.'

'The house did not deserve her fate.' Senara wiped a tear from her eye. The air around her was now filled with birdsong. 'It should be loved and cherished.' She laughed. 'What a strange thing for me to say. My fancies are overtaking me today.'

Adam shook his head. 'Not so strange. That is how I feel about Trevowan.'

He stopped speaking. His carefree mood changed, his expression bleak with silent longing for the home he adored and which he would never possess.

Senara's heart ached that Adam was not welcome in the home he loved because his family still had not fully accepted her.

Again with the swiftness of the wind, his mood veered. 'Come, wife, I will race you to the Druid stone. It is on the way to Hannah's farm.'

Adam took off before she could voice her misgiving. Would the rift with his family never end?

It was a month before Dr Bell considered Meriel fit to return to Trevowan. She had been enjoying the fuss and attention of being waited upon by the numerous servants of Lord Fetherington. Lord Wycham called every day and spent an hour recounting the gossip of the town. With each meeting Meriel became more enamoured of the earl.

St John resented the earl's visits and now that Meriel was able to leave her bedroom and spend her day lying downstairs on a day bed, he found Lord Fetherington also paying an unwarranted amount of attention to his wife.

St John found Meriel lying on a couch in the blue morning room with its pale walnut and gilt French furniture. Six large gilded Venetian mirrors reflected the morning sunlight. The colour was back in Meriel's cheeks and she had been up until midnight the previous night following a dinner party which had ended in the guests playing charades.

'The doctor has declared that you are able to return to Trevowan without detriment to your health,' St John informed Meriel. 'Father sent the carriage four days ago and we shall leave tomorrow.'

'But I am enjoying myself. Tomorrow a dozen guests will dine and next weekend a musical evening is planned.' Meriel spread out her new gown which the seamstress had delivered two days after her attack. Her hair had been dressed by Lady Fetherington's French maid and fresh rosebuds had been inserted between the curls. There was a ruby bracelet on her wrist which St John had not seen before.

'Where did you get that bracelet?'

She sighed languidly and held it up to the light to admire the warm vibrant colours of the gems as they sparkled in the sunlight. 'Lord Wycham gave it to me as a birthday gift. He said I had been so brave throughout my recovery from my ordeal.'

It had been Meriel's birthday ten days ago and St John, who had brought her a silk shawl, had found his gift overshadowed by a silver and pearl trinket casket from Basil Bracewaite and a sapphire pendant from Lord Fetherington. 'It is not done for a woman to receive jewels from other than her husband. I did not approve of the other gifts you have received. And you scarcely know Wycham.'

'I know him well enough for him to have saved my life.' She continued to admire the bracelet. 'And they were insistent that I accept them. They were to cheer me when I had gone through so much. It would have been discourteous to refuse.' Meriel pouted. 'It is mean of you to expect me to leave Truro so soon. Lord Fetherington has extended his hospitality to me until the trial.'

'I am surprised that you even remember that I could be facing a murder trial.' His sarcasm had no impression on her. 'And what of Rowena? You have not seen your daughter for weeks. Any natural mother would be fretting to return to her side. I want to spend some time with her.'

He missed his daughter and, though he had shown a brave face to his friends about the forthcoming trial, it was thoughts of Rowena which were the most crippling.

A liveried footman entered the morning room. 'Mr Loveday, Sir Gregory Kilmarthen has called, sir.'

St John frowned, not recognising the name, then remembered his father had mentioned that Kilmarthen had been the English spy whom Adam had rescued in France. The man had agreed to make investigations about the night of the murder. St John felt his fear become acute. It had been with him ever since his arrest. He raised a shaking hand to his stock, which felt uncomfortably tight around his neck.

'Show Sir Gregory Kilmarthen into the study,' St John replied.

'His Lordship is working there, sir.'

'I wish to meet him,' Meriel protested.

St John nodded to the footman that he would see the visitor in the morning room. When Kilmarthen appeared, at first St John thought it was some kind of joke that he was receiving a dwarf. He had only seen such men and women in sideshows at fairs. He hesitated briefly to wait to see if this was a servant whose master had yet to appear, then recovered quickly as soon as he realised his blunder. This man held his life in his hands; he did not wish to offend him. Meriel began to giggle.

'Sir Gregory, my father has spoken highly of you.' St John flushed with embarrassment at Meriel's rudeness.

'I am never what people expect,' Kilmarthen announced to St John, 'but I have discovered facts which may help your case.'

'Shall we talk in the garden? We are unlikely to be disturbed there. A few of Lord Fetherington's guests are still here.' St John led the way to a paved courtyard at the rear of the house. Roses climbed over the high brick walls enclosing the courtyard and a dozen large Italian urns were filled with lilies and violas. 'I apologise for my wife. She has been unsettled since the attack upon her.'

Sir Gregory did not answer. Once they were away from the house he told St John of his findings which were all concerning Lanyon. 'Lanyon was a violent man. I've found a family, name of Renfrew, who will testify against him. The father and sons were arrested for the murder of a man called Grimley. The body was found on their farm by a pack of hunting hounds. The Renfrews' case is to be heard at the same assizes as yourself. The Renfrews rented the farm from Lanyon. They say that he came to their farm after his wife disappeared, and stayed until Grimley arrived. Renfrew has no reputation for violence in the past, but is known as a smuggler and there was a string of pack ponies in his barn.'

'So how can this help my case?' St John could see no connection.

'Renfrew's story is that Grimley told Lanyon that he'd killed the servant girl as Lanyon had ordered and disposed of her body on Bodmin Moor. The servant had run off at the same time as Lanyon's wife. Lanyon killed Grimley and told the Renfrews to bury him. Showing the evil of which Thadeous Lanyon was capable, while still having no clear proof that you actually murdered him, can only help your case.'

'But I did not murder him. How can they bring a case against me if there is no evidence that I did?' St John kicked a pebble on the garden path.

'They will bring witnesses testifying to the threats you made. There is fresh evidence that you had a pistol on you when you left the Red Lion. It is no longer in your possession.'

St John now knew what a drowning man felt like when there was no help in sight and the shore was a distant blur on the horizon. He closed his eyes, fighting against the bleakness of despair. 'It was stolen from me.' He peered down at the little man, irritated by his inane questions. 'I was so drunk I probably passed out in a gutter somewhere, then eventually got myself back to the inn.'

Long Tom shook his head. 'The loss of the pistol will be looked upon as suspicious in the circumstances, especially as your dagger had not been taken.'

'The devil take it! How am I supposed to know what happened to the pistol? I cannot even remember where I was. That pistol had a mother-of-pearl handle. It was worth a great deal of money. I was so drunk it would have been easy for a pickpocket to steal.'

He slumped down on to a stone bench and dropped his head into his hands. 'Who are these witnesses?'

'A couple of men from St Austell who heard you threatening Lanyon over the incident of the *Sea Sprite*. Dr Bell and Lord Wycham have also been called to testify as to your state of mind when your wife was found attacked. But any threats under such circumstances will likely be discounted, as those any man would make concerning his wife's assailant.'

St John looked into the square face of Sir Gregory on a level with his own. 'Is that meant to reassure me? I thought you were supposed to find witnesses to testify where I was that night.'

'If a man had set out to cover his tracks that night, he could not have been more efficient. You were not seen at any respectable establishment. You enquired of your cousin Japhet at the Crown where he was staying, and were told by the landlord that he was at Lord Fetherington's house for the evening. You had several drinks at the Crown. The barmaid noticed you had left midway through the evening.'

St John bristled. 'But I had no idea where Lanyon was staying. How could I have found him?'

Long Tom regarded him gravely. 'Wandering around the town you could have seen him in a tavern or street and followed him. You did not return to the Red Lion until four in the morning. The potboy who was sleeping behind the bar was woken by you demanding entrance. You collapsed on a settle, demanded a brandy and fell asleep before he served you. You were still on the settle when the constables arrested you.'

St John became agitated. 'Then if no one saw me kill Lanyon, why am I still to face trial?'

'Because of another witness who saw you pull a pistol on Lanyon in St Austell and threaten his life. Lieutenant Francis Beaumont.'

St John slumped on the seat and shook his head. 'The man hates our family.' He swore roundly, then looked up at Kilmarthen and accused, 'What about Harry Sawle? He has threatened Lanyon in public. Why he is not facing trial? The man is always fighting and has a reputation for violence.'

'Sawle has an alibi: Guy Mabbley, who was Lanyon's coachman, as it happens. Mabbley had driven Lanyon to

Truro, then was sent on an errand to Looe by his master.
That's where he met Harry Sawle.'

St John frowned. 'That sounds strange to me. My cousin
thought he saw Sawle in Truro. Sawle must have bribed
Mabbley. I can't see him having anything to do with Lanyon's
man.'

'Mabbley has stated he was with Sawle. I am sorry,
Loveday. From other enquiries I have made Mabbley seems
to be working for Sawle now.'

'Mabbley had been with Lanyon for years. Harry must
have bought him off.'

'That will be impossible to prove.' Long Tom took a
snuffbox from his pocket, sprinkled some on the back of his
hand and inhaled it, before adding, 'I have recommended a
London barrister of great repute to your father, Mr Adolphus Maddock. Maddock has agreed to take on your case.
He will arrive in Bodmin three days before the trial to go
over your defence with you.'

'Will you not be continuing to search for witnesses?' There
was fear in St John's eyes as he regarded Long Tom.

'I will continue to do what I can. I have one further lead,
but that is also to the detriment of Lanyon's character. It will
not help to prove your innocence.'

'Someone must have seen me,' St John groaned.

'It was a misty night and visibility not at its best.'

St John sat in the garden long after Sir Gregory left. His
despair did not lift. He could stand it in Truro no longer and
ordered the Loveday coach readied, and a maid to pack his
wife's belongings. Within an hour, a protesting and angry
Meriel was haranguing him as the coach pulled away from
Lord Fetherington's house.

St John wanted the peace which Trevowan could bring
him. He had never felt so drawn to his home before. He had
felt pride in his family but his home had always been just

bricks to him and a comfortable accommodation. In later years he had even resented the acres of land, for the hours they demanded of his time and labour. But not now. His life and freedom were precarious, whatever Sir Gregory had said. Trevowan was his future, his security. And at Trevowan waited Rowena.

An image of her made his pain and despair deepen. He had never thought it possible to love anyone as he loved his daughter. She was his reason for living and he wanted to continue his life and see her grow to womanhood.

Meriel's shrill voice blasted the peace of the journey. 'I shall never forgive you for this. I had no time to say goodbye to Lord Wycham. After all his kindness, he will think us discourteous that we left before he called on us this afternoon.'

What galled Meriel most was that her lettering and spelling were too poor to attempt to leave a letter for Lord Wycham to explain their hasty departure. Though the earl had called every day to enquire after her health, they had never been alone and she was uncertain of his intentions. But she was captivated by him.

Her glare was disapproving as it settled on her husband. Her marriage bored her; the thought of an affair with Lord Wycham was all that cheered her as she contemplated the future.

As the date of the trial approached, an article appeared in the *Sherborne Mercury* relating some scandalous incidents about Thadeous Lanyon's life. When Adam read it, he guessed much of the information had been collected by Long Tom. It stated that Thadeous Lanyon was a man with much to hide in his past, relating his years as a pedlar and of how his father had been hanged as a cattle thief on the information given by his son. It painted an uncompromising picture of a violent man who had always managed to evade justice for his crimes.

Adam frowned as he read the account of St John's forthcoming trial and the details about the Loveday family, Trevowan and the shipyard. He was not pleased that the report also included mention of Lanyon's grievance against the yard though it did state that the yard had been vindicated by Mr Tregurrian's findings.

As in all times of crisis, the Loveday family would assemble in Bodmin to support St John through his ordeal. A letter had arrived from Aunt Margaret in London, and Thomas and his new wife, Georganna, would also be present. Even Senara was to attend, for Edward insisted that in this the family showed solidarity.

There was one other Loveday converging on Bodmin for the trial. Tamasine had seen the report in the paper which she had scavenged from a bench outside an inn on their daily walk through the town. Tamasine was always eager for news of the outside world, and on several occasions had appropriated a paper in such a fashion. She had been amazed to find the report and details of the Loveday family. There were too many similarities for the family referred to to be other than that of her new guardian, and the report had details of their home as well as the trial.

Two nights after she'd read of the impending trial Tamasine Loveday Keyne slipped undetected from the Mertle Moxon Academy for Young Ladies and caught the morning flyer westwards from Salisbury. To pay for her fare she had pawned the ruby brooch from the set of jewellery Lady Keyne had left to her. The loss saddened her and she was sure that the wizened old Jew in the shop had cheated her of its true price, but fifteen shillings was all he would offer her. It was enough for her fare and would pay for lodgings and food in Bodmin. She had no intention of returning to the school. If Edward Loveday would not openly accept her into his family as his ward, then she would join a troupe of travelling players and become an actress.

On the flyer Tamasine did not like the way a middle-aged gentleman on the seat opposite kept eyeing her. She kept her head turned away and refused to answer his questions. Fortunately he was not the only other occupant: a merchant and his wife also shared the carriage. When they stopped at the coaching inn for the night, Tamasine pulled a chest across the door to her room before she slept. Clarinda Derwent had regaled Tamasine and Cassie with tales of young women who went to London to make their fortune, and were preyed upon the moment they stepped off the coach. According to Clarinda it was not just men who would seek to entrap a pretty virgin into a life of debauchery. Women would try and befriend them, taking pity on their naïvety and would offer to show them rooms where they would be safe. They were then taken to a brothel and sold into near slavery.

An hour after Tamasine had retired, she heard the handle of her door rattle and she awoke with a start.

'Are you in there, my pretty? I have something special for you, my dear.'

Tamasine recognised the gruff voice of the man who had been watching her throughout the journey.

'Go away or I shall scream.'

'No need for that, my pretty. Open the door. See, I have something you will like. A trinket which will match your lovely blue eyes.'

'I have a pistol, sir, and I know how to use it,' Tamasine bluffed. 'Go away or I shall scream for the landlord.'

'Is that any way to speak with a man who would make you

a fortune? You are too pretty for the drab grey dress you are wearing. I will give you a dress of scarlet, and lace for your hair.'

'You would make of me a whore, sir. Get you gone. I will not warn you again, I shall scream for the landlord.'

There was a deep mumbling and shuffling from outside the door and Tamasine held her breath but the noise subsided. She got out of bed and picked up a heavy brass candlestick to hold in her hand as she attempted to sleep. Despite her bravado she was trembling and frightened.

She refused to think what would happen to her if Edward Loveday turned his back on her and she was cast alone into the world.

Chapter Twenty-Eight

The assizes in Bodmin were held in the old Franciscan refectory. The long hall, with its soaring roof, was both magnificent and daunting. The early morning mist had lifted, and the sunlight streaming through the stained-glass window cast rainbow coins over the faces of the expectant assembly.

Since the Reformation with its desecration of the monasteries, the hall had become a seat of power. Armed guards stood by the dock and around the perimeter of the room. Bewigged barristers and scribbling notaries shuffled papers on their desks. The jurors sat in their best clothes with an air of false importance, or with ill-concealed impatience for the proceedings to begin.

An orange-seller sauntered in, carrying her wares in a wicker basket. She leaned provocatively across the rows of people, displaying an ample cleavage as she passed a purchase to a customer. Lewd comments followed her passage through the courtroom until one of the guards ushered her out.

The Lovedays gathered to await the trial with uncertainty and apprehension. The only members of their family not present were Lisette – for Amelia had proclaimed that the Frenchwoman's volatile moods would be too great a strain on her already overwrought nerves – Peter, who was still away, and Hannah, who could not afford to leave the farm at harvest-time.

The family had arrived early to secure places near the front of the hall and to sit in unified dignity. Other spectators were far from decorous. Trials, as well as the punishments levied by them, were a welcome diversion to the populace. The courtroom was full. The trial of St John Loveday had aroused a greater interest than most. It was not often that a member of so eminent a family stood accused of murder.

St John's friends Percy and Basil, together with Lord Wycham, Lord Fetherington, Squire Penwithick, Sir Henry and Lady Roslyn Traherne and Gwendolyn Druce were also present. Less salubrious spectators shouted across the room at acquaintances, and odds were taken up on wagers as to which defendants would go free and which would be imprisoned.

Harry Sawle swaggered in. He made only the most cursory greeting to Hester, her face hidden behind her widow's weeds. She sat between Keziah, whom she had begged to attend with her, and her father, Jim Moyle. Harry seated himself on the opposite side of the hall to Hester and did not look in her direction again.

The rising clamour in the court was deafening. Men sneezed and blew their noses loudly as they inhaled snuff. Ladies frantically waved their fans and held perfumed pomanders to their noses to combat the smell of tightly pressed, unwashed humanity.

Edward greeted his friends with a calm demeanour, though inwardly he was queasy with fear for his son. Amelia was pale and held tightly to his arm, and he could feel her shaking. He patted her hand and whispered words of reassurance which he was far from feeling. The Reverend Mr Joshua Loveday similarly consoled his wife, Cecily, who was weeping softly. Joshua and Edward's elder sister, Margaret, who had arrived from London two days ago, nodded to old acquaintances and introduced Georganna, the wife of her son, Thomas. The couple drew the interest of the Loveday neighbours, who had yet to meet Thomas's new bride.

'Georganna has become the daughter I was never blessed with and is a great comfort to me,' Margaret proclaimed. 'Thomas works far too hard in the family bank. Georganna has become my companion. It was her idea that we hold fortnightly soirees at our house and invite notable poets to attend. She is a great patron of the arts.'

Thomas Mercer looked like no owner of a bank any of those present had encountered. He was tall, slim and with the Loveday striking looks, though his hair was blond. His attire of a black-striped, sapphire-blue cutaway coat and primrose waistcoat and black breeches was considered by the country gentry to be dandified. Many of Thomas's friends in London would consider such dress as unfashionably restrained. His long tapering fingers rested on the gold-topped malacca walking cane he carried.

'I had not realised that Tom Mercer was connected to the Lovedays,' Lord Wycham observed. 'He is my banker in London.'

Basil Bracewaite, who was sitting next to Lord Wycham, guffawed. 'The man looks something of a fop to me. Are you sure you can trust such a popinjay with your investments? His bank was in trouble last year, so I heard.'

The earl smiled. 'I was one of their new investors after Thomas Mercer made the merger with Lascalles Bank. Mercer and Lascalles have paid interests on my investments yet to be equalled by another bank. I have no complaints. And Mercer is not such a fop that I would risk calling him one to his face. He fences regularly with the same master as myself. He is an expert swordsman, one of the finest.'

Bracewaite did not look convinced. 'His wife is rather plain, don't you think?'

The earl lifted an eyeglass to survey Georganna. She was

as tall as a man and boyishly slim. Her eyes and mouth were too large for beauty and her nose unfortunately long, but as she spoke to her husband her expressive features were transformed. It was a face alive with intelligence and interest, and her hair was a thick luxurious hazelnut brown.

'Not a beauty in the first mould like Meriel Loveday, I grant you,' Lord Wycham observed, 'but she has a sharp wit and lively intelligence for a woman. Tom Mercer had a play performed on the London stage in the spring. Prinny himself attended and was vastly amused.'

Meriel had seen the earl watching their party. She was about to rise and greet him, when Elspeth gripped her wrist in a bruising hold and jerked her back down on to the seat.

'At least have the grace to look like a stricken wife. It is unseemly the way you are staring around you, and showing interest in those who have come to ogle at your husband's humiliation.'

'Our friends have come to show their support for my husband,' Meriel returned with a haughty toss of her blonde curls. 'The least we can do is acknowledge them. Many of them have shown me kindness in the terrible weeks since I was attacked.'

'As always you think only of your own problems.' Elspeth regarded her with ice in her eyes. 'Your husband is on trial for his life, because you forgot everything that was taught to you about correct behaviour. If you had not ventured on to the streets of Truro without an escort—' She broke off to control the anger consuming her, but was too incensed to hold her tongue. 'Has it even occurred to you that had you waited for your husband to accompany you, none of the ensuing events would have happened?'

Meriel's mouth dropped open in shock and she burst into noisy tears which drew exasperated glances from Edward and Adam at the far end of the row. Elspeth turned away from

Meriel, her tone scornful. 'You are overdoing the theatrics, Meriel. If you cannot conduct yourself in a civilised manner perhaps you should leave.'

'You must try to be strong for St John's sake, Meriel,' Amelia leaned across Elspeth to whisper. 'Do you need my smelling salts?'

Meriel dabbed at her eyes and sat with a rigid back to stare at the empty judge's seat behind the bench. She muttered through clenched teeth, 'Does no one care what I feel? How I suffer?' She waved her fan erratically.

The whine in Meriel's voice grated through Senara, who sat next to Adam. She could sympathise with the woman's loss of a child but had been upset when Meriel had snubbed her. The other women of the family had treated her with polite civility.

On the other side of Senara was Thomas Mercer, who had greeted her warmly when she met him yesterday.

Long Tom entered the court and signalled to Edward. Adam went with his father to talk to him. Conscious that she was alone with his family for the first time, Senara felt her flesh sting with embarrassment. She swallowed against the sudden dryness in her throat, aware of curious glances and of the whispers about her behind fluttering fans.

'Such a pity that we could not get to your wedding.' Thomas addressed Senara. 'The roads are impassable by coach in winter. The occasions become rarer when all the family are together. Of late we seem to meet only to avert a new tragedy.'

She was grateful to him for taking the pains to put her at ease. 'And you are but recently wed yourself, are you not?'

'A year come September.' He smiled fondly at Georganna, which surprised Senara. Thomas had married Georganna to ensure the financial security of his bank, and had for some years been the lover of the poet Lucien Greene. 'It has passed quickly.'

'Your wife has a warm and vivacious manner which is charming.' Senara was sincere in her compliment.

'Georganna is quite remarkable.'

Georganna smiled at her husband, then leaned forward to wink at Senara. 'I am the most ardent admirer of Thomas's play writing. I encourage him shamelessly. We both long for the day when he can retire from the bank and spend all his time on his plays. He will not do that until every penny his family lost when the bank nearly failed has been repaid. He owes an immeasurable debt to Edward.'

Thomas nodded. 'And to you, my dear. The merger with your family bank restored the faith in the City in Mercer's Bank.' The easy way they smiled at each other was not of a couple madly enamoured, but of close friends and allies.

Georganna nodded towards Meriel and Elspeth. 'I hope those two have not been beastly to you. Elspeth terrifies me. *En masse* the Lovedays can be a formidable force to contend with!'

The sharp rap from the clerk of the court's gavel brought a hush to the gathering. There was a shuffling of feet and rustle of petticoats as everyone stood as the Hon. Mr Justice Catchpole was announced. His long curled periwig and scarlet gown accentuated the grim, sallow, hatchet face. The dark eyes were pouched with flesh and the thin lips scored by deep lines. It was not a face which looked capable of compassion. Catchpole's reputation was for harsh justice.

The assizes had already been in session for two days and St John's case was the first one on the list that morning. When he was led in, there was a stirring and murmuring within the court. Edward and Adam slipped back into their seats as St John took his place in the dock. Senara was shocked to see him wearing manacles on his wrists.

St John was pale and hollow-eyed from lack of sleep. He held himself rigid, his hands clasped in a stance of stalwart reserve. He felt nauseous and was trembling. He had spent a harrowing two nights in the gaol after having presented himself to the sheriff before the trial. Those two nights in a cramped cell with just a thin straw mattress and a slop bucket had been horror enough. His sleep had been destroyed by the thought that if the jury found against him, he could face months enduring the squalor and greater deprivation of prison. He had paid for water to be brought in so that he could wash this morning. Edward had brought him a clean shirt and jacket so that he would present a respectable figure. St John wished his skin did not itch so much from the score of flea bites he had received from the mattress he had laid upon.

His expression remained impassive as the charges were read out, including divers disturbances of the King's peace by threats to the murder victim. At each charge he felt his despair rise. They sounded so malicious when read out by the clerk of the court.

The prosecuting Counsel for the Crown, Mr Jerome Winthrup, had the booming voice of a town crier. His diatribe was delivered in a thundering monotone, which in the heat of the court drummed with the persistence of a hornet in a honey trap. 'In these troubled times of grain riots and general incitement amongst the populace to rise up and take the law unto themselves, men of position and standing in the community have a duty to maintain order. Wealth and position do not make a man invincible against the law. Examples must be made. The Bible states that a life must be taken for a life. St John Arthur Loveday, with malice aforethought, wilfully set out cold-bloodedly to take the life of one Thadeous Lanyon . . .'

The voice droned on in a seemingly endless stream of

accusation and St John rubbed at the sore flesh beneath the manacles on his wrists. Their weight pressed as heavily as his darkening mood. St John could not look at his family and felt the eyes of his friends judging him.

Mr Jerome Winthrup ended, 'Good citizens of the jury, see not this man's status or position. Judge him upon his intent on that dastardly night when a man was deprived of his life. Wilfully and with grievous revenge in his mind, St John Loveday hunted down a man who, it will be shown, he loathed and despised. A man who had at that time not been proved as the attacker of his wife – and with evil retribution that mocked the laws of our land, St John Loveday committed a foul and cowardly murder. No man may take the law into his own hands with impunity.'

The clerk of the court demanded, 'St John Arthur Loveday, how do you plead?'

He attempted to answer but found his voice had locked. He cleared his throat and was relieved his voice was strong. 'Not guilty.'

Mr Adolphus Maddock stood up and raised his hand, his forefinger pointing at the ceiling. 'A man has been accused of the most heinous crime of murder. Yet where is the foundation of this case, other than in hearsay? When family honour has been maligned, a man roused to outrage will defend that honour heatedly. In such a moment of righteous anger, his words could sound like a threat. When a man learns his wife has been attacked in the street in so craven and odious a fashion, and as a result of that pernicious and bestial assault, she has miscarried of a son, what man here would not vow vengeance in his hour of grief? It is quite one thing to voice a threat, and another altogether to commit murder in cold blood. A man of repute and honour does not stoop to common villainy . . .'

St John found it impossible to follow the words. He

needed all his control to present a calm appearance to the court. The flea bites were a minor irritation compared to the turmoil of the nightmare he was living. Even Maddock's argument appeared to him to take on a tone of condemnation.

Mr Adolphus Maddock was a master of rhetoric with a voice which resounded with passion. He expounded with an eloquence which was mesmeric. 'I put to our esteemed jury that the evidence presented by the prosecutor of this court is no more than circumstantial, brought against a God-fearing and reputable man of honour and integrity. Whereas the murdered victim was all that was despicable in humankind. A man who by his felonious and nefarious deeds had made many enemies.'

Mr Jerome Winthrup boomed out, 'Thadeous Lanyon was killed by underhand means. Gentry and nobles are too fond of duelling over a point of honour. A man's life was wiped out in its prime by a wanton act of vengeance. Thadeous Lanyon died by a single bullet entering his temple, a perfect example of death from a duel.' He paused to draw breath then expounded as he walked along the line of jurors, 'And I put it to you that St John Loveday was seen leaving the Red Lion carrying a pistol but the weapon was not on him upon his return. He declared it stolen when other items of value had not been taken from his person. Was it stolen? Or deliberately lost so that no one could discover that it had recently been fired?'

St John started as though a bullet had entered his heart. He had to bite his lip to stop himself crying out in his defence. A gasp followed Winthrup's statement and loud mutterings broke out in the court. Mr Jerome Winthrup puffed out his substantial chest. 'I call the first witness, Lord Wycham.'

His Lordship proceeded to the stand with an air of boredom. He stated how he had rescued the defendant's wife from an attacker who answered the description of Thadeous Lanyon. He vividly described the condition in which he had found Meriel, upon which she burst into loud tears. His Lordship raised his voice so that not a single word was lost. 'I would have been shocked if St John Loveday had not been so distraught. Not only was his wife viciously beaten but she miscarried their child. The man who was capable of such brutality deserved no mercy.'

'But your Lordship had no proof that the attacker was Thadeous Lanyon?' Mr Jerome Winthrup demanded.

'I had never met the man.'

'Your Lordship was heard by the landlord of the Red Lion in Truro to offer your services as second, if Mr Loveday called out his wife's attacker.'

'Any honourable man would have done the same.'

Mr Jerome Winthrup paraded along the line of jurors. 'And therefore be a party to murder.'

The Earl of Wycham did not answer. St John had thought Wycham would appear as witness for his defence, not for the prosecution. Duelling was the resort of gentlemen, whereas St John's only hope had been that Lanyon had many enemies amongst his own class.

St John glanced towards Meriel with loathing. He regarded her as the cause of all his problems. She was not even looking at him. Her gaze was rapt as she stared at Lord Wycham. Anger blazed through him. Meriel was infatuated with the man. His title alone would have impressed her, and Wycham was handsome and wealthy as well. Did they seek to cuckold him? His wife certainly picked her timing to play the faithless baggage.

As the silence stretched out and the earl did not respond to Winthrup's statement, the prosecutor looked smug. St John's fear increased. He had to grip his hands together to stop them from shaking.

'I have no further questions of this witness,' Winthrup declared.

Mr Adolphus Maddock approached the stand. 'My lord, did St John Loveday take up your offer to act as his second?'

'He did not.'

'Then from that, it was not likely that he intended to call Lanyon out.'

'Objection, your honour, that is speculation,' Winthrup leaped from his seat to protest.

Mr Justice Catchpole fixed a rheumy eye upon Maddock. 'Do not make inferences which cannot be upheld.'

'Very well, Your Honour. But then is not most of the evidence against the accused founded upon speculation?'

'You risk contempt, Mr Maddock.' The judge banged his gavel. 'I will have the proper respect shown the proceedings of this court.'

Other witnesses from St Austell were called who had heard St John threaten Lanyon in the High Street. Then Mr Jerome Winthrup called his next witness. It was Lieutenant Francis Beaumont.

St John closed his eyes against the fear gnawing at his gut. Beaumont hated his family. And St John had made an enemy of the man by winning his money and insulting him in St Austell. That brief moment of triumph tasted foul as ashes in his throat. To combat his anguish, St John watched the officer approach and kept his manner and expression aloof.

The officer was in full naval regalia, though no uniform was mandatory for an officer within the revenue service. There was a commotion from the side of the court. St John saw Gwendolyn Druce push past her mother. The Lady Anne was hissing at her in distraction. Gwendolyn moved through the court to the row where the Lovedays were seated.

Japhet, who was directly behind Adam and Edward, rose as she approached. Gwendolyn squeezed in next to him, her face flushed and angry. 'That odious man, how can he speak against St John and call himself a friend of our family? I told him I will not be at home if he speaks against St John.'

Japhet's eyes sparkled. 'Does that mean you are no longer cross with me?'

Other conversation broke out as the officer swore his oath on the Bible.

Gwendolyn tutted. 'I was never cross with you, Japhet.' Her glare was mutinous as she regarded Lieutenant Beaumont who was watching her through narrowed eyes. 'Mama wishes me to marry that buffoon. I cannot bear it at Traherne Hall. I am never free of Mama's plots to see me wed.'

'Order in court!' the clerk shouted.

A hush fell on the gathering as Lieutenant Beaumont gave his evidence, placing emphasis on the threats that St John had given Lanyon. 'Mr Loveday swore that he would see Thadeous Lanyon dead before he allowed him to destroy the reputation of his family and shipyard.' Beaumont leaned forward, his hands gripping the rail of the witness stand. His glare flickered over Gwendolyn and Japhet before he continued. 'And it was not the first time they had quarrelled and threats were uttered.'

'Threats from both men towards each other,' Mr Adolphus Maddock announced. 'Is that not so, Lieutenant.'

'I heard only Mr Loveday threaten Mr Lanyon. The Lovedays may present a respectable persona to the world, but they had every cause to see Lanyon dead. He had commenced proceedings to bring their shipyard to court. He had purchased a ship from them which had proved unseaworthy.'

Mr Adolphus Maddock stood up and declared, 'Lanyon's cutter was proclaimed by the Inspector of Sloops and Boats to be seaworthy. Lanyon had no case against the Loveday yard.'

'Sit down, Mr Maddock, or I will hold you in contempt,'

Mr Justice Catchpole demanded. 'Continue with your evidence, Lieutenant Beaumont, if you please.'

Beaumont pulled himself up straight and assumed a stance of pious condemnation. 'I have long suspected that Thadeous Lanyon was a free-trader but he was never caught. And according to certain informants, St John Loveday is the leader of a rival gang. Though again he has evaded capture.'

Mr Adolphus Maddock leaped to his feet and vehemently protested: 'That is hearsay, Your Honour. My client is not on trial for free-trading. And this witness also spoke against the Lovedays when the Inspector of Sloops and Boats investigated the allegations made by Mr Lanyon. Lieutenant Beaumont is master of a cutter of the same design built in the Loveday yard. He declared that the cutter was unstable in high winds. This was disproved by the Inspector of Sloops and Boats when he boarded her and took her out in one of the worst storms of this year.' He then brought up the incident of the duel with Adam and the long-running feud between the Lovedays, and ended by declaring, 'This man has a grudge against my client's family. His evidence is coloured by his vendetta against them. I ask the jury to discount his evidence.'

Momentarily, St John felt some of the tension slide from his body until Mr Justice Catchpole overruled Maddock. That flaring of hope, fragile as a house of cards, crashed down, pitching him into greater dread.

Three other witnesses were called, all stating that St John Loveday had been drinking heavily in Truro on the evening of Lanyon's death and was heard to vow 'to see the man dead'.

'I have no further witnesses, Your Honour,' Mr Jeremy Winthrup announced.

Mr Justice Catchpole rose and announced that the proceedings were adjourned for lunch and St John was led back to his cell. He laid his head against the wall. The manacles placed on his wrists jangled, reminding him that he had been reduced to a common felon. The hearsay and half-truths all pointed an ominous finger that he had every reason to have killed Lanyon.

The door opened and his father entered. 'You are innocent, St John. If the best they can bring against you is Beaumont's insinuations, and a few people hearing you threaten Lanyon, they have no case.'

'It does not seem that way when you are in the dock and by law are allowed no voice to state your own case.'

'You have done well to follow Maddock's advice about saying nothing unless directly addressed by the judge. It cannot have been easy at the way Beaumont blatantly twisted the truth.' Edward forced a laugh. 'I could have struck the pompous ass myself. The man is insufferable.'

St John grimaced. 'Wycham did not help. I thought he was on my side.'

'If he was called by the prosecution he would have had no course but to attend.'

St John's anger returned at his wife's interest in the earl. 'Perhaps he had his own reasons.'

The turnkey opened the door. 'Time is up.'

Edward was moved to embrace St John. 'You are innocent. Justice will prevail.' He was shocked at how St John seemed ready to accept defeat.

Long Tom had left the courtroom before Adam could question him and was not seen until the trial resumed. He was looking pleased as he walked in. Meriel had slipped away from the family to exchange a few words with Lord Wycham.

'I was mortified when the prosecution called you as their witness, but you gave no evidence which would incriminate St John.'

He smiled. 'I had no intention of causing you distress. I do not believe that there is enough evidence to convict your husband. You must not worry about your future, dear lady.'

'You showed how much I have come to rely upon your support, my lord. I owe you so much, including my life.' The admiration was heavy in her voice and she was breathing unnaturally fast at standing so close to his handsome and commanding presence. 'I am for ever in your debt, my lord.'

'I did little enough. I am your devoted servant, dear lady.' He bowed to her and rejoined his party. There had been a wealth of promise in his words, and the look in his eyes set Meriel's pulse racing. She returned to her seat with a lighter step as the court reconvened.

Mr Adolphus Maddock called Squire Penwithick and Sir Henry Traherne to testify as to St John's character. Both men declared that St John was not of the disposition to challenge a man to a duel, and certainly it was not within his nature to kill a man in cold blood.

Mr Justice Catchpole regarded the barrister with a jaundiced eye. Lunch, and the three glasses of port he had drunk sat heavily on his stomach. He was feeling the first twinges of gout, which was making him irascible. 'This case is too circumstantial. Are there no witnesses to prove that St John Loveday was with them at the time of the murder?'

'I regret not, Your Honour,' Mr Adolphus Maddock conceded with reluctance. 'But it is my intent now to prove that Thadeous Lanyon was a man whom many would wish dead.'

'We are not here to malign the murder victim, sir,' Mr Justice Catchpole snapped, 'who after all is unable to defend his good name.'

The comment roused a laugh amongst the spectators, and Mr Justice Catchpole banged his gavel to bring order to the court. His expression was growing more sour by the moment.

Adam wiped his brow with a kerchief and stared at St

John, who seemed to have turned to marble, his face and stance were so impassive. Adam whispered to his father, 'It does not look good, does it?'

'But there is no proof that St John committed murder.' Edward's face was strained with tension. 'Maddock knows what he is about. He said Sir Gregory Kilmarthen had found a surprise witness who could make all the difference.'

'Who is that?'

Edward shrugged. 'Some woman. He was vague about it. It all depends whether she arrives here in time.'

Adam glanced across at Long Tom, who was again leaving the courtroom.

Mr Adolphus Maddock addressed the court. 'My client is accused of a murder where there is no direct evidence against him. We do not dispute that he on occasion had heated exchanges with Thadeous Lanyon in public. The incident in St Austell followed upon Lanyon himself striking my client in a demented fit of anger. Yet a threat delivered in the heat of anger is a far cry from the heinous crime of murder. The court needs to know the character of the murdered man and I therefore call Bill Renfrew to the stand.'

'Are you sure this witness is necessary?' Mr Justice Catchpole grumbled.

'My client has the right to establish that the man he is accused of murdering led a violent and evil life.'

Bill Renfrew shuffled into the court wearing manacles, his shirt and breeches grey with dirt from a week in the gaol. He was in a nervous state. His eyes darted around the court, and he was wringing his large hands together as he took his oath on the Bible.

Mr Justice Catchpole frowned. 'This man is in shackles. The word of a convict is not something we would judge as reliable, Mr Maddock.'

'With respect, Your Honour, Mr Renfrew is to be tried at

these assizes later in the session, together with his two sons, for the murder of Joseph Grimley whose body was found on their land.' There was an outbreak of talking within the court and Maddock raised his stentorian voice to transcend the voices. 'The murder of Grimley is relevant to this case, Your Honour. If you will bear with us and hear the evidence of William Renfrew . . .'

'It had better be relevant, Mr Maddock,' the judge barked. He sat back in his chair and a spasm of pain creased his face.

The judge's manner alarmed St John. Catchpole was growing more surly by the hour. That could affect the severity of any sentence passed upon him.

Maddock turned to Bill Renfrew, who was sweating and fidgeting in the witness stand. 'I want you to tell the court what happened at your farm the last time Mr Lanyon visited.'

Renfrew shuffled, his eyes fearful as he beheld the judge. 'We rented the farm from Lanyon. Had done for years. Lanyon came and said 'e'd be staying for a few days till some business were dealt with. Two days later a man turns up. Grimley 'is name were. Grimley said 'e'd dealt with the maid as Lanyon 'ad ordered him and buried 'er on Bodmin Moor.'

'And why would Mr Lanyon want this maid "dealt with", as you put it, Mr Renfrew?' interrupted Adolphus Maddock.

'Lanyon were in a rage. 'Is wife had left 'im and the maid 'ad gone with 'er. 'E wanted 'em found. Grimley told Lanyon that the maid were on 'er own and 'ad no idea where Lanyon's wife 'ad gone. The maid 'ad stolen some money from Lanyon which Grimley returned to 'im. Grimley said he'd strangled the woman. Lanyon pulls a pistol and shoots Grimley dead, right there in the middle of our parlour. Me and the boys were told to bury 'im. We did as Lanyon said. 'E be capable of doing fer us as 'e did fer Grimley. We didn't murder Grimley, 'twere Lanyon.'

'I discount the evidence of this witness.' Mr Justice Catchpole waved Renfrew away. 'One case cannot have bearing upon another.'

'With respect, Your Honour, I believe it must be taken into consideration,' Mr Maddock defended. 'It is testament to the evil of which Thadeous Lanyon was capable.'

'Very well, Mr Maddock, but any future witness must be relevant to this case alone.'

Mr Maddock bowed to the judge in agreement. 'I call my last witness, Mistress Marigold Lanyon.'

'I did not know Lanyon had any kin,' Adam whispered to his father. The gaze of everyone present was upon the thin, middle-aged woman in a scarlet dress and black feather hat atop a bright yellow wig, who entered the court with Long Tom. Her face was whitened with powder and several patches adorned her sunken cheeks.

'Madam, will you give the court your name, occupation and place of residence?'

'I be Marigold Lanyon, mostly known as Goldie. I bain't used me wedded name after that bastard sold me off, like I be no more use than a mangy dog. I live in Bristol and run a lodging house for sailors.'

Mr Adolphus Maddock said, 'And who was your husband?'

'Thadeous Lanyon. Not that the world will miss the scurvy cur.'

'Will you tell us why you have come forward to testify, Mistress Lanyon?' persisted Maddock.

'Thadeous Lanyon be me 'usband, as I said. We were wed proper at St Nonna's in Altarnun. Lanyon had a pedlar's wagon then. Me pa had just died, leaving me a farm. Lanyon sold it, but it didn't fetch much and the money ran out after a year. That's when he got nasty. Beat me most weeks. He wanted rid of me. One night he got me drunk and sold me to a brothel. I were lucky 'e didn't kill me. 'E would've if I hadn't 'ave been pretty enough to fetch him a shilling or two. 'E used to boast that 'e'd killed the pedlar whose wagon 'e used. I were a prisoner at the whorehouse for six months . . . locked in a room unless a customer wanted me.'

A stirring and murmuring in the court was halted by the demand for silence by the judge. St John stared at the brassy-haired woman in astonishment. Dare he hope that the trial was going in his favour? Long Tom had said he had learned that Lanyon was married years ago, and could find no evidence that his first wife had died. The man was a magician to have found Goldie Lanyon. He had certainly been thorough in his investigations. A glance at his father showed the strain lifting from Edward's face. That encouraged St John to believe that the evidence was going well, and he could be acquitted.

St John's gaze fixed on Harry Sawle. He was furious that Sawle had not been implicated in Lanyon's murder. Harry had uttered more threats than himself against Lanyon's life. But Harry was a wily scoundrel. He had apparently sworn he was in Looe at the time of the murder and two witnesses vouched for him. Had he paid them? And now Harry was deathly pale and his glare was hostile as he heard the witness's statement.

Goldie Lanyon was rambling in her haste to give evidence. The judge, to St John's consternation, seemed to be dozing, but the jury were wide-eyed at the new revelations being presented to them. Goldie was clearly playing on their sympathy, but why should she be so obliging as to help him? Then St John realised that Goldie was not merely denouncing Lanyon as a violent man – she had proclaimed him a killer. Also, by declaring that she was his first wife, she was his only legal wife. Lanyon was a bigamist – three times over. Her voice was shrill, recapturing his attention, as she continued her story.

'Once I stopped trying to escape from the whorehouse, I were given more freedom. It were a lousy life and several of the women died through mistreatment or disease. I reckon Lanyon thought the same would 'appen to me. I survived and took up with a sailor who treated me proper. 'E never beat me like Lanyon. Twice I nearly died at that bastard's hands afore he sold me. I reckoned I were better off in the brothel than the life I had with 'im. That's all I gotta say.'

The pause was brief before she launched forth with greater passion. 'Except, as God be my witness, I be 'is only true wife. I got the marriage lines to prove it. He thought they'd been destroyed. I reckon now I be a wealthy widow and I come to claim what be mine.'

Goldie pulled a yellowed, crumpled paper from her bodice and handed it to Mr Maddock. 'That do tell all I be the wife of Thadeous Lanyon.'

There was a scream from Hester and she fell forward in a faint. A buzz of voices rose within the court and the judge hammered frantically with his gavel for silence. Mr Maddock passed him the marriage lines which he read and handed back to the barrister.

'This woman is speaking the truth, but it still has no bearing upon the murder of Thadeous Lanyon,' Mr Justice Catchpole declared.

The courtroom door banged shut as Harry Sawle marched from the room.

Adolphus Maddock had the determined expression of a man who had taken the bull by the horns knowing his strength to overpower any adversary. 'Your Honour, I believe that we have proved that Lanyon was a bigamist, a murderer, a liar and the worst of blackguards. St John Loveday is a man of impeccable honour and integrity. No evidence has been presented which can place him at the scene of the crime, or indeed in the company of the deceased on the night of

Thadeous Lanyon's murder. I ask your clemency, Your Honour. The case brought by the prosecution has no foundation.'

There was a bout of cheering from many of the crowd who were friends of the Lovedays. Mr Justice Catchpole used his gavel with such force that the end flew off and hit the clerk of the court on the ear. 'Silence. I will have silence, or the court will be cleared and each one of you charged with contempt.'

The shufflings and voices subsided to a murmur and finally there was silence.

Mr Justice Catchpole turned to the jury. 'The jury will consider their verdict. You may retire.'

The foreman consulted with his fellow jurors. 'There be no need to retire, Your Honour. We be unanimous in our decision.'

Mr Justice Catchpole eyed them sternly. 'Do you find the prisoner guilty or not guilty?'

'We find him not guilty.'

There was a momentary hush, then Japhet let out a triumphant yell and the courtroom erupted into loud cheering. St John vaulted over the rail of the dock but was immediately restrained by two guards.

'I will have order!' the judge bellowed. 'The prisoner will return to the bar and await my judgement.'

St John had thought the trial over, and now felt crushed at this new blow, which might yet deprive him of his freedom. Mr Justice Catchpole waited until every voice in the courtroom was silent – the long seconds straining St John's nerves to breaking point.

'St John Arthur Loveday, you have been tried before God and your countrymen and have been found not guilty. However, the evidence has shown that you are a man of heated disposition, with a wildness in your blood which could lead you into lawlessness. The laws of this land are for the good of all and, if flouted, whether by commoner, gentry, or noble, then the severest penalties should be their punishment. You have been granted your freedom and should review your life with humility and gratitude. May God grant you the wisdom to take warning from the consequences which could have befallen you this day. You may leave this court a free man.'

As the manacles were unlocked from St John's wrists, there was joy on his face and he held his father's relieved stare. Then Japhet and Adam lifted St John on their shoulders and carried him through the cheering crowd into the street. Edward laughed with relief and kissed Amelia. 'Thank God that ordeal is over. We can now get on with our lives in peace and security.'

Amelia sighed. 'I trust in this you are right, my dear. This cannot have helped the need to re-establish the integrity and reputation of the shipyard. I think St John and Meriel should leave Cornwall for a time until this regrettable incident is forgotten.'

'Yes, you may be right.' Edward had seen Basil Bracewaite and Lord Wycham on either side of Meriel as she left the court. The way Meriel had been gazing up into the earl's face had alarmed Edward. And St John in his moment of triumph had not even glanced towards his wife. Throughout the trial St John had ignored Meriel. There was much that was wrong with that marriage which must be put right if further scandal was to be averted.

From the corner of his eye he caught sight of a dark-haired young woman and his heart jolted. She had looked so like Tamasine. He scanned the dispersing crowd. He could not see her and relaxed; it must be the strain of the day telling on him. Tamasine was safe in Salisbury. She could not possibly be in Bodmin. He realised then how his own marriage could become unstable if Amelia discovered the truth about his daughter. An unexpected appearance by her could cause the scandal which Amelia so dreaded.

★ ★ ★

Tamasine fought her way through the press of people in the courtroom. The trial had both shocked and exhilarated her. To be involved in such a case the Lovedays were not quite the respectable family she had envisaged. That lack of convention had heartened her.

From her position at the side of the hall she had studied each member of the family closely. The older woman, who she had learned was an aunt, looked to be a martinet. It would be Edward Loveday's wife who could destroy Tamasine's dreams of acceptance. The woman was beautiful but there was a stiffness to her features throughout most of the trial which showed that she found it an ordeal. The wives of the younger men Tamasine did not regard as a threat. Most of her attention was riveted on the younger Loveday men. They were handsome with a bold devil-may-care manner that set her heart racing. For years, trapped by the staid formality of the ladies' academy, she had yearned for a life of adventure. She had listened avidly to the gossip whispered about St John, Adam and Japhet. Were they truly a smuggler, a merchant adventurer who was rumoured to have risked his life saving French *émigrés*, and a professional gambler? In her wildest dreams she had not conceived so exciting a family. They were part of her blood – nothing would convince her otherwise.

Tamasine longed to throw herself upon Edward Loveday's mercy but discretion held her back. This was not the time. When she presented herself to him, she had to be confident of success. She had no intention of returning to the dreary routine of the academy.

Chapter Twenty-Nine

H ester was desperate to find Harry. The look of fury on his features as he stormed from the courtroom alarmed her. She pulled the hood of her cloak around her face to avoid being recognised. As it was too late in the day for Harry to reach Penruan before nightfall, she guessed he would be drinking in one of the inns. It took her four hours of searching to find him. She was swaying and near to exhaustion as she peered through the dingy window of a rowdy backstreet tavern. From inside she heard Harry's distinctive laugh. At last she had found him, and he sounded in a good mood.

She had to steel herself to enter such a disreputable place, and pressed the edge of her cloak over her nose and mouth at the unwholesome stench which assailed her.

The tavern was poorly lit and Hester shuddered at the coarse language and ragged clothing of the people surrounding her. Harry was slumped on a battered settle in a corner with a bare-breasted harlot sitting on his lap. He was kissing her and his hand was fondling her beneath her grimy skirts. The agony of his betrayal slashed through Hester. At her cry of pain the couple broke apart. Harry's eyes were glacial as they regarded her. 'What you be doing 'ere?'

'Get rid of that whore, Harry.'

He laughed, but pushed the woman from his lap and gave

her buttocks a friendly slap to send her on her way. 'Maybe later, my lovely.'

'How could you do this to me, Harry?' Hester accused.

He glowered into a horn cup and swigged back his ale before scowling at her. 'Get back to Penruan, Hester. I bain't got nothing to say to you.'

'But we got plans. Our future . . .'

He did not look at her and his voice was low and dangerous. 'Go home, Hester. That is, if you've still got one. You'd best get what you can from Lanyon's house before his real wife takes possession of it.'

'I don't care about the money. Why are you being so mean? Lanyon is dead. We can be together now, like we always planned.' She could not believe that he was being so cruel.

Harry drained his horn cup and when he turned to regard her there was contempt in his eyes. 'I bain't got no plans to wed a penniless widow. Lanyon had the last laugh on us, didn't he?'

Hester began to tremble with fear. 'But we be gonna wed, Harry.' She put a hand over her swollen stomach. 'This be your child.'

His lips drew back over his teeth. 'It bain't the first of mine another man's wife has carried.'

'But you love me,' Hester wailed. 'Why you being so mean?'

'You made a fool of me when you wed another. No one gets the better of Harry Sawle.'

Hester put her hand to her mouth and backed away from the menace in his eyes. It was as though a stranger stood before her – but this was the ruthless, brutal Harry Sawle her family had always warned against, and she had never listened to them. 'All this time you've been lying to me. I loved you. I risked Lanyon's beatings to see you. And all you wanted was to get back at me. Did you never intend to wed me?'

'As Lanyon's widow you would have been worth getting hitched to. I wanted all Lanyon had taken from me. The Sawles were the most important smugglers in Penruan before he got above himself.'

Her reddened eyes rounded in horror. 'You killed Lanyon, didn't you? And you intended to wed me not from love but from revenge. To get his money.' Her face screwed up in anguish and she sagged to the floor, clutching her stomach in her misery. 'And it turned out I bain't even Lanyon's true wife. There bain't no money. You killed him. You be the murderer, not St John Loveday.'

He stooped over her, gripped her chin and wrenched it up to stare into her eyes without pity. 'Now you know what I be capable of, you know to keep your mouth shut – that's if you don't want to end the same way as Lanyon did. Go back to your father. He'll take in a wronged widow even if she be with child. Bain't no shame in that. Lanyon tricked you. He tricked us all.'

Harry stepped over Hester's crouched body and ignored her outstretched hand. Hester screamed after him, 'And you be just like him. Heaven help your sinful, evil soul.'

Harry walked out into the darkening street with an evening mist beginning to obscure the houses. It had been just such a night when he had seen Lanyon in Truro and followed him. By chance he had learned where Lanyon was staying. Harry had dressed in rags to disguise himself as a beggar and waited in the street until Lanyon left his lodgings in the evening. He had followed him, and at a secluded spot called out Lanyon's name. As the man turned, he had fired – shot him through the head. The fog had shielded him as he heaved the corpse over his shoulder for the short walk to the river where he had disposed of the body. Yet Lanyon's death meant little. He had wanted his empire – that would have been the true revenge.

As for Hester . . . She'd wronged him by marrying Lanyon. She had got off lightly by his reckoning.

After the trial the Lovedays and their friends had celebrated St John's acquittal by dining in a private room of their hotel. Neither Lady Anne Druce nor Gwendolyn attended. Japhet had been puzzled by Gwen's absence. He had planned to travel from Bodmin to join his friends in Bath after the trial and would be leaving in the morning. He had learned that Lady Anne and Gwendolyn had quarrelled, and that her Ladyship had taken to her bed with a sick headache, demanding that Gwendolyn attend her all evening. The knowledge had angered Japhet for Lady Anne became more demanding of her daughter's time with each year. Also he suspected that Lady Anne had been annoyed at Gwen for snubbing Lieutenant Beaumont and sitting next to himself at the trial. The memory had made him laugh and he decided to say his farewells to Gwen before he left Bodmin.

He arrived at the hotel where the Druces were staying at mid-morning, knowing that Lady Anne never rose before noon, and tipped a pretty brunette maid to take a message to Gwendolyn that he would await her in the hotel parlour until eleven. He sat down and prepared himself for a long wait and was astonished when Gwendolyn hurried into the parlour before a quarter of an hour had passed. Her hair was simply dressed, drawn back from her face and falling in natural curls over her shoulder, and she was wearing a pale blue morning gown which flattered her figure.

'This is a surprise, Japhet,' she said as he bowed over her hand.

'I leave for Bath in the hour and wished to bid you farewell now that we are friends again,' he smiled. 'You look lovely. It was cruel of your mama to keep you from the celebrations last evening.'

The parlour was empty of guests besides themselves and Gwen hid her disappointment that Japhet was to leave Cornwall so soon. She was used to his impromptu departures but that did not make them easier to bear. She walked to the window, too nervous to sit down. 'I thought you would stay at Trewenna until Adam sails. He is to become a privateer now that he has letters of marque. Such a dangerous life. Senara must be worried for his safety.' She paced the room as she spoke and fidgeted with the lace on her cuffs.

With a laugh Japhet caught her elbow and turned her to face him. 'I cannot talk to you while you dart like a butterfly around the room. It has been so long since we have spoken.'

'I should not be here now. Mama will be furious.' Her voice was breathless as she stared into his teasing hazel eyes.

He glanced around the room and his eyes sparkled when he realised that they were alone. 'Your mama does not approve of me and perhaps rightly so, especially as we are alone. Your reputation could be quite in shreds.'

Her eyes sparkled with a wounded light. 'You have proved that I am safe with you. Did you just come to tell me you are leaving? I am honoured, for I have not seen you most of the summer.' She turned away but when she would have broken free of his hold, her arm was held tighter and he drew her closer so that her breasts grazed against his chest.

'You know me for all that I am, dear Gwen, yet you never judge me. But now I have made you angry.'

She stared at him in exasperation. How could he be so blind – so stubborn not to see the love which consumed her? She shook her head in a vague denial of what she did not know. He always confused her, drugged her senses so that sane reason was impossible. All she could see was his full lips parted in the smile she adored. And then those lips were closer and their sweetness closed over hers. Their warmth was

509

all-pervading, rousing a sensuality within her which turned her body to fire.

'Oh, Japhet,' she sighed as he crushed her in his arms.

There was a tension in his body as his lips moved over her face to kiss her hair. 'Gwen, sweetest Gwen. There is no one like you.'

Then again her mouth was pliant under his. The hotel parlour and her surroundings blurred as she clung to him, oblivious to propriety – all that mattered was that she was in his arms.

A shocked gasp from the doorway tore them apart. Japhet was staring over her head at the intruder. His features had turned to an alabaster mask. Before Gwen could recover her composure, the door clicked shut and Lady Anne's fury descended upon them.

'You scurrilous knave! Lecher! Blackguard! How dare you compromise my daughter in this manner? I always feared you would taint her with your corruption. You are despicable. Get out before I call the constables to have you arrested. You are not fit to be in the company of a decent woman, Japhet Loveday.'

'Mama, you mistake us—' Gwendolyn pleaded.

'Get to your room, miss.' Lady Anne turned on her daughter. 'I forbade you to see this man and with just cause. Have you no regard for your reputation? This man is the worst reprobate in all Cornwall. No woman is safe from him.'

Japhet stood tall and rigid, his eyes dark with outrage. 'My last intent was to harm Gwen's reputation. I hold her in the highest esteem.'

Lady Anne bore down on him. 'You do not know the meaning of the word where women are concerned. And even if your intentions were honourable – *which I doubt* – I would never allow my daughter to marry a profligate, a man who shames the Loveday name by his base living and gaming.'

'Mama, that is not true,' Gwendolyn defended Japhet. 'And when I wed it will be to whom I choose.'

'Gwen, every word your mother has said is true enough.' He clipped the words out with bitter self-accusation. 'Though it was not my intent to have wronged you this day. Your pardon, most revered lady. Unworthy as I am, I shall always be your devoted servant. I shall not risk endangering your reputation again. Goodbye, my dear friend.'

He marched from the room and Gwen made to run after him. Lady Anne barred her way and slapped her cheek. Gwendolyn reeled back against a chair and as she recovered her balance declared, 'I will not give Japhet up. I love him.'

'I will not listen to this nonsense. Japhet Loveday will never be your husband while I have breath in my body. I thank God that maid had the sense to come to me when she remembered Japhet's reputation was unsavoury. You will forget that man.'

Gwendolyn did not listen. She ran towards the open door and through the hotel foyer to the street. Japhet was nowhere in sight in the busy jostling crowd. Tears stung her eyes. She had seen the tenderness in his eyes before he kissed her and she vowed that her mama would not come between them. Japhet had gone but he would return to Cornwall. He always did. And Gwendolyn was now convinced that Japhet loved her. That was all that mattered.

Two days after she and Adam arrived back at Mariner's House after the trial, Senara woke with a start and sat up in bed. Her heart was throbbing from the fear she had experienced in a dream. The memory of the dream was as elusive as mist – only the sensation of being trapped and enclosed remained. She turned to embrace Adam and was dismayed to find that he was already up and she could hear him moving about downstairs.

She looked out the window and saw by the height of the sun through the branches of a tree that it was time to rise. Outside she could hear the voices of the shipwrights as they began their work for the day. She rose and pulled on a gown, but the unease of the dream clung tenacious as a cobweb to the edges of her mind. Adam had been away from the yard for most of yesterday and he had been in a distracted mood on his return. Nathan had been teething and Senara had spent the evening trying to soothe his tears.

As she slipped her feet into her shoes, Adam was at the bedroom door holding Nathan in his arms. The child was happy and laughing as he pulled at his father's hair, which was flowing loose about his shoulders. Adam was in black breeches and his shirt was open at the neck. It was how she loved him most. He smiled at Nathan and the faintest frown creased her husband's brow as they regarded her. Scamp ran past him to leap on the bed and Adam shouted at him to get off. There was tension in Adam's eyes as they lifted to regard Senara.

Then she knew. He would be leaving Cornwall soon.

'How long before you must sail?'

'A few days. My letters of marque have been granted. If I take any French ship then I am entitled to a large part of the money she will fetch, though obviously, the Crown wants its share of the spoils of war.'

'Do we need the money so badly that you must now become a pirate?'

'A gentleman privateer is the correct term, my love. It sounds far more respectable.' Adam laughed and handed Nathan to her. 'Our son needs changing, from the smell of him. Let Carrie take care of him for the day. I want us to be together. And you have not forgotten that you are to dine at Trevowan this evening?'

'How could I when it ends the rift between you and your

father? But I have been dreading it.'

He kissed her. 'You will charm them. But to take your mind from this evening we will enjoy this day together. I have ordered the horses to be saddled.'

She leaned back in his arms and her smile hid the heaviness in her heart. He was sailing sooner than she expected and the voyage would be dangerous, that was why Adam wanted to spend this day with her.

The joy of a ride with Adam was overshadowed. Her sense of foreboding was increasing. Yet none of this showed as she rode with her husband out of the yard and across the countryside. She had promised herself she would never criticise him for the life at sea which he had chosen. He was a man who needed that freedom of adventure, and she had known and accepted that when she fell in love with him.

With Scamp keeping pace with them, they took the route they had ridden before St John's trial. Senara again felt the enchantment of the abandoned estate. When Adam halted by the gateway to the house, it was to see it with the full sunshine on it. The lichen on its walls and shingles glowed golden against the grey stone and house martins flew around the eaves where they had nested. A fox had been crossing the shadows of the courtyard and paused to look at them, its amber eyes fearless, before it turned its head and trotted away. Scamp had been running through the trees behind them. When he saw the fox the dog yelped and bounded after it.

'Senara, what would you say if this was to be our home?' Adam dragged his gaze from the house to regard her solemnly.

'We have Mariner's House. I am happy there.' She felt a rustling of panic in her stomach.

'I would have more for our children. This is to be our home. Once I knew Trevowan would never be mine, I asked

Squire Penwithick to find out who owned it. The heirs are willing to sell for a reasonable price. I intend to buy the house and land.'

'But how can we afford it?'

'I have raised loans which will be repaid out of the profits of future voyages. You said Pegasus was a sign of our good fortune. The land must be cleared and money must be spent on the house before it will be inhabitable. I may even decide to build a new house on the land. It is our future. I want it to rise up and be more glorious than Trevowan.'

Senara knew the source of her earlier panic. She had no wish to become mistress of a manor house – yet that was her destiny as Adam's wife. The child moved within her, reminding her of Adam's hopes for his children's future. She pushed her own misgivings aside and gazed at the trees of beech, oak and rowan surrounding the property. The nearest oak had a large growth of mistletoe on its branches – the sacred bush of the ancient gods.

She tilted her head to one side and listened to the voice of the wind in the leaves. If it was her destiny to live on a large estate, then here she could find a measure of peace. 'What is this place called?'

'Boscabel. It means place of the beautiful woods. There is also a waterfall.'

Her face lit with pleasure. 'Show me.'

'Do you not want to see inside the house?'

'Later. No house can hold sway over my gypsy blood. It is the open land and the life-giving power of water which flows freely and strongly from its source into streams, rivers and eventually the great oceans which are important. And a waterfall is most especially blessed.'

'This one is known as the white lady,' Adam said as they approached it. The rush of its cascading water was loud enough for him to have to raise his voice.

'As are so many,' Senara laughed. 'The Celts venerated them as the form of the goddess.'

Senara stared in wonder at the green bank with its forty-foot drop. There was a huge boulder at the top of the fast-flowing stream which parted the waters as they tumbled over the edge. They rejoined ten feet lower, forming a slim column, like the robes a woman would have worn in bygone times. The sun filtered through the treetops and a rainbow haze formed in the fine mist. The water flowed in the form of a white figure with arms raised to the heavens in homage, or that of an angel hovering in an evergreen glade in veneration of nature.

Adam saw the rapt expression on his wife's face and laughed. 'I take it that your new home will please you?'

'I could live here in a tent if I had to,' she replied. 'Let us explore the house.'

They wandered through the rooms, the floors strewn with dead leaves which had blown in through the broken panes. The shingled roof was damaged from years of neglect and countless storms. Where the rain had poured in, black and green slime covered the walls. In many places the oak panelling had warped and fallen away. Adam had to bend his head to walk through the low Tudor door arches. The winding staircase which led to a turret, with a view of the river, was blocked with debris where the roof had fallen in. The plaster work was peeling in the oldest part of the house which was once the great hall and main living quarters of the house. Senara fell in love with the play of sunlight through the tall oriel window in the solar. Another delight was that the roof over the long gallery, which ran the entire length of the main building, had not been too badly damaged. Senara ran to each window to look out across the overgrown gardens and caught glimpses of the river.

'This house is lovely. It would be a shame to build another.

One day it will be a home worthy of you, Adam.'

'There is much work to be done. But Pegasus will provide the fortune we will need to restore the house and estate.' He pulled her to him and held her tight. 'But it will never be Trevowan.'

Her heart wrenched at the sadness in his voice. 'No, it will be Boscabel. Our Boscabel – blessed by the ancient ones and resurrected to its former glory with the blood of a new dynasty raised upon its land.'

Adam smiled but there remained a shadow in his eyes. Boscabel would never replace Trevowan which had pride of place in his heart. 'Boscabel will be the equal of Trevowan.' It was a vow spoken from determination and rivalry. 'Indeed, I will make this estate greater than anything St John is capable of achieving.'

Amelia heard the arrival of a horse and carriage and glanced out of the window of the green salon. She was expecting Lady Anne Druce to call. A bright yellow phaeton had drawn up outside the Dower House and she frowned when she saw Lord Wycham alight. The earl was visiting Meriel far too regularly, and often when St John was working on the estate. Amelia decided to go to the Dower House and ensure that Meriel was properly chaperoned. The earl must be informed that such visits were not acceptable.

She got no further than the entrance hall when the phaeton sped past the house and Meriel was perched on top beside Lord Wycham. Amelia had seen enough.

By the time Edward returned from the shipyard Amelia was shaking with fury. She poured out her censure of Meriel. 'I will not permit another scandal to break over our heads. St John and Meriel must leave Trevowan until the gossip of the trial blows over. And that baggage St John has married must be far from anywhere she is likely to encounter Lord Wycham.'

Edward sighed. 'I agree with you that St John and Meriel should leave Cornwall for a time, but for different reasons. St John's trial has not helped the situation at the yard. He has been gambling since his return and Fraddon informs me that Prince was missing from the stable two nights ago. St John is involved with the smugglers again. The good name of the family is being jeopardised by his irresponsible conduct and Meriel is making matters worse.'

Amelia was relieved. She had expected Edward to defend his son. 'Where can they go? London would not be a good idea, not from the way Meriel has been encouraging Lord Wycham.'

Edward nodded but his eyes were weary with resignation. 'We have a cousin in Virginia, Garfield Penhaligan. He wrote at the beginning of the year inviting us to visit. William stayed with them for a month a few years ago. Where better for St John to spend a year until the scandal of his trial dies down. I will speak to St John this evening. He can sail with Adam at the end of the week. Adam has agreed.'

'Because Adam has not given up hope of one day inheriting Trevowan despite his purchase of Boscabel,' Amelia replied.

'His motives are unimportant. A year in the old American colony will do St John no harm.' Edward now considered the invitation a blessing. He needed to re-establish the reputation of his family as one of integrity and diligence.

Amelia put her hand on her husband's arm and gazed into his face. 'But with Adam at sea and St John abroad, how will you manage the yard and the estate? You will make yourself ill, my love.'

Edward laughed. 'Until five years ago I managed well enough on my own. Thomas is optimistic that he will be able to repay us another seven hundred and fifty pounds at the next quarter. I can afford to hire extra farm labourers now.'

'And how will St John view your plans for his future?'

'He has no choice. He caused the scandal to the family with his trial. If he wants to keep Trevowan as his birthright, he will do as I say.'

When Edward left to inform St John of his decision, Amelia wrung her hands. She could see no other solution. It would put a halt to Meriel's antics and bring an end to St John's involvement with the smugglers.

The arguments which blazed through the Dower House could be heard in the main house. Amelia held her head and winced. Would there never be peace in this family? Adam sailed in two hours. Perhaps then normality would be restored. Even Lisette had been behaving herself in the last weeks, though Amelia did not believe her exemplary behaviour would last for long.

Across the lawns of Trevowan, Meriel faced her husband with mutiny in her heart. Their baggage had been taken to Trevowan Hard earlier. Meriel was frantic with panic. 'For the last time, I will not go to America.'

'Father has ordered it. And your conduct is the reason behind our banishment. People are beginning to talk about you and Wycham. You are my wife and for once you will do as I say.'

'I wish I had never married you.'

'The feeling is mutual, madam,' St John raged. The sight of Meriel filled him with revulsion. He blamed his enforced exile on her.

Rowena ran into the room crying. 'Papa! Mama! Stop shouting.'

Meriel ignored her daughter and stood with her hands on her hips in front of her husband. 'I am not going with you, St

John. I am going to London with Lord Wycham.'

St John scowled. He suspected Meriel was having an affair with the earl. He would not allow himself to become a laughing stock. 'Do you think I would allow that? Or that Father would permit you to drag this family into another scandal? I rue the day I met you. I was a fool to wed you.'

She smiled maliciously. 'You were always a fool, St John.'

Rowena sobbed louder. 'No! Stop! Mama, Papa! You mustn't shout.' Their arguments had been upsetting her all day.

St John picked her up and kissed her cheek. 'It is all right, sweetheart. Papa is not cross with you. Go and make sure all your toys have been packed. We are going on Uncle Adam's ship. Will that not be exciting?' He kissed her again and put her down. 'Papa loves you. Don't cry.'

Rowena ran from the room and when St John turned to Meriel her expression was filled with such loathing and cruelty, he was shaken. At first he had been angered at Edward's banishment, but he could live well in Virginia from the money he had amassed from smuggling. 'Unfortunately, we have to make the best of our marriage, Meriel, for Rowena's sake.'

'Everything is for Rowena's sake, is it not?' Meriel was pacing the floor, her eyes wild and her step agitated. 'She was even the reason I entered this ridiculous marriage.'

St John was appalled. Meriel had never been that vindictive before. Before he could reply, her lips drew back into a snarl. 'You would do anything for your precious Rowena. I have never been important to you. You were right: you are a fool. A blind fool. I am not going with you. I never wanted to marry you in the first place. It was Adam I wanted, Adam whom I would have done anything for to ensure that he wed me. But Adam had to rejoin his ship . . .'

St John stared at Meriel with horror dawning in his eyes. She laughed. 'Yes. I gave myself to Adam. I loved Adam, not you.' Meriel had to break the bonds of her marriage and this was the only way St John would let her go. Her tone was scathing. 'And Rowena is no eight-month child—'

Her words were snapped off at the force of St John's slap. 'You lie,' he raged. 'This is a cruel trick.'

'Look at her and you will know I speak the truth.' Meriel continued to laugh. 'Rowena is the image of Adam. Senara guessed last year and also Sal. How long before others notice?'

He lunged at her to stop her lies. Meriel nimbly side-stepped. 'You lie!' he shouted again.

She shook her head, impatient to be free of him and to be able to enjoy the riches Lord Wycham had promised her. 'It was so easy to trick you. You hated Adam so much you would do anything to beat him. That's why you raped me – to take something that you thought Adam wanted. But Adam had won me weeks before.'

'Papa. Papa.' Rowena ran into the room, holding up a wooden doll. 'I nearly forgot, Honey.'

St John stared at his daughter and the colour left his face. He did not see Rowena. It was Adam's face looking at him – mocking him.

'I hope you end up rotting in the gutter where you belong, madam.' He marched from the house.

Meriel called to Rachel, 'I think you should take Rowena up to the main house.' She did not want to be encumbered with a child in her new life.

When the maid and child left, Meriel walked out of the Dower House. Through the trees she could see the outline of Lord Wycham's phaeton waiting for her. That she took nothing with her but her secret cache of jewels, which were hidden inside her bodice, she did not care. Lord Wycham would have her dressed in the latest fashions. Every luxury she had dreamed of would now be hers. Meriel left Trevowan without a single regret.

There was a cold and deadly fury locked in St John's heart as he was rowed out to *Pegasus*. Sir Gregory Kilmarthen was on deck smoking a pipe. Two weeks at his home, Athel Grange, had been enough to show Long Tom that he could not tolerate living with his mother and sister. Adam's invitation to sail with him had been an irresistible lure.

'Your brother said we were to hoist anchor as soon as you boarded, St John,' Kilmarthen informed him. 'Are your family not with you?'

'Plans were changed at the last minute. I go to Virginia alone.'

'The captain is in his cabin if you wish to see him.' Kilmarthen shrugged. His own bizarre experience of family life enabled him to accept anything as normal. He turned to Melthrop, who was waiting for orders. 'Weigh anchor. Captain will want us to take full advantage of the tide.'

St John did not go immediately to Adam's cabin. He needed to calm down before he saw his brother. He had much to consider. The old rivalries and vendettas remained. He had wanted to kill Adam when he learned of Rowena's parentage and his hatred for his twin was stronger than ever. He had lost Rowena – or had he? He could not cut the love he felt for the child from his heart, and she had always adored him. He despised Meriel and did not regret her leaving. It was a relief to be rid of her and her greed and scheming.

He gazed up at the moon reflected in the water as they left Fowey for the open sea. At first Virginia had appeared to be a punishment. Now he wondered otherwise. Did it not herald a new beginning with unlimited opportunities? The ship was small and the ocean large. And there was time enough on the weeks of the voyage to end the rivalry between him and his twin once and for all.

Chapter One

It was an hour before noon and Senara Loveday was enjoying what had become her daily walk around the grounds of the estate that would one day be her home. The land which had been neglected for decades was overgrown and the healing herbs she used for her remedies grew in abundance. Boscabel, as its name suggested, had a magic of its own, and the wildness of nature reclaiming the once-formal flowerbeds and knot gardens held its own beauty for Senara.

She tilted her face towards the sun, her skin the colour of palest amber from the long hours in the open air, her hair the warm brown of freshly tilled earth. She breathed in the scent of the roses and honeysuckle which climbed unrestrained amongst the ivy which covered the walls of outbuildings, hiding the scars of crumbling wattle and daub walls, broken window panes and disintegrating thatch. Through an archway leading to the garden, marigolds and marguerites had self-seeded to form a white and gold carpet around the borders. In the stableyard, brambles laden with dark, succulent fruit twisted around a rusted plough and harrow and spread across the flagstones.

Her wicker pannier filled with blackberries for preserving, Senara turned to study the Elizabethan manor house. The stone cladding around the porch was cracked and mottled with lichen. No one had lived here for over twenty years nd the winter storms had taken their toll on the beautiful house. The stonework was broken on the upper storey of the turret. Tall brick chimneys rose above the long gallery whose lattice windows ran the entire length of the house and whose rotted roof struts and shingles were being replaced by pale new timber beams. From a bonfire in the courtyard rose blue spirals of smoke as the flames consumed timbers riddled with woodworm and deathwatch beetle. One of the apprentices from the Loveday shipyard threw more wood on the fire, and two carpenters unloaded a wagon of cut timber.

As the wife of Adam Loveday, Senara had accepted that the heir to a shipyard owned by one of the oldest families in Cornwall would wish to raise his family in style. Yet a grand mansion with immaculate gardens would have stifled Senara's gypsy blood. Adam had promised that the grounds of Boscabel would be her domain and should be landscaped as she desired. The renovation of the old house would be Adam's creation and responsibility, for she knew nothing of grand mansions and felt uncomfortable in large buildings.

Outdoors was a different matter and she delighted in exploring the estate. She hummed softly as she walked to the wood at the edge of the gardens to collect the herbs she needed to attend her patients. Boscabel Wood was purpled in places by deep shadows. The late summer sun was low in a cloudless sky, its rays piercing the canopy of foliage to cast golden arrows against the gnarled tree trunks. Senara paused to collect some lady's mantle, a herb which was effective in the healing of wounds, vomiting and the bloody flux. Engrossed in her work, she could push to the back of her mind the duty expected of her that evening. She had been invited to the end-of-harvest feast at Trevowan.

Trevowan was the home of Adam's family and this was the

first time she had been invited to visit without her husba
She should be delighted that the Lovedays were holding c
an olive branch and finally seemed to be accepting her a
Adam's wife. Yet with Adam at sea it would be a traumatic
ordeal, especially since the family expected her to stay the
night at Trevowan. At least the harvest feast was a simple
celebration for the tenants and farm workers and she would
not be forced to mix with the local gentry who she knew
disapproved of Adam's choice of bride.

Senara rubbed the tender spot at the base of her spine. She
was carrying her second child, though little evidence showed
as yet in her slim figure. Senara was under no illusions that
the Lovedays approved of her. They simply wanted to
present a united front to their neighbours following the trial
of Adam's twin brother, St John, for murder. St John had
been declared innocent but the scandal had been the gossip
of the county and it had harmed the reputation of the
shipyard.

Senara pushed her misgivings aside as she walked to the
grass slopes at the edge of the wood in search of horehound
to ease cases of consumption or rheum of the lungs. As she
worked, raucous cries from pheasants in the undergrowth
and magpies and rooks in the treetops were accompanied by
the songs of linnets and blackbirds. A fox carrying a dead
rabbit peered at Senara through a curtain of meadowsweet
and tansy before continuing to his lair.

Senara gathered a bunch of comfrey and laid it in her
basket, enjoying the tranquillity and solitude of Boscabel.
Here, she could enjoy the peace which only nature could
bring her. The constant hammering and shouts of the shipyard which was her current home were the sounds of an alien
world where she still felt ill at ease.

A distant shout made her look towards the crest of the
next hill, which sloped down towards an inlet of the River

ey. A woman in a blue riding-habit galloped at a ...gerous pace over the rough grounds dappled with ...anite boulders. Recognising the Arab mare belonging to ...wendolyn Druce, Senara frowned. It was not like Gwen to be so reckless. Then a second rider appeared – a man in pursuit of Gwen. Was the second rider another suitor encouraged by Gwendolyn's mother, the Lady Anne? How galling that must be for Gwen. She would love only one man and he was as feckless as he was charming. Gwen had been in love with Japhet Loveday for years, but Japhet relished his freedom far too much to consider marriage. Unfortunately, whilst Gwen steadfastly refused all alternative suitors, the Lady Anne Druce was equally resolved that her daughter would marry any man except Japhet Loveday.

Senara shook her head as she stooped to slice the sharp blade of her dagger through the stems of a bunch of St Peter's wort which she would use in a purge to ease the sciatica of a shipwright's wife. Dew from the morning mist still clung to its leaves. Unaccountably, the hairs at the back of Senara's neck tingled, a sign that forewarned her something was amiss. Her eyes narrowed as she straightened to study the two riders once more. Gwen's mare had stumbled and her companion was gaining on her. The man was dressed as a gentleman and, as there was no accompanying groom, Senara surmised he was known to the family. There was a grim determination in the posture of Gwen's companion which increased Senara's unease, and she could not dispel the feeling that the woman was in danger. Her intuition was rarely wrong.

Senara ran to where she had tethered her mare, Hera. Abandoning her herb basket, she called to Scamp, her husband's dog. As she swung into the saddle, the liver and white cross-breed spaniel appeared out of the undergrowth where he had been chasing squirrels.

Senara had covered less than half a mile when she heard a scream which was abruptly cut off. Her unease turned to a sickening dread and she urged Hera faster. Senara was a fearless horsewoman, raised by her gypsy father to ride bareback as a child, but a fast-running inlet of the River Fowey cut her off from the direction of the scream. The two riders would have crossed by the stone bridge further upstream but Senara, fearing for the safety of Gwendolyn Druce, plunged Hera into the reed bed at the edge of the bank. Startled moorhens and coots squawked and flapped their wings noisily as they flew away from feeding in the reeds. The water was several yards wide but not so deep that Hera would lose her footing.

Scamp loved water and shot like an arrow into the river at her side. The cold water swirled around Senara's legs, drenching her green riding habit, but she did not falter.

A horse whinnied in the trees on the opposite bank, followed by the sound of scuffling and a muffled cry. There was a flash of blue through the branches and waist-high bracken, then silence. The wood was too thick to ride through and Senara dismounted, staggering under the weight of her sodden gown which wrapped around her legs and made walking difficult.

Fear churned her stomach. 'Is that you, Gwen?'

A loud growl was her only reply. Senara pushed through the bracken into a small clearing to discover Gwen pressed against a tree trunk, striving to push away a man who held her tightly and forced his kisses on to her reluctant lips. The pins had fallen from her chestnut hair and it was in disarray about her shoulders, while her lace stock and the lapel of her jacket had been ripped in the struggle.

'Stand away from Miss Druce, or the dog will attack,' Senara commanded. 'Are you unharmed, Gwen?'

Gwen nodded, too shaken to speak as she struggled to regain her composure.

The man turned and pulled a pistol from inside his jacket. 'Set that cur on me and I shall shoot it.'

The arrogance of his tone roused Senara's anger. She recognised the thin figure and haughty features of Lieutenant Francis Beaumont. All summer Lady Anne Druce had encouraged him to call upon Gwendolyn. 'Sir, how dare you force yourself upon Miss Druce in such a despicable manner?'

Senara summoned Scamp to her side and ordered him to lie down before moving forward to confront the man. As she approached, his expression became sullen at her intrusion. He viewed her wet skirts with a chilling derision and Senara could feel his scorn for her gypsy blood. But if he intended to intimidate her he had failed. Senara despised such men.

'You mistake the situation, Mrs Loveday.' The words were a venomous hiss. 'I hold Miss Druce in the highest regard. We are betrothed. I have the blessing of her family.'

The colour was returning to Gwendolyn's cheeks and she shook her head, her voice shaking with her outrage. 'You lie. I never agreed to wed you. You do not have my blessing, sir. Neither shall you. You sought to compromise me this day. I will not be browbeaten into a marriage which is repugnant to me.'

He rounded on Gwendolyn, his thin lips twisting into a sneer. 'Your conceit astounds me, Miss Druce. You should be grateful that a man of my family and position would consider you as his wife. Your reputation has been tarnished this summer by consorting with that rakehell, Japhet Loveday.'

Gwendolyn flushed but the anger continued to spark in her eyes. 'It is your conduct which is reprehensible, sir. Japhet Loveday is a man of honour. He would never give false evidence in a court of law as you did at the last Assizes. Your

530

lies could have hanged St John Loveday. You sicken me.'

He squared his shoulders and stuck out his chest. 'I was carrying out my duty as an officer of His Majesty's Excise Office. St John Loveday is a smuggler and murderer. I spoke the truth.'

Senara had heard enough. 'Mercifully, your evidence did not hold up in court. St John was acquitted. There was no evidence that he murdered Thadeous Lanyon. Lanyon had won many enemies as a smuggler and he killed anyone who crossed him.' She strode to Gwendolyn's side, the two angry women flanking the officer. Senara bristled. 'No gentleman would force their unwanted attentions upon a gentlewoman of Miss Druce's position as you have.'

'What would a gypsy brat know of gentlemanly conduct?' Beaumont sneered.

The insult had no power to hurt Senara for she felt no shame in her heritage. Pride lifted her chin. This man had been her husband's enemy for years – since the days when Beaumont and Adam had served together as midshipmen in the navy. After instigating a duel with Adam, Beaumont had been dismissed from the navy to serve upon an excise cutter. Unable to get his revenge upon Adam, Beaumont had taken up a vendetta against Adam's twin, St John. Again he had failed. Beaumont had abused his position as an excise officer, taking bribes from Thadeous Lanyon to turn a blind eye to the smuggler's trade.

'A true gentleman is a man of honour and integrity in both word and deed.' Her tone was scathing. 'I see no evidence of that in yourself.'

There was hatred in his eyes as he glared at Senara. He clearly held her responsible for thwarting his plans to damage Gwendolyn's honour in such a way that she would be forced to marry him. It was not love that drove him but greed for her substantial inheritance.

Beaumont grabbed Gwendolyn's arm. 'You will marry me.'

She cried out at the pain he was inflicting and wrenched her arm free to slap his face. 'I will marry the man I love or no man at all. And certainly not an arrogant bully as you have shown yourself to be this day.'

Beaumont did not move and his face was rigid with fury. 'I will have you as my bride.'

The menace of his threat was charged with the malevolence of a lightning bolt. Senara's flesh prickled in growing fear for the heiress. Scamp growled, his fangs bared as he edged closer to the lieutenant.

'You are on private land, Lieutenant Beaumont,' Senara informed him. 'My husband's land. Leave now or I shall summon the gamekeeper and bailiff to arrest you for trespass. I will also bear witness if Miss Druce presses charges of assault. That would ensure you are never accepted within polite society again.'

His belligerence was frightening but Senara refused to back down. She had lied, for there was no gamekeeper or bailiff at Boscabel – Adam had acquired the property in recent months and they could not afford servants to work here while they continued to live at Mariner's House.

Gwendolyn added her vehemence. 'If you present yourself at Traherne Hall again I shall inform my mother and Sir Henry of your conduct today.'

Lieutenant Beaumont smirked. 'The Lady Anne said you would be difficult. She has already placed an announcement in the *Sherborne Mercury* and informed the Reverend Mr Snell that the ceremony will take place in the old chapel at Traherne Manor in one month's time.'

'Mama would never—'

Beaumont's cruel laughter cut across her words. 'It is all arranged. Unless you wish to create a scandal and be shunned by society, you have no choice but to marry me.' He turned on Senara. 'The Lovedays think they are invincible. But they are not. They had better stay out of my affairs in the future.' He bowed mockingly to the women, and marched away.

'I will never marry you, Lieutenant Beaumont.' Gwendolyn sagged against the trunk of a beech tree, her legs stripped of the strength to support her.

He whirled round and flung out his arm in an intimidating manner. 'Marry me you will, or you and anyone who crosses me will live to regret it.'

Gwendolyn put a shaking hand to her temple. 'Does Mama hate me so much that she wishes me to wed that monster?'

The heiress's pain was heartrending to witness. Gwendolyn had been one of the few people of her class to accept Senara as Adam's bride. Putting a comforting arm around Gwen, Senara was fearful of Lieutenant Beaumont's warning. He was a vindictive man and his threat was no idle one.

Gwendolyn ripped off the torn stock and crumpled it in disgust. 'I love Japhet. He is the only man I will marry.'

Senara shivered, chilled by the premonition that if Gwendolyn continued her infatuation with Japhet against the wishes of her family, it would bring further retribution to the Lovedays.